ALSO BY JACK RIGGS

When the Finch Rises

The Fireman's Wife

THE
FIREMAN'S
WIFE

A NOVEL

JACK RIGGS

BALLANTINE BOOKS · NEW YORK

A Ballantine Books Trade Paperback Original

Copyright © 2008 by Jack Riggs
Reading group guide copyright © 2008 by Random House, Inc.

Published in the United States by Ballantine Books,
an imprint of The Random House Publishing Group,
a division of Random House, Inc., New York.

BALLANTINE and colophon are registered
trademarks of Random House, Inc.
RANDOM HOUSE READER'S CIRCLE and colophon
are trademarks of Random House, Inc.

Library of Congress Cataloging-in-Publication Data

Riggs, Jack.
The fireman's wife/Jack Riggs.—Ballantine trade paperback ed.
p.   cm.
ISBN 978-0-345-48006-4 (pbk.)
1. Self-actualization (Psychology)—Fiction.   2. South
Carolina—Fiction.   3. Domestic fiction.   I. Title.

PS3618.I395F57   2009
813'.6—dc22   2008043275

Printed in the United States of America

www.randomhousereaderscircle.com

246897531

Book design by Elizabeth A. D. Eno

In memory of LB.
You left us too soon, Bro.

For Debra, Madison, and Chris.

You let me go on this journey,
but you wouldn't let me go it alone.

You are all so strong and lovely.

The water is wide, I can't cross over,
And neither have I wings to fly,
Build me a boat that will carry two
And both shall row, my love and I.

—Traditional folk song

JUNE 1970

Cassie

I AM A PASSENGER in my own car, eyes closed, head lying against hot vinyl as Clay Taylor drives south through Murrells Inlet toward Litchfield. Even with all the windows down and Clay easily doing sixty miles an hour along the straight stretches, the heat feels oppressive. Sweat pours off my neck. It trickles down the small of my back, sticks my legs to the plastic seats. I try to imagine sitting here naked, the top of the car ripped away so that the breeze would become a tornado and blast away the heat. But I don't think even that would bring relief.

It's June in the low country of South Carolina. The heat should be just starting to build in for the season, but instead it feels like it never left from last year. It's been hot and dry for so long, nothing wants to move, animals are laying down dead, the salt creeks drying up to nothing. Peck talks about the drought all the time, seven months and counting. He's a fireman and feels the heat in ways I could never understand. He's nervous about the dry land, worried that a fire will take off and he and his crew won't have enough bodies and equipment to put it out.

The music on the radio is something Kelly insists we listen to, rock and roll, a scratchy man's voice screaming out *who'll stop the rain?* The song is annoying, makes me wonder when the rain might actually come. Everybody who lives on the marsh year-round prays for as much water as possible to fall from the sky. Some are even joking a hurricane would be welcome relief.

The storm season started a couple of weeks ago, the Gulf Stream warming up, pulling bad weather from the far side of the world toward us. It's the serious season mixed into the tourist one, but people down here aren't thinking straight when they talk about hurricanes like that. Peck tells them to be careful what they ask for.

The drought's put a sharp edge on everyone except Clay. He's not talking about rain. He's driving with his elbow hanging out the window, both hands on the steering wheel, a cigarette pinched between his lips. He's going on about us all taking a trip to the North Georgia mountains where a tightwire walker will, in a month's time, cross Tallulah Gorge using only his feet and a pole to hold him there.

He's been talking nonstop ever since we left Garden City Beach because Georgetown Steel is fabricating the cables to be used in the crossing. "That walk across the gorge is going to make history," Clay says, the tip of his cigarette bobbing in the air. "And we're a big part of making it happen, Georgetown Steel. You got to go, won't see anything like it ever again, not in your lifetime." I say nothing, letting the smoke from his cigarette swirl in the breeze around me. "Besides, it would be easy," he says. "I'll come up from Walhalla, pick you and Kelly up in the morning, and drive on over. It's not that far from the Highlands."

I raise my head then, nervous that he's looking right at me, not watching the road, and Kelly right there in the backseat hearing everything. "It's not *the* Highlands," I say. "It's just Highlands. You're being lazy with that, you know."

The car's tires hum along the packed shell and gravel road. I shade my eyes to read the sign just past Pawleys Island telling us Georgetown is still fifteen miles away. I smile, reach over to touch him so he won't be offended by the mild scolding. "Let's just wait and see," I say.

I don't tell him that I've seen acrobats before on *The Ed Sullivan Show*, a man walking a wire, bouncing for a moment before turning a somersault and landing again on his feet. This is different, though. There is always a net on TV, the distance only ceiling to floor in some television studio. Clay says the gorge is a thousand feet deep in places, and one small mistake, one slip or miscalculation . . .

I lift myself up in the seat, find sunglasses on the dashboard, and then turn to face Kelly. She is stretched out, eyes closed, though I know she's not asleep. She has heard every word about Tallulah Gorge and how Clay plans to visit me in Whiteside Cove when I take her up to visit Momma this summer. When I tell her to sit up and rejoin the living, Kelly just lays there, eyes closed, her softball glove propped on her stomach like it's the very thing holding her down.

The land outside the back window runs away from me simmering in mid-afternoon sun. The whiteness of the road, the sand edging along its shoulder, stands in stark contrast to the brown beyond. Here, away from the ocean and salt creeks, trees seem to wilt, shrubbery, salt myrtle, straggling cordgrass, all dry and brittle.

Once Kelly's song is through, I run the dial, find a crackling AM station trying its best to keep Marvin Gaye tuned in. Clay lights another cigarette, the blunt end of the lighter flaming when it touches the tip. I smile and sing along. *"Ain't no moun-tain high, ain't no val-ley low . . ."*

Our hands touch palm to palm as he passes the filterless cigarette to me. It's then I hear Kelly turn over in the backseat, the words *good God* tumbling out of her mouth in what I know is disrespect. The harsh smoke burns my throat. I hate the habit, the nastiness of the taste, but the nicotine has its effect, and I lean again on the seat letting the song and cigarette be enough until we are across the Intracoastal Waterway and into Georgetown, where my baby girl will be an All-Star pitcher this afternoon.

We find the field squeezed in between steel and paper mills, smokestacks belching black and gray soot into a sky already filled with an uncomfortable haze. Kelly won't talk to me when we park the car, just gets up from the seat and runs out to the field where her coach gives her a ball, lets her know she'll pitch the first three innings. The Bel Air sits beneath a small stand of trees where Clay spreads a blanket, unfolds lounge chairs for us to sit in while Kelly's team takes the field.

I watch her on the infield dirt, so much like Peck, her arms and shoulders strong and balanced, skin the color of honey. I'm as white as sun-bleached shell, skin too pale to do anything but burn if I'm outside too long. Worshipping the sun was never part of growing up in the mountains. Whiteside Cove was breezy, cool enough even in midsummer to wear long sleeves by late afternoon, a sweater at night. Here along the salt creeks and beaches, the sun demands that you disrobe to nothing, sink knee-deep into black mud, dig out oysters, or empty crab pots. Seining nets are like bridal veils thrown into creeks capturing shrimp and minnows, their transparent bodies nearly invisible in the turbid muck. It is all part of the land's requirement that you become a living part of the rivers and creeks. But it has never been very livable to me. It is unbearable at best.

I watch Kelly warm up, so poised and unafraid at fifteen, so much like Peck. I wonder if she even needs me. I remember after she was born, how Peck could calm her when she cried, the way he would carry her outside onto the dock by the marsh or drive along the beach until she fell asleep. When Kelly was old enough to walk, he took her to play in the ocean and later taught her to surf and fish, catch crabs or dig for clams at low tide. They were inseparable. When I began our trips back to the mountains to get away from the heat and the marsh, her time away from Peck was tolerated. And even though I know Kelly loved being with her grandmother, the mountains were just too far away. She would climb up Sunset Rock or to the top of Whiteside Mountain, look as far east as she could, take a deep breath only to announce that there was no smell of the ocean in the air, and that would seem to negate the legitimacy of our stay. Low country is in her blood, but not a drop pulses through me. It used to disturb me to think Kelly was more Peck's than mine. It used to tie me up in knots for days, but now it seems to matter less.

I have read in magazines that everyone has the right to go and find themselves, *do your own thing,* they say. I tried talking to Clay about this when we stopped for lunch today, but Kelly was mad at the world because Peck wasn't the one bringing her to the game. She was just ugly—not a good way to start out my new life, but I didn't care. I ignored her, ate my Hardee's hamburger, and told Clay that today was the first day of the rest of my life. I said, "I feel like Jonathan Livingston Seagull."

Kelly looked up from her meal then, said, "Momma, seagulls are dumb birds. All they eat is other people's trash."

Jonathan Livingston Seagull was an assigned book from Kelly's high school English class, so I know she read it. I know she doesn't think that about Jonathan because she's the one who told me to read it. Right then she was just so angry at me. I told her to shut up, said, "You know what I mean." Clay sat there with the dumbest look on his face. A fireman like Peck, I don't think he's read a thing since college, unless it had something to do with smoke and flames. "I feel free," I said, looking at both of them. "I just feel free, that's all I was trying to say."

I watch seagulls differently now, the way they float out on a breeze, cut loose, free. *No limits, Jonathan,* that's what the book said. I don't want limits either, no matter how mad Kelly gets at me.

She's on the mound when a gust of hot wind gets itself tangled up on the infield, the sand and shell surface whipping up into a small tornado. The girls cover their faces with gloves, arms over eyes until it passes, leaving the air dusty and parched.

"They could have done this in the evening," I tell Clay. "The heat could hurt these girls." He is standing up watching Kelly throw strikes, smiles at me when I say this.

"You never liked it here, Cassie," he says. "I don't think anything could make you happy." He looks into the sky, scans the edge of the field. The whole neighborhood surrounding us seems to be a victim of the steel mill drowning in grime and soot. "Besides," he says. "No lights."

"What?" I ask, shading my eyes when I look at him.

"No lights for a nighttime game," he says, then yells encouragement when Kelly's team closes out the first inning.

In the second, Kelly gets a hit and is then thrown out at second. When she pitches in the top of the third, a girl from Aynor hits her good and scores a couple of runs. Clay shouts encouragement, but Kelly ignores us both. By the time she is finished pitching, she leaves the mound to applause, pats on her back from the coach.

Some people tell me that my daughter is a phenom, that at fifteen she is better than some seniors who are winning college scholarships. Her coach says there could be something for her down the road once college coaches get a whiff of her. I don't like the way he put that, the idea of someone sniffing at my daughter like she's some kind of dog in heat, but I understand what he means. When I see her play, the way she's different on the mound or in the batter's box waiting on a pitch, I know she's not the same girl I see at home when I ask her to clean her room or help with the dishes. I've been taking her to two-a-days, that's all the responsibility for her talent that I can claim. The rest is of her making.

During the next three innings, Kelly is in the outfield. Clay walks over behind the backstop and talks to some man who's been watching the game with a clipboard and pencil, scribbling notes while Kelly pitched. They talk like they're friends from way back. Clay stands with his arms crossed, spitting onto the ground, rocking on his heels, pointing out at Kelly and then over to me. I act like I don't see this because I really don't like it. Sometimes Clay will just take over. He doesn't ask or tell me what he's going to do. He just leaves me unannounced to go somewhere and then comes back with something new to tell me.

My affair with Clay Taylor has been going on for as long as there has been a drought in the low country. He keeps joking that if he quit seeing me maybe it would start raining again. But he won't do that. Whenever Peck's working at the station, Clay makes sure he's off duty so he and I can be together. It doesn't work all the time, so lately he's even started calling in sick.

Clay and Peck used to be equals, friends. But he thought he'd be chief instead of Peck when Garden City opened, thought they passed over the better man. Now he's leaving the low country altogether to become the new chief in Walhalla, South Carolina. Earlier this afternoon, before we left for Georgetown, Clay came to me and asked if I would move up there with him.

I heard his boat come through the salt creeks navigating the high tide. He called for me by tooting his horn, the reverse of his engine boiling the water as he glided up to the floating pier. He waited there, shirtless, the sun sparkling against his heat-drenched skin, a dark perpetual tan that seems dyed into all men who live their entire lives along the marsh. We dangled our feet in the creek, letting the dark water push at our ankles while he told me about Walhalla.

Clay made it sound like a new life though he would still be a fireman. It was closer to the mountains, he said, a new world that he didn't know, so it would be like starting all over. That's when he asked me to go. "You can be my guide," he said, "show me the ropes up in them thar hills." He smiled, and then lit a cigarette.

"But you know the mountains," I told him. "You went to school in Cullowhee."

"You should have been there too," he reminded me. "I expected to see you on campus that fall, but when I heard what happened, I couldn't believe it. Peck stepped up and did the right thing. But it should have been different, Cassie. I won't let another chance get past me."

I didn't know what to say. The fact is, he was right, everything would have been different if I would have stayed at college and not come here married and pregnant, just out of high school. That summer, Clay and I talked about going to school every day. Peck was always quiet, maybe a little jealous, though he never would admit it. Clay and Peck were good friends while they were life-guards, and after Peck started taking me out at night, Clay kept his distance. Near the end of summer, though, he would drop by the cabins when Peck wasn't around, and we'd talked about looking for each other on campus. It seemed innocent enough at the time, flirtatious maybe, but I never told Peck about it. I didn't want it to bring up any trouble between them.

On the pier this afternoon Clay's eyes were dark, serious, holding me there until I promised that I would go with him. When I did, he smiled, breathed heavy like he wasn't sure I was going to say yes. He flicked the spent cigarette into the marsh, leaned over and kissed me hard on the mouth for God or anyone else who might have wanted to see it.

We sat on the edge of the dock, the black creek water lapping against the side of Clay's boat. I felt there wasn't a place in the world that I couldn't go now. I had met Clay when I was seventeen years old and from that moment on we were living our lives separately, waiting to arrive at this moment together. I needed Clay and he needed me. Walhalla would be a new start.

When I heard Kelly coming home from the beach, I tried to get up, but Clay held my wrist. "Let her see," he said. "If you pretend nothing's going on, then nothing's going on." He raised an eyebrow as if he was flaunting some sort of hard-earned wisdom.

Ellen Thomas's Volkswagen stuttered down the stretch of dirt road and coughed to a stop in the backyard. Both girls were laughing, slamming car doors, running into the house when Kelly caught us sitting like high school lovers, our feet wet, bodies touching. "Where's Daddy?" she asked. She averted her eyes, searched the yard as an obvious and uncomfortable excuse.

"He's at work, where else?" I told her.

"Is he coming with us?" Ellen had walked back down the steps. The two girls stood frozen, arm in arm so naturally, so unassumingly that it angered me how easy it was for them to protect each other.

"No," I snapped, "but we need to leave soon, so go get your things." I watched Ellen whisper something into Kelly's ear. Then she waved and hurried off to her car.

Kelly stayed put, alone now, shifting on her feet, one arm

reaching behind her back to catch the other at the elbow. She squinted in the sun, this time looking straight at me, defiant. "I thought he was coming."

"He got called out, a boy drowned or something at the pier," I said. "Didn't you see them down there?"

"No," she said, her voice breaking, giving her away. "I should have gone by there myself and picked him up."

"You know what kind of good that would have done," I said.

Kelly stood there like she was waiting for me to say something more, like this was one of those moments where if I opened my mouth, whatever came out would explain the whole world to her. I know she deserves someone who can give her that, a way for her to understand what she can't see through her own eyes yet, but I wasn't in the mood. I was caught up in Clay's offer in Walhalla and the possibility of a new life. I just sat there, looked at her and raised my hands. "So what are you waiting for?" I said. "Scoot." She turned, running into the house, the door slamming shut behind her.

There is no letup in the heat on the field, the high sun bleaching color out of everything. Stagnant air from the paper mills finds us when the breeze shifts, making breathing all that more difficult. The umpires change out for the second time in the top of the fifth inning. All the girls hover around the water buckets, drinking and pouring it over their heads and necks to keep cool.

Clay is still talking to the man behind the backstop. They concentrate on a clipboard, watch Kelly field a pop fly to end the inning. Clay turns and shakes the man's hand, then takes an envelope before he leaves to return to me. Kelly comes in from the field. I watch her cross the third-base line, throw her glove into the dugout, and dowse water on her face.

"I've got more good news," Clay says when he sits down. He

opens the envelope, hands me papers, some sort of application to be filled out. "Coach Lambert over there," he says, pointing to the sheet of paper I am holding, "guess where he's from?"

"Where?" I say. I look at the man as he writes on his clipboard.

"Guess," he says.

"Clay, I have no idea. He could be from Mars for all I know."

"He's from Cullowhee," Clay says, his face broadening into a smile. "Cullowhee, North Carolina."

"That's real nice," I say. "But I don't know what that means." I glance back to the papers in my hand looking for answers.

"He coaches softball for Western Carolina. He likes what he sees in Kelly."

I look toward the man again, this time seeing more of a threat than anything else. "She's only going to be a sophomore, Clay."

"He knows that. He wants her at his camp this summer."

"Where?" I ask, though I heard what he just said. Cullowhee's less than an hour from Momma's house in Whiteside Cove.

"At Western Carolina," he repeats while pointing to the application, tapping it with his finger. "Camp starts on Monday."

"Monday," I say. My heart races when I realize I am holding papers that give our plans legitimacy, a real reason to leave early and be with Clay.

"Monday," he says, winking at me. He takes a drag from his cigarette then flicks the ash into the sand. Around us, the trees drop leaves like it's fall. "It's perfect, Cassie. I've given Surfside my notice, so Peck won't find out until Monday. You can take Kelly up to Cullowhee. Peck won't stop you. Then we can meet up in Walhalla for the summer, get things started."

At first I'm elated, my heart racing, remembering the promise I made to Clay on the dock earlier in the afternoon. Then hesitation like a cold tide rises through me, a question forming that I did not expect. It surprises me, almost takes my breath away. Clay Taylor is a fireman too, and what good would it do to live with him, trade one fireman for another? It's odd that I would feel this as soon as there is a chance to go, as soon as there are no more excuses to keep me from leaving Peck, but there it is, hesitation enough that Clay asks me if I'm all right.

"Yes," I say. "I'm just hot, this heat is stifling."

"Well, if you're worried about it, let's talk," he says. "We've waited too long."

"I'm fine," I tell him. "It's just happening so fast, that's all. I need time for it to sink in. Now let's watch the game." I touch his hand for reassurance, but it's too brief, a light pat, affectionless, a touch that I know will confuse him more than settle any concern.

I don't tell him that after almost seven months of scheming to be together, I am suddenly questioning my motives. I can't afford the doubt. I'm too close to finding a way out of this life for good. In my reasoning, I remind myself it's his way out too, so I let Clay enjoy the moment. "I'm excited about the future," I say. "It's all going to work out."

He smiles at me then. "It's going to be perfect," he says, then turns, like a proud father, to watch Kelly come to bat.

He stretches his lips with forefinger and thumb to let out a shrill whistle when Kelly steps to the plate. It's her last at bat. She looks at me, her stare cold, her stance angry when she lifts the bat to her shoulder, stabs the ground with the toe of her cleat to plant it firmly in the batter's box. And then, taking the first pitch, she sends the ball out over the fence in deep center field.

It flies through air hot enough to catch fire, doesn't stop until it is in the street rolling toward the steel mill. The crowd sitting around the field erupts while she stands watching the ball leave the field. Then, as if Kelly couldn't care less, she turns and looks at me, her face expressionless, pale in the heat as she begins to run the bases. She jogs like what she has just done means nothing, but I know it does. I know how important it was to her to do well here today. She is a standout, the one everyone is talking about, heads leaning to ears, voices whispering about her future.

Though she no longer looks at me, I can still see her there at home plate, our eyes locked before the ball had even cleared the fence. While I watch her run the bases, I cannot help but feel she is trying to leave me, trying to get away because I am here with Clay and not her father. Kelly is a child and will not understand for years what is to come, even though she will have to endure it all. I have to wonder if I will destroy her very understanding of love and family. "I'm sorry," I whisper, apologizing for what I am about to do.

Clay asks what, thinking my words are meant for him. I smile, say "Nothing, never mind," and then watch Kelly touch home plate, raising her hands to the high fives of her cheering team-mates. Peck is in that girl more than me. It's as plain as the heat and sweat of this boiling summer. It's a shame he's not here to see it all, but then he never has been. Peck Calhoun Johnson is first and foremost a fireman and saving a life is more important than living his own. I wish he could be here to see Kelly's home run, but he has trouble on the beach. There's trouble everywhere now, I think. Peck always told me that in a fire there's nothing good for anyone, not those caught in it or those that have to fight it. "Flame don't choose who or what to burn," he says. "It burns blind."

When the game is over, Kelly walks toward where Clay and I sit. She drags her bag, the sun blanching the world around us.

Peck

IT DOESN'T OCCUR TO ME until we get the call, an eight-year-old boy off the pier at Garden City Beach. I'm not supposed to even be here. Clay Taylor is scheduled for rotation, but he's been about as dependable as rain lately, so I stick around, take the call. I'm over at the window that closes off the small office from the rest of the station when it comes, a feeling that pulls at my stomach, washes across me like a faint breeze. It makes me wait a second longer than I should. Intuition maybe, I don't know. It's just all over me when I stick my face into the small hole in the glass and yell at Lori, the sound of the fire bell and the Pirsch pumper roaring to life hiding any signs in my voice that I feel something's wrong, somewhere something's not right. "Call Cassie," I say, "tell her there's a drowning. I'll get there when I can." I can see the disappointment when I tell her this. Lori knows what I'll be missing, knows what it will mean. I'm last to get into my turnouts, J.D. already behind the wheel waiting as I lift myself up to ride shotgun. J.D.'s new, a rookie in his first year, but he's got an old heart. You can't hide much from that boy. "You all right there, Chief?" he asks.

"Right as rain," I say.

He looks at me then, a question growing in his eyes that I won't let him ask. "Well, are we going," I say, motioning toward the opened garage door, "or do you want to sit here all afternoon and talk about the weather?"

J.D. smiles at that. "Well," he says, putting the Pirsch into gear, "you're the one who brought up rain." He turns on lights, pops the horn twice to let Lori know we're on the move. I keep quiet about what I felt when the call came in. I don't want to raise any concern. Everything we do out here on the beach is about danger and death. I can't tell my crew that something I don't even understand myself has come over me. If they think I'm worried, it could put us in even more danger than we'll have to face, so I stay quiet and look around for my sunglasses. A chief has to be a chief, mind clear and eyes wide open. I yell at J.D., "You seen my shades?"

He looks over, a smile pulling at one side of his face, his eyes bright when he yells back, "Yeah."

He swings the Pirsch pumper out into oncoming traffic, emergencies flashing, the siren piercing the mid-afternoon heat, warning other drivers to let us get on through. I pull the hand mike from its cradle to let dispatch down in Surfside know that we are on Atlantic Avenue, 10-76, responding and en route.

J.D.'s young, twenty-four back in April. He's been with the station since last fall. It looks like he's lived on the beach all his life, even though he grew up in Columbia, his daddy a retired firefighter up there. I can see by the way Lori watches him that he's a real looker. He's got a strong jaw, sandy blond hair that I need to remind him to cut. He has a fortress face, looks like it was chiseled from stone. It makes people turn around and listen when he speaks. "I ain't got all day here," I yell. "Where are my shades, J.D.?" He taps the top of his head with a hand to say *right where you left them,* then grabs the wheel with both to whip the truck onto South Waccamaw.

The road across from the beach is full of pedestrians watching us run up to the Kingfisher Pier. We pull in underneath the decking, a small arcade and snack bar full of tourists right above us. It's the only place on the whole beach where there's good shade, where the breeze tries its best to be cool. We're the first on the scene—no law enforcement or ambulance yet. I don't like it, but it happens.

"Radio Lori, tell here we're 10-23," I say, "and keep your radio on. No one else is here yet."

I head out toward the end of the pier to assess the situation while J.D. preps the gear. All the while I'm wishing that I was going home to pick up Kelly and Cassie for the drive over to Georgetown. It would be hotter than scorched earth at the softball field, but that's nothing compared to what I'm about to confront out here.

On the end of the pier, it's not good at all. There's a man and a woman huddled in chairs, the woman hysterical to the point that she's probably going into shock. The man is trying to console her, but he's not getting anywhere. I can tell they've been drinking. It's all over them, and it's not good.

Out off the pier, a boy is floating limp and facedown in the water. Several men have him on their lines. They've hooked his shorts to keep him from floating away. There're kids screaming and gawkers trying to take pictures. One of the men pulls me off to the side, his breath full of alcohol when he tells me that the boy's been in the water a long time, that he's got to be dead. He leans closer, whispers about a spinner that's been hanging around that's nearly six feet long. Even though the shark's not likely to care about a dead boy, the idea worries me. I don't need a spectacle like that going on down here.

Another man smelling of hot sun and booze comes up while

I'm looking over the side. "We got a net, but ain't got no rope to tie it off," he says. "Jimmy over here was going in after him, but I said wait."

This guy Jimmy's wearing a pair of cutoffs and no shirt, his skin burned a bright pink. His eyes are almost slits. He's drunker than his buddy who's telling me about the net.

"Show me the net," I say. The man hurries me around the back of a small covered shed while I radio to J.D. to bring the hundred-foot lifeline from the truck. I settle in to the call now, measured patience taking over.

The man brings me around the shed to find a round wire mesh four feet in diameter leaning against the rail. "We got it sitting here just in case someone hooks a turtle or a skate or something like that," he says, "but it'll hold that boy too. We just need a rope." He smells like a brewery when we're out of the breeze.

"Let's see what we can do with this thing," I say. When we get back, the father is at the rail. It looks like he wants to go over, and we don't need that happening. J.D.'s right there doing what he needs to do. I can hear him talking, the man's wife screaming from her chair. It's like something out of a bad movie, the screams notching up the tension.

Now some man who doesn't belong on the pier decides to take charge. He gets up in my face. "Somebody's got to get that boy out," he screams. "What the hell's taking so long?" I put the net down and walk him over to the middle of the pier.

"Sir," I say, "you need to move on back, right now."

He seems startled that someone's put a hand on his chest and is pushing back on him like this, but I don't care. I don't need any more chaos out here than I already have.

"Are you in charge of this?" he asks, his words slurred in the air.

"Yes sir, I am."

"Well goddamn, man, get a rope. We got to get that boy out!"

"We're working on that," I say. "Now I really need you to move on back, sir, please, right now."

That's when I see Teddy coming down the pier. He's the Horry County deputy sheriff who works Garden City Beach during his weekday shifts. We go way back, past high school even, still surf together when schedules allow. It always helps when he's on scene. Teddy's a stand-up guy. I let him have this one and go back to the net and J.D. at the rail. The father is down on the decking, J.D. holding him there asking him to be a good man and go back to his wife.

The men who told me about the net have started tying off the rope to the lead lines. They've mangled the job, and that pisses me off too. It's part of the problem, being thin in personnel on a beach that is busting out of its seams. I take a minute to look around, assess the situation, make sure that everything is falling into place. I learned a long time ago that you have to pull yourself out of a call to take account of things, to make sure nothing's overlooked and that we don't invite any unnecessary danger.

Teddy's pushing the public back, putting chairs out in a row to move onlookers a safe distance away from the scene. J.D.'s with the mother and father, checking vitals, trying to console. The men with the lines on the boy keep him there, spotting the water just in case that spinner shows up. With everything accounted for, I get busy untangling the line, the circus of dunces watching me undo their mess when Teddy comes over and tells them to leave. "You okay?" he asks.

"Yeah, now that you're here."

He looks at the spaghetti of rope tangled around my feet and says, "You must have been a Boy Scout."

"All the way to Eagle," I say, and then we both smile.

When the rope's ready, I look over to the boy's parents for J.D. The mother's on her knees throwing up, maybe going into shock. The father's crumpled down next to her, no help at all. I know this is a recovery, not a rescue, so their boy won't need what J.D. can offer. I leave him where he can do some good and call Teddy in, tell him what I want to do.

There's nothing that can be done to save this child, but we still hurry, lower the net, the wire mesh slipping beneath the water when a wave slops past. When I feel the tug against my grip, I say "Pull," and Teddy starts backing toward the other side of the pier. He's a mule of a guy, the half-inch line wrapped around his thick waist two or three times, a firm counterweight to the bloated body we catch on the first try.

The boy rolls down into the basket and stays there in a fetal position, small crabs falling off his back as the rope is drawn up to the top of the pier. For a moment there's hope that he's alive, his mouth almost in a smile, his eyes opened. The movement of the net and the lines still attached gives the impression that the boy is moving. It's macabre, a little puppet on strings rising out of death. The image taunts, fools those on top who don't know any better. The father is holding on to his wife, and they have edged out onto the pier, J.D. standing with them.

"You might want to get them back," I say, but he can't make the boy's parents leave the rail. I don't blame them; if it was my kid, I'd be there too. I don't know how you live without your child. I see this too much, and I still never get used to it.

An ambulance crew arrives just as we get the boy on the pier. He flops out of the net like some kind of odd fish, water pouring out of his mouth. It's horrible and Teddy doesn't waste any time pushing the crowd farther away. The mother starts screaming again, tries to crawl into the net, the father too. They're so torn up they're just crazy. The ambulance crew holds them back so J.D. can get to their boy. He's over the body checking for vitals and clearing airways, trying to do what he can to find any signs of life. But the boy's just dead, that's it. The father walks over to ID the body, while the mother is put on a stretcher and rolled back down the pier. There's a few on the beach who cheer when the stretcher rolls away thinking the boy has survived, but the father knows better.

He knows they let the boy get away and the most horrific thing that could have ever happened did. J.D. stops working and lays a blanket over the body. The man walks to the end of the pier still holding on to a beer and that sort of pisses me off until he heaves the can out into the ocean, his cry so full of hurt and grief that it makes my stomach hurt.

And though the man doesn't come right out and say it, I know he wants to be under that blanket instead of his boy. He'd trade anything so his boy could live. I'd want that if it was Kelly. It hurts to see it, but it hurts more to think all of this could have been avoided. Somehow the boy just got away from them, got on the beach and then the ocean had its way. Fault will be for Teddy to figure out, to see if the parents might be charged with some kind of negligence, though I doubt he'll want to do anything more to these people. I mean, my God, what more could be done to punish them?

We wait for the second ambulance and Teddy's backup to come before we wrap our gear. I call Lori to request a 10-79 because a coroner's going to have to be involved in this. There's going to be an investigation, which means more paperwork before I can get away.

"How does that happen?" J.D. asks when he comes up beside me.

"What?"

"The boy drowning while his parents are on the pier like that. How does that happen?"

I look at J.D. for a minute because I forget he's still a rookie. "I don't know," I say. "It's just life, brother. And sometimes we get to clean it up."

He looks at me and I can see that's not going to do it for him. He's going to be a good fireman if he learns to let it go. You got to learn to do that if you're going to last any time on this job. "Let's finish this up," I say, and he hikes up the gear onto his shoulders, moves down the pier to the truck where small boys have gathered. They ask him if he can turn on the siren, but J.D. ignores them, just keeps storing the gear and dwelling on something he can't change.

"Hey, let the boys have a look inside," I say. "I'll finish up out here." I stow the ropes and J.D.'s medical supplies. He uses a large tackle box to carry his gear, and when he pulls it out, it looks like he might be going fishing instead of heading out to save a life. We tease him all the time, tell him there's nothing in that box a fish would care to eat, that we'd never let him on a boat with that thing. He's a good rookie, a good sport with all the shit we dish out. I look up toward the front of the Pirsch. J.D.'s letting the boys sit in the driver's seat with the lights flashing. One of them is wearing his helmet. They all seem to be having a good time, the tragedy out on the pier finding a perspective. It's a good sign.

When the truck is packed, I tell the boys to stand clear, then I jump in shotgun, and we are on our way back to the station. My watch says 4:45, so there's no way I'll make Kelly's game.

"Think she pitched good?" J.D. asks. He looks over. I can see his eyes, dark pools of blue. He knows Cassie and I are having trouble.

"Guess so," I say, "but she's just fifteen. I don't think it matters much."

"She's got an awful good arm, Peck. Fifteen or not, I bet she's good."

"Still, it won't matter much," I say.

J.D.'s seen Kelly pitch. Early in the spring, she called Lori to remind me about a game in Litchfield. J.D. was rotating off duty at the same time, so he volunteered to tag along. I was staying down at the fire station pretty regularly because Cassie didn't want me at home. We were fighting then as we are now about disappointments she felt had ruined her life. I know there are things she didn't get to do because of what happened with Kelly, and at times I wish I could just tell her to go, come back when you're finished doing whatever it is you got to do. But I don't say that. She has a daughter to raise, and I've told her time and again that Kelly's more important than anything bad between the two of us.

She told me she needed space, so I started staying at the station, checking in when Kelly would come to the beach to surf or just drop by to let me know how her mother was getting along. I probably take more rotations than I should, stay at the station when I ought to be home trying to make it work with Cassie. But life becomes a habit if you live it the same way long enough, and we've been at this for years.

We drove over to Litchfield in my truck, rain threatening the skies, but it never showed up. There were only a handful of folks at the game when J.D. and I got there, mostly parents of the kids on the Socastee team. We watched Kelly throw six perfect innings, miss the no-hitter, and end up losing the game with four hits in the top of the seventh. Kelly's only in the ninth grade, pitching against girls three years older. I can only imagine what she'll be like in a couple of years.

The game helped Cassie and me get along that afternoon. She let J.D. come back to the house, and he took it on himself to cheer

Kelly up. He let her pitch for about an hour out in the backyard while Cassie and I tried to work things out. I think Kelly's crush on him started that day. She's fifteen, J.D. twenty-four. I know couples who are married and have more years between them, so I'm not telling J.D. anything about the crush. There're some things he doesn't need to know.

When we get back to the station, only Partee's there for the shift change. He's looking around like he lost something when J.D. kills the engine. "Where's Clay?" he asks.

"He called in sick," Lori says, rolling her eyes. She's waiting when I climb out of the Pirsch waving forms in my face that need filling out already. The loss of life makes the pile of paperwork that much more urgent.

"He ain't sick," Partee says. "He just ain't here, again."

"I know that," I say.

Partee leans a hand against the Pirsch, sweat darkening his shirt into a half-moon under his arm. "Who wants to stay this time?"

J.D. walks around from the front of the Pirsch, gathering and putting equipment back in order. "I'll stay," he says. He looks at me then. "You go on and try to make some of that game."

It's a nice gesture on his part, but I just shake my head. "Nah, it's probably over," I say. "You don't need to do that."

"Rookie wants to stay, let him stay," Partee says. "Otherwise it's going to be you again." He smiles then, his wide white grin glowing against his dark skin.

Partee's black, the darkest black I've ever seen. He still has family that lives out on one of the old barrier islands. They've been around these parts for generations, descendants of slaves who worked the rice and tobacco fields. Some of the firemen have a problem with Partee being black. But hell, Partee's always got your back, and that's a lot more than I can say about Clay Taylor right now. There're still a lot of people in these parts who can't see past a man's color. But I hardly ever think about it with Partee, except when he smiles. It's just too hard to miss it then.

"Seems you should be out doing something more exciting than taking an extra shift," I tell J.D.

Partee smiles that smile again. "Rookie's too young to do that, ain't he?"

"They still card him at Maggie's," Lori says, turning to leave. We all get a good laugh out of that, the way she just throws it out there like it's truth.

I look at the boy. He's doing all right with the teasing. He's a good rookie. "You don't mind hanging around then?"

"Nah," he says. "You go on home, see Cassie."

I think about that for a minute, but I know I won't go. "Better I just head on down to the beach for a while," I say. "Let Cassie get home before I do."

Nobody argues with that. They all understand my situation. Partee says, "You go on then, enjoy yourself. We'll take care of business around here." Then he offers to help J.D. finish cleaning the Pirsch.

I tell the boys to be safe. J.D. looks out from around the back of the Pirsch, says, "Let me know about Kelly now. I want to know how bad she smoked them."

I give him a thumbs-up as a promise, then Lori comes out of the office to tell me she's radioed Surfside that I'm 10-42, off duty.

In my truck, I reach over and pop the glove box, fish around inside until I come up with a small Skoal tin. In it are a few roaches, good weed that Teddy shares with me when we get together. The traffic has quieted down, everyone out to dinner or getting ready to go. I make it across fast, the evening light raking the cordgrass, burning the back side of the cottages along the shore. I pull a right onto South Waccamaw, head out to the dunes where the marsh and the ocean meet. There's still room on this end of the strand, Myrtle Beach not yet reaching its tentacles this far south, but it's coming. There's talk of a private beach somewhere out past the marina headed toward the point, but I haven't heard much more than rumors about that.

I remember 1954, after Hurricane Hazel. We could drive out here and be on deserted beach for miles, but I was just nineteen back then. The storm destroyed all but two houses along the strand, swept across the marsh on an eighteen-foot tidal surge and wreaked havoc for miles inland, killing more than a thousand people before it ended its path of destruction somewhere in Canada. In the aftermath of the storm, many wondered if Garden City would stay deserted forever. That was nearly sixteen years ago, and it's becoming hard to find anywhere along the strand that's untouched, where I can surf and not see houses and people crowding the beach.

Still, there's nothing that can take the place of an evening on the water, the way the light pearls the sky and the ocean so flat you can see a wave form long before it gets to you. I climb into the back end of my truck, shed my uniform and underwear right there, change into my cutoffs, and grab the board. I climb the dunes and walk down the beach past a few tourists who are starting to take their evening strolls. We exchange glances, but I don't want to think about people who come here for a week and then disappear, skin burned and nursing weeklong hangovers.

Right now, I'm looking out on the ocean, watching the lineup coming in, waves I should be catching. I wish Kelly were here. I taught her to surf when she was just ten, and I bet if you asked her where she'd rather have been today, pitching softball or surfing,

Kelly would say the beach, riding waves with her old man. It's all that matters when you're out here. It's all I care about once I feel the water float the board, my arms pulling to take me out beyond the break, out beyond where anything can get in my way, until the light is gone from the sky and I have to return to shore. And when I feel the lift, the push a wave gives me sliding down into its trough, the board no longer floats still but is caught in motion moving forward, slicing toward the beach, my mind clear, wet and cool, easy.

WE LIVE ON THE OTHER SIDE of the marsh, down along the salt creeks, but to get there takes time. The roads are narrow, congested with ribbons of tourists, two lanes not enough to keep the flow moving. It gives me time to think about Cassie and what she might be like when I get home. We haven't talked for a few days. When I call she's not there, or just won't answer the phone. I know she's suffering, but I don't know what more I can do. We've been at it for fifteen years, a love that comes and goes, more going than coming lately, and now Kelly's getting in the middle of it. She can see it when we fight, knows that I stay away from the house, and that worries me. I don't want her hurting about her mother and me; she's not supposed to. It just seems everything down here is suffering right now, Cassie and me further apart than I can remember. I try and do what I can to keep Kelly out of it, keep the calm.

Once I turn off pavement, there's no light at all for about a mile. The land's so dark it moans. My truck finds every rut in the sandy unpaved road as it winds through thick old-growth oak and magnolia. Kelly and Cassie have often begged to sell this house and move farther toward Conway. "We need to be closer to civilization," they complain, but I won't budge. I just can't leave this place.

When Pops saw the house for the first time, he stood on what little of the pier was left after Hurricane Hazel came through. He looked out across the marsh like he was measuring the distance to open water. On the beachfront a mile or more across, they were struggling to rebuild where the storm had shifted land and re-shaped the point. He came back up into the yard after a few minutes, a heaviness already settled in on his life. He said, "This house was built before Hazel came through and look, it's still here." He turned then, his arm making a great sweeping motion to take in the whole of the marsh. "You can't say that about anything else."

Cassie was still in the truck, Kelly not yet born. But already, her attitude had turned against the place. "If Hazel didn't get this house," Pops said, "nothing will. Now count your blessings and move on in."

And that's what we did; at least, that's what I did. It's the one place I come home to, where I can leave everything else behind. Living out here on the marsh helps me get through the rest of my life. I wish Cassie understood that, and I wish it were true for her, too.

I take a curve. Spanish moss, like the fingers of ghosts, pulls at my truck. The headlights keep me from driving into swamp on ei-ther side until the road abruptly dead-ends into our backyard. The house is two stories in need of a paint job. It's surrounded by red cedar and oaks, tall trees that keep us cool except during the hottest part of the season. The house looks out onto the salt creek, seems abandoned in the darkness of night. I park behind Cassie's Bel Air, can't see any lights, but I know she's up. I know she's wait-ing for me to come home.

When I step into the screened-in porch, I see the living room is lit, the pier too. There's a familiar boat tied up, Cassie talking real friendly with someone. I know who it is, but I won't go down there yet. I want to say hello to Kelly first, see how she played this afternoon. When I come through the door, she's stretched out on the couch, still in her uniform, reading a book.

I head to the refrigerator for a beer.

"Hey," she says, the word short like a bark. She holds the book on her belly, not lifting her eyes from the page. I pull a cold bottle from the fridge, know I need to answer, but I wait. Down on the pier Clay Taylor is talking to Cassie, their laughter floating through the opened windows of the house. "Sorry I missed the game," I say. "Did you win?"

"If you'd have been there, you'd know." Kelly drops the book like a curtain, her eyes watery, tired. She holds me in her gaze, challenging.

"I got a job, Kelly, you know that." We look at each other for another minute before she gives up.

"Whatever," she says and then starts reading the book again.

I stay put, look out to where Cassie and Clay are standing. Cassie glances toward the house then back to Clay, wrapping herself in her arms like she might be cold, impossible as that is. She's never been comfortable here, winter or summer. In the fifteen years we've been on the marsh, I think she's lived alone, even when I tried to help her live with me. From the looks of it, she's got a new helper now.

I watch Clay flick a cigarette into the black water. All this is pissing me off, but I don't want to take it out on Kelly. It's hard to hold back. "You didn't answer my question," I say. "I asked if you won. You want to answer me this time?"

"It's not about winning in an All-Star game," Kelly says.

"That still doesn't answer the question, does it?"

"We lost four to two," she says, putting her book down to look at me again. "I pitched three innings and then played center field."

"Anyone hit you while you pitched?"

"Only this girl from Aynor. I really just lobbed one over and she creamed it."

"Little nervous out there?"

"Yeah, I guess." Kelly stretches, the couch no longer easily holding her. She's not a little girl anymore. At fifteen, she's starting to look like a woman. She's sleepy, bone-tired. I can see it in her eyes, half-mast and red, so I try to ease up. Even though I'm happy for how well she's done in her freshman year, I'm glad it's over and she can have some fun again. It's summer, let her be a kid without the pressures to be something more.

"I wish you'd have been there," she says. "That's all."

"I know you do," I say. "I couldn't make it this time, but I imagine there'll be others, don't you?"

"Yeah, I guess." She thumbs the pages of her book. Dark outlines of dirt cross her ankles to mark the shadow of her shoes. "Did the kid drown off the pier?" she asks.

"Yes ma'am," I say, but I don't want to talk about that. "Rather have been watching you," I tell her.

I walk over to stand in front of the couch, lean over and kiss her forehead. I can taste salty skin, evidence of the hard work done earlier in the day. "You don't need to hear the particulars," I say. "Besides, it's time for bed."

"Well, I was just waiting up for you,"

"To give me a hard time?" I say.

"You deserve it," she says, smiling finally.

"I probably do at that."

She closes the book, lifts herself up. "Think I'll go take a bath."

"I caught some four-footers this evening," I tell her. "Might be around tomorrow morning if you want to go."

"Okay, but Momma needs to talk to you about my softball," she says, her words pushed out through a tired sigh. "She's down on the pier with Clay."

"What's he doing here?"

"You need to ask her that," Kelly says.

"Hey." I walk over to the stairs. Kelly stops, her eyes nearly shut. Her hair falls in tangled curls around her face. She's growing up fast, but in the shadowy light of the stairs, I can still see my little girl. "I didn't miss your game because I went surfing. By the time we took care of the boy, your game was over. I don't know what your momma told you, but I never would've made it to Georgetown."

"She didn't say anything about that, Daddy. She was too busy talking about seagulls."

"About what?"

"Just ask her, I'm too tired to tell you." She reaches down from the step and wraps her arms around me, squeezes tight.

"Hey, I'm sure you did just fine today," I say. "You got a lot more All-Star games left, so don't go worrying over lobbing some pitch to a girl from Aynor."

"I won't, I promise."

I can smell her skin, sweet, earthy, and I want to hold her there forever. I don't want her to grow up, but I won't ever tell her that. I don't want her to feel guilty for doing what we all do. I just love her so much because when I look at her I see Cassie before things went bad. I see in our little girl another chance at life, and I want to make sure she does it right, college and a career, wherever she wants to go in this world.

Maybe that's one reason I stay out here in the middle of

nowhere. I know, when it's time for Kelly to go, there will be no hesitation in her steps. She'll be okay when she leaves because she'll take some of this place with her. The marsh gets into your bones and settles there, good or bad. I want her to come back often. I want her to need salt in the air for the world to seem right.

I wait, watching her climb the stairs, the darkness at the top swallowing her before I turn away. Down at the pier, Clay's engine sputters to life, the small flat-bottom scow disappearing into the marsh before I can join them. Cassie sits alone at the edge of the pier. The few lights I've strung up along the dock fight to push back the night. From the porch, I can tell she is dressed up more than she should be for a softball game, her skin white, almost glowing under the sundress she wears.

Suddenly I am aware of the afternoon again, the call about the boy drowning off the pier, how I felt something wrong, a fireman's sixth sense that told me danger was too close. My throat clinches up as I find the reason for my hesitation this afternoon. I watch Cassie light a cigarette. She pushes a hand through her hair then looks toward the house waiting for me to walk down so it can all begin.

The sudden feeling of loss takes my breath away.

Cassie

PECK COMES TOWARD THE PIER, the silence broken only by the sound of Clay's boat fading in the distance. He blamed the tide, said he needed to make it out before the water was too low, but I wonder if Clay just didn't want to face Peck, afraid of what might happen in the darkness of the marsh. It doesn't really matter, though, his words from this afternoon are still there to hold me steady, to remind me of what I have chosen, what I must do. *If you pretend nothing's going on, then nothing's going on.*

Before today, we kept our visits in the shadows, alone in places where we would remain strangers to those who might see us together. We would come no closer than Georgetown, though even that was not far enough away. People from Garden City and Surfside have business in Georgetown all the time, but we were lucky and never got caught. Sometimes we'd drive to Pawleys Island at night and walk the beach while Peck was on duty and Kelly sleeping. We were almost caught there once when Kelly showed up in a car full of her friends and parked on the other end of the lot.

She has always been forbidden to do such a thing, to ride out to the beach after dark. But Ellen Thomas has her license and is a troublemaker, always coaxing Kelly to be an accomplice to her crimes. That night I hid on the floorboard of Clay's truck until Kelly was on the beach and we could drive away. I couldn't punish her for fear of being found out myself, nor would I ever let Clay take me to Pawleys Island again.

After that, our trips moved farther south toward Charleston and north just across the state line to Calabash, North Carolina, all day trips to small, out-of-the-way motels. Rooms that were dark and sullen, so dirty and dangerous tourists would never think of staying there. It was always exhausting and guilt-ridden, but the pleasure of having Clay, pretending we were on our own, rehearsing plans that are now truly going to happen, made it worth the risk.

I watch Peck walk quietly along the dock, his eyes cast downward, the marsh so quiet it puts an ache in my bones. The sharpness of this moment makes me shake even though the heat has refused to let go of the air. He comes to stand next to me. The muscles along his jaw ripple like waves, his back rigid and wet with sweat. "Couldn't he stay to say hello?" he asks, then offers a cigarette before I can answer. When I accept with a shaky hand, Peck notices, holds the cigarette back. "You cold?"

"No," I say, "just tired."

He gives it over then, lights the tip. The flame of the match forces me to close my eyes.

"He was here to see you," I tell him, which is true, at least in part, "but he needed to get away, make sure the tides stayed in his favor."

He looks a minute longer, calling me a liar with his eyes. "You don't have to explain yourself," Peck says.

"I'm not explaining myself," I snap back. "Just thought you'd want to know, that's all."

He turns, his arms catching the weight of his body as he leans against the rail. When he spits into the water, he smiles like he's keeping a joke to himself. It raises the heat along my neck until my face burns. I get up and stand beside him, the air dark and hot, smelling of wet mud as the tide pushes out. I want to come right to the point and tell Peck that I'm leaving to meet Clay in Walhalla, but I can't do it. It frustrates me, my indecision, the fear really of telling Peck to his face. I've tried before, but it never goes right, and with Kelly up at the house, I just can't do it again. She doesn't need to hear it when our marriage finally fails.

Peck's wearing a T-shirt, the sleeves pulled up to his shoulders, his hair tousled like he just woke up. Jeans hang on his waist without a belt to hold them. I know he's been in the water. "You think being on that surfboard is more important than being at your daughter's game?" I say, wanting it to hurt.

Peck doesn't move, just turns his head to look, his eyes tired and narrowed. "No, I don't, Cassie. I had no choice."

"There's always a choice, Peck. You chose surfing instead of your daughter."

"You got Lori's call about the drowning?" he asks.

"Yes," I say.

"Well, then you know where I was. You know what I had to do."

There's silence then. I won't ask about the boy drowning. I don't want to know about a tragedy like that, so close to home, a child wandering off somehow and then it being too late to do anything about it. I can't imagine that happening to Kelly, but it could. Peck taught her to surf when she was ten, but trying to watch that small spot of a girl struggling to get out beyond the break was too much for me. It kept my heart in my throat. Even now, though she is strong and athletic, ready to be taller than me, I don't like her doing it, pushing out there at all hours of the day, and night if we'd let her.

Tragedy shows no favorites, Peck says. We have to be ready for anything. Of course he's talking about the station, accidents and natural disasters, hurricanes and fires that don't ask you anything before wreaking havoc upon your life. But it can be meant for other things too. I've seen tragedy in the mountains when death stalked those who never saw it coming, took them with a whisper, not a shout like the accidents Peck sees.

I want my daughter safe, the world so much more dangerous than a fifteen-year-old could ever imagine. I want Peck safe too, even though it's harder to feel that right now. What I feel mostly is the impossibility of staying here any longer, the urge to leave almost desperate. "Did you see Kelly?" I ask.

A small breeze breaks across the marsh lifting the strands of hair around Peck's face. "Yes, she told me about the game, said some girl hit her hard."

"It was early," I tell him. "She settled down."

Peck looks at me then, his blue eyes so sharp even in the darkness that I have to look away. "Kelly said you had something to tell me."

Up at the house, there's a light on in Kelly's room, her window open, so I try to be careful, weighing my words. "Yes, I do," I say. "There was a coach from North Carolina at the game. He saw Kelly pitch and wants her to come to his camp."

"And where would that be?" Peck asks.

"Up in Cullowhee, near Momma."

Peck thinks about this for a minute, studies me with his eyes, then says, "I think that's a good idea." His response surprises me. Still, I'm careful not to mention Clay, not give too much away. "It'll be good to have more time up there," he says. "That will make Meemaw happy."

Whiteside Cove is a day's drive from Garden City Beach, but to me, it's a whole world away. That place put a mark on me so deep that I have yet to figure out the flatness of the low country.

Peck can see a storm coming for miles before it hits the marsh. He told me once he could hear the tide rise and fall, knew where it lay by just standing quietly and listening, never looking at a chart or a clock. I told him that was the craziest thing I'd ever heard. "You can listen to anything you want," I told him, "but I'm suffocating out here."

He said he understood, but I had my doubts, and so after my father died, I started going back to the mountains every summer to escape the heat and the ugliness of the marsh. In the last couple of years, the trips have been even harder because when I return to Peck, I'm like a cornered dog. I'm just all twisted up inside. Peck sees it in me every day. It's been a fight from the beginning to stay here as long as I have.

"I think it would be good for Meemaw and Kelly both," I say, trying to agree. Peck squints at me, smoke from the cigarette curling into his eyes when I show him the application papers for the camp. I tell him that it will last for two weeks, that we will need to extend our stay in the mountains because of it.

"That's a lot of her summer, Cassie."

"She'll love it, Peck. Besides, it will be good for her game."

"Her game," he says, laughing dismissively under his breath. "She's only fifteen."

"But this is when it starts. Clay says they look at girls Kelly's age. He knows the coach, says he's one of the best."

Peck turns away when I mention Clay, looks out on the marsh. "He said all that?"

"Yes," I tell him. "He went to school in Cullowhee. Did you know that?" The question goes too far, of course he knows. Peck looks back at me, his stare reprimanding, reminding me there are still parts of his life that I should leave alone. He was as close to Clay as he was with Teddy. They all fished and swam the creeks together, surfed along the beaches, and lifeguarded in the summer until Clay left for college. The great distance, the changes that occurred over four years' time changed their friendship forever. Clay tried to push against the grain of things when he came home, expected more because of his college degree. He expected Strachen to recognize how much more he brought to the table. "An educated fireman ought to get a station," he told me after Peck got the call to run Garden City Beach. They had a falling-out shortly after that and Peck seemed hurt when I tried to argue Clay's point.

"You can't fight a fire with books, Cassie," he had scoffed. "Next time you see him, tell him that." The words *next time* stunned me. Clay Taylor and I had begun to talk about things, accidental meetings that became planned and calculated so we could be together for longer periods of time. It wasn't an affair yet. We wouldn't sleep together for some time. But there was enough going on that I was scared Peck was calling me out that afternoon. Tonight, as back then, he's hurt by my words, by my taking sides with Clay. He turns to walk across the dock. "What else?" he asks.

"What else what?"

"What else did old Clay want? If he was here to see me, he sure didn't wait around very long."

"He's going to quit," I tell him.

"Quit what?"

"Quit you, Peck. He's quitting the force."

"Well, he doesn't need to tell me that. He needs to tell Surfside."

"He has," I say. "Today in fact, then he came out to tell you, and when you weren't here, he left."

"He knew where I was."

"He thought you were already off," I lie. "He was out here about three, went on to see Kelly play, and I'm glad he did because he knew that coach. That was worth it, don't you think?"

I look up to the house. The light in Kelly's room is off now, but I bet she's there, watching, listening from the window.

"What's he going to do with all his spare time now," Peck asks, "help our daughter get a scholarship to college?"

"He just knew the coach, Peck. You don't have to be so ugly about it. He's going to Walhalla. He's going to be chief up there."

"That's convenient," Peck says. "Walhalla's less than two hours from Whiteside Cove."

"He's getting a promotion. You got what you wanted, so why can't anyone else have something? Can't you be happy for Clay?"

"He was needed at the station today when that boy drowned, that's all I know."

"He's got the time," I say.

"Time? Time for what?"

"Vacation time, time off, Clay said he had time off."

"You know a hell of a lot about his time off, about becoming chief in Walhalla," he says. "Why all of a sudden have you become interested in a fireman and his promotions? Seems to me just yesterday you didn't give a rat's ass about mine."

I look back to the house and see Kelly moving in the darkness, listening to things a fifteen-year-old should never have to hear. "I'm leaving tomorrow," I say. "She needs to be there Sunday to check in. He's holding her a spot." I wave the papers to Kelly's camp in front of him hoping they might hide my lie, but Peck's not buying any of it.

"Are you coming back this time?" he asks. His eyes hold me, dare me to take the next step.

"I don't know," I say and then hold my breath for the weight to fall.

He stays where he is, looks away, releasing me for the moment. His toe pushes against the weathered wood like he's grinding a cigarette dead. "You know, today, taking that call on the drowned boy, I felt something—" But then he doesn't finish his thought.

It hurts to see Peck like this when he's not in control. I think about taking it all back, telling him of course I'll come home from Momma's. But I don't. I stay strong, and hold my ground. It's enough, I keep reminding myself. Fifteen years of trying to stay is enough.

When I don't respond, he seems to accept what has not been spoken outright. "All right then," he says, his hands lifted into the air. "I'll stay at the station tonight, but you tell Clay he better not come around, just tell him to keep away from me."

"He told Surfside he'd work this week for his notice."

"You tell him, I got it. He can go with you tomorrow, promote himself in Walhalla a week early."

I sit on the bench, weakened, head in my hands, afraid Peck might offer something more and I won't be able to fend him off again. Instead he smiles, a hand thrown up in a wave as he turns to walk back toward the house, leaving me alone with my little mess.

Peck

INSIDE, KELLY'S WAITING, something I didn't want to have to deal with, but here it comes. "Where are you going?" she asks when I walk through the door.

"Nowhere special, just back down to the station."

"I thought you were off duty," she says, more a statement of fact than a question.

"Well I was," I say, opening another cold one. "But Clay's just quit the force so we're shorthanded. I got to help carry the load. You know how that is."

"I don't want you to go," she says.

I look at her on the landing, leaning against the rail. It makes me ache to know what her mother and I are doing to her. But there's really no choice. "Sorry," is all I can say, "it's just a matter of circumstances."

Kelly moves down the steps in her stocking feet, sits on the bottom of the stairs, her body nearly invisible in the dark shadows. "I wish you never made lieutenant. I just wish you were a fireman like you used to be."

I come over, take a seat beside her. "Well, young lady," I say, "you get more because I work more, so don't be forgetting that."

She grabs the beer from my hand, takes a quick swallow to make a point. Her face turns up like the brew's spoiled, so I don't have to say anything about her insolence.

She leans into me, wraps her arms around her bare legs. "I don't want to go to the mountains," she says. "I don't want to go to some camp for two weeks. Let me stay here with you."

"You can't do that, angel. You know how Momma is about you going up there to visit Meemaw. Besides, a two-week softball camp sounds like fun. You'll have a blast."

"Then you stay here," she says. "You take me tomorrow. That's only fair."

"I'd love to, baby," I tell her, "but I've got to go help at the station. That's the honest truth."

Kelly raises her face to look at me, her cheeks moist with tears. "Don't lie to me."

"Honey, I won't lie to you. I've got to go because of Clay." Kelly puts her face into my shoulder, and it really pisses me off that she understands my lie in a way that makes it truth. I hold her for just a minute more and then I get up, tell her to go on to bed, that she's got to go with her momma. I can hear her door slam after she runs upstairs crying, but I don't have time to fix it right now.

I don't take any clothes when I go. I've got a small stash at the station. I want to be gone before Cassie decides to come back inside and start the whole thing over again. I leave the house and don't look back until I'm in my truck driving away. The house remains visible through the side mirror until I take a curve and it disappears around a dark corner of sweeping Spanish moss and low-hanging oak trees.

Alone, the wash of dashboard lights paints the inside of my truck a sick green. I turn on the police scanner like a habit to pull me up, get me thinking about anything other than Cassie and Clay going off somewhere together. She's going to leave me and I just can't fight for her right now. I've let her go until the space she put between us got too wide. Now Cassie needs something more than I know how to give. I love her more than life itself, that's a fact, but sometimes, I guess that just doesn't seem to be enough.

After we were married and Cassie was disowned by her father, we moved to Garden City Beach. We weren't on the marsh then, just in a small house two rows back from the beach. It was hard, Cassie sick all the time carrying the baby. We didn't have good money coming in. I don't know what we would have done if my father hadn't helped out. Pops took some extra work in Georgetown at the steel mill, stayed over on weekends to make a little more so we could survive while I tried to get hired on with Surfside Fire. Pops didn't want me going to Georgetown, didn't want me working in a mill like he did all his life. "It breaks a man too far down," he told me once. "It would be nice if you could take a step up."

Cassie and I split up three times that year before Kelly was born. It's a lie to say I gave her some room to breathe because we were damn sure broken up, so much to the point that Cassie moved all her stuff out twice during that time. And then after Kelly was born, we nearly killed each other because of the child's colic. She cried like she was hurt, like we were doing something to her that she didn't like. Cassie could never find the herbs in the low country Meemaw would have used to help calm Kelly down, and when she tried to call home, the phone either rang forever or was picked up and then put down immediately. No hello or good-bye—nothing. My mother tried to help, but Cassie was just beside herself and wouldn't listen to anyone.

She would go crazy and leave the house, take Kelly and drive along South Waccamaw, drive all night sometimes. She never drove all the way to Cashiers, but she drove to Florence a couple of times, and then once to Spartanburg. That's as far as she ever got, Kelly sleeping soundly in the seat beside her.

She always came back. Funny how that worked. She'd leave me, clean out everything, and then drive all over the place only to end up at Pops and Mom's house in Conway. I think they both knew what we were going through. I never asked if they did similar things. But I know we never would have made it without them.

I wish I could at least pass all of this by one of them now, see if they could help me out again, but that won't happen. Mom's been dead eight years and Pops isn't doing too well over in Conway. We grow up when we have children; we grow old when our parents die. I've already grown old once, and I'm afraid I'm getting ready to grow a bit older a lot sooner than I want to. Pops is withering away in a rest home. I need to go see him. It's been awhile.

Suddenly the scanner on the dashboard of my truck lights up like a Christmas tree, a dispatcher's voice crackling out codes, Garden City station and Surfside responding. There is no time to think anymore, Pops and Cassie put on hold for now. I only have time to react and do what I have done my entire adult life, be a fireman and respond. My headlights push hard at the darkness along the narrow ribbon of road. I hit a switch, red lights spinning like a tornado against the night as heat lightning catches fire across a dry sky.

WHEN I GET TO THE station, it's empty, the Pirsch gone, the Quonset hut deserted. I move fast, grab my turnouts and check with Surfside while in route, confirm the location of the 10-52—a wreck with possible fatal injuries. There is a second code, 10-53, all lanes blocked. My emergencies pierce the darkness, spinning and flashing off windshields and into the eyes of unsuspecting motorists. They slice panicked looks into rearview mirrors before slowing down to pull over so I can get past, make it to the scene and do my job. The drive in is awesome and terrifying at the same time, as I come up on traffic that's building from the blocked highway up ahead. The pulsing emergency lights of fire and police already on scene reach out to pull me in so the whole grisly dance can begin.

I drive down the shoulder, careful not to create another accident by hitting a curious pedestrian. They always show up, gawkers, onlookers who don't realize how much of a hazard they're creating when they walk up or slow down to rubberneck at the misfortunes of others.

Surfside has a pumper and a ladder unit working alongside our Pirsch. Floodlights attached to the trucks pour down an unnatural kind of daylight onto the wreckage. Ambulances wait nearby. I pull over into what should be a left-turn lane and park. Glass and car debris are scattered everywhere. It's hot as hell putting on turnouts during the summer, even in the middle of the night, but you've got to wear them. You've got to protect yourself, always, so I slide the fire retardant pants and boots on, buckle the jacket tight before going to locate my crew. When I find them, Partee is pulling a line from the Pirsch, J.D. inside the car looking at a boy who is dead and a girl who is dying.

A Plymouth Barracuda ran a red light and plowed into a Ford Gran Torino full of teenagers, T-boned the shit out of it. Couldn't have planned it any better, a perfect bull's-eye. It pushed the middle post on the left side of the Torino almost to the other side of the car, propelling the whole mess into the southbound lanes and clogging up the entire highway.

The impact nearly split the Torino in two. There's a girl trapped, pinched tight in the backseat, but she's still alive. The boy in the driver's seat is dead, two others are on the ground, having been ejected from the car, dead. The Barracuda is local, and the kid who was driving it is alive and drunk, his face messed up, but that's about it. When I walk up to the car, I can't imagine how he escaped injury. The engine compartment is pushed completely into the front seat. He keeps saying the car's not his, keeps telling a patrolman that he wasn't driving. But there's no one else here, and this boy, somehow still alive, is so drunk that he can't stand up. I count ten beer cans in the backseat, empty.

The Torino is from Ohio, a long way from home. I look inside where J.D. is laying a canvas covering over the boy's body. He's got to get some room to work and needs to sit on top of the dead boy if he's going to have any chance at the girl in the back. Nobody asks me why I'm here when I'm supposed to be off duty. Nobody has time to care about that.

"What do you need?" I ask.

"I need to get her out and fast," J.D. says, his voice calm and even. "I think there's an artery cut, lots of blood, and I don't know if I can get to it without freeing her first."

"Okay, then," I say, scanning the chaos for someone from Surfside who might have a Jaws of Life. Of course no one does. "Next in line to get one," Bob Strachen tells me as he pulls a crowbar from a cabinet on his pumper. "We got a ram tool and a saw. What you got?"

"Same," I say and then go over to Partee, tell him to pull the saw and tool. "We're going to lose everyone out here if we don't get the girl out now."

The crowd is growing. Four Horry County Sheriff's cars and three State Troopers control the perimeter of the accident. Flares are scattered all over the place. An attempt is made to reroute traffic in both directions, but then the patrolmen give up and just shut the flow down cold. Everyone has to wait, those closest getting more than they bargained for on their vacation.

The problem won't be solved with just cutting sheet metal. They can cut it, but the ram tools will have to pry the metal back if we're going to get in there anytime soon. J.D. and the girl are covered because of the debris the saws might kick up. Two lines are laid out, primed and then sprayed around the car to keep sparks from igniting the gasoline. The smell of fuel sits heavy in the air. Once everything is up and online, three rams and two saws start to work on the car, J.D. and the girl buried under a pile of metal shavings and glass.

Early on, it looks like nothing is going to budge, sparks flying all over like we're trying to catch the whole mess on fire. Then there is a sudden shudder, a crack followed by a loud *Pop!* and the car falls apart. It cracks right open like an egg and falls into two pieces in the middle of the goddamn road. It's like God said "Enough of this," and just flicked His finger and broke that son of a bitch right in two. The girl falls to the ground, J.D. there to tie off the bleeding artery and then stabilize her on a backboard.

Strachen comes over and tells me a medevac from Florence is coming in.

"Where?" I say.

"How about up the road a bit? We'll need to set flares."

I agree and then hustle across the scene, moving around broken bodies and destroyed vehicles to pull torches off the Pirsch. Fifty yards out, I set up a perimeter of flares just as the chopper's lights come into view. Its blades raise the air into a torrent, sand whipping up, going under my mask into my face and eyes. Flashlights lead him in, bring that bird down on the mark, and he's on the ground before the sand can settle.

J.D. hands the girl off to the flight nurse, a breathing bag going, her artery the least of the injuries as far as I can tell. She was on the side of impact so has extensive head trauma. J.D. tells the flight nurse, "Keep the bag going. I don't know if you got enough time. It took us too long to get her out."

The nurse has no opinion about that. She just takes control of the bag and the rest of us get the girl into the helicopter. It's ready to lift off in a matter of minutes. When everyone is a safe distance away, I release him back into the night. The chopper dips its nose, turns a hundred and eighty degrees in a tight maneuver, and heads for Florence.

The boy who did all of this is from over in Conway and only has a broken nose, cut lip, and some glass in his face. He's put in an ambulance in handcuffs, a Sheriff's deputy in the back with him so he can be patched up at the local emergency room and later booked on multiple counts of vehicular homicide. The kids from Ohio leave in the other three ambulances with flashing lights on, but no sirens. There's no rush since there's no one to be saved.

It seems like we're here for about five minutes doing all of this, but when I look at my watch, it's three-thirty in the morning. Someone says traffic is backed up all the way to Myrtle Beach north and Pawleys Island south. I wouldn't doubt it one bit. I walk over to Strachen and thank him for coming down. "We're short-handed with Clay resigning," I say. "So it was good to see you fellas out here tonight."

"He's still got a week to go," Strachen says like he thinks he ought to be here. But I shake my head, raise my hand and tell him no.

"He won't be back at Garden City, Bob. I can't have him calling out sick with our crew as light as it is. I'd rather know who's going to be here than have to second-guess who might not show.

Besides, he's going to Walhalla to be chief, so let him go be a chief."

Strachen looks at me real close like he's trying to figure out my point. It's been a hard night on everyone, still a lot to be done to get us out of here and back to our stations where we belong. He knows I've never refused help or equipment before, yet here I am standing in the middle of Highway 17 with blood and human remains, car parts and all kinds of hell surrounding us, and I'm telling him I don't need a man on my crew. I know it doesn't make good sense, but I'm not going into details just yet on something that doesn't need a public airing.

"We'll keep him down at Surfside then, or hell, maybe we'll just let the son-of-a-bitch go, but I can't give you anybody else right now. Maybe later this summer, but until then you've got to double it up, see if there's a man who can come over from the volunteer squad and help out. I can't give any overtime on this."

I look at J.D. as he wraps up his gear, all the patients gone, the victims' positions replaced by fluorescent orange spray-painted silhouettes, ghosts on the ground, as the highway patrol finishes marking and investigating the accident. "I want J.D. to have overtime tonight," I say. "He's on for Clay because the guy never showed up. That's only fair, I think. He may have saved that girl's life because he took the shift."

It takes him a minute, but he agrees. "I'll do that," Strachen says, "but that's it. You guys figure this out, and let me know what you come up with."

I thank him and then walk over to J.D., his uniform covered in blood and dirt, his hair flecked with glass from being inside the Torino while we were cutting it apart. "You okay?" I ask.

He looks up, and for the first time I can tell he's surprised to see me, wasn't expecting this. "What are you doing out here?" he says. "Thought you went home."

"Oh, I did, but then I was thinking, what the hell, I can't miss the rookie earning a merit badge. What kind of chief would I be if I did that?"

A smile pushes against J.D.'s face. He looks over at Partee who's laughing along, pushing a broom, removing the debris from the roadway. I'm glad he can still have a sense of humor after what's just happened out here. It's a good sign, because tonight we tried to save a life. You've got to find ways to remember that. Lots of kids died and there are families from Ohio whose lives will never be the same because some kid from Conway got drunk and then went on a killing spree. We tried our best. That's what I want to focus on, even when our best comes up short.

On the ride back, I make the call to Surfside, ask that we be taken off-line so we can get some rest and reload. According to statistics, nothing happens this time of the morning, the night nearly exhausted. People who dodged any trouble will just be going to bed while others are starting to get up for work. Nothing's bound to happen until at least eight, if not later. Surfside agrees and takes us off-line until 8 A.M.

At the station, no one wants to sleep. It's too hot, too much to process with the young kids who died tonight. I could insist that we all try to lie down because we have to be ready in just a few hours to go back on call, but I don't. We make ourselves busy, Partee taking care of the Pirsch, J.D. working on his emergency kits, restocking bandages, IVs, blankets, and extrication kits. We sent the neck brace and backboard with the victim, and so J.D. breaks out our backups, but not before letting me know we need to get that equipment back, if we can. I promise to make the call later in the morning.

I walk out of the station, leave J.D. and Partee there to do the cleanup. I need some time alone. Tonight hurt more than that drowning did in the afternoon. I saw a girl not much older than Kelly dying in the backseat of a car. I'd hate to get the call that someone's parents got tonight in a hotel room, or worse yet, back home in Ohio. No parent's supposed to outlive their kid, that's about as unnatural as anything in the world, but it's precisely what we've had to deal with all day.

I'd like to hide Kelly away somewhere until she's thirty, then I'd let her out and say, "Good luck," but I know I can't shelter her like that. She already sees too much that's between her mother and me. When Cassie and I were good, there was nothing sweeter. But the low country just seemed to drain it all out of her over the years. The mountains probably would have done the same to me if I'd had to go there against my will.

That first night back in Conway, Cassie was almost inconsolable. It was the fall of 1954, and she was to have already started college. Instead, we were staying with Mom and Pops. Cassie's anger at her own father was so deep and hot that she seemed to give up inside; burned beyond recognition is the only way I can explain it. It was like the girl who spent the summer with me died when Cassie went home, and the pregnant girl who returned when her daddy kicked her out was someone else entirely. Her whole world stopped, and Cassie floated free of anything that had grounded her in life.

She never settled things with her father. He died before she could find a way to work it out. Parker had remained silent in life, and now for the past ten years, silent in death, though I think he haunts her. Cassie tells me that she sees her father in Kelly's eyes. She says, "Sometimes I think he's watching me through her, sometimes I can hardly look at her face and not feel I'm being spied on."

"Don't be unfair to Kelly," I tell her. "She's got nothing to do with this." But I don't know if Cassie believes that. I'm not close enough to her anymore to tell.

Out before me, the marsh is finding the early light, the salt creeks just beginning to wake. Along the fringes of cordgrass, black mud disappears beneath a rising tide. Skimmers rake their beaks across the water for an early morning meal. Even before the sun is on the horizon the air is thick. It's going to be another hot one with no chance of rain, and here I am working on a twenty-four-hour day when I was supposed to be off duty, so tired I can barely breathe.

Cassie

I︢t is S︢a︢t︢u︢r︢d︢a︢y︢ m︢o︢r︢n︢i︢n︢g︢ and I am following Clay, watching his taillights weave back and forth, the small boat he pulls behind the truck teasing the yellow line whenever we take a curve. We pass through little inland towns, Conway and then Lake City, Turbeville, until we are finally on a long stretch of 378. Here the land begins to rise, the road warning that the distance I have already traveled has meaning. To continue, it says, will mean that I have finally done it. I have left Peck.

My spirits lifted the minute Peck left the house last night and went back to the fire station. I went inside and packed my bags, knew it had to be done right then, that in the morning if I wasn't ready to go, I might never leave. Clay called early, said Surfside had let him go, that he was packing too. "I got no reason to stay now, so let's eat breakfast over in Conway and get the hell out of here. Oh, and don't worry," he continued, "it's better we leave like this. I can watch your back."

I felt like I was back in high school and it was the first day of summer, my whole life in front of me. Kelly was mad from the moment I woke her up, just plain ugly, but I didn't care. I ignored her and packed the car. In Conway, Clay was excited too. Strachen had let him go with a full week's pay—a good omen, Clay called it.

He talked about his new job, the trip to Walhalla, and the coming summer. He promised to take us to Tallulah Gorge in July to see the great Flying Wallenda walk across it on a wire, like that single event was going to be the great send-off to this new adventure, the new life we were beginning that morning. I was excited and wanted Kelly to feel the same, but that wasn't going to happen. I said, "You can invite Ellen to come up, if you want to."

"What for?" she said, like she hadn't heard a word that Clay had spoken.

"You know what for, young lady."

"Cassie, we got time," Clay said. "Kelly can decide about that later." But I was having none of it.

"I don't care if we got until doomsday, she's going to be respectful."

Kelly sat playing with her link sausage and the little bit of egg left on her plate. She was so rude. "I don't want to see some old man walk on a rope across a gorge. I don't see what that's got to do with anything anyway."

She slouched down in the booth. "Sit up," I said, but she didn't move.

"Cassie," Clay pleaded.

"Sit up, Kelly, right now." I kicked the booth between her feet, pushed it back against the wall. Her fingers lost the fork and it fell off the table and onto the floor, the whole restaurant watching what was going on. It got really quiet, and then Kelly pushed back on the table, sending it into me and Clay, stood up and stormed out of the restaurant. Everybody watched her walk out, and then it was like they all waited to see if someone was going to follow. Clay looked at me with disappointment. "You didn't have to make a big deal about it," he said. "There's plenty of time."

"No there's not," I said. "Just pay the bill and let's get out of here."

I ran out after Kelly, my embarrassment hidden in the anger I felt when the cashier just stood there looking at me like I was the plague or something, chewing gum, her lipstick smudged, mascara tired on her face from the all-nighter she'd just pulled. "He's paying," I said, and then I smiled at her like the next thing out of my mouth would've been *Eat shit and die* if I was going to say anything at all.

I walked out, found Kelly standing at the edge of the driveway looking back down the road toward Garden City Beach. We had always rubbed against each other. I think it's just the way it is when a child is having a child. Kelly kept me sick until she was born and then she was a colic baby. By the time I thought I had figured her out, she'd change or go through some other phase that scared me more than the last. There were days that I didn't want her. I feel horrible thinking about that now, but I didn't. Momma used to say children were empty vessels that we fill. If that's the case, then I was only half full myself when Kelly came along. I don't know how we made it this far.

Outside the diner, I hoped her attitude might change, but she still wanted to fight. She just turned her back like she didn't want to have anything to do with me. "Look," I said. "We're going to Meemaw's and you're going to play softball. That's all."

"Why isn't Daddy taking us?" Kelly asked. Her words were muffled by the cars passing along the road. I wanted to grab her arm and pull her back, but didn't. I was afraid if I tried, she'd pull away, maybe step out into oncoming traffic and there'd be no time to react. I stood next to her, arms crossed, trying to explain, my heart softening. "Does Daddy ever come up to the mountains with us?"

"No," she said. "But we could have asked. Did you ask him?"

"He knows we're going," I said, wanting that to be enough.

"Does he know Clay's taking us?" She turned then to face me, her cheeks wet with tears.

I stood looking at Kelly, her features so much like Peck's that I didn't want to tell her the truth. Clay finished up inside the restaurant and came out, watched us from the distance of his truck. He lit a cigarette, leaned against the cab and waited.

"He doesn't know, does he?" she said defiantly. "You should call him and tell him the truth."

"And what's the truth, Kelly? What am I going to tell your father when I call him?" My questions seemed to stump her. It was like her young mind could only take what I was doing so far and then it shut down. All she could say was, "I want to talk to Daddy."

The moment passed, cars whizzing along the highway, the air whipped up into a hot wind. I could see Kelly was exhausted by everything. I had roused her early from sleep, and we had been at each other for the better part of the morning already. I put my arms around her, walked back toward the car. "You can call him later, after we get on down the road a bit." I looked to Clay, motioned quietly for him to get in his truck, to get going. We left Conway, Kelly in the seat next to me, still mad because I had involved her in my messy life.

She is just like her father, a hard-set chin and silence. She won't tell me I'm wrong, but the way she stares out the window, a stranger, a hitchhiker here only for the ride, is telling enough. I have tried to tell her that there was no other way. I could not look Peck in the face and say good-bye. It would never have worked if

I did that, so to leave a quick note and be gone was the only way, no hurtful words or stares.

"Do you want to turn on the radio?" I ask, but she won't give me the pleasure of an answer. I try to keep my eye on her, but it's hard to do that with Clay slowing down to check on me. I honk my horn. "Just go on," I say as his hand comes out of the window to give me the okay sign.

It's getting on my nerves the way he drives, assuming I can't do it without him leading the way, but I dare not share this with Kelly. She would like it too much. She would look at me with that *so why are you following him, then?* look on her face. I just let it go and turn the radio on myself, punching buttons, running through the stations but finding only static along the dial.

"There's nothing out here," Kelly says, reaching over to turn it off. "We're in the middle of nowhere, can't you at least see that?" Then she is gone again, her head turned away from me, body scrunched up in the seat, feet on the dashboard. Her comment is something like smoke disappearing into the hot air, giving me nothing to reply to. Just like Peck, I think. She is so like her father, it's annoying.

When we stop outside Columbia for gas, Clay checks his boat and then comes back to the car where I'm filling the tank myself. "Let me get that for you," he says.

"No," I say. "I can fill my car."

"I know you can," Clay says, "but I can finish it so you and Kelly can freshen up. You need to freshen up, don't you?"

Clay's getting frustrated, and for whatever reason that irritates me even more. "I can *freshen up* when I finish *filling up*," I say, using my fingers to hang quotation marks in the air.

My attitude is enough to send Clay back to his truck where he slams the door and sits inside the cab. Everything is suddenly so uncertain that I lose confidence in what I'm doing, feel too alone to keep going by myself. I know I need Clay's strength right now. I don't need him mad at me too, so I walk over to his truck and stick my head inside, kiss him on the lips. "Sorry," I say.

"For what?" He won't even look at me.

"For being such a bitch to you. I'm sorry."

"It's nothing," he says, reaching for the cigarette lighter. He lights one, takes it from his mouth and puts it in mine, then reaches for another. "We still got a long way to go. Are you going to be all right?"

"Yes," I say, but I'm not so sure, the uncertainty from Kelly's softball game returning, that feeling of treading water, starting over with something so familiar that I wonder if I'm really starting over at all. I don't want to tell him this. I don't want to believe it myself, because to do so would make my leaving Peck seem that much more useless. Instead, I smile. I nod my head and say yes again. "Yes, I'll be all right."

The rest of the trip is uneventful. We stop for gas again, eat sandwiches at a Stuckey's, then more coffee. Kelly turns on the radio around Greenville and follows stations all the way to Clemson. We drive on late into the afternoon and then into cooler evening air. The upstate favors opened windows, the cool air acting like a balm to ease the tension as we rise and fall along the rolling farmland, crossing over into Oconee County. And when we are on Main Street in Walhalla, I feel like I have arrived at another life altogether. The evening light feels good here, Walhalla, a good place to be. I look over at Kelly, but she's still ignoring me. She knows where we are, but there's nothing she can do about it.

We follow Clay as he looks for the fire station. I try to stick my head out of the window and tell him to just stop and ask directions. People are sitting outside the Rexall with ice cream cones. There's a cafeteria right next door. But he just drives on, passes a gas station twice.

"Momma, can we just stop and let him come and get us when he finds the thing?" Kelly comes alive now, just when I need her to be quiet. "If he can't find his station, how can he find a fire?" she says.

"Honey, this town's small enough that he'll be able to see the smoke." We both laugh at that, knowing it's just ridiculous that Clay won't stop and ask. And when he finally does bump into it, the station is right there, right under his nose, one block off Main on East North Broad.

"Shouldn't that be Northeast Broad?" Kelly asks.

I look at my child.

"Well, it's just weird, that's all," she says and then slouches back down, leaving me alone again.

The station is a big, brightly lit cave, not like the dirty garage Peck works in. There are two engines inside and a fire chief's car. It's a two-story building with big opened doors, the painted floor glistening like it's still wet. No sand anywhere. I point to the car, all red and shiny. "That's what Clay will drive to the fires. He won't have to ride on the engine anymore."

"Probably a bright idea to keep him away from real firemen," Kelly says.

I'd like to reach over and smack her face because of the way she disrespects Clay. He's a good fireman, but he'll make a better chief. He told me he's better watching from a distance, seeing the problems and following through with the right procedures. He's a thinking fireman, he says. Once when I told Peck that, he just said, "Well I'd like to know what he's thinking about, because he sure isn't doing anything else." Peck can be such an asshole.

We pull into the station, Clay's truck and the boat and then me and Kelly. When he comes over to the window, I put my arms on the door, lean out and smile. "Hey, Chief, where's the fire?" I say, but he's all business.

"I need to check in, see how the crew's doing, let them know I'm here."

"Okay; want us to wait?"

"I'd rather keep going," Kelly says. "We still have an hour and a half to Meemaw's."

Clay looks at me hard. "Haven't you two talked?"

"About what?" Kelly says.

"About tonight." He looks at Kelly like he's daring her to keep it up. "You're not going any farther. You're staying here tonight."

Kelly looks out the window. "At the fire station?"

"No," Clay says. "You're staying with me."

Kelly says, "No I'm not."

"I'll talk to her, Clay, just go on over and see your new firemen." But he doesn't leave. He eyes Kelly, waiting for her to turn and look back, but she won't. She stares out her window, cheeks sucked in, defiant. "Go," I say. I can feel the car shake when he pushes himself off the door to turn and walk away.

I look at my daughter. She's as unhappy again now as she was when we left. The radio is on, the volume too loud for sitting here without the wind blowing into the car, so I turn it off. I kill the engine too, and then we are surrounded by uncomfortable silence. In her eyes I see something I have never seen before. There is hatred staring at me, a hatred I don't know how to answer. It sends a cold chill through the center of my body.

Clay is talking to the firemen over at the opened doors. A couple are sitting, two or three standing around him. He scuffs at the ground, motions back, but it's not to point toward us. He's talking about his boat, I can hear that. The men nod and then shake their heads, point in a direction that is up the road. "On up there," one of them says, "about five miles."

One man comes from inside the station with a piece of paper, hands it to Clay, and then points in the same direction, his hands and arms weaving in the night air like he's trying to draw a map. Clay nods, looks back at his boat, then to us with a slight wave. I hear one of the men ask how his wife and daughter are doing, how they fared on the long trip and all.

"Wife and daughter," Kelly says. "My god, Momma." She slumps hard in her seat, feet against the dashboard.

"Hush," I tell her. "They don't know any better. It's just a mistake. Don't you say anything about that."

When he's finished, he shakes hands around and walks back over to my window while slipping the folded paper in his shirt pocket. He lights a cigarette, takes a long draw before bending into the window. "Got a little more to go," he says.

"Where?" I ask. He can tell I don't want to drive anymore. It's been a long day.

"Just up the road. It's a new station they're opening. I won't be down here." I can tell this disappoints him. He seemed more excited when we first pulled up to the brightly lit firehouse, the chief's car all polished and parked out front. "I can take you two over to the house first," he says, "then I'll go drop the boat off."

"No, that's all right," I say. "We've come this far." He smiles, glances over at Kelly, and then walks back to his truck, flicking his cigarette into the darkness.

The rest of the ride is up a winding unlit road, treacherous when I'm this tired. Kelly is even sitting up keeping an eye out, keeping tabs on Clay, who's driving too fast for us to follow. "Where's he going?" she asks, breaking the silence between us.

"To his station," I say, "but I have my doubts. I think he's lost again."

When we catch up, Clay is pulling into a small graveled parking lot. My headlights sweep across a building, an unpainted cinder-block garage with no fire engine inside. The place seems abandoned in the night. We make the small donut turn and wait for Clay to back his boat in against the far side of the building.

The trees rise around us, a black wall that feels warm and comforting. We are past the foothills now. Cicadas and tree frogs fill the cool air and somewhere off in the distance I hear a small stream running down along the roadside. I am on the cusp of being home, and think maybe Kelly is right that we should just keep going, push higher into the mountains until we are beyond South Carolina and back home in Whiteside Cove.

Clay comes toward the car, his dark figure moving away from the building like a prowler who has failed to find a way inside. "Where are they?" I ask.

"It's volunteer until Monday," he says, "then I'll have a crew. Two of the firemen I was talking to will be up here with me. Later there'll be more."

"It's a long way from Walhalla," I say.

"Only five miles, but it takes a while to get up here with the roads." He acts for a moment like he's unsure what to do next, like maybe he's made a mistake in taking this job. It makes my stomach sink to see it, a feeling of disappointment flushing hot across my face.

"Are you okay?" I ask, my voice pulling Clay back.

"Sure," he says. He smiles, looks around like he's sizing up the possibilities. "This is going to be great." He looks out over the top of the Bel Air, then leans into the window, points with his hand up a road that disappears quickly into the black night. "See that right there? It goes to the Highlands," he says. "You take that, then head on down 106 past Scaly Mountain until you hit 441 toward Clayton. You get that far, and you're almost to Tallulah Gorge, where they're building that rope walk for Wallenda right now." He smiles at the both of us, but I think we're just too tired to care.

"Let's get going," I say. "If I don't get something to eat soon, I might never make it to Tallulah Gorge." I can see Clay's disappointed that we don't play along, so I smile, try to be more reassuring. "Why don't we get some dinner at that cafeteria, maybe some ice cream afterward?" He smiles then, his spirits raised.

Back in Walhalla, our luck keeps running out. The cafeteria is closed, the Rexall too. There's no place to eat this late on a Saturday night except a small roadhouse all the way back down in Westminster. Retracing our steps makes me feel I'm losing ground, falling farther away from where I want to be. By the time we have eaten and found the house that Clay has rented, it's midnight, Kelly asleep in the car. When I try to wake her, she calls out for Meemaw in a small voice.

"No honey," I say. "We aren't there yet. We'll go tomorrow." And then she remembers about Walhalla, and refuses to move.

It's not worth the fight to pull her out of the car, drag her into the small house Clay has rented for himself. "Stay in the car," I say. "I don't care." I slam the door and leave her, forgetting to lock the car until I hear her push the buttons down. "This has been the worst day of my life," she yells through the closed windows. "I hate you. I hate you more than anything in the world."

What do we do to our children in this life? If I could change it all in a moment, I would. If I could walk over and tell Kelly that everything will be all right, I would, but I can't. I'm just as scared as she is, and I have no idea how all of this will turn out, but I won't stop now. I can't. I've come too far, even if I fail, to give up trying now.

Inside, the house smells of spoiled summer heat. There is no air-conditioning, but the nights here are not as hot as in Garden City Beach, and a breeze slips through the raised windows. The carpet is worn through in places. The walls need a good coat of paint, cobwebs shadowing the corners along the ceiling. The kitchen is tiny, the linoleum peeling on the floor, the pine cabinets dark and oily to the touch. "Seems the chief of a firehouse could live a little higher than this," I say, sorry as soon as the words escape my mouth.

"I'll do better once I get settled in," Clay says. He looks out at my car where Kelly has grown silent, the windows beginning to whiten on the inside. "Think she'll be there in the morning?"

"She has no idea where she is," I say, "so I imagine she'll stay put."

"Want me to go out there and say something?" he asks.

"No, let her stew. Maybe a night in the car will do her some good, the hardhead."

He watches her for a minute more, then draws the shade while I make the bed where we will sleep tonight. "I won't lock the door," he says, "just in case she changes her mind."

"Thank you, that's kind," I tell him, "but you don't need to be on her side."

"It's not her side I'm on, Cassie. It's ours." I know he wants me to say something, give some kind of reassurance about what we are doing, but I can't. I just find my nightgown and toothbrush, then head to the bathroom to get ready for sleep.

By the time we are in bed together, it is after one, Sunday morning, and I am thinking about Peck, wondering if he knows by now that I have left him for good. I did not say that in my note, just a quick line to tell him I would call. But if he looks around, he will see things are missing.

It is the first time that I will spend a whole night completely with Clay. In the past it has been only stolen afternoons or evenings at the house when Kelly was out or asleep, short hours together that never had the sense of permanence that this night carries. It is more uneasy than I had imagined it would be. The fight that has raged all day with Kelly has taken something away from the moment, and I can't summon the strength to bring it back. In the past just being with Clay, even if it was only an hour or two, was easy. I didn't have to think about what I was doing. I was desperate to just be there, and my reward was always a renewed strength to continue, a strength that I had thought I would find here tenfold tonight. Instead, I am exhausted. My daughter is angry and alone in a car and Clay is beside me waiting as I struggle to decide if I should turn to him.

"It's the beginning of our life together," he says quietly. I can feel his finger trace my spine, the way he lets his hand settle on my hip. He smells of heat and tobacco.

"I know," I say. "It's taken a lot out of me to get here. I hope you don't mind—"

"Shhhh," he says, his mouth close to my ear as he pushes up next to me. His arm drapes over my side, holds me close. I stare at a dark wall, relieved he will let me be, pray he won't sense my sudden disappointment in all of this, or that I am thinking I should be sleeping with Kelly rather than in here next to him.

Peck

It's Saturday, traveling day at the beach, when one set of tourists moves out and another set moves in. The roads are packed with cars and motorcycles, the worst time in the world for an emergency to happen. J.D. is laying on the siren, but the cars sitting in front of us are doing nothing to get out of the way. He looks at me, can see I'm pissed off at the world. "What do you want me to do?" he asks.

"Hell, I don't know," I say. "Bump him."

"What?" J.D. asks, his voice rising with surprise.

"Bump him," I tell him again. "If he won't move over, hell, let's move him ourselves."

"Okay, Chief." A smile creeps across J.D.'s face as he lets off the air brake and inches forward.

When he taps the car, I can see a man's head jerk forward. His body jumps in the seat like we just woke him up. "There, that ought to do it," I say. But it takes another bump and a blast from our air horn for the man to figure it out and get his car to the shoulder of the road. When we move up beside him, I can tell he's pissed off, but I don't say anything. I just look out the window and eyeball him real good to let him know it's the law, move over for emergency vehicles, just get the hell out of the way.

It's like dominoes after that, each car seeing the one behind it slide to the side, and we are able to move to the front of the line where we find the car fire. I spot a Ford station wagon, its engine compartment billowing black smoke and flame. The father's trying to unload the back end, save some of the family's luggage, while his wife and three kids watch from the embankment.

"He shouldn't be doing that," J.D. says.

"Nope, he needs to get on back," I say, but before I can yell that, the whole inside of the car ignites, and in one sweet *Poof!* flames shoot out the back just as this poor fellow is reaching in to pull out a suitcase.

The explosion—flame and smoke, an unbelievably powerful fist of exploding pressure—hits his face. The impact knocks him down and sends his whole family into a fit. Rule one: Never stand near a burning car, not with all the fuel around, inflated tires, plastic upholstery that can explode without warning. It's just best to get the hell away and wait until a fire unit arrives on scene.

We pull the Pirsch pumper on the grass between the car and the family. J.D. looks after the father while Partee pulls and primes the line. He fogs the nozzle while I engage the pumper to send a white wall of water into the car. The temperature inside is probably two thousand degrees or more by the time we hit it, so when our spray touches flame, it turns to steam, white clouds filling the inside to suffocate the fire.

Toxic clouds roll out the windows and mushroom upward. A highway patrol car pulls alongside, sits on the shoulder as traffic builds. He puts on his lights, doesn't even get out. Acts like it's too dangerous for him to do anything else but sit there.

The station wagon is a smoldering wreck by the time J.D. finishes bandaging up the father's hands and face—minor burns that will heal fast, a lucky man. He comes over, and we coordinate how to open the hood so we can get to the engine. We keep our masks on, tighten helmet straps, button collars tight. We make sure there's no crease or a loose buckle that might leak flame onto exposed skin if the fire decides to start up again when the top comes off.

J.D. goes down on his knees to crawl up to the front of the car, gets right up next to the grille, puts his hand on the hood so it won't pop up on its own when he releases the latch. "On three," he says, and we count together. When he pulls the release, Partee shoves the hose right up under the hood and we shoot that sucker back against the front windshield, drown an already dead engine with what's left of the five hundred gallons of water that we've brought with us.

By the time we're finished, the tank on the pumper is empty. We put out too much water, sort of overkill, but when you drive up to a car fire and the first thing you see is a man being hit by an explosion, it gets your heart pumping. You just want to knock the shit out of it with everything you got.

We get the highway patrolman to help out with finding accommodations for the family. Partee goes through the car with J.D. They look for anything that might be salvageable that they can take with them, clothes or toys, souvenirs from a trip no one's going to forget for a long time. Nothing's left except the burned-out frame of a Ford Country Squire station wagon and a metal bucket full of blackened shells. J.D. walks over shaking his head. "What?" I ask.

"My old man used to say, 'Can't buy a car, buy a Ford.' Guess I know why now."

I look over at Partee. He's trimming the hose, getting it back up on the truck. He's heard what J.D. said. "Better go tell Partee about your daddy's idea there."

"Why's that?" J.D. asks.

"He's got a Mustang over in Aynor he's been sinking money into for over a year. I think his kids have gone hungry while he stashed away enough cash to hop up that thing. He'd probably like to know that Fords ain't worth a shit before he picks it up next week."

Now, Partee is big. J.D. is too, but not a size that could compete. We've all watched Partee lift weights back at the station. He puts anything and everything he can find on that bar and still can hold it above his head all day. He's lifted the back end of cars when we've been out on calls, kicked down doors faster than we could go through them with an ax. He tore a phone book in two a few months back, swear to God.

Partee was looking at a *Mr. America* magazine that day. The picture on the front showed a man built of pure muscle, his hair curly and long, pumping his arms on a beach with women hanging all over him. Partee said, "I'd like to do some of that down on our beach."

Clay Taylor just happened to be working, or hanging around looking like he was working. He grabbed the magazine and said, "Shit, Partee, that's Frank Zane, Mr. Universe. You ain't Mr. Universe."

"My wife thinks I am," Partee said, and we all got a good laugh out of that. But what Clay said got to Partee, I could tell. He didn't say anything else, just got up after a little while and went into the office and asked Lori for the phone book, not Garden City Beach, but the one from Myrtle because it was big and fat, had all the Grand Strand numbers listed in it. He brought the book out and said, "I'm going to tear this thing in half because you said that."

Clay looked up from the table where he was sitting and said, "Shit you say, Partee."

"Shit I do," Partee said back at him and then ripped that son-of-a-bitch right down the middle all the way to its spine, let the two sides dangle there like tassels on a shoe.

I made Clay hoof it back up to Myrtle Beach and get us another phone book that afternoon, told him it was his fault, not Partee's, that the book was destroyed. "You don't tell Partee his wife ain't right," I said. We all got another good laugh out of that, everybody but Clay Taylor. Served him right, if you asked me.

I don't have to remind J.D. about that phone book. I just take my hands and tear the air in two, tell J.D., "Go on, you go tell Partee what your daddy said." But he'll have none of it.

"Naw, that's all right," he says. "Wouldn't want him to think his kids went hungry for nothing." Partee looks at us then, smiles that big old gap-tooth grin, shoots us the bird and says he could use some help with the hose. I just look at J.D., don't have to say another word.

Back at the station, Phil Roddy, the volunteer replacing Clay, walks in. I thank him for coming to relieve me, then take off, head out after thirty-six hours that saw us answer six calls, a new record for this station, one I'm sure we'll break before the season's out.

I'm driving in the same thick traffic that we endured going out on the call. I can still taste the smell of burning car in my mouth, and I'm anxious to get home, the traffic making the wait all the worse. I can't bump them like we did this morning, or use my emergency lights to move the traffic, so I sit letting my anxiety build until it feels like my head might blow off my shoulders like that car did today, one sweet god almighty *Poof!*

I inch along until I can finally turn left across traffic, accelerate down a road that is more like a sandy path for the last mile.

Speed is more dangerous out here, the truck fishtailing in the curves, but I need to get home. After a tight turn to the left, the road runs out in my yard. I kill the engine, look around. No Bel Air is waiting. I'm alone.

The quiet that falls around me is as dead as driftwood. Usually Kelly's playing the stereo too loud, Cassie yelling at her to turn the damn thing down. In the past when Cassie's taken Kelly to Meemaw's, there have been things left undone, clothes drying on the line, trash cans waiting for me to take out to the main road. But the emptiness feels deeper this time. It looks like a house that has been abandoned, empty, hot, and dark, shades drawn on all the windows. Inside I can see Cassie's packed things she wouldn't normally take on a vacation. Her jewelry box is gone, and pictures of her and Kelly. The missing frames have left dusty silhouettes where they used to sit on shelves and tables, more ghosts on the ground, I think. The pictures with me in them are still here.

In our bedroom, Cassie's cleaned out the cedar closet. She's taken all her bras and panties, her skirts that she never wears down here, and a whole pile of sweaters she never takes off in the winter because she complains the house is too damp and cold. Her shoes are cleared out, not just her flip-flops and the pair of hiking boots that she usually takes. Every pair she owns is gone. When I look in Cassie's drawer in the bathroom, her diaphragm is gone. She never took that before because she never needed it until now.

I find a sealed envelope on the kitchen counter with my name written across the front in Cassie's chicken scratch. Inside is a piece of paper that reads, *I'll call you later.* That's it, nothing more.

I walk back through the house feeling damned depressed. I know in my gut that Clay Taylor's with Cassie, even though no one's told me this. It's no coincidence they left the same day, headed pretty much in the same direction. Strachen called earlier to tell me Clay was gone, that I didn't have to worry about him anymore. I wish that were the truth, but I know it's not. Right now, all I want to do is get some sleep and then maybe when I wake up everyone will be back where they belong.

In the living room, I plop down on the couch and watch the television for distraction. It gets three channels, but nothing good. The only one with any reception is Channel 5, NBC, and they're playing golf. I can't watch that, so I turn the set off, lay my head on a pillow, stretch out on the couch to rest my eyes for a minute before figuring out what to do next. When I drop off to sleep, it is deep and silent, dead like this house.

It isn't until I am on the other side of the weekend, Sunday afternoon, that my eyes open again. My body creaks like an old hinged door. It's late afternoon, and I'm hungry and groggy, sore. I need to take a bath, need to regain some bearings, catch up with the world that's already deposited another batch of sunbathers and partyers on the Grand Strand—the exchange completed while I was asleep.

I search the refrigerator for food and find fresh clams from the creeks, saltine crackers in the cupboard. There are pickles and a bowl of leftover mac and cheese that Kelly never finished. It will do for dinner. I don't feel like trying to go somewhere to buy something more. I take my makeshift meal and walk to the dock, a cold beer to wash the whole mess down. I have lost a whole night and the better part of the next day to sleep, but somehow it feels like more. It feels like a life.

When the sun leaves the marsh, the light flattens and dies. It reveals the fractured salt creeks and mudflats in a way that makes it all feel too vulnerable with the heat and drought hurting everything. I cannot imagine something like this great body of water, the marsh and all the life that exists in it, burning up, being lost forever. Or for that matter, that I would voluntarily leave this place, whether Cassie returns or not.

I was born in the low country and this is home, no place better in the whole world, though at times it's hard to make it work the way it should. When Mom died, I wasn't sure Pops would make it on his own. He became frail, seemed lost without her there to do things for him. When I moved him into the rest home, I told him I was sorry, that I didn't know what else to do, that I hated taking him away from his home, away from everything he had known up until that day. Pops just smiled and touched his chest. He said, "A man builds his home in his heart, son. That way it's always safe. You can't take it away. You'll be a rich man for the rest of your days if you come to understand that, a guaranteed deposit in any bank in the world."

I understand this as truth right now more than ever, standing here eating a crappy dinner, my family gone for good, my heart bankrupt, about to break wide open while I wait for the telephone to ring, for my wife to call.

THE BEER AND MAC and cheese aren't enough to make the hurt go away, and I find myself back on the road heading into Conway to see Pops. I look at my watch. Eight-thirty and I know he will be staring at the TV. He always has it on, likes watching *Let's Make a Deal* during the week. Pops loves it when the contestant picks the wrong box or curtain and gets a broken-down car or coop full of chickens as a prize. "Serves them right," he says, chuckling like he's talking to a friend who's always there. On Sundays he won't miss watching Ted Mack's *Amateur Hour* and *Bonanza*. I know he's lonely and I don't get over to see him as often as I should. It's just hard to do right now with the season in full swing. It's going to get even harder.

I pull up in the parking lot off Fourth Avenue and Kingston, park near a small building that looks like it's as old as Conway. Kingston Convalescent Home sits on the river, a white brick and clapboard house that has been added on to, a rambling old structure that looks like it's tired of all the extra weight. There are cypress and oak trees shading the place, Spanish moss floating through the limbs like torn gray sailcloth. At night it's all black except where the bug lights feather out into the dark, painting the limbs and overhanging moss a sick yellow. Fireflies blink high up in the trees, but won't come down in this heat. Along the river, it's eerily quiet like winter, hardly any sounds coming from the water. The building's paint is peeling, the white bricks mottled and cracked along the foundation. When I walk up onto the porch, there's a feeling like the whole place is sagging under my weight.

There are only a few residents left in the home, five or six old men including Pops. Every year the people who run the place write me a letter saying they might close the doors, but they never do. The men inside did a lot for Conway in their day, so they keep it going out of respect if for no other reason.

After World War II, Pops came here to work in the turpentine industry. He was taught how to tap a tree to harvest the sap and later worked in the mill cooking it down. In the twenty-five years Pops has lived in Conway, he's made turpentine, cut timber, and moved it down the Waccamaw. He went to work at Georgetown Steel because he could make better money than the sawmill offered. He did that until he was injured in an accident. Both his legs were crushed by falling steel, and one never healed right. He could only do odd jobs around Conway after that because of the struggle to get around on a bum leg.

He's been here in the Kingston since Mom died eight years ago. He just couldn't do for himself anymore, and a couple of his buddies were already here. Back when he moved in, the place was better than it is today. The old nurses still take care of him, but his friends are gone. He's got the best room in the house, the only one that has a good view of the river.

When I knock on his door, I don't get a response. Inside, I find him sitting in near-dark, the light from his television keeping him from disappearing. He's asleep in his chair, his head lowered to his chest, arms gathered in his lap. He's covered at his shoulders by a frayed afghan Mom knitted for him years ago. The room smells like camphor, a cold, half-eaten dinner on a tray near his bed. I put my hand on his shoulder and call out his name. "Pops, hey Pops," I say. "Wake up. You got a visitor."

I'm not sure he knows who I am, even after I turn on a lamp beside his bed so he can see me. The space is a small square box just big enough for a bed and a bureau with a mirror attached to the wall. There's a worn La-Z-Boy against one side that he's sitting in. The RCA black-and-white is on a rolling rack pushed against the opposite wall. When I open a window to let clean air into the room, he looks up at me through rheumy and unfocused eyes like he's been drinking. He's done his fair share of that, but I don't think he's thought about the bottle for years. He's sick. That's what's doing it to Pops now. His eyes are telling me that he's sick.

"You okay, Pops?"

It takes him a minute to figure things out, but then he smiles. "I found a penny," he says like it's fresh news. He lifts his arm to point toward the small bedside cabinet. On it is his watch, a glass of water, Kleenex, a jar of Vaseline, a tin of Vick's VapoRub. Momma's picture is in a small wooden frame and beside that lies a dull copper penny.

"When did you get that?" I ask.

"Yesterday," he says. "That might be the one."

"Might just be," I say, reaching over to touch his hand. "Can't stay long," I tell him, "but I was thinking about you and thought I'd come by, maybe watch *Bonanza* for a while."

"That don't come on until Sunday," he says, like that's not what day it is. "Give me that penny, will ya?"

Pops always collected pennies, picked them up off the ground for as long as I can remember. He told me once that a penny was all you needed to start making a million dollars. He'd find one, pick it up off the ground, look at it real good, then spit on it to make it shine. He said, "Rich people know the value of this. How do you think they got rich?" Then he'd put the penny in his shoe, said it would only bring good luck if you walked on it.

When we cleared out the house, I found pennies everywhere, boxes full, jars too. He had a drawer that had nothing but pennies in it. An old ammo box from a World War II army surplus store was fat with them, and one of Mom's old shoe boxes was full to running over. Pops always said that the next penny he found might put him over the top, so he saved every one he picked up, carried them in his shoes until he'd come home on the weekends from over at the Georgetown Steel Mill.

I watched him once shake six or seven copper coins out of each shoe. We read the dates and then put them in an empty cigar box. Cassie collected what she could find after Pops was moved, took it by the bank so it could be counted and cashed. There were more than ten thousand pennies in that house—a hundred dollars and fifty-seven cents' worth to be exact.

I give Pops the penny and he looks at it in the dull light, squints his eyes but then gives up. "What's the date on this one?"

I pull his hand to me, my eyes not much better than his in this light. "Nineteen fifty-four," I say.

"Nineteen fifty-four," he parrots back. "Your momma cried that year," he says, turning to look at me like it was my fault.

"How's that?" I ask.

"Don't play stupid with me, boy. You got that girl pregnant in nineteen fifty-four. Your momma cried for days over that, she was so worried."

"Pops, that was Cassie," I tell him.

"I know who it was," he says back, his voice agitated. He pushes himself up into his chair, rearranges his body like the thought of my mom crying is too much for him to take, even if she's been dead eight years. "You shouldn't have done that."

"Done what?" I ask.

"Knocked that girl up like that," he yells at me.

"Pops," I say, trying to be patient with him. "It was Cassie who got pregnant. I married her and now you have a beautiful grand-daughter because of it." This pushes hard against his mind. He can't put two and two together.

Pops is dying, his body letting go a little bit more every day, and when it does, he speaks his mind, truth in a kind of craziness. His memory gets loose and I find out how he really felt about me at times when I was growing up. Tonight it's Cassie. He's scolding me for something I did that really pissed him off. He never showed it, never let me know how much it hurt, and I've learned over my own years how much pain comes with being a parent. Anger gets swallowed along the way when what you really want to do is knock some teeth out. I appreciate Pops not doing that. I'm better with my own child because of it. He's too old to take a swing at me now, so he just cusses me out and then we watch TV.

When the commercials are over, I turn up the volume on *Bonanza*, try to help Pops let go of his memories. Hoss is riding into town with Little Joe, Ben Cartwright is in trouble with the law and sits in jail. Hoss's jaw is set tight. He's seething at the injustice taking place, but Little Joe calms him down, tells him to believe in the law, that when they get to Virginia City, everything will get figured out. It's early in the show, so I know that won't happen. Little Joe is going to be disappointed, at least for another half hour or so.

We're quiet for a bit until a nurse comes in to get Pops's dinner tray. She's surprised to see me. The nurse is black, one of the older ladies who have been here for a while. She's big, with deep charcoal skin that makes her white uniform and hat glow. Her eyes are lazy, sleepy like she might not care, but she's a friend and knows more about what's going on with Pops than most anyone else here. "Well hey, Mr. Peck. Ya'll doin' all right in here?" she asks.

"Yes ma'am," I say.

Daddy looks up, knows who's in front of him. "Margaret, I need to go pee."

"You do now?" Margaret says, looking at me.

I just shrug my shoulders. "First time I heard that," I tell her.

"Well, can you wait until the next commercial?" she asks. "Or do you need to go right now?"

"Next commercial," Pops says. Margaret smiles at me as she goes over to close the blinds. She pulls the window shut even though it's hot enough to sweat a pig thin in the room. I don't say anything about it, don't want to mess up the routine. Even when it seems so much less, it's his life and he has people like Margaret to keep him company, to keep things regular.

She fusses around in the room, fluffing Pops's pillow, straightening his sheets to make sure they aren't soiled, her commentary running along with the action on *Bonanza*. "Hmmmm, mmmm," she says. "That Hoss Cotright is sure aimin' to get hisself in trouble," she says. "That sheriff won't put up with any of that. Now where's his daddy anyway?" She sits on the bed next to Pops's chair like they're old friends. "What you got in your hand?" she asks him.

He looks at his hands like he has no idea until he sees the penny. "It's my penny," he says.

"You found that today?" she asks. Her eyes lift up to me, shining in a way that says she's not just humoring Pops. She's keeping his mind going, pushing him to use the brain cells even if many of them no longer want to work.

"Nineteen fifty-four," he says. He reaches out to let Margaret look at it. "Think it's the one. What do you think?" He watches Margaret as she takes the penny, turns toward the lamp, and examines the piece of copper through glasses perched on the tip of her nose.

"That's a good one, all right," she says. "Better keep that in a special place."

"In my shoe," he says. The comment makes Margaret laugh.

"You don't wear shoes much no more, Mr. Johnson. And those slippers won't do you no good. Better find some other place to keep it safe."

Margaret's words catch Pops off guard, make him use some more of those dying brain cells. He holds the penny in his shaky palm, closes it into a fist, then reaches over to hold it out in front of me. "Here," he says.

"What?"

"You can have it," Pops says. "Put it in your shoe. It'll be lucky then."

Margaret looks at me, her eyes droopy, a smile breaking up the deep richness of her black skin. "It's a gift from your daddy. You best take it."

And I do. It's silly, but they both sit there watching, waiting for me to put the damn thing in my boot. I sit on a stool, shove the penny down along my ankle, then shake the boot until I can feel it slide across my arch.

"I'll probably pull up lame walking on that thing," I say.

Margaret stands then, pushes her tired body up off the bed with hands on her legs. "You never know what a penny might do for you," she says, her lungs exhausted from the work to get herself up. I stand up next to Margaret, look at Pops, his body swollen, weakening with each labored breath.

Besides the diabetes, the doctor says he's having congestive heart failure now. They give him these diuretics to keep him flushed out, but he's pretty swollen around his ankles and feet. He's wearing slip-on bedroom shoes like Mom used to wear because he can't get his feet into regular shoes anymore. I don't know if he can stand or not. I don't know if he can get to the bathroom on his own.

When *Bonanza* goes to commercial break, I ask him again if he needs to go. "Where to?" he says like he might be going on a trip.

"You know, Pops—do you have to go to the bathroom?" I say.

He looks at himself, then at me like he can't quite figure out who I am. "Might need to do that," he says.

I get his crutches and have Margaret hold them while Pops positions himself to stand. From in front his chair, I put both hands under his arms, lift his swollen torso up, steady him until the crutches are firmly planted. "You go on now," he says. "I can do it from here."

"No Pops, I'm going to walk you, just in case."

And then he becomes lucid, his smoky eyes clear, the liver spots on his loose skin quivering when he speaks. "No, boy," he says. "I can get there myself. Now you go on. Come by again when you can."

We compromise and I stand with Margaret watching Pops hobble down the hallway. "Is he going to be all right?" I ask.

"He's having a good night," she says, smiling. "He'll be just fine." I want to wait to make sure he's okay, but I trust Margaret's word. "You just go on," she says, "and don't worry about him. Your daddy is doing just fine."

Outside, I smell smoke, pungent and full on a hot breeze. I can't see anything in the air, so maybe it's just a small backyard fire, leaves left over from the winter being burned in someone's garden. Still, it worries me, smoke this far inland on a Sunday night in desperate drought conditions.

I pull into Barker's Servicenter, let Goose Hetzel fill the truck up. Goose is an old friend from school, a mechanic who also works the full-service pumps. He's checking my oil and the pressure in my tires when he tells me that there's a fire starting to burn out toward the paper-mill land. He says the sheriff was in talking about it early in the evening, tells me they have it under control. "Got to it quick," he says like he was there himself. Then Goose walks up to my window, tells me I'm lucky to be on the beach. "Lots of water around you," he laughs.

I pay with cash, remind him that Horry County's big, lots of dry land on the beach and off. If there's a fire out here, we'll all be fighting it sooner or later. Goose acts all hurt that I don't believe him when I ask again where the fire started, when I tell him I'm going to go take a look. He reminds me that the sheriff told him the fire was small and under control, but I don't buy anything that's more hearsay than truth. I don't care how long I've known Goose.

I leave Barker's and ride a ways out 701 toward the paper-mill land just to see for myself. The breeze kicked up by my truck moving down the road feels like a furnace. I can smell smoke but can't find fire, can't see anything illuminating the sky that would tell me one is burning inland. I start feeling bad about the way I treated Goose. Figure he was telling the truth about it being a small fire, practice for the big one everyone's afraid is coming this summer.

I slow down after taking a sharp curve past a trailer park where kids are shooting fireworks off in the drive. I don't like that, but I don't say anything. It's not my place out here. It's all going up into the air anyway, the embers arcing like a crooked smile out into the dark sky and then dying before they get near ground. It's not wise to let them do it, but no one in authority has yet said you can't shoot fireworks. No one's put a moratorium on anything except burning brush. They're even letting campers have fires still. The politicians are afraid that tourists will stop coming if there are safety regulations put in force, but I question their wisdom. Someone should have shut the whole mess down until we got rain, but they didn't, so we wait, keeping our eyes open and noses turned to the air.

Just past the boys is a shoulder deep enough that I can turn the truck around. I've gone ten miles out and seen no fire, so I'm thinking whatever it was is over with, gone. It's a good feeling accelerating back down 701, the town of Conway the only thing glowing off in the distance. I keep the windows on my truck rolled down, the wind blasting through.

There's a big old full moon over the trees in front of me casting shadows across the road. I'd love to head straight down to the water, get some relief with my board kicking up onto a wave, dropping me down into its trough, a silky smooth ride on a moonlit wave. I need to do that for my own sanity, but I won't go. I'm still exhausted. I need sleep more than I need to ride a wave, so I floor the accelerator trying not to think about Cassie and where she's sleeping tonight.

It's something I've never had to do before, worry about Cassie like this. It's impossible to avoid, so I just tell my truck to do its best to get me the hell out of here. I thank Goose Hetzel for his words of wisdom when I pass back through Conway, Barker's dark and closed up for the night.

Cassie

In the morning, light fills the room in a way that makes this house seem more livable than just hours ago. I can smell bacon cooking, coffee already done. I stretch, feeling a coolness in the sheets that I had forgotten about after living so long in the low country. In Garden City, the air will be unforgiving for months. You go to sleep sticky, wake up with bed linens damp and hot like fever. But nearer the mountains, there is a coolness that comes back on evening breezes swept down from higher elevations to settle you in sleep, wake you up chilled.

It's Sunday morning and in the distance there is a record playing over a loudspeaker, some nearby church broadcasting familiar music to call out the congregation. The scratchy pops of an organ playing "The Old Rugged Cross" echo out across Walhalla. My father used to sing the hymn when he ministered at Whiteside Cove Baptist. He died ten years ago while still working and praying for the same small congregation that forgave him after his only daughter sinned and was forced to leave the cove.

Bitterness rises in my throat even now when I think about how he treated me, choosing his congregation over his own flesh and blood. For fifteen years I have felt like an outcast, a visitor only allowed to return to the mountains for a few short weeks in the summer. But now I am pushing my way back, trying to re-stake my claim and return home for good.

Out in the kitchen, I hear Clay's voice and feel the bitterness soften into a sudden rush of fatigue. I remember earlier this morning when he came to me again before there was light in the sky. He touched me with warm hands, a soft voice telling me he was about to go crazy. "I can't be here like this and not touch you," he said. He kissed my neck, let his fingers part me below the covers. This is what we had wanted. This is what we had talked about, being here in Walhalla, alone together, far away from those dirty little motels and our dirty deeds. Yet, this morning I could not be a willing partner.

He sensed this and moved away, lay quietly for a few minutes longer. "It's been a hard time," he said finally. "You rest as long as you need to." He stood then, stepped into pants that were laying on the floor beside the bed, pulled a T-shirt out of his suitcase before leaving the room, the door closing quietly behind him.

I stayed in bed wanting to sleep for a hundred years, thinking that might be how long it would take to feel strong again. But now I'm awake. It's only a few short hours later and I'm hidden here beneath the covers listening to the old music fade away, the room falling quiet so that now I hear Kelly in the kitchen too. She's talking to Clay, trying to get along. I'm glad to know that she has come in from the car and not run away. For a moment, I can imagine that it will all work out, that Walhalla will be home and Kelly will accept our new life and no longer consider me an enemy.

Only then do I get up, caught naked in a mirror on the bedroom door. I feel like I am looking at a picture of someone else, my body beginning to let go of its part of the bargain. So much wasted time. I slip on a pair of shorts, find a blouse. I need to move faster, I think, faster before it's too late and none of it matters anymore.

The hallway is dark, cool on my bare feet. I can hear Clay talking, both of them laughing at something. When I enter the kitchen Kelly stops abruptly, the flush of old anger falling across her face.

"Good morning," Clay says. He looks at me kindly, reaches over to find another cup for my coffee. "We've got eggs and bacon," he says, "and if Kelly hasn't eaten it all, we've got some French toast for you too."

"There's plenty left," Kelly reports, but she's not looking at me when she says it.

I sit down and Clay puts a plate on the table, hands me a mug of coffee.

"Where did all this come from?" I ask, knowing last night there was nothing in the house to eat.

"Got up early," Clay says. "Kelly did too." He looks over at her, but she's not going to give him any help in this.

The fresh coffee feels good going down, the room's chill falling away quickly. "Well, this is quite the surprise," I say as I cut into a plateful of French toast. The room is silent until Kelly decides to get up. She pushes hard on her chair. The back legs like a pair of heels dig into the linoleum, sending a tremor through the whole floor.

I stop eating and watch Kelly as she walks over to the cabinet, reaches up for a mug, then lifts the pot to pour herself a cup of coffee. It's the first time I've seen this. "When did you start drinking coffee?" I ask.

She raises the mug to sip gingerly, the steam thick on top. "Daddy lets me, so I figured who cares."

"I care," I say, putting my fork down, waiting to see how far she will go. "I think you might be too young just yet."

Clay tucks his head, an uneasy smile pulling at his face. He rubs at a smudge on the linoleum with the toe of his boot.

"Give Clay that cup, please," I tell her.

He looks up, shifts his eyes between the two of us like he doesn't want to be part of any of this. "It's just a cup of coffee, Cassie."

Kelly's eyes roll when he says this like she doesn't need him to defend her. I raise my elbows onto the table, clasp my hands together and look at both of them. "I don't want her to drink coffee yet," I say. "She's just fifteen years old, so please take it back."

Clay looks at Kelly, shakes his head. "Better give it here then."

"No," she says. "I can have it."

"Kelly, this isn't the time to fight me," I say. "I know what you're doing."

"I'm not doing anything except drinking coffee."

Clay looks at me hard. "Pick your battles," he says.

"This isn't going to be a battle." I can't let her win, though I'm thinking Clay's right. Whatever I've done, it's too late to retreat, and I feel myself get up from the table, move toward my daughter to take the cup away.

"No," she says. She moves over to the sink where I can't get to her.

"I want you to pour that out," I say. "You're too young to drink coffee."

"Daddy said I could," Kelly says, her voice raised, sassy now, like she can do this to me because of what I've done to her. "So if you want to call him about it, let's do it. If not, then I'm drinking the coffee."

"Cassie, why not—" Before Clay can finish his thought, I cut him off. "Don't Cassie me, Clay Taylor. She knows what she's doing."

"And I know what you're doing," Kelly snaps back like a smart-ass, "and that's a million times worse than me drinking a cup of coffee."

When she raises the mug up to her face, something just snaps inside of me. I don't know what it is, or where it comes from, but I look on the table, see the keys to the car, and without even realizing what I'm doing, I grab them in my fist and throw them at her. The angle is bad, and I regret it before the keys are even out of my hand. They hit her forehead. The force of the throw, the surprise of such an attack, pushes her back against the door frame. The coffee cup drops, shattering on the floor.

For a moment we stand in silence, Kelly in shock, her mouth opened, tears forming in her eyes. And then she screams, "I can't believe you did that, goddammit."

Clay turns around to the sink. "Jesus," he says.

I follow Kelly into the living room heartbroken over what I have just done. "Come here," I say. "Don't walk away like that."

"Leave me alone." Kelly pushes through the screen door, the frame popping against the side of the house, rousing dogs down the block. She takes the front porch steps in one leap, heads out into the road walking like she knows where she's going. We're both barefoot on a gravel road. I'm scared as hell and I want to tell her I'm sorry, that she can just go on back to the beach and live with Peck, drink all the coffee she wants, but I don't. Kelly is crying and holding her head and I'm afraid I might have really hurt her, so I walk faster, almost run as I catch up and then get out in front, stopping her from going any farther. "Hey," I say, "hey baby, I'm sorry. I'm really sorry." I try to hold her but she pulls away.

"You hit me with your keys," she says, her forehead red, a small welt where the keys struck, but no blood drawn.

"That was a stupid thing for me to do." I hold her at arm's length. "Let me look at it."

"No, get away," she says, turning, trying to get loose, but I won't let her go.

"Kelly, listen to me. Listen to me, baby." I pull her in, hug her tight, let her cry on my shoulder, her limp body heaving against me.

"Honey, I didn't mean to do that," I tell her. "I don't know where that came from, but it won't ever come back, I promise."

"You tried to kill me," she says.

"No I didn't."

"You could have put my eye out or worse."

"I wanted you to listen to me, that's all. I didn't mean to throw the keys at you. I didn't mean to throw anything at you. I'm sorry, baby."

"I want to go home," Kelly cries. "I want to go back to our house and the beach. I don't want to be here. I don't want you to be here."

"I know, baby. I know. But we have to go see Meemaw, remember? We need to go see Meemaw and you need to go to Cullowhee for your camp. After that, we can see how you feel. If you want to go home, you can."

This seems to help, Kelly's body no longer heavy. "I want to talk to Daddy," she says into my shoulder.

"We can call him later today," I say, though I don't want to do that. I need more distance between us before I hear his voice again. I don't know what might happen if we talk. I don't feel that I'm strong enough yet to stay here, to not go back like all the other times before.

"I want to get out of here," she says. "I don't want to stay at Clay's one more minute."

"You two seemed to be having a nice time before I came in," I say.

"It wasn't that nice."

"Look, we can go," I say, "but we have to go back there and get our things. And we need to get out of this street, baby." I look around, see a few faces in windows, and think this isn't the way Clay needs to start a new job.

Kelly looks up and is immediately embarrassed. "Where are we?" she asks.

"Down the street," I say. "If I hadn't stopped you, we'd probably be in the middle of Walhalla by now and then what would people say?"

Kelly says, "Oh my lord," and then turns, holding on to me as a shield as we walk back to the house arm in arm.

Inside, Clay is in the kitchen cleaning up the mess, waiting. His face shows hurt, but in all honesty, I don't care. I tell him I'm sorry; his acceptance of my apology is tepid at best. He stays out of it, cleans up the breakfast dishes while Kelly and I shower and dress. Nobody says anything, and by early afternoon when we are ready to go, the tension inside Clay's house is strung so tight that I'm happy to be leaving. From the car, I tell him good luck with his first day. He waits, seems vexed when I offer nothing more. Finally he asks, "You coming back?"

I key the ignition, the engine turning over and over like a broken record. "Yes," I say, though I know it sounds like I don't mean it.

The Bel Air coughs to life. Kelly looks over at me. "You're not coming back here, are you?"

I shush her, pump the accelerator to wake the engine up good, black smoke pouring out from the tailpipe. "If I come back, it'll be while you're in camp," I say. "I won't make you come here again."

"I don't want you here, Momma. I don't want you staying at Clay's anymore."

"You'll be fine," I say, trying to play it all down. And then the war is back on, Kelly's body balled up into a tight little fist, her feet on the dashboard, her face staring out into the afternoon as I roll my eyes at Clay, a hopeless situation with this girl.

"I'll be here" is all he says. He turns his back on both of us and walks inside, the screen door slapping against the house.

It's not the way I want to leave, but we go anyway, find our way out of Walhalla and onto the road headed toward Cashiers. The curves tighten, the slant of the highway pitching upward, the Bel Air working hard to make the climb. I welcome a lull in our war when it comes, Kelly leaning against a locked door, a pillow beneath her head, her breathing heavy when she falls asleep. The sun is warm on my arm. Where shade still covers the road, the asphalt is damp.

Just over the border the car snakes past the small hamlets and crossroad towns of Jack's Branch and Bull Pen, signs that we are close. Whiteside Cove is a small gathering of houses at the end of a mountain road outside Cashiers. It spreads out below Whiteside Mountain, a sheer rock face that my father used to say was the oldest piece of rock in the world. He would take long walks through the property until he could feel Whiteside towering over him, and there he would pray each day.

When I was a child, I read about Moses saving the Israelites and how he went up onto Mount Sinai to be given the Ten Commandments. I remember thinking of my father like that when he would leave us on his walks early in the morning before the cove awakened. I'd watch him disappear into the quiet veil of fog that blanketed the world, and I would believe that he was going to talk to God directly, that he would bring back the message written in stone for his congregation. When he returned, it was always empty-handed, yet there was something about him that made me believe he had seen God. Because of this image I held of my father, I tried to please him, so that God would be pleased with me.

In the end, when his faith and that of his congregation was tested by my pregnancy, there was nothing I could do or say that would get him to let me come back. For the longest time I believed God had disowned me. Peck didn't help since he was not raised in a church. Only with time have I come to feel my father was wrong, that God has looked after me and is now giving me a second chance.

When I turn off the highway, the asphalt narrows, becomes gravel. The trees drop down into a thick canopy. The change of speed and surface makes Kelly stir, and she lifts herself up, her eyes struggling to open, strands of hair glued to her face and mouth. "Are we here?" she asks, her voice high and childish.

"Almost," I say.

Along the road, I see earthmovers, blue and orange ribbons marking off the land, *No Trespassing* signs where once there was nothing but woods and rocks and mountain streams to explore. My heart sinks at the sight. Momma had told me it was bad, but this is more than I ever imagined. Someone is cutting up the earth, reshaping it into fairways and acre lots, subdivisions with silly names like Cherokee Sunset, Beaver Run, and White Water Ridge Estates. It is only toward the end of this road that familiarity returns and I can see the remainder of the cove as it was when I lived here.

We take a final curve breaking into sunlight. In front of us is a tired house of worn wood and peeling paint, two stories with a rusting tin roof. It's the old parsonage, the house that my father was given title to shortly before he died. He was securing something for Momma. It was as if he knew he would not be here long enough to protect her, and so he gave her this house and the land he walked every day to live on forever.

She is outside when we drive up. A low-slung porch like a gardener's hat holds flower baskets bobbing along its edges. Even at this late-afternoon hour, Momma is there in her nightgown and robe watering. When she sees the Bel Air, I sense panic, the way she pulls her robe close to her neck until she finally recognizes us.

"You should have called," she scolds. "I didn't know when you were coming and here I am all a mess. You should have called."

I hug her, feel her soft damp skin against my arms. She seems smaller, her body more frail than when we came for our visit last year. Then it was a *real* visit, Kelly excited to spend the few weeks with her grandmother, and me happy to be away from the marsh and what had become of my life. Now I am here with intentions of staying, cut loose and on my own for the first time in fifteen years. "We should have called," I say, "but something came up. Besides, we're only a couple of weeks early."

Momma holds me out in front of her, intuition taking hold. "Is there something wrong?"

"No Momma, nothing's wrong," I lie. "Kelly has a wonderful opportunity to attend a softball camp up in Cullowhee at the state college, so I thought we'd surprise you."

I look at Kelly, wink like what I am telling Meemaw is just a little white lie, but it's bigger than that and she knows it. I don't want to say anything about leaving Peck just yet. Momma worries more since my father's gone. When he passed, the way he passed—his body discovered one Sunday afternoon at the foot of Whiteside

Mountain—seemed to ruin her spirit. When I came home for the funeral there was less life in her eyes. Some of it seems to have returned, but Momma is a step slower now, my father's death having taken part of her with it and then refused to give it back. She seems frail.

"I'm going to let Kelly visit with you for a little while," I tell her, "and then we'll go up to Cullowhee. I have to get her there by six this evening. Her camp starts tomorrow morning. She's really amazing, Momma. You'll have to go up there with me and watch her play."

Before we can get inside, a neighbor of Momma's drives up. John Boyd Carter honks his horn, stops behind the Bel Air, waves, and says, "Hey, Mavis." His large body squeezes through the car door. He's wearing Red Camels and work boots, a white short-sleeve shirt with sweat stains, his tie loose at the collar. He stands stiffly like he's finding his bearings, eyeballing us—a nosy neighbor. "Looks like you got company," he says. He grins at Momma, steps up onto the porch, and leans over to give her a kiss on the cheek.

I'm friendly watching this, but I don't like John Boyd. The history between us soured years ago. Momma smiles. "How are you, John Boyd?"

"Fine, Mavis, just fine," he says before looking at me. "Cassie? Is that you?"

I nod to let him know he's right. "Hey, John Boyd," I say.

"I thought that was you," he crows. "Goodness it's been a while." He reaches over to hug me, his body smelling of cigarettes and cedar, the sweet fragrance evidence of summer's clothes just beginning to come out of storage.

"You know my daughter, Kelly," I say.

"Yes I do, but I don't remember her all grown up like this. How are you, Kelly?"

She smiles, but then turns away, ignoring us.

"We're a bit tired from the drive," I say, apologizing for her behavior. "Seems like it takes me longer every year to drive in."

"You're down on the coast, is that right?" John Boyd asks like he doesn't know.

"That's right," I say, "Murrells Inlet and Garden City Beach."

"Well, that's a distance all right," he says. John Boyd sits down on the rail of Momma's porch like he might stay awhile. The flowerpots above drip water onto his shirt, though he seems not to notice or care. "I saw you drive in, and well, we don't see many cars driving down this way anymore. I just wanted to make sure Mavis was all right. Are you all right, Mavis?" He smiles saying this, winks at me like he's enjoying his joke.

"I would have been if I'd known they were coming," Momma says.

I look over and explain, "We're here early. Kelly's going up to the college for two weeks, a softball camp that starts tomorrow."

He nods. "Well I'm sure she'll enjoy that. They're really growing up there from what I hear." He looks at Kelly, smiles in a way that bothers me, like he's waiting for more information, wanting to know more. "You'll be here then," John Boyd asks, "for the two weeks?"

"Yes, and then some," I lie, knowing that Clay will be expecting me to stay with him in Walhalla. Kelly's sitting on the side rail, her eyes out toward land I used to roam as a child. She knows I'm lying and I can only hope she'll keep her mouth shut.

I'm uneasy with all of this, wishing John Boyd wasn't the first person we saw as soon as we arrived. He was a deacon in the church when I became pregnant with Kelly. He kept my father in the pulpit, but told him he would have to make an example out of me. "Cast out the weed," he'd said. He's changed over the years since the church closed its doors, but looking at him, I feel he could do it all again.

"Well, I hope you stay as long as you can, Cassie. I know how much Mavis would appreciate that."

I thank him for stopping by to check on Momma, and he asks if I might see him later to talk about what's happening to this end of the cove. "No one usually comes out here unless it's some real-estate agent or construction company trying to get at the land. I didn't recognize your car, so thought I ought to drop by, just in case. I try to keep my eye out, you know, be a good neighbor and all."

"And I appreciate that, John Boyd," says Momma. She looks at me, her face suddenly pulled with worry. "They want this land for some private country club or something like that."

"Momma, you should have called," I say. "I didn't know."

"Well, it's nothing to worry about. We're not selling." There's defiance in her voice, a hint of the old fire Momma had in her when I was growing up.

"It would just be good to talk," John Boyd says. "Now that you're here, I think it might be a good time, that's all it is."

I promise him to find some time, and, oddly, that seems to end his visit. He's off the porch with barely a good-bye, his car quickly disappearing past the end of the drive.

"Why didn't you tell us they were trying to get your property?" I ask.

"Because they won't get it," Momma says. Kelly and I follow her through the screen door, the smell of Sunday dinner cooking on the stove, filling the house. I marvel at that, how even when there's no one to cook for, Momma still does it, a part of her life so deeply learned that she'll continue doing it until the day she dies. "John Boyd's got the most to sell," she says, walking into the kitchen. She bends over, opens the oven to check on her casserole, chicken broccoli, enough for us to eat off all week. "But with my land, we hold a large block. They can't do anything about it, so he keeps an eye out for me. John Boyd's a good man." She pulls the casserole from the oven with dishtowels to protect her hands, sets it down on the stove top and turns to look at us both. "Now," she says, "go wash up and we'll have dinner."

I don't tell her of my distrust of John Boyd—I'm not sure she would listen to me. Loyalty here in the mountains is nearly as deep as blood. My father turned against me in favor of John Boyd, so my suspicions of this man will never fade. You don't do something like that unless there's a debt to be paid. You don't give up family the way my father gave me up.

I won't upset Momma with my concerns now. There will be plenty of time for that. Instead, we eat Sunday dinner, chicken-broccoli casserole, field potatoes, and fresh green beans from the garden. We take our sweet tea outside in the backyard, sit in low-slung Adirondack chairs under a small grove of oak trees, and visit quietly for a while before Kelly has to leave for Cullowhee. I watch a deer move along the edge of the woods to graze. Kelly is out in tall grass halfheartedly looking for June bugs. When she was younger, Momma would help her hunt them down, June bugs as big as bottle caps. We would tie strings to their legs and Kelly would squeal as she flew them through the air, silvery green bodies flashing past her head, winking each time they came around through the sun.

She's out there by herself now acting all hurt and sullen. Momma notices, but she leaves it alone, doesn't ask about her standoffishness. Beyond the tree line, Whiteside Mountain rises straight up like a giant wave cresting, nearly two thousand feet above the lowest point in the cove. I can't imagine a life in which I would never come here again, never set foot in this house or look out into the backyard and see Whiteside Mountain—this land that I grew up on no longer here as it is right now.

Momma is quiet in her chair. She works on a bowl of green beans she's picked from her garden, her head down, fingers quickly snapping and stringing each. "You need to let me know what's wrong," she says without raising her head. "We'll talk when you're ready."

Her intuition is unsettling, but I don't let on that I'm worried she has found me out. I'm not ready to tell her anything more than she already knows. Kelly and I are here for our summer visit, that's enough for right now. "There's nothing to say," I assure her. But she's not buying my bluff. I can see it in her hands, the beans taking the brunt of her impatience. Still she remains quiet. Momma will wait for me to come around. She always has.

CULLOWHEE IS ANOTHER HOUR into the mountains. Western Carolina is there, the college where I enrolled for the fall of 1954. I went to be a freshman there after a summer working at a church camp near Myrtle Beach, but never finished. By the end of September, I was married to Peck, Kelly still just a speck inside me. Hurricane Hazel had devastated our small home—the storm surge came in on us at the highest lunar tide of that year. All of Garden City Beach was part of the sea for days, the marsh disappearing with everything else under the powerful surge.

"Now you belong to the low country," Peck said grimly when we finally got a boat and could get back to where our small house had stood. It was just gone, along with everything that I had brought with me.

After I was married, I held on to my hopes that I would one day come back to Cullowhee. I kept a catalogue of classes to the college, along with a letter promising a scholarship, in a small drawer in the bedroom. When I was alone, I would look at it as a source of strength, say to myself that the pregnancy was just a momentary pause in my life. I really believed, as foolish as it was, that I would deliver Kelly and then return to my life. But as we floated past where our house had sat just days before, I felt all of that die deep inside my body.

Now here I am again with my daughter, traveling along the Tuckasegee River and then onto Cullowhee Road until the college is before us, a cluster of buildings gathered like ancient outcroppings against the side of a mountain. When I pull onto the campus I cannot help but think of what I missed, what my life might have been like had I stayed and graduated. I wanted to be a teacher, that's all I can remember now. If there was more, it has long since faded into what became my life. It is Kelly's turn, I think. Then maybe it will be mine again, maybe. I catch my heart racing at the thought.

Kelly is out of the car before the engine is off. She has no idea where she's going. "Can you wait a minute?" I say.

"No," she says back to me. She is walking away fast, legs pushing her up a steep sidewalk.

"Where are you going?"

"To camp, Mother. I'm going to camp just like you want so you can go back down there."

"Kelly, that's not fair." I look around to see if anyone else hears us, but we are late, nearly seven o'clock, the last ones to arrive it seems.

I pull her clothes bag from the car, carry her softball equipment in a large canvas duffel slung over my shoulder. When I finally catch up, she has stopped and sits on a wall, legs crossed, elbows on her knees to rest her head. I toss the bags at her feet, accidentally scraping them against her tanned skin.

"Hey," she whines, "that hurt." She rubs the spot where the keys hit her face, the wound still fresh.

I look at her wishing I wasn't angry, wanting Kelly to understand in a way that might help us get along. "I'm sorry," I say. "I didn't mean to hurt you. Let's just go register. I think that will help both of us."

"I can do it by myself," Kelly snaps, giving up any chance of a compromise.

I look up the hill to where girls are pitching balls in front of the gym. There's laughter, and I can only hope that Kelly will fit in once I am gone. "Well good," I say. I feel tears in my eyes that I don't want Kelly to see. "You can do it all on your own then." I pull the paper from my pocket containing information she will need, her application, and the check to pay for her camp. "That's Breese Gym over there. Go sign in, and I'm sure someone will help you find your dorm. Have fun."

When I leave, I see Kelly's face fall, but I don't turn around. I understand there is no history in all of this for her and that mine is tainted by the mistakes I have made, but for the moment I don't want to be the adult here. I don't want reason. I just want to leave.

I walk down the sidewalk, the steep angle pushing me into a little jog until it bottoms out and I am by the car. When I look back, Kelly is gone, the stone wall where she sat empty. Then I start to worry. I can't see much from the car. The street is narrow, draped by trees that cast deep shadows onto the cars parked along one side. The only thing I can do is drive beside the gym and look for her.

It's hard to make out the faces of the girls darting by, weighed down with bags and backpacks. They walk in twos and threes, joking and getting along, creating new friendships so this new world won't be too hard. It had been that way for me the summer I worked at Myrtle Beach. Had it not been for Kimberly Jordan, my best friend, I never would have made it to the end of that first week. After I met Peck, everything changed, nothing was unfamiliar.

I had heard of the camp during revivals that spring. A minister my father knew in Franklin encouraged him to let me go. The camp was for the month of August. There would be a group of teenagers from the mountains working around the arcades, cleaning the beaches, handing out tracts, visiting local churches to sing on Sunday mornings. There was chapel and a sermon every morning, Bible study and prayers in the evenings. Kimberly's parents talked to my father, but it did little good. He was still afraid of idle time, what such a place might encourage if young minds weren't kept busy enough with the work of the Lord. It wasn't until he returned one morning from Whiteside, two days before the bus was to leave, that he reluctantly gave his approval.

Myrtle Beach was like living in a dream, and when Kimberly left early to go home, sunburned and homesick, I stayed on by myself, and Peck changed my world forever. I met him one day when we all rented air rafts to float on the water. He was surfing with Teddy that afternoon, and when a wave washed me off the raft, he was there to pull me out of the swirling tide, sandy and wet to the bone.

After Vespers that evening, I snuck away, walked to the beach, and Peck picked me up in his truck. It was a routine we would keep the rest of the month I was at the beach. He showed me the low country that summer—sunsets along the marsh that made my heart break. We slopped through black mud at low tide to harvest clams, the musky slick meat a foreign delicacy to me. There were conversations and promises of how we would trade off summers until I finished college. It was hot and sweet and full of love that summer, and when I left at the end of August, my heart broke hard for Peck Johnson, but I knew it was probably over and I was excited to go to college.

I left for Cullowhee soon after I returned home, excited about school and the fact that Clay Taylor would be there, that I would see him again and hear about Peck. We had written a few letters, but I longed to hear Peck's voice, feel his touch on my skin. Clay would carry good news, I hoped. We promised to look each other up when school began.

It was a hard summer for my father with the beach and my packing to go to school following so quickly after my return. He brooded constantly, irritated by both. He thought high school was enough, that there was plenty for me to do to help Momma until I met someone of faith, who I would marry and then start my own family. He stayed away while I packed, his walks to Whiteside lasting all day instead of just a few hours. Momma scoffed at his behavior. She could be strong when it was necessary. She stood beside me, took my side of the argument when I went to the beach and later when she drove me to Cullowhee.

On campus, I threw up each morning for the first three days I was there. I wanted to find Clay to ask how Peck was doing, but the morning sickness and what it surely meant consumed me. Instead, I made trips to the infirmary and was finally told the grim news by a nurse who knew the symptoms. "We can test you, if you'd like," she said, so matter-of-fact that I assumed she said it all the time. But I knew, so I packed my bags and called Momma to come pick me up.

When she arrived, I didn't have to tell her anything. "Are you quick?" she asked, as soon as we were alone.

"Yes," I said. "I think so." And then I broke down crying, my body emptying out all the hope I had for my life, all of it lost. We sat in the car as kids walked past us going to their classes. Momma seemed to grow distant, my betrayal of her trust and loyalty during that summer a deep cut between us. My father would have to know the truth, and then she would have to endure the harsh accusations he would throw at her for not listening to him in the first place.

It wasn't the first time Momma had seen a girl in trouble, and I knew there was a way out. From time to time, there were girls in my father's small congregation who came to him in need of help. Some men back in the mountains could not keep their hands off their own children. It hurt my father deeply that men sinned against the word of God and would lay with their own daughters, but he would never judge them or condemn their actions. Instead he put it up to Momma to right the wrong.

These girls would come to her in the middle of the night and she would drive them deep into the mountains to see a woman who administered herbal contractors, blue cohosh root, pennyroyal leaf, or angelica. These toxic poisons could kill if not properly administered, and would certainly abort the pregnancy, remove the sin, and wash the child clean.

Some daughters were brought more than once, an issue that came as close as anything to dividing my parents. I heard the arguments from their room. How could God allow this, and how could a minister turn a blind eye, Momma would say. My father reprimanded her for questioning his wisdom, told her that it was his job to prosecute the teachings of Jesus, to carry out the burden of God in this cove. He forbade her from discussing it, told her it was a sin to deny God's judgment of redemption and salvation. "Don't be the sinner," he said. "Lucifer has already made his mark. It's up to you to help erase it."

She would always go into the mountains and stay for two or three days, depending on the stage of the pregnancy and the effects of the abortifacient. I thought that afternoon when she came to pick me up, she would turn the car toward the mountains to pay a visit to some Cherokee woman whose tonics could kill the very spirit of life inside my womb. I figured she would take me there, unknown to my father, to have the devil's mark removed from inside me. But she never did. "You have to call that boy," she said. "He needs to make this right."

When I asked about the woman in the mountains, she winced like the very words caused her pain. "Will I need to go there, like the rest?" I asked.

"No," she said, her body rigid, her face torn with grief. "I imagine your father will never forgive me, but you won't go. I won't take you."

I have seen Momma cry twice in her life, at my father's funeral and the day I asked if I would be taken into the mountains for an abortion. That day she wept in the car, sitting on the campus of Western Carolina, holding me so tight, I thought she might squeeze the child right out. "You won't go," she said. "You will never go, because you're not like them. You're my child."

I told Momma we could try to find Clay, let him know that I needed to talk to Peck, but she wanted nothing to do with that. "You'll call him yourself," she said. "You don't need to tell no other boy about this." We left Cullowhee that afternoon, my life already moving along a path that would bring me to this moment, where ghosts of an earlier life have long awaited my arrival.

I'm sitting in the middle of the road when the gym door opens and Kelly walks out. She doesn't see me there as she walks alongside another girl, easily carrying her bags, smiling, seemingly happy again. It makes me feel better. Still, I have to watch her walk away, see that her direction is toward a dorm, before I can leave and drive back to Walhalla.

When we left Momma in Whiteside Cove, I told her I'd be staying the night in Cullowhee, a mother-daughter thing. But that wasn't true. Here I am, a thirty-three-year-old woman, and I am still lying to my mother about where I'm going. How silly that I still do this, that I cannot live my life open and free like I always dreamed it would be. I thought I would have my whole life to right myself after Kelly was born, that I would find a way to do it all, but in the end I did nothing.

I find my way back to Cullowhee Road and then Highway 107 to drive out of the deepest part of these mountains, past Glenville and Cashiers, Whiteside Cove, where I don't even think about stopping. It is nearly seven o'clock when I arrive in Walhalla, a black leaden sky swirling above me. Clay is there, impatient that it has taken me all day to return to him.

It has been so long since I have seen rain that I get excited when it finally comes. It is the freshest sound I think I have ever heard. The drops touch my face. I feel the wind blow in my hair, the air cooling under the dense clouds, the temperature dropping. It is like a miracle to feel this change in weather, something the low country needs, deserves more than Walhalla right now. But it is here, and so I take what is given, and stick my tongue out to taste the raindrops as they gather intensity, a solid sheet of wet descending on Walhalla.

Thunder rattles the whole house. I run back inside, watch lightning illuminate the backyard where someone has left what looks like half a car in ruins. Its body parts have been torn out and strewn between the house and a small shed that is padlocked as if it is trying to keep the car from coming inside to save itself. "I'll get that cleaned up out there," Clay says, apologizing for a mess he didn't make. He comes over to stand behind me, his hands on my shoulders. "You could plant us a garden out there, if you feel like it."

There's an empty bird feeder on top of a pole and a clothesline, its wires limp, rocking side to side in the storm. We stand there watching a cardinal attempt to light onto the feeder, its bloodred body frantic in the wind until it gives up, becoming a momentary fleck of debris blown against the slate sky. Clay's hands move down my arms. His touch tries to be soft, but there's just so much softness in a man's hand. The rest has to be accepted for what it is. "How was it," he asks, "being back at school?"

"Hard," I tell him. "It reminds me just how close I came."

"You'll be all right," he says. Clay stays behind me pushing his body into mine. "You can have anything now, Cassie. You can go back to school, if that's what you want." He turns my head so he can kiss me. When he puts his mouth on mine, it is not gentle, but full of a hard need.

I can feel his hand move to my breast, sliding across it, cupping it for a moment before he starts to unbutton my blouse. I need Clay Taylor to keep my head on straight, to let me know I am doing the right thing. I let myself go and Clay's strength is all that I have left. He lifts me in his arms, takes me to the bedroom where I lay watching him undress.

There is a scar on his chest that I have never asked about, a tan as deep as Peck's all over his body. He has a small patch of hair running up to his belly button. He smells of cigarettes and sweat. He removes my shorts and panties, his hands sliding the wet clothes from my body. I can feel the tightness of my nipples in the cooling air when he unsnaps my bra, the tug between my legs when I feel his fingers there.

"Slow, be slow with me," I whisper, as I pull him down on top of me.

And then in the middle of it all, I feel my world begin to crash. I have never felt so alone and lost in a bed as I do at this very moment. Clay asks if I'm all right, and I whisper that it is the storm, that I'm sorry. "You're just not used to seeing rain," he says. He sits up on the bed, lights a cigarette, but this time he doesn't offer one. His back is to me, the lingering storm holding us there in silence.

When the phone rings, Clay leaves and I hear him talking to

someone at the fire station. "All right," he says. "I can do that. I'll be up there in a half hour." He comes back in to tell me that he needs to be at the station just in case there are fires started from the storm.

"How can there be fire in all this rain?" I ask.

"Other things can happen," he says, "lightning strikes and such. Besides, the chief needs to be there to set an example."

I tell him that I need an example set too, that I need to know this life won't be the same life I just left, a fireman for a fireman. "That's not what I bargained for," I say.

"Just what was it that you bargained for then?" he asks. I can tell our poor attempt to make love has hurt.

"You," I say, but that doesn't seem to do it for either one of us. It is the second time in all of this that I have been unable to be with him when he wanted me.

"Look, I need to go," Clay says, running a hand through his hair. "Will you be okay by yourself?"

"Sure," I say. Then I tell him that in the morning I'll go to stay with Momma for a while.

This stops him, something unexpected that disappoints.

"I need to go, Clay," I try to explain. "She has no idea about us. She thinks I'm sleeping on campus with Kelly tonight. God, I'm thirty-three and I still lie to my mother about where I'm going."

He stands in front of me, his eyes sullen and dark. He's given all he can. I know this. It's up to me now. "Call before you leave," he says. He grabs a T-shirt and then stands at the door, his body hardly visible in the darkening hallway. "Stay in touch, please."

I tell him I will, then turn over to watch the storm intensify again, the thunder—empty barrels rolling over the top of this house. It is more rain than I have seen in a whole year, the moisture chilling my skin. I listen to water pour off the roof, Clay's truck starting up and leaving the driveway, his headlights sweeping through the bedroom when he backs out like he is searching for me one last time before he goes.

I sleep on and off, watching the alarm clock flip the hours, the sound of storm and rain fading into a quiet morning. The world begins to dry out as I eat and shower. I dress, pack what little I have brought, and leave the key Clay had given me on the kitchen table, nervous that he might show up now before I can get out. I don't want to talk about any of this right now. I want to go home to Momma and feel there are no strings attached to me anywhere. I hurry, pull the door shut behind me, almost running to where my car waits at the curb.

Peck

WEDNESDAY DAWNS SLOW and easy along the strand. People who have come down for vacations have by now exhausted themselves. They arrived on Saturday or Sunday and immediately started trying to kill themselves, drinking on the beach, drinking and burning their skin, drinking and swimming in the ocean, drinking and driving to seafood restaurants in Murrells Inlet and north up to Calabash.

This occurs like a habit every week, the exhaustion taking over like someone set an alarm to go off inside their bodies. By Wednesday, they're moving slow and only far enough to eat breakfast at a pancake house or get donuts and coffee at a Krispy Kreme. They stay inside nursing hangovers and blistered sunburns or head into one of the arcades to play Skee-Ball. They fill up putt-putt courses in the late afternoon or take in a movie, making it easy on the rest of us, the people who live here year-round.

We call it Hump Day, the best day of the week, and I am happy to be sitting in a rocking chair outside the station with my first cup of coffee from a fresh pot Lori made as soon as she got in this morning.

"Hump Day," she says when she brings me my three packets of sugar.

"Yep," I say, smiling, "best damn day of the week."

"You got that right," Partee says. He pulls up a chair to sit next to me, takes one of my sugars before I can dump them all in my cup, but that's okay.

All season we plan our routine chores around Hump Day. Any errands that need to be done are scheduled then. The traffic's easy and the stores less crowded up and down the strand. We go light on crews some Wednesdays. If it rains or is even overcast, we know the chances of a fire or accident drop dramatically, so we let some of the boys take a day's vacation if they need it. We always look forward to Wednesday, and this one feels good this morning, the air a bit less humid, a breeze in the shade if you sit still and feel for it. This week's hump has a little something more to it. Everyone has come in early or stayed on duty because someone decided it's the perfect day to throw me a birthday party.

I have tried to persuade them not to, but they won't listen. Surfside has okayed taking us off-line for the day barring any major disaster, and Lori has taken on the job of organizing everything. She seems to be leading the charge. I know she's thinking about Cassie not being here. She told me the other day that it wasn't right for someone to spend their birthday alone. "It's the day you came to this world," she said. "You always have to celebrate that with someone."

I won't stop them if they want to do it. Matter of fact, it makes me feel better. I was at home the other day and the place seemed so empty that I got up and left, came back down to the station. Cassie hasn't called yet, and it's got me thinking that she might really be gone for good. It hurts like hell to think about it. I nearly called up to Meemaw's yesterday to see what was going on, but I didn't. I wasn't even sure she'd be there.

Partee comes into the station with grocery bags under each arm. He's in charge of food. I tell him he's always in charge of food. That's the law in this firehouse. Partee Mathis will cook for God when he dies. He's that good. I'd never say this out loud, but I try to schedule Partee to be on duty when I'm here. I don't want to miss his meals, good meals that he cooks from scratch and with everything that's grown fresh in the season.

I've given him venison roasts that he's performed miracles on. He has a fresh mustard sauce that could bring about world peace if everyone would just sit down and eat it. Lamb kabobs, barbecued chicken, and smoked pork loin are specialties we all look forward to at the station. Mud pie and his ambrosia around the holidays keep the crew happy and on time. All the boys need to smell is his scrambled-egg casserole smothered in salsa and they are up and ready to roll, as long as the fire bell holds off until the meal is done. I hate to say it, but Partee puts Cassie's cooking to shame, though I would never tell her that. I'm not stupid.

He's ordered the boys from Surfside to cook up the low country boil, told them where to go to get the best sausage, the vegetable stands where they would find the corn, onions, and red potatoes. Teddy promises imported beer but Partee tells him Pabst will be better for the boil. He's got lists for everyone with directions on how to start it all up until he gets back from the marsh. And then he grabs me and says, "Let's go, birthday boy."

"Where to?" I ask.

"If you going to eat it, you going to help get it," he says, a big old grin breaking out across his face. The gap between his front teeth makes it look like one's missing, big enough he can stick a straw through to sip on a milkshake from down at Sam's. We get up and head out the back side of the station, Partee's Mustang GT convertible waiting to take us for a ride.

"Mustang Sally, better slow your mustang down," I sing, the pitch less than perfect. I do a little bit of the twist there in the parking lot, grinding gravel into the sole of my boot. Partee winces like he's just put something bad in his mouth.

"You better stop doing that," he says, "if you want me to cook for you." We both laugh, get into the Mustang, and Partee kicks up dust leaving the parking lot.

He just got this killer car, 1965 convertible, Rangoon red inside and out. It's loaded, with a 289 V8, four-barrel carb and power steering and power brakes. A center console separates bucket seats up front. It's got an AM radio and eight-track tape player, factory air-conditioning that he turns on even with the top down.

He talked about this car all last year. Even had the used-car dealer up in Florence hold it back on layaway, until he could get all the money together. He bought it back in the winter for a good chunk of change, put it up on blocks and spent more when he ordered a new top and a factory rally pack—a clock on the right and a six-thousand rpm tach on the left of the steering column. A guy at the Aynor station helped him install it all so he would be ready to ride by summer. Now it's June, and we're cruising in a car that has shit-kicking speed and Partee's ready to open it up for the very first time. "It's my last child," he says over dual exhausts that vibrate us in our seats. "I ain't having no more."

We're headed over the Intracoastal Waterway, past Conway to a place outside Aynor near where Partee lives, to pick up ribs. "After we get this," he says, "we're going down to your place, got to go get them clams out of the creek." That's why he's got me here, I realize. He needs my boat and my hands.

"I wasn't planning to spend my morning in the mud," I tell him, but Partee just smiles and downshifts, turning onto a small sandy road that takes us up past tobacco fields, the rows of young plants flickering past as he fishtails side to side.

A half mile in, he pulls up under a grove of pines, brown nearly to the top of every tree. Needles blanket the sand below us, the air still, hot as a furnace. Out in the fields, the tobacco is wilting and will die if it doesn't rain soon.

Behind a small house, a man is boiling water in a large pot that sits on an open fire. Several large buckets of water are positioned around it to dowse any errant spark or ash that might find its way from under the pot. I look at Partee and shake my head. "That's against the law right now," I say.

He holds up his hand to stop me there, the palm gray to the deep rich blackness of its back side. "He's been slaughtering hog like that for years," he says. "It won't be Pacman who starts the big one. He ain't that stupid."

Walking back, I look around the pot and see small black burn spots where Pacman's been putting out loose hot ash. I worry when I see something like this, but I know this old guy isn't the only local working with fire every day inland of the beaches, so I keep my mouth shut, let Partee do the talking.

If my partner is black, then Pacman is a piece of midnight cut out and thrown into the light of day. He is black as tar, deep sunburned black, his skin leathery thick. Behind the pot, a dead pig hangs by its hindquarters to bleed out. Its eyes are waxed and dead, the tongue loose and thick in its opened mouth. It's been gutted and some woman is washing out the inner cavity. I can't look at it long. The smell back here is musty and raw, blood in the air, the innards of the hog in a bucket, the intestines saved so the skins can be used to stuff sausage.

A stout black girl is sharpening knives, razor-sharp edges glinting in the sunlight. She lays them down on a clean white cloth like she's preparing an operating table. It's the wrong time of year to be slaughtering hogs. Pops used to help Colin Murphy kill hogs in late October or November after the heat broke. He was a black man Pops worked with over in Georgetown at the mill. They'd drive over to Colin's farm outside Litchfield and kill two, split the meat up between the families.

Pork was plentiful for the better part of the winter if you had a good freezer. Pops would give away whole roasts and chops to families he knew needed them for the holidays, but for the most part we ate everything he cut up. This time of the year, the meat will spoil fast, so the work has to be done without hesitation, the meat cut and stored in a cooler before it can turn. Out here there are no butcher stores, and if there was one, it would still be for whites. It might be 1970, but in some places in the low country, it's not even 1950 yet.

I watch Partee talk to Pacman, tell him what he wants in the way of pork ribs and how many. The man smiles over at me, waves his hand and says, "Happy Birthday, Mista Peck."

I smile and wave back. "Appreciate the meat," I say.

"Pork," Pacman says, and that gets a laugh out of the woman sharpening the knives.

The man whistles up a young boy from the house, who walks out like he's molasses poured from a bottle. He's barefoot, dressed only in cutoff jeans, his skin deep black like his daddy's. He takes Partee's order and then scuffs off with indifference into a small garage that's painted pink. Partee looks back at Pacman, raises an eyebrow.

"His dog got kilt yesterday," the man says, shaking his head. "Stray bitch in heat took him right across the road out yonder. They's a whole pack chasing that thing around. Should have been the bitch to get kilt the way it's been treating all the dogs around here." He raises his head, nods toward the door, a black empty rectangle where the boy entered. "I'm letting him heal a little for it," he says like it's an apology for the boy's behavior.

"Bad when a boy loses his dog," Partee says. He looks at me and I nod in agreement.

"Part of growing up, I reckon," Pacman says, then clicks his tongue like it's a real shame.

The boy comes out carrying a large package of white butcher-block paper. It steams in the heat, ten racks of pork ribs just pulled from a cooler. "I can get this, Partee," I say. I pull out my money, but Partee will have none of it, puts his hand on my chest—something he's never done before. He cuts a look down at me like he's my father, sweat pouring off his face. He never wears the county-issued T-shirt that would make it a lot cooler on him. Partee's always got on his long-sleeve shirt buttoned at his collar and cuffs, the T-shirt underneath. "I never heard of a man paying for his own birthday party," he says, "so let it go, Chief. We took up money. It ain't no skin off my back."

He turns and finishes paying off Pacman, then as if an afterthought strikes, he looks at me again, his hand pushing his wallet back into his hip pocket. "But if I wanted to go buy these ribs for you, I could, no doubt about it. You'd get these ribs for your party no matter what." I can't tell if he's saying this to prove something or just wanting to say I deserve fresh pork ribs barbecued like no other in the world.

"It just seems like a bit too much," I say, "all this about my birthday."

Everyone in the yard laughs, heads shaking like I'm crazy to say such a thing. When we say good-bye, I look back, give a wave. "Ya'll drop on by, if you can," I say.

"Love to, Chief," Pacman says, "but this here pig won't last that long, so we'll have to take a rain check. Next year." His laugh is big, deep like he really means it. Partee puts his arm over my shoulder, another first, and says, "Come on, Chief, before you invite the whole county."

He puts the pork in his trunk, packs it in coolers for the wait while we head toward the marsh where the tide's going down and we'll walk in knee-deep mud to pull out clams as big as our fists.

We're back in the Mustang cruising, the road flat and straight in front of us. Partee's winding it out, showing me what the car can do. We're in backcountry, deep in Horry County, so I don't much worry about highway patrol or a Sheriff's deputy busting us. Out my window I watch the countryside fly past, look for signs of smoke, remembering Goose Hetzel back at Barker's in Conway. I can't help but look because I can smell it in the air. It's hot and dry, and it's not right people are using fire back inland like Pacman. Someone's going to get careless, it's human nature.

Partee's not worrying like me. He's got the eight-track cranked up with the Temptations. *I know you wanna leave me, but I refuse to let you go.* The top's down, the land blurring past us. The sun's moving quick up the sky, heat melting the air, rolling it in oily waves on top of the hot road in front of us. A ways ahead, we both see a car come up to the road from a dirt driveway, a Plymouth Roadrunner pushing dust up into the air when it brakes. I can see it wants to turn right in front of us. I glance at Partee. "Be careful," I say.

"No problem," Partee says, letting off the accelerator to pull the Mustang back, but it won't slow enough to help. He flashes his lights to let the driver know he's on him, to stay put, but that doesn't seem to do any good. The Roadrunner spins dirt and pulls on out. Partee sees it, this bright orange body with a spoiler on the back, knows he's got to keep going, that he's too fast to stop. He checks the oncoming lane, downshifts, then hits the accelerator, lays on the horn as he comes up on the car, its back window filled with a Confederate flag. He weaves the Mustang into the empty lane, passes the Roadrunner, startling the driver so much he runs off the road, a tornado of dirt kicking up behind them.

I turn and look, can tell this isn't going to be over just yet. It's obvious the boys in the Roadrunner don't like what just happened. There's more dust when they spin tires getting back onto the road. They come up fast, redneck boys from out this way who aren't going to take a pass like that without doing something about it. "Shit," I say. "Now what?"

"Nothing," Partee tells me. I see him look into the rearview mirror, can tell he's a little bothered by this. We're both in our uniforms, but I'm betting these two could give a rat's ass about firemen out for a ride to get ribs and clams for a birthday party. They pull up behind us, tailgating so close if Partee lets off the gas they'll ride right up the trunk of the Mustang. "That's too close," Partee says when he gives the car more gas.

We separate for a minute, but then the orange Roadrunner is right back up our ass. I look at the speedometer. Partee is doing eighty-five. The road remains straight, nothing coming up in front of us until we find a long arching curve, tall pines on either side trying to cool the air around us. It's at the end of the curve I see the truck, a logger pulling out from the sand road leading back into paper-mill land. It's long and heavy, slow to pull up onto the pavement with its full load. The Roadrunner pulls out into the oncoming lane, accelerates to hold up next to us, trap us from getting out of the way of the truck.

Its windows are down, the boys in the front with white T-shirt sleeves rolled up to their shoulders, hair cropped close to the scalp. There's a girl in the back, but she just looks scared, like she doesn't want any part of what's going on. The driver looks over, screams something about learning how to drive, and calls Partee a coon. The boy on the passenger side looks directly at me and says, "Niggers ought not have cars like that." Then he spits out the window, the force of air taking it past us so it misses the car.

All the while, we are quiet. Partee's trying to slow down to stop the fast approach of the logging truck. It's picking up speed, but we don't have the room to stop unless Partee hits the brakes hard and that's exactly what he does. "Hang on," he says, then slams on the brakes, catapulting the Roadrunner on down the road, where it disappears amid whoops and hollers, white hands hanging out of the windows shooting us the finger.

The back end of the logging truck comes up quick. A piece of red cloth is sticking out of the tree trunks like it's trying to wave itself silly so we'll see it and stop. Blue smoke from skidding tires fills the air behind us. We slide hard, Partee able to control the Mustang until the last second when the front wheels slip off onto the shoulder grinding at the sand and shell, the whole thing rattling to a stop in a storm of white dust. We don't hit the truck, which is a miracle in itself, the Mustang unharmed, just inches from going down an embankment and into swamp. Out in front, the Roadrunner has disappeared, the truck moving on, never even a clue as to what just happened.

We sit there for a minute, the heavy bass and screaming guitar of the Temptations pushing air around the car. The high voice of the singer pulls us back to the side of the road, *An eye for an eye, a tooth for a tooth.* . . .

"Shit, did they do that on purpose?" I ask.

"I don't know," Partee says. He turns off the eight-track, his head against the steering wheel, the silence suffocating.

"Goddamn," I say. "They weren't going to let us out of there."

"That ain't the first time," Partee says. He lifts his head, looks at me. "I seen those boys, that car at least. They like that all the time."

"We'll wipe them up off the road one day, I'll guarantee you that. You okay?"

"Yeah," Partee says. He waits another second watching the road like he's afraid those boys will be back. "We got shit like that out this way, Chief," he says finally. "Wouldn't mind living closer in, but can't afford it."

I can see in Partee's eyes that he's telling me this for more than information. I nod, tell him that I'll see what I can do. "Hell, you can come live with me now," I say.

Partee shakes his head, smiles when he starts the engine again. "Cassie won't like that when she comes back," he says like he knows that's going to happen no matter what I'm thinking.

I smile, pat Partee on the shoulder, my nerves finally catching up to what almost happened. "Drive the speed limit, how about it," I say, and then laugh out loud, too loud.

Partee smiles, pulls out onto the highway just about the same time Teddy flies by. He recognizes the car, flashes his lights, hits his siren. He holds a six-pack of Pabst out the window.

"Think he's going to drink that before he gets back to the station?" I ask. We're laughing hard when the Mustang accelerates.

The rednecks in the Roadrunner soften on our mind until they are just a shadow. Still, every now and then, a car comes up from a side road, a logging truck passes going the other way, and we just have to shake our heads, look at each other and say, "Unbelievable."

WHEN WE GET TO THE HOUSE, I don't go inside. There's nothing in there waiting for me but empty air. The johnboat sits in a shed that I can enter from an outside door. Partee helps me carry it to the dock, the barrels that float it up nearly sitting on mud. I pull the small motor from the wall of the shed, hurry to carry it and the gas tank down while Partee holds the boat in shallow water. We've got to move quick to get to the clam beds. It will be hard making it back to the house at low tide, but there's enough water to move through if you know where to steer the boat.

The marsh is quiet because of the drought, the wind weak as we push off with oars past browning grass to follow the shallows to deeper waters. The best clams are found on the other side of the marsh, and once we are deep enough to use the motor, we're over quickly, the tide lowering to reveal clam beds all around us. They sit along the edges of the grass where the water is shallow. When it recedes the clams reveal themselves as little lumps in mud so thick and deep that the minute we step out of the boat we will sink to our knees.

I have watched the prison crews come through here over the years on big pontoon barges that put the men right up in the mud.

They clean out oyster bars, the piles of dead shells that build up and clog the creeks. They gather clams for restaurants along Murrells Inlet, keep some for themselves, and eat better than any other prisoners in the state. They walk in the mud shirtless, wearing prison-issued pants, and stick long rakes into the muck. The backs and shoulders of the black men absorb the sun, leaving a deep richness like coal freshly plucked from the earth, while white men burn red raw. They move fast, stay just ahead of a low tide that could strand them for hours in the hot fetid muck.

My johnboat is a baby compared to the prison barges, and what we are after here today is just a spit of what they do every few years to keep the creeks open and the clam and oyster beds healthy. I try to maneuver in as close as I can, cut the engine and drop anchor to hold us there. "We need about six dozen," Partee says.

"Six dozen?" I say. "Damn, Partee, who all's invited to this thing?"

"Everybody," he says, "now get pickin."

We slide into waders and then into the water, black mud sucking at our legs. Our hands feel for lumps, then we hoe with small potato rakes until we can yank the clam out. It's dirty hot work as we go fighting off the few midges and deerflies that seem to be hanging in with the drought. I almost don't mind them because I know they're just trying to survive like everything else until we can get some rain.

We work fast floating the boat from bed to bed until Partee is satisfied with what we have. Then he picks a couple out of one of the buckets, slices the shells open with his knife, offering them up as just reward for the hard labor. We share the clams, tipping the shells into our mouths, the soft, sweet meat of the marsh slipping down our throats. "Goddamn, show me something better than that," I say. Partee just laughs out loud.

All around me small crabs peek in and out of holes in the mud, much like insects. Shrimp, translucent ghosts, ripple the surface. Partee finds three fat flounder, gigs them quick to add to the bounty. Egrets stalk the shallows along the grass, their necks cocked, ready to launch arrows stabbing their prey. Even in the height of this drought, there is life here—the briny water taking care of its own, waiting for the rest of the world around it to catch up.

I think about this morning sitting with my cup of coffee studying the creeks. Now here I am up to my ass in black mud and mucky water pulling clams for my own party. There's got to be something wrong with this picture, I tell Partee. I just don't know exactly what it might be. Partee laughs.

I'm muddy from head to toe when we finish, ended up with water and a crab in my waders somehow. My socks are ruined. We use oars to push out into water deep enough where I can start the engine again. On the way back across, we spot Annie Lee, the crab lady of Garden City Beach. She's been in the creeks for years, left South Korea during the war and has been crabbing for a living as long as I can remember. She's all of five feet tall and is dressed head to toe in orange rain gear, waders, and a knit hat. It's the way everyone knows her, never changes winter or summer, a constant like the tides. She's like a channel buoy bobbing up and down in her small skiff while struggling to pull crab pots off the bottom. It's late for her to be here, low tide the least agreeable time to be pulling pots out of the marsh.

We come alongside Annie's boat, her eyes dancing around us suspiciously. I've heard talk of those who steal her crabs, taking them right off her boat if she's out alone, or emptying her crab pots before she can arrive. I imagine she's out here in low tide for just such a reason. She's making sure no one gets what is rightfully hers, and I can tell Annie's concerned about our approach until she recognizes Partee. He waves, calls out her name and then his own. It's all smiles after that, a round moon face peeking out from under the knit cap.

I stay quiet as we pull up beside her, wave a friendly greeting, let Partee barter some of our clams for a bucket of her blue crabs. Annie's boat is loaded down with bait, frozen fish and fish heads. She has buckets full of crabs, flounder in the bottom by her feet. The boat seems top-heavy with all the weight, and I don't see a life jacket anywhere within her reach. It's another law being broken, just like at Pacman's.

All the locals seem to live by their own rules, and I don't mind really. It's part of the low country, an ingrained sense of right that holds everyone together. Annie and Partee singly have been on the marsh longer than I can claim, and their years together leave me no right to say anything to either one about rules or regulations, so I sit with the engine in neutral until the deal is done. Partee trades a pail for a pail, tells her it's my birthday. The news draws a smile my way and the only words to me while we are there. "You enjoy my crab," she says. "Good birthday present, best one ever."

I thank Annie, tell her to be careful with the tide, but she just throws up an impatient hand to my words. We leave her standing, straddling her catch, arms reaching over to let loose a crab pot she has just baited with a fish head fixed to the bottom of the metal cage with wire. She watches it sink out of sight, the line slipping through her tiny hands until she knows the pot is safely planted, a small white buoy bobbing on top of the briny water to mark its place.

When we return to the house, the tide's still out, so we have to wade through mud pulling our catch up to the dock. We secure the boat so it won't wash out on the rising tide, the motor hung and locked up in the shed. It's necessary that we go inside this time to use the sink and clean the mud off our bodies, but I don't wander around. Don't feel like being inside any longer than I have to. The air carries a familiar grief that's hard to breathe. Besides, it's nearly noon and we're riding the hump. We got to get going if there's to be any time for a party.

When we pull into the station, everybody's already there. J.D., Lori, Roddy, and some boys from Surfside are standing near the back door smiling. A fifty-gallon drum has been split down the middle longways to make a barbecue grill, and Teddy's hovering a hand over the charcoal to feel the heat of the fire. The pot for cooking a low country boil is heating up on the other side of the parking lot, the propane tank safely secured and marked. A few of the boys from Surfside come by Partee's Mustang while we're unpacking the ribs and clams, their hands full of blue crab and shrimp for the boil, Teddy's Pabst to throw in too. They can't wave so they just tip their heads, smile real big and yell Happy Birthday.

I'm thirty-five yesterday. It went right past me and I didn't even notice it until I pulled in this morning and remembered Lori saying they were throwing me a party. It's all reminding me of the one thing I don't really care to celebrate.

Teddy walks over to the truck, ignores my gesture to shake his hand, and grabs me in a bear hug, lifting me off my feet. "Happy Birthday, bro," he says. "You boys all right out there on that road today? I almost turned around to check on you."

"Nothing to check on," I tell him. I'll speak to Teddy about the Roadrunner later. He probably knows those boys from trouble and I don't want to bother him right now with something like that. He's been drinking already, so I keep quiet and say, "Getting the beer here was more important than turning around."

He hugs me again. "If you weren't so ugly, I'd kiss you," he says.

"I'm glad I'm ugly," I tell him, pulling at his cheeks like a baby.

Lori's next. She gives me an easier hug. "Hey, Peck," she says, sounding apologetic, "I'm sorry I'm making you go through this, but it's your day."

"Yesterday," I remind her, but she'll have none of that.

"Close enough," she says. "No matter how much it hurts." She winks at me so I won't take her words the wrong way. They're meant to tease and that's the way I take them. I let her kiss me on the cheek, and then return the same before letting go.

J.D.'s standing behind everyone smiling. I look out over heads to catch his eye. "And you, boy, I know you encouraged her to do all of this, but don't come over here expecting me to kiss you too."

J.D. just laughs at that, shakes his head. "It's not in my nature," he says.

I give Lori another hug because it feels good to hold on to a woman again, say, "You did good, girl. Guess I need the distraction."

"Of course you do," she says, holding on a little longer than both of us know she should. Everybody's excited so no one sees that Lori keeps her arm around my back.

I don't think it's so much that it's my birthday, but that it's a party. The station is off-line. Surfside is rotating crews in shorter shifts so those off duty can come by and enjoy the party too. Teddy's off until midnight and shouldn't be drinking, but he's got a beer in his hand every time I look over and catch his eye.

Strachen's here too. He's okayed the brew as long as we keep the empties in trash cans and cold ones in coolers. Teddy's trying his best, but my bet is he'll have to call in sick tonight. He's got the music started, stole Partee's eight-track of the Temptations. A couple of the boys get pulled out onto the cement drive with their girlfriends or wives because everyone's been invited and everyone wants to come to a party whenever there's one going on.

I don't know what it is about firemen, but they like to hang it out when they can. We keep so much bottled up, so much pressure when we go out there to fight a fire or save someone in an accident that when we get the chance to party, we bring the whole family along. I watch the dancing, Teddy over by the stereo singing so loud and off-key that people start to yell at him to shut up. I want Kelly to be here to enjoy all of this. I want Cassie here so we can dance like we used to early on before living together became such a burden. I tighten my arm around Lori, the feeling achingly familiar. She looks up and smiles, says, "It's your birthday, you need to enjoy yourself."

I let her pour me a beer. "I'm still trying to figure out why I let you do this. I could have gone on without any fuss."

Her eyes turn down to my cup, carefully watching the brew pour in. "Well, I guess sometimes I just know what's better for you, Peck."

We still have our arms wrapped around each other's waists when we turn to watch Teddy. He's over by the tunes in another world, drinking and singing, dancing with Roddy's wife, then with Billy Perkins's girlfriend, taking them off their man's arm each time one or another gets close enough for him to grab a hold. He twirls them, shags as good as anybody half his size.

The air is sweet with the smell of Partee's grill and the low country boil, the music loud, kids running around inside the Quonset where J.D. has wandered with his plate of food looking for a little more peace and quiet. He gives up on finding any and stands next to the front door of the Pirsch holding his plate in one hand while boys and girls, the sons and daughters of these firemen, jump up into the driver's seat turning on the lights and siren. It's that first taste of what already exists there inside each, bone and blood, the old pull toward smoke and fire.

"Where's Partee's family?" Lori asks.

I look over to where he is working the grill, pulling ribs off to serve people who are already waiting in line. He's working harder than anyone else here. "He doesn't bring them around the beach," I tell her. "It's not all that right down here yet, so he won't let them come."

"He knows we're all family. He doesn't need to do that."

"Most of us get it," I say, "but there're still some boys inland that have a hard time getting past color. Strachen's crews are all right. Garden City Beach is a good spot for Partee. He worries more about the people down here on vacation. I ask him to bring his family along all the time, and he always politely declines. I don't think I need to go any farther. It's up to him."

J.D. comes out of the Quonset with three little boys in tow. He's down on one knee taking orders, relaying them to Partee, who fills paper plates full of ribs, throws on some clams on the half shell for J.D. He gets the boys Cokes from the tub of iced drinks, takes a beer for himself.

"You should go talk to J.D.," I tell Lori, trying to change directions, the sudden shift taking her by surprise.

"Now Peck," she says, "mind your own business."

"Well, it's just, you know, you aren't married and J.D.'s not married."

"Neither is Billy Perkins," Lori says, pointing with her beer to where Teddy's twirling Billy's girlfriend around on the cement, "but I'm not going over there and taking him away from Janie."

"You might get him while Teddy's here," I say. "Janie looks like she's enjoying herself." Lori hits my arm, spills beer all over me.

"Serves you right," she says, and then goes to find a roll of paper towels to clean up the mess.

When she brings me another beer, I tease her some more. "Look, you wouldn't be taking anyone away from J.D. He's not attached."

"Peck," Lori says, "I really haven't thought about it."

"Well, maybe you should," I say.

Lori finally stops, looks at me hard like she's had enough.

"Okay, I tried, Peck, some time ago. It didn't work."

Now that surprises me, it really does. Lori is a fine woman, finer when you really get to know her. She comes from a good family over in Georgetown, a local all her life. If I didn't have a ring on my finger, I'd be asking her out in a heartbeat, no doubt about it. I don't tell her this. I just tell her not to worry. J.D.'s got to get his head out of those books he reads all the time. He needs to find someone to come home to. "J.D. doesn't know what he's missing," I say. "He's got smarts growing out of all the wrong places, if you ask me."

Lori comes into me again, puts her arm back around my waist. She squeezes just enough that I can feel her shoulder on my rib cage. "Thanks, Peck. But I shouldn't have done it anyway. Work romances never work out, do they?" Before she leaves, Lori pulls me down to her size and kisses me on the cheek again, the smell of her hair sweet, like coconut and beach. "If you weren't so old, I might ask you out. You're a sweet man, Peck Johnson. Cassie should know better than to let you loose. Happy Birthday."

I watch her walk away. The wetness of her kiss makes me want more. I'm lost without the touch of a woman, though Lori's almost young enough to be my own kid. She's J.D.'s for the taking if he wants her. I need to talk to the boy about that sometime. I think of Cassie then, what we had when it was good. I still want more of her if she would have me, if she would ever call, if she would ever come back home. It doesn't matter what she's done. You can't erase fifteen years over something like this. If we can talk, I think we can figure it all out.

Partee is some kind of barbecue man, a magician with hickory. He could make an old shoe taste good if you gave him enough hickory chips and charcoal. I swear to God the ribs we bought from Pacman melt off the bone, sweet and juicy, heaven in your mouth. I almost cry when I eat that first bite. It's been so long since I had a good meal that it's almost criminal how good this tastes. I eat potato salad and baked beans, Texas toast and home-made fruit salad that Lori has whipped up from her momma's recipe. I'm so full from ribs and beer and beans that I nearly forget the boil that the boys from Surfside have been watching for Par-tee. But I find a way to get that down too, the sausage and corn, shrimp and crab, baby potatoes. Teddy brings out the birthday cake with thirty-five candles burning hot, compliments of his wife, Mo, who, of course, is not here. She's never around for these kind of parties either, but I imagine it has nothing to do with who vacations on the beach. Teddy just never tells her she's invited.

Strachen heads back over to Surfside after the food is eaten. And when the music starts to repeat itself, when the last sparks of the party seem ready to be extinguished, someone suggests that we go surfing, and the spirit is revived. I ask Partee to go with us, to stop working for a while and enjoy himself. He seems reluctant at first until Lori starts pulling him along, tells Partee there's no reason for anyone to sit in an empty station if it's going to stay off-line. When he says yes, we get him in a pair of swim trunks out of Teddy's car and then all pile into my truck.

It's blazing on the road, the whiteness of the light blinding, the sun bubbling tar seams, black scars that crisscross the asphalt. On the way down, Teddy makes me stop so he can buy more beer, ice it down and stow it in the bed of the truck. He changes clothes in the back while I'm still driving. Lori holds a hand across her eyes when his exposed butt comes up and lies flat against the back window, Teddy's off-key voice singing loudly, *"I see the bad moon rising."* Partee's back there shaking his head, probably wishing he'd stayed at the station. It's all crazy and on the edge of being out of control, but we get to the beach without incident, without losing Teddy from the bed of the truck, and for the rest of the afternoon, we're on the water.

Teddy coaxes Partee out, gives him a surfing lesson, then lets him use his board for a couple of attempts at riding a wave. He's awkward in the water, a little unsure of himself, and I think he notices the way people along the strand stare. He's the only black man on a white beach even though there's no law left that can keep people from coming out here. All that's been gone for a long time, but it takes more than changing the law to change people's minds. Partee's good at keeping it to himself. He's had a lifetime to learn. Everybody else just got started.

He gives up sooner than Teddy wants him to, but the surface is mostly flat, so I don't blame him. The rest of us wait until a set rises high enough to bring us to life. We point the nose of our boards toward shore, paddle furiously to catch the tender top of a curl, the force downward just enough to push us across the front of the wave. Partee is in the shallows whistling and whooping it up as, for that brief moment in time, he watches us walk on water.

The late afternoon rides along, drops into evening, the waves flattening out for good when the tide changes. We leave the beach, and I take Partee back to pick up his Mustang. He's had enough, as have others with children or those who don't care to keep it going. I say good-bye, thank him for all the good food, leave him in the deserted parking lot behind the station as the party rekindles itself, the changing shift from Surfside complaining that they didn't get in on any of the fun. Teddy thinks that's unfair and so he leads the charge, says they're all expecting me at Maggie's where the beers are free and there's another birthday cake waiting.

We roll into Murrells Inlet where Maggie's is already hopping, listen to southern rock and roll, Lynyrd Skynyrd and the Allman Brothers, ZZ Top and Marshall Tucker covered by a local band. Teddy has no idea who the boys are on stage, but that doesn't stop him from running up there to sing along with "Fire on the Mountain." He jumps around hogging the microphone, his voice so off-key that we laugh until our stomachs hurt, beg anyone who can hear us over the ruckus to please stop him before he makes everybody sick. A generous bouncer goes up there, tells him that the band needs to move on, convinces Teddy to jump off the stage.

At eleven-thirty he goes to work. Teddy's so drunk that he can't walk straight. Earlier he had given me the keys to his car and I handed them straight to Lori. When he asks me for them back, I pull my pants pockets inside out and lie, tell him that I lost them.

"Well goddammit, Peck," he says. "I got to go to work in a taxi."

We all laughed, want to be there when he drives up to the Horry County Sheriff's Department in a cab, drunk out of his mind and ready to go out on patrol. He won't make it, but the idea's funny enough that even long after old Teddy's gone, he's still talked about. He remains the life of the party.

After another round or two, J.D. leaves. He comes up before he goes and shakes my hand. "Happy Birthday, old man," he says. I want to tell him he's a hell of a partner. I want him to understand that I think he has magic in his hands when it comes to saving people's lives, but I'm drunk. "You're a pussy for leaving so soon," I say.

He smiles at that, kisses me on the cheek. "I love you too, Chief." He tells Lori to take good care of me, and then J.D.'s gone.

Someone says "Let's cruise," and I find myself in the back end of a truck flying out through the low country passing a joint around. These are firemen, responsible men most of the time, lighting up, whooping and hollering, singing to the eight-track music coming out the back window to fill up the bed where I sit with Lori. We end up in some field outside Conway where somebody brings out fireworks of all things, air bombs and Roman candles, to light up the sky.

There's more beer and pot and everybody sings Happy Birthday again, and I get hit on the back more than I want to be hit, hugged and kissed on the cheek by men I stand shoulder to shoulder with when we are told to enter a burning building, our lives put on the line every day. I'm out here in a dried-up field in the middle of the night, drunk and stoned at the same time, dead tired and watching grown-up men act like little boys who've snuck out of their houses to party for the first time.

It's the best birthday that I can remember, but one that comes to an abrupt end when a deputy shows up threatening arrest if we don't stop with the fireworks and go home. Someone asks him if he knows Teddy, but that just seems to make matters worse. He lectures us about some small hot spots already burning inland, tells us that they're expecting winds to shift, a bad sign. It looks like we're in big trouble here until Lori steps in. She's over by his car, talks the deputy out of doing anything to us, then comes over to the bed of the truck, says, "Everybody just shut up and leave, right now."

We're out of there, back on the road headed home. We don't talk about the fires inland. We just keep our eyes on the sky scanning for the light from growing flames. No one asked how far inland the fires were, but the deputy seemed tired, like he'd been up longer than he should have watching for foolish behavior like our own. I sniff the air like a dog looking for love, find nothing there but the musty smell of a low-tide marsh as we ride into Garden City Beach.

There's nothing left of Hump Day but loose ends and smoldering grills when we pull back into the station. Everyone quickly scatters, talking quietly about the deputy's concerns, worrying what it might mean for all of us if the fires get out of hand. Inland fires and changing winds—which way they will go is a roll of the dice.

Lori gets my truck and drives me home. I can smell her hair even when all the windows are rolled down and we're going fifty miles an hour. I tell her she smells good. She says, "That's because I take baths."

I laugh at that, tell her, "I'd take them more often, but I hate going home alone." She's quiet like what I've just said is filled with poison. I can feel her turn left onto the sand road leading to the house even though I have my eyes closed to try and stop the spinning. When we get there, Lori turns the engine off and we sit in thick air, the marsh silent. Tree frogs chirp in the distance behind the house. Somewhere far away, I hear an owl haunting the dark. Out before us the marsh is undefined, nothing but a big black hole.

"God, that was stupid out there tonight," Lori says.

"Which part?" I ask, rubbing my temples, pulling my hand through greasy hair.

"All of it," she says, "but the fireworks were the stupidest thing I've ever seen. We could have started a fire, and then what?"

"We're firemen," I tell her. "We'd have put it out."

"With what, Peck Johnson, your good looks?"

We laugh when Lori says this. "I didn't think I was that pretty," I say.

"Well you are," Lori says, her eyes turned away, "but I doubt that would've helped to put out a fire."

For fun, I pull the rearview mirror over to look at my silhouetted face, rub my jaw, the rough stubble reminding me I need a shave. "Let's stay out here," I say, "make out all night."

Lori rolls her eyes, pulls the keys from the ignition, then opens her door. "Not with me, Peck Johnson. You're a married man." She comes around and opens my door like we're going to a prom. I put out my hand to pull her back in, but she slaps it away. "Get out, Peck. It's late."

When I try to stand, I stumble into her arms. She holds me good, tells me I'm a sight. I don't remember the last time I got this wasted. It's bad and getting worse. We work our way around the house and onto the screened-in porch. I can't find my house key, so Lori has to search my pockets, her hand in places that should raise more than an eyebrow, but she isn't embarrassed. I'm too drunk to get into trouble like that. She finds it, keys the lock, and we fall inside. I'm on my knees, Lori about ready to give up when I ask her to stay.

The moment is awkward because she can tell I'm serious. I crawl to the couch, pat the cushion for her to sit down next to me, my head spinning so fast it feels like I'm on the Tilt-A-Whirl down at the Pavilion in Myrtle Beach. "You can't drive yourself back tonight," I tell her. "Just stay, I could use the company."

She's like stone when I lean over and kiss her on the lips, don't even know I'm going to do it until it's done. It feels odd kissing Lori like this. I try to hold her there, keep my balance, but I can't. And when I fall away, the spell is broken.

"I can't," she says. "I can't do it like this, Peck."

"Do what?" I say, a grin pushing at the corners of my mouth.

"You know what I'm talking about. It's unfair to Cassie, even though—"

"—even though she's off fucking Clay Taylor in Walhalla?" I say, finishing her sentence with the wrong words.

"That's not what I was going to say," Lori tells me. "But if you want to know what I think—" She stops there, the space abruptly empty when she gets up off the couch. "I'll make a pot of coffee."

I can hear her in the kitchen finding things, my head spinning the world crazy. "I guess you were right, then," I say.

"Right about what?" Lori asks from the kitchen.

"About having a relationship at work. Won't work, no doubt about it."

There's nothing from her after that, my words stuck in the air, sarcasm gone sour. Lori busies herself with the coffee, and that's good for both of us. When she's finished, she finds me outside where I've managed to park myself on a bench on the floating dock. We sit there with steaming mugs saying nothing more, watching the light come back into the marsh. Lori lays her head on my shoulder. "I need sleep, Peck."

"I know you do," I say. I tell her to go on in and take the bed, that I'll sleep on the couch.

"You don't have to do that," she says. She raises her head to look at me, the offer made with her eyes, that after all the innocent sparring tonight, she's ready to go the distance, give me what Cassie won't.

"I need to be a good Boy Scout here," I say.

She watches me a bit longer, her hair falling across her face, loose strands that I pull back, my hand brushing against her cheek. I can tell she's thinking about it, holding me there with her eyes until they too give up. "You're a good man, Peck Johnson."

Lori kisses my cheek, leaves to walk up the yard. I can hear the screen door popping against the frame as she enters the house. When she's gone, I sit alone watching the marsh come to life, the sun yet to break across the water along the beaches. I close my eyes, imagining that I'm in bed with her, my hands moving across flesh I have never touched before, the draw incredibly strong. I rub my hands through hair that feels wet. I need a bath and a few hours of sleep. I'm beat up, thirty-five and two days old, too old to be staying up all night and partying like this. When we were surfing earlier in the afternoon, Teddy told me to be glad I wasn't a dog. He said in dog years, I'd be dead. I don't know why, but for some reason, that makes me feel a little bit better. Right now, I don't mind being compared to a dog.

Cassie

I WAS SICK this morning when I woke up. It came over me while I sat with Momma in the kitchen. She stood by the stove poaching eggs and frying bacon. There was bread in the toaster, and I was doing just fine until she brought out the sweet butter and a jar of homemade sorghum. She set it there on the table right in front of me, and it sent a current pulsing into my throat, a burning sensation that raised me off my chair. Momma knew immediately what was happening. A dishcloth across my mouth, she helped me run to the bathroom. I knelt at the toilet, my body shivering against the cold floor. I threw up what little was in my stomach, Momma's hand on my back rubbing slowly to help calm me down.

Afterward, nothing smelled good. Every time I tried to leave the bathroom, the nausea hit again, the smells so rancid that the air seemed poisoned. I stayed there on the floor for I don't know how long while Momma opened doors and windows to let cool mountain air in. She helped me back to bed where I slept until noon. And then, it was as if nothing had ever happened. I woke up hungry, feeling no ill effects at all.

I lay in bed for a while longer with my windows opened, the sounds of the summer birds chirping, a breeze light and cool holding back the heat of the afternoon. Momma made lunch, sweet tea, fresh cucumber and tomato sandwiches. She asked that I join her on the front porch, where we sit now. I'm still in pajamas, the afternoon beginning to push light up against the face of White-side. When she lifts herself out of the chair to water her flowers, I ask if she would like my help, but she declines, says this is her exercise. So I sit quietly watching her lift the can on tiptoes to pour fresh well water into the soil. "Besides," she says, "you're pregnant again."

The water overflows the hanging pots, splashing onto the worn planks below like a sudden outburst of tears. "No I'm not," I say.

"Yes, I believe you are." Her voice is more stern this time, like I should know better than to doubt her. "How late are you?"

She won't turn around to look at me after her question, and I know what this means. I have to answer, though I don't want to because I know that I am; late I mean—maybe six weeks, maybe a little more. Looking back, I realize I didn't have my period in May—I figured then it was stress that delayed it, but now it's pushing the middle of June. "I don't see that I need to talk to you about this," I tell her. My denial, the avoidance of saying more, is not enough for her, but she lets it go, remains silent while finishing her watering, and then leaves the porch when the phone rings.

From where I sit, I cannot see Whiteside Mountain, but I feel its presence on the land as I feel my father's presence in this house. When I was pregnant with Kelly, Momma knew the trouble it would mean. "This is going to kill your father," she said as we sat in the car that day. There was little hope in any of it. My father walked off after being told, didn't come home by the time the dew settled across the fields. I stood with Momma watching from the kitchen window, waiting for him to return that night, my chances for college vanished.

You're pregnant. The words hang in the air like one of Momma's dripping baskets. If it is true, if I am pregnant, I cannot say if it is Clay's or Peck's. Either way it's not what I want because to have a baby right now is to resume my old life, and all I want is to leave that behind.

When she is finished on the phone, Momma returns to the porch. "You'll need to get dressed," she says. "John Boyd just called to say he would like to talk to you today. He's coming by in about an hour." I look at Momma, her face expressionless. I know this conversation is not over, not yet.

The morning sickness is a distraction that slows me down. When John Boyd arrives, I am still in my room dressing, fretting about what I should wear when I talk to him. The man is so intertwined in my past that I don't remember growing up in Whiteside Cove without him somehow being here. He helped my father lower me into the Cullasaja when I was baptized. I used his car for my driver's-license test because we didn't own one when I turned sixteen. He was the one, ten years ago, who found my father at the foot of Whiteside Mountain on his knees, head bowed, dead. He carried him home in his arms, told Momma that it was as if God had come down in the middle of his prayer to take him. He was at peace.

For a time after that, Momma was not capable of living alone. She stayed in bed refusing to eat, sat for hours on her porch forgetting to take care of her flowers. John Boyd was there. And even when she told him to leave her alone, that she would just as soon lay there and die, he came to the house day after day until the pall passed and Momma found her feet. Now he is coming to talk about the land and how best to save it—John Boyd in our lives still.

When I come into the room, he is standing by the door, his

hand extended. Momma smiles from her seat. She seems so small sitting there, so vulnerable that I walk over ignoring John Boyd's hand and lean down to kiss her cheek. "You two go have a good talk," she says.

"No," I say, "I thought we would all sit down and discuss this together?" I look at her concerned that she so willingly excludes herself from what will be said.

Momma takes a Kleenex from the waistband of her dress. "Your father never talked to me about such things and I don't want to tread on his grave by starting now. You and John Boyd can do all of that. He'll tell us what we need to do." With that Momma is up and out of the chair, her small frame walking so softly that she seems to float off the ground. She touches John Boyd on the shoulder as if anointing him her caretaker, and that worries me even more.

It's obvious from the way I am silently led down the steps and into the front yard that I am only here to listen, to follow John Boyd's direction and do as I am told. "I thought we'd take a walk out over the fields," he says, pointing in the direction of my father's daily retreats toward Whiteside.

"That's fine," I say.

When we pass the gate, I look for the old narrow pathway that is no longer visible. In the ten years since my father's death the cove has reclaimed any evidence of his presence. Momma remains in the house, her small figure diminished in the kitchen window by a single lightbulb wrapping a halo around her gathered hair.

"I want to thank you for taking care of Momma," I say.

John Boyd smiles at that. "She can be set in her ways. But we get along. She's been a good neighbor."

We walk through wild fields, carefully navigating large growths of blackberry and thorny bush, our clothing caught and pulled. The mountain's massive rock face rises nearly two thousand feet from this point in the cove, high enough that it forces you to look straight up to see sky. I cannot look at its sheer face and not think of my father. To me it is his immortality, his spirit that will never leave this place, though there have been times I wished for that whole of the mountain to disappear into the earth's core. We walk at a brisk pace toward the tree line, sweat beading in the small of my back. I am about to tell John Boyd that I cannot go any farther, that I did not intend to return to where my father died, when he stops and turns to look back over the land we have just covered.

"Let's stop here for a moment," he says. "This is such a pretty view, don't you think?"

"I don't even know how far Momma's land extends," I say. "I don't think I've ever walked the whole parcel."

"Your father and I discussed his desire to own the land to the base of Whiteside, but this is about the extent of it, right here."

"It's smaller than Momma thought," I say, surprised, though John Boyd remains silent beside me. It's as if he's letting his words sink in and become truth before he continues.

Through the stillness comes the sound of earthmovers working the land. It fills the hollow air and makes me think the cove is being torn apart. "God, are they tearing up everything at once?"

"No," John Boyd says, "they're still down by 107, but they want to come up here, that's for sure. They want to make this whole cove a golf course and residential area. Arnold Palmer's designed it. The ninth green would be right back down yonder." He points, his finger settling right on top of Momma's house.

I look at him when he does this, surprised that John Boyd would know such specifics of something he has promised will never happen. "Arnold Palmer," I say. "They've already designed the golf course, already taken into consideration all of this?"

"Sure," he says. "They've designed the whole resort area. Not just this parcel, but many different ones around Cashiers and over near Glenville. They can get hold of maps and make designs. Anybody can do that."

"And you've seen them, the maps and designs?" I ask.

"I have," he says. "They keep me abreast of what's happening. I met Arnold himself when he came up here to do a flyover."

For the first time, I realize that in the length of our walk, John Boyd has yet to look at me. "And what are these developers telling you?" I ask. "What are they saying?"

"Well, one thing is that they're getting close, Cassie. They want the land."

"Want our land?"

"Yes, this land, all of it from Whiteside to 107."

"Can we fight them?"

"Probably not," he says, the words so matter-of-fact that they make me wince. "I'm trying to make some deals, trying to keep your mother in a good place when this happens."

"*When* it happens?" I say, "How can that be? It's her property. She'd have to agree to sell it, wouldn't she?"

John Boyd turns and walks until he is at the edge of the woods, my father's old refuge somewhere near where the earth and mountain meet. He sits down on a rock that is protruding from the ground. "Look, Cassie, come here, sit down, please." His hand moves in front of him like he is swatting flies, a motion meant for me to follow, but I remain a good distance away.

My distrust of John Boyd resurfaces hard and fast. I have carried it with me for years after finding out about his part in having me sent away. Kelly had already been born when Momma wrote about John Boyd's involvement. She was trying to be the peacemaker and heal the wounds between my father and me. She said John Boyd made him choose, me and my baby or the church. It hadn't been a blunt order, Momma wrote, something direct and out in the open, but more a threat implicitly made when he told my father that there would not be an illegitimate child born into Whiteside Cove Baptist. "It was better to send you away," she tried to explain. "It might be hard for you to understand this now, but your father made the right choice."

I was so angry at the time that I couldn't understand what she was saying, couldn't see my father was, in his own way, going against John Boyd's orders that I experience the same fate as any other girl who became pregnant in the congregation. I wrote her back in anger, one line: "This wasn't *my* choice." The response, I'm sure, hurt my father greatly, if he ever saw the letter and read it.

I don't know what he thought about me in the end. If he were alive today I would talk to him, tell him about his granddaughter, say, I still love you, no matter how much hurt we caused each other. I would not let what happened all those years ago stand in the way of our reconciliation. If he were alive, we would talk and make amends. But my father is dead and I'm here with John Boyd, the man who found him along the base of Whiteside, talking about what is to become of Momma and our land. His impatience makes me uneasy, my refusal to come, do as I'm told and sit with him, unacceptable. But I won't do it. I stay put, tell him that I'm fine where I am.

"Just tell me what we need to do," I say. "It's getting late, Momma will worry."

It's then that he tells me—the land is not really hers. It has always belonged to the church, the agreement between the deacons and my father never made legal in the eyes of the law.

"Parker knew our agreement," he says. "He knew we would take care of Mavis as long as we could. But when the church closed its doors, well, it sort of changed."

"I don't understand," I say. "I thought there was an agreement, written and signed, that deeded the land to her. I thought it was all taken care of before Daddy died."

"No, there was never a paper, Cassie." John Boyd shakes his head, clicks his tongue like he's scolding me for such a suggestion. "Your father knew that at the time. Parker agreed with the way we handled it. Who would have thought the church would close its doors? No, I wish there would have been a contract or something, I really do. It would make all of this much easier."

"How has all this been handled over the years?" I ask. "Who's been in charge of all this property?"

"Well, I was the last deacon," he says. "It's been up to me over the years. When we sold the church property down on 107, I took that money and set it aside for Mavis because we weren't tax exempt anymore. It's all gone up over the years, Cassie. It's costing an arm and a leg to keep her there. The money I was using to pay the property tax, repair the house, things like that, is about gone. We're going to have to do something. I'm trying to work out a deal that she'll get one of the condos to live in, sort of part of the trade—you know, to let her still believe that this is her land. But I need you to talk to her. I don't want her to be upset when it all has to be done."

"When is that?" I ask.

"What?"

"When do they want her out?"

"I'm not sure, maybe August."

"August, my god, that's like six weeks or something." I count it out on my fingers just to make sure I'm right.

"It could be longer, Cassie. I just don't know."

"But there *was* a contract, something written down that might help," I say.

"I'm sorry, Cassie. There's nothing. I would have told her myself some time ago, but then the way she is with me sometimes, well, I just didn't want to risk her shutting me out. I promised your father I would look after her, if anything happened to him. I've tried, Cassie. But now I need you to tell Mavis what's going on. She needs to know."

"I don't know if I can do this," I say.

John Boyd pushes himself up, hands pressing against thighs, the exertion of this long walk hard on him. "Cassie, there's been some hard times up here, bad blood between us, I know that. I want to do what's right, and what's right is to get her to understand the situation so we can all move forward." He puts an arm on my shoulder, looks at me for the first time. "You're really the only one who can talk to her."

What John Boyd has just told me about the land makes me sick to my stomach. And if I had any nerve at all, I would slap his hand right off my shoulder. I don't know what to believe about any of it, but I know John Boyd is not to be trusted. I smile, but promise nothing, tell him that there's a lot to think about and that we need to start back.

It bothers me, his insistence that there are no papers or a deed. It was not in my father's character to leave loose ends. He ran his church from top to bottom. He was in on every major decision concerning its upkeep, knew by name his entire congregation, who was tithing and who gave in other ways, canned vegetables and smoked meat, a new roof on the parsonage, painting the church—good works done when money was not an option. My father worked tirelessly, and I can't imagine that he would have let John Boyd just shake his hand over something as important as land.

When we reach the back fence, John Boyd peels off from our walk and heads toward his car. Momma is on the front porch watching, one hand holding on to the rail, the other pulling a sweater closed across her dress. I join her on the steps. "I'll be in touch then," he says, climbing into the front seat, a smile faint on his face like he's not so sure he has made his point with me.

I wave. "That'll be fine," I say.

When I watch him drive away, I feel I have been talking to the enemy. I think about how he never really looked me in the eyes, always glanced downward or out over the land like he was sizing it up, imagining what the cove would look like after it was carved up and divvied out to those who would be able to afford to live where Arnold Palmer might play a round of golf. Then a question enters my mind. "Momma, where did Daddy keep all his papers? You know, business papers and such?"

"Lord honey, I don't know," she says. "Some of it was at the church, and some of it was kept here at the house."

"What about the deed to your land? Where did he keep that?"

This stops her for a moment. It is as if she realizes for the first time that there are things lost to her, memories and events in her life that have left her for good, or else are buried so deep that they require more than she has left to dig them up. "I don't know," she says. "Your father and John Boyd took care of all of that."

"But Daddy had something, right? He signed a paper, a contract or a deed or something?"

I can tell the questions frustrate her, the details about things that happened ten years ago, details my father kept to himself because he never wanted her to worry over them, but now she has to. "He would have shown it to you," I remind her, "you might have even signed it."

And then the confusion clears, memory of what I am asking for returns. "Yes he did," she says, her eyes brightening. "I remember. He brought the paper home. We sat at the kitchen table and looked at it. He felt after all the years he had sacrificed for his congregation, that he had finally done something for me, something that was really just for me. He was proud."

I smile, touch her face. "Well, we need to find that paper," I say. "We need to find it very soon."

"John Boyd will know where it is," she says. Her words have a sense of finality that this man will somehow come to her rescue.

"John Boyd wants us to look here first," I lie. I cannot tell her that she doesn't own this land. I cannot because I believe she does, and that John Boyd is lying.

Peck once told me that the eyes are a window into the soul. When someone won't look at you straight on, they must be missing something inside or withholding something that they don't want you to see. He told me this after his suspicions about Clay began. After he failed to come in on time for one of his shifts last year, Clay avoided eye contact with Peck, and he knew something had changed. Peck said it was strange, but at the time I knew why Clay had been late on call. He was with me that afternoon for the very first time. It was the beginning, the first step that has brought me this great distance, standing here with Momma on her front porch and pregnant again. But John Boyd won't run me off this time. I'm here to stay.

Peck was right about a man's soul. John Boyd is hiding something. The man is up to no good.

Peck

BACK LAST WINTER, Surfside sent us all to Bennettsville to watch a demonstration on the dangers of mobile-home fires. The chief over there loaded us all into a school bus and took us out into an empty cotton field near Clio where they had put up a trailer. They made it look real, with toys outside and a car parked in front. J.D. thought it was somebody's home, but I said they just wanted us to take it seriously by making it look as real as possible.

They circled us around the trailer a good distance away, told us to wear our masks and turnouts because of the smoke and heat, and then someone went inside and lit a small flame on a couch like a cigarette had been left to smolder. They had two pumpers nearby, had built and filled a pool for drafting just in case something got out of hand. Over by the bus, they pulled out this big old clock that someone said came from the Bennettsville YMCA pool, a lap clock is what they called it, and turned it on when the fireman inside said, "The candle's lit."

We all stood out there in the cold wind and watched that clock to see just how long it took the trailer to go up. I noticed J.D. taking notes, watching and scribbling whenever the chief announced what was happening inside the trailer at each moment during the fire. In a couple of minutes, the couch was completely involved, black poisonous smoke pouring out the windows and doors. Flames danced at the windows and licked along the bottom of the door. At the twelve-minute mark, there was a sudden explosion that caught us all off guard, blowing out windows as the fire found more oxygen. The whole thing took off like it was made out of dry kindling.

The trailer itself began to glow red hot, every window full of flame. The siding and lower frame radiated a great heat we could feel even though we were a safe distance away. At about the twenty-minute mark, the whole goddamn thing just exploded. Some of the men whistled, some walked backward, some just said "god almighty" and pulled their masks on, especially those who were downwind. In thirty minutes, the trailer was gone, the car that sat outside the door gutted. The windows in the vehicle had been left down, something I do all the time when I drive up to my house, and when the radiated heat got hot enough, the interior ignited like someone had poured fuel on the seats.

When the point had been made, the chief sent his firemen in on the burn. They got the pumpers up close and hit the fire hard. It wasn't an easy one to put out because of all the plastic and siding material. Trailer construction is largely unregulated, so there's no thought put into fire safety. No thought on how the trailer is built without proper egress. There's only one door, and if the fire starts between you and that escape route, you have nowhere to go; your chances of being killed increase tenfold.

On the way back, we stopped at a Piggly Wiggly for some beer, the smell of burning plastic clinging to our clothes and skin. The young checkout girl saw my insignias and smiled when she rang up the brew. "Ya'll been working hard today," she said.

I watched her bag the beer, gave her a ten-dollar bill to pay for it all. The boys deserved that much. "Not as hard as you, darlin'," I told her. She smiled and I could see she was probably Kelly's age, maybe a year older. It was in the middle of the school year, in the middle part of the afternoon when this girl should have been in school, not working behind a cash register checking out firemen who are buying beer in a Piggly Wiggly. It made me want to make sure Kelly has choices. That no matter what happens between me and her mother, she will have a good life ahead of her. I smiled when she handed me my change, grabbed the bag of beer, and got the hell out of there. We drove back talking about trailer fires, hoping to never have to fight one more than twenty minutes away because after that, you might as well roast marshmallows. You're not saving anything.

That's what we learned on a cold day last year when we stood there in that field outside Clio. It's something we're all remembering right now as J.D. fights traffic to get us out to McDowell Road. It's the day after the birthday party and nobody's feeling like fighting a fire. Lori and I got into the station late, everybody there clicking tongues and shaking their heads when we walked in. Roddy said, "Anything we need to know here, Chief?" Everybody laughed at that, and I told Roddy to shut up.

J.D. was up on the Pirsch. He looked down at us both, said to Lori, "When I said take care of him, I didn't mean take him home with you." They all laughed again and then I told J.D., "She didn't take me home with her, I took her home with me." That got enough woofs and howls to be heard all the way down to the strand. Lori looked at me like *you got to be kidding* and then just walked off into her office and started working.

We all thought we were going to get a pass today, that the fire gods would let us be to heal our self-inflicted wounds and get over the party. But that didn't happen. The bell rang at eleven-thirty, got us real good, and now here we are driving out to the edge of the county.

The boys are betting good money that we're on our way to put out a trailer fire. Mobile homes are strung out along the way. Most are old and run-down, and the county has yet to pave the sandy roads or set a water line for hydrants this far out. In front of us, I can see black smoke behind a grove of trees climbing into the sky fast. Whatever it is, it's alive and well, and we'll be the ones, hungover or not, who'll have to go in there and kill it.

Where we turn off, the road is hard sand. When we get nearer the fire, the ground turns to mush. The Pirsch has difficulty maneuvering down into the small dead end where a trailer sits fully involved. There's a dog out in front of the fire barking like it knows the flames aren't supposed to be inside. It looks like Clio last winter, but this one's real and getting worse by the second. There are people standing around watching, staring at us as we struggle with the sand just to get to the fire ball sitting in front of us. Finally J.D. says, "Fuck it. We'll pull from here. It's not like we got a fire hydrant waiting."

I radio back to Lori that we're 10-23. J.D. and Partee start pulling lines while I go over to see if anyone can tell me who's living in the trailer. A boy straddling a homemade minibike, barefoot and shirtless, points to a young woman sitting under a palmetto with her head in her hands. She's trembling, a cigarette dangling from her fingers. "Is that your trailer, ma'am?" I ask, kneeling down, my hand touching her shoulder.

"I think so," she says, talking to the ground. She doesn't lift her head to look at me. "I think it's mine."

I can tell she's nearly in shock, maybe drunk too, so I yell to J.D. to radio for an ambulance and that gets him interested. I let him take my place and then help Partee throttle up the pumper.

Behind the trailer sits a propane tank. It's far enough away from the burning structure that I think it will be okay. But I remember the radiating heat and that car back in Clio and make a choice at that moment not to try and fight the fire. We're out here alone and there's only five hundred gallons of water in the pumper and lots of people I can't get rid of by myself. I make the decision to cool down the propane, let the fire burn itself out. Partee concurs and we move in, fog the nozzle, and watch the tank sizzle and steam when the water hits it hard. I look at my partner when he says, "Good call, Chief."

"Lucky call," I say.

The air burns my face through the mask while we cool the propane. I'm starting to think we got lucky on this one, that we can handle it alone, when J.D. walks up and tells me the girl's mumbling something about her boyfriend still being inside. "Jesus, get some backup down here," I tell him. Then I yell at Partee to keep on the tank. I need to go talk to this girl.

Teddy pulls up, an ambulance right on his tail. The girl is hysterical now trying to get up and run toward the fire. I'm holding her, wanting her to sit back down. There are people coming out of the woods from God knows where to stand too close. "We need to get a perimeter," I tell Teddy.

"Everybody out of that thing?" he asks.

"I don't know," I say. "She says her boyfriend might still be in there."

"Holy shit." Teddy walks toward the gathering crowd and begins to push them back. He's a big guy. It makes his job easier, but these people are curious and the sand is deep, so it's like trying to chase them down in low tide creek mud.

J.D. comes back over, tells me Lori is radioing Surfside for backup. He goes into another gear then, getting an IV bag ready for the girl, making sure he's saving one life out here today. I try talking to her again, asking her questions. This time I smell the alcohol on her breath, see a dark bruise under a swollen eye. She looks familiar, but I don't know why, and I don't have any time to think about it. "Where's the last place you saw him?" I ask.

There's a chilling moment when everything goes silent. I look into her eyes, trying to draw an answer out of her. I don't hear the sirens of other emergency vehicles arriving on scene or the fire eating away at what's left of the trailer. It all falls into the background as I watch the woman's face recognize my question, register its full intent, the understanding of what has occurred exploding so deep inside her soul that it can only pour out in some kind of animal-like scream. "Inside the trailer," she screams. "He's inside the trailer." She collapses onto the ground, J.D. over her with the ambulance attendants at his side.

I go to Partee, tell him what's up, and ask what he thinks about trying to put the rest of the fire out. He's still hosing down the propane tank, chasing small runners that try to spread fire along the ground. "We ain't looking at a rescue, are we, Chief?"

I look at the burning trailer, now nothing more than a red-hot skeleton crackling and hissing in the cooked air. "No, it's not a rescue," I say.

"Then let's keep this tank cool so nothing else gets burned."

I don't say anything more. I just pat him on his broad shoulders and leave him to his job.

When Surfside arrives, they throttle their pumper and hit the trailer hard. I help Partee turn our hose from the Pirsch now and we hit the trailer too with what little water we have left. Before it's over there are five fire engines and two ambulances on scene. Teddy has half the Horry County Sheriff's Department helping keep the perimeter clear. A news truck from Channel 5 is talking to Surfside because I told Strachen I had nothing to say to anyone about this tragedy. J.D. is with the girl. She's beat up, talking about a fight inside the trailer last night. None of it looks good. There'll be a full-blown investigation, a line of officers already waiting to talk to her.

Where there was fire, there remains smoldering ash, remnants of a home, and no doubt now, a life. Remains of the boyfriend are found in what used to be the hallway from the bedroom, where he must have been overcome with smoke, suffocated, and then eaten by the flames. The initial investigation suggests the fire started in the kitchen. It's a bad design when a stove and oven are built into the same wall that someone sleeps against on the other side, a wall filled with foam insulation and other materials primed and ready to burn if given the slightest chance to ignite.

The preliminary report, the one we talk about on scene, is pitiful. After the fire got going real good, the boy inside woke up, then tried to get out. He knew he was in trouble. We're talking about it while we wait for the coroner to finish up, wonder what he thought when it occurred to him that he wasn't going to make it out. Everyone's smoking cigarettes, trying to relax, when Partee walks right up to me and asks if I see anything familiar. "It's like Clio," I tell him, but he just says, "No, that's not what I'm talking about."

We walk over by the burned-out trailer, and then I see it—the car. It's the Roadrunner. The side nearest the fire is all bubbled up and black. The spoiler on the back end is melted and leaning toward the remnants of the trailer. The windows are blown out, the Confederate flag barely recognizable. "Jesus Christ," I say, and then I remember the girl's face.

"Ain't that many Roadrunners around here with rebel flags in the back window," Partee says. He nods toward what's left of the trailer. "That boy in there was driving."

"The girl was in the backseat," I say, but it's something Partee already knows.

He nods. "I figured that out too."

We stand together watching the coroner do his work, the girl-friend gone in an ambulance. If she was still here, I'd try and get a name from her, find out who the boy was that died, but that will come with time. We'll know soon enough.

When the coroner is finished, I have no choice but to take Partee into the burned-out remains of the trailer to retrieve what's left of the body. "You okay with this?" I ask.

Partee nods quietly. "He ain't the one who spit," he says. "He was the driver."

I stop him there. "What if he was?" I ask.

Partee looks at me, his eyes tired, worn out like the rest of us. "You mean the one who spit?"

"Yeah," I say, "that's what I'm asking." I don't take my eyes off Partee because I want him to think about this, to know I'm asking a serious question about being a fireman. We don't have many moments around here where life and work collide and choices have to be made. "What do you think?" I say.

"Well," Partee says, the word pulled long and hard from his mouth, "maybe I'd move a bit slower getting in there. That's about it, Chief." He looks at me when he says this, and I can see in his face he's being honest.

"Don't matter what he did in life," I say, "he's not apt to do that anymore." My hand touches Partee on the shoulder.

"Then let's go, get this over," he says.

We work with silent respect, but goddamn, it's the hardest part of the job that I have to do. If somebody walked up to me right this minute and said I could leave, I'd do it and not look back. I didn't join the force to put remains in bags. It's something that sticks deep inside your gut, something that wakes you up at night, makes it hard to breathe.

I can't begin to tell you what human beings are all about, there're just too many different kinds, and we all have our weaknesses, frailties that can get us in trouble if we don't work at minding our own business. But what I can tell you is this, we're not invincible. We die like anything else that lives and breathes. And sometimes you have to clean up death to understand that. It keeps us humble, reminds us just who we are.

After the body is removed, there's no more recovery or salvaging to be done. This particular cleanup is hard because of what the fire leaves behind, the way plastic and fiberglass materials burn. It takes us the better part of the day to finish this out; a trailer fire with a death inside is about as bad as it gets. Everybody hears about Partee's story, pisses them off for the most part and makes the work that much more difficult. We're at it until early evening, finally off the call by six when I help J.D. guide the Pirsch back into the station.

Teddy drops by with word that the boy who died was some bigwig's kid over in Columbia, says the fire might have been set by that girl. We look at Partee, who just shrugs like Teddy's news isn't really news at all. "The coroner's got his ass all tied up in knots over this one," Teddy says.

Even though the news is tragic, we have to laugh at Teddy—he's a mess after being out in the sun and sand all day, his body drooping, sweat and ash ruining his uniform shirt. He looks like he could use a drink. But before I can offer, Lori informs me I have a visitor.

"Who?" I ask.

"I'll let that be a surprise," she says, "but she's on the beach. Said she was bored waiting for you."

"Is it Cassie?" Though I know as soon as the words are out of my mouth that the beach is the last place Cassie would ever go.

"No, but you're close," Lori says.

Teddy volunteers to drive me down, so we get into his patrol car and follow Atlantic Avenue until it dead-ends into South Waccamaw. When I get to the beach I find Kelly in the water on her board, she and Ellen Thomas trying to ride waves on a flat ocean.

"Jesus," Teddy says. "I thought she was with Cassie."

"She was," I say. And then I walk down to the water's edge, my finger pointing toward Kelly until she sees me. I draw her in, pull my hand toward shore as if I am grabbing her through the hot air. I'm tired and angry because I have been around fire and waste and death today. Tomorrow I'll be glad she's home, and I'll ask her why she left camp after only four days. But right now, I tell Teddy to watch me because I'm not sure what I might do to this girl when she gets within my reach. I stand there waiting, wanting to know how in the hell she got home. Wondering if her mother knows she has run away.

Cassie

Momma sits in the chaise lounge. Wisps of evening air sweep beneath the awning rich with the fragrance of the cove, magnolia and rhododendron, the light scent of honeysuckle. Her azaleas are still in bloom. I close my eyes and imagine I'm young again, the weight of my life yet to draw down on me. The land below the cove is not cut and scarred or ripped away for things so unnatural as an Arnold Palmer golf course, of all things. It angers me to think what is coming, and I want to do whatever I can to stop it, to stop John Boyd, but I'm afraid it's already too late.

I have made small efforts to look for the deed, sifting through drawers when Momma was out of the room. Out in the shed behind the house are boxes from the church, but nothing is there either, just a few old hymnals and fading bulletins from long-ago Sundays. I found Momma's prayer shawl, knitted by women in the congregation when my father died, moth-eaten and full of dirt. Momma said it was nothing she wanted to wear on her shoulders. It wouldn't bring my father back. There are needlepoint pillows and flyers advertising my father's tent revivals, but there is nothing as official as a deed. I have not told Momma about John Boyd. How can I tell her that the land is not hers, has never been hers, and that now, though she never had a clue, time is about to run out?

I watch her in the deepening shadows of the front porch. She sits quietly in the length of this evening, her eyes closed. Toes push against worn wood planks until her head nods with sleep. What will happen to her if she loses the land? She has struggled all her life, one of a dozen children who grew up on a farm outside Waynesville until the Depression scattered them all so far apart that she has never reconnected, never found anyone to reclaim as family. She stayed in Waynesville, lived with her mother until she died, then with a distant cousin, then with others, strangers who would take her in as long as she earned her keep. Washing, sewing, cooking meals was the full extent of her life, simply a means to survive. That is the one thing I can say about Momma— she always survived.

In her late twenties, she met my father at a camp meeting and was so taken by him that he became her world. After they married, Momma never once strayed from her duty to him, except when I was pregnant and she tried to repair the relationship between us. In the end, she even backed away from that, held steadfast to her place here in Whiteside Cove alongside him. When I look at her and think about my life, sometimes I just have to ask, am I really any different from her?

It's incredibly similar, I think, that in her sixty years, Momma never lived more than thirty miles from where she was born. And though fifteen years ago I traveled hours away to live along the flat salt marshes of the low country, I never really left either, haunted over a life unfulfilled. I remind myself that I have come here to change that. I cannot, in the end, judge my life by what I did not do. I have regretted too much already.

Inside, the phone rings, the shrill bell startling Momma awake.

I tell her to let it go, but she won't do any such a thing. She hurries off the porch fixing the bun in her hair, the bottom of her dress wrinkled and sticking to her legs. I listen to her answer the phone, recognize the banter, the other man in both our lives. Her voice lifts when she calls out to me that Peck is on the line.

The coolness of the dark hallway makes me shiver when I enter the house, goose bumps along my arms as I take the phone from Momma's hand. My first thought is that it is the note that he is calling about, and I am here to take the call, not at Clay's like I was supposed to be. "Hello, Peck," I say, and then wait for his voice. I place my finger into my ear to hear more clearly. "Hello," I say again.

"Hey, Momma, it's Kelly."

To hear my daughter's voice is like waking up in an unfamiliar place. I look at Momma. "I thought you said it was Peck."

"It is," she says.

"No," I say, "it's not." And then we are both confused.

"Kelly?"

"Yes, Momma."

"Are you all right, honey? How's camp?"

Peck's voice is behind her. I can hear him coaxing, demanding, really, for her to tell me more. "Tell her," he says. "You tell her what you've done."

"Kelly? Where are you?" I say, though I know exactly where she is now. There is more silence than I can hardly stand, pressure building in my chest. I look at Momma, her hand to her mouth like she has had the breath knocked out of her. "Let me talk to your daddy," I say.

"She wants to talk to you," says Kelly, her voice off the phone, even more distant when she speaks to Peck.

"You're not finished yet," Peck says. "I'll talk to her in a minute."

Then silence as I wait for whatever is happening back at home to play out, my mind spinning, trying to find my daughter's path in the last four days.

"Momma," Kelly says. "I'm at home. Ellen came and picked me up. I came home, Momma."

I stand in the hallway frozen by what I have just heard. I can hear Peck interrupt. He takes the phone from her hand. "That's enough," he says. "Now go to your room and stay there."

Somewhere in what becomes the rest of this conversation, Peck tells me the story, that Kelly called Ellen Thomas and the girl drove all the way up there and back in her Volkswagen "in the middle of the goddamn night," he says. "She's not doing shit like this. We'll be up there sometime tomorrow."

"Is she all right?" I ask.

"She's all right," Peck says, "but I could've about killed her when I found out. She was down on the beach surfing like there wasn't a goddamn thing wrong."

"Did she say why she did it?"

"Well she's keeping a tight lip about it all," Peck says. "Just said she wanted to spend her summer at the beach, not in the mountains. I told her she was full of shit."

"Be easy on her, Peck. It's me she's doing this to, not you." I pause then, twisting the phone line around my finger like a schoolgirl waiting to be asked out on a date, knowing that I won't go.

"You took more things this time than you did before," he says. "Was that on purpose?"

"Peck," I whisper into the phone. "Don't do this."

"All right," he says. "I just expected something more, I don't know. A note that said you would call. That was it. When, Cassie, when were you going to call?"

"It's only been a few days, Peck."

"It's Thursday night, Cassie. You left on Saturday. Now our daughter is back at home and you don't even know a goddamn thing about it. I don't know what's going on here. Where the hell are you?"

"Peck, you know I'm at Momma's," I say, trying to keep this conversation from becoming more than I want it to be. "I can't believe she would do something like this."

"Well she did," he says. "Look, we'll leave soon as we can tomorrow, try to be up there before dark. You plan on being around?"

"Of course I'll be here," I say.

"All right then. I got lots to do before we head out. There are fires inland that are being watched. I got to make sure we're ready."

When he says this, it stops me. "What kind of fires?" I ask.

"Brush fires over near the paper-mill land. Nothing big yet, but everyone's getting worried. I'll have to bring her up there and then get right back."

"Just let her stay then," I say. "That's where she wants to be, and you don't need to be driving up here and back like that."

"No way," Peck says. "There's another whole week of this camp. We'll be there tomorrow. She's not getting away with something like this." And then he's gone, the phone line dead in my ear.

I look at Momma, know she is waiting for answers. "She's at home," I say. "Kelly got one of her friends to drive up to Cullowhee and get her."

"My lord, why on earth would she do that?" Momma asks.

"I have no idea," I say, the lying so much easier when I'm tired. I tell Momma I want to go to bed, that I have no more information than she does for the time being until Peck arrives with Kelly tomorrow.

"When tomorrow?" Momma asks.

"I don't know. He didn't say. It'll take a while."

"Is she upset about something, because I've never heard of Kelly—"

"Momma," I interrupt. "She's fifteen years old. I have no idea what's going on in her head. When I was her age I thought about running away or jumping off some cliff and killing myself, anything to get out of here."

"Cassie, no you did not," Momma says.

"I wrote poetry about slitting my wrists, for godsakes. I hated my life at fifteen. Kelly will be all right, just wait until she gets back up here. Everything is going to be just fine." I have upset Momma, and so I leave her there in the kitchen, walk to my room, where I close the door and free-fall onto the bed. The covers bury me.

I'm relieved to know Kelly's safe at home, though I feel foolish that I didn't even know she was gone. What kind of mother could I be to not see that she might do something like this? Why didn't the camp know she was gone? I have been so preoccupied with my own life that I have forgotten to be a mother, my intuition dulled or missing altogether. And now Peck is back on my mind, a good father bringing our daughter back to me while fires are beginning to grow in the low country. It all keeps me from sleeping, Kelly's misbehavior, the danger Peck will face sooner or later.

In the years we have been together, I have thought of fire every day. The possibility of losing him to flame and smoke haunted me each time he went to work. Many days I sat waiting for his crew to come home, wondering if he was safe, praying he made the right choices, remembered his training when it was time to walk into fire. In the morning, Peck will bring Kelly to Whiteside Cove, both of them safe, alive and well. I don't know what I will do when they get here. I don't know what I will say to Peck.

I WAKE BEFORE THERE is light. I'm not sick, at least not yet, which is a good start. The air is cool in my room, so I slip on a robe Momma has given me, my father's old robe that is big and warm. It smells of cedar, an old smell that reminds me how long it's been, how the world has changed since he died.

Ten years have come and gone since he passed away in the spring of 1960. He became a part of the history of the cove on that day, the rest of the world spinning ahead. A president was killed, as was his brother, and Martin Luther King. Men rocketed into space and now walk on the moon. There is color television, though not in this house. Kelly listens to FM radio that would have sent my father into fits. When we visit here, Kelly can find stations from Gatlinburg and Knoxville, Tennessee, the high towers of FM built on the peaks of the Smoky Mountains to penetrate deep into the surrounding coves.

When I think of how hard my father tried to keep AM stations tuned in on Saturday nights, the Ole Opry and Charles Fuller's *Old Fashion Revival Hour,* it all seems so primitive now. He would gather us all in the kitchen on Saturday nights listening to Reverend Fuller preach the amazing grace of God all the way from Los Angeles, California. The reception faded in and out as he moved the dial trying to catch the best signal so we could listen to the sermons and sing all the gospel hymns my father knew by heart. He would be appalled by what's on the radio today. My father would not allow FM radio, or for that matter television, in this house if he was still alive.

I go into the kitchen for a cup of coffee and find Momma in the backyard sitting quietly, looking out toward Whiteside. It is blanketed in hues of deep purple and blue, the air still holding on to the nighttime chill. I join her and can tell she is still upset with me for not being forthcoming about Kelly, about what is going on. "I just don't understand it," she says, her voice full of surprise as if she breathed it in last night and held it there until now. "Why would Kelly run away like that?"

"I guess she didn't want to come up here so soon," I tell her.

"But she's always enjoyed her visits," she says. "What's wrong, Cassie?"

I mistake her question as being about Kelly's behavior and say, "She's a teenager, Momma. You just don't remember me that way. When Peck gets her back up here, everything will be okay."

"I wasn't talking about Kelly," Momma snaps back, "I was talking about you. Something's wrong, beyond that baby inside you, and you're not talking about it." She gets up in a huff and walks back inside. She's had it with me.

I sit quietly watching the light catch fire along the rim of Whiteside, the sun finally rising. Momma returns, having changed into her gardening clothes, a large brimmed hat and gloves, a small hand rake and hoe. She's on her knees in her garden removing weeds, complaining about me to her tomato plants, checking the lettuce for bugs. It's my being here that brings disruption. I know that, but what about John Boyd? When he gets through with her, she will have nothing left at all.

I think about Clay, see him as another part of my life in chaos. I need to talk to him too, let him know I am here and that things are not as I expected them to be when we left Garden City Beach. I leave Momma in her garden to go inside and find Clay's number in my purse, a number I haven't memorized yet, though it is almost exactly the same as Peck's down at the fire station—just the first three digits rearranged and, of course, an entirely different area code. My hand shakes dialing the number. I tell myself that he can't be home this time of day, it's too early. He will still be at the station because there is so much to do with a new crew and all.

I remember Peck's first weeks at Garden City Beach, how he stayed on-site around the clock to prepare the station to come on-line. They poured concrete, helped raise the Quonset over the cured slab. Surfside gave him one truck, a pumper that came late and was in need of repair. He and Partee had to fix it all by themselves. I made lunch and dinner, helped Lori move in furniture and arrange the office once the walls were raised. Clay will find the same at his station, the small cinder-block garage in need of more than just paint and a fire engine.

I'm about to hang up, relieved that Clay isn't home, when I hear his voice on the other end, an odd, flat, monotone "Hello" that I don't recognize at first.

"Clay," I say. "It's me, Cassie."

There's a brief uncomfortable silence, and then his words stretched out of a yawn. "Well hey," he says, "where you at?"

"I'm here at Momma's," I say. "Did I wake you up?"

"That don't matter," he says. I can hear him push himself up off the couch or the bed or maybe the floor for all I know. "I've needed to talk to you," he says. "I didn't know what happened. I thought you were coming back down here."

"I wanted to," I lie, "but things have gotten sort of complicated. Kelly ran away from camp."

"I know that. Coach Lambert called," he says. "I needed to talk to you, Cassie, find out what happened, but I didn't have a number."

"I know. I'm sorry I didn't call sooner."

"Kelly didn't give her real address or phone number when she registered on Sunday. Did you know that?"

"No, I had no idea. We had a fight, so I let her go in by herself and do all of that."

"Well, you shouldn't have done that," he says. "Coach Lambert couldn't find a way to get ahold of you, so he called me." I can feel the heat in his words, his anger close even though he is back in Walhalla. "I wanted to come up there 'cause I got worried. I wanted to see if there was something wrong, like maybe she had wandered off, gone off the side of a mountain or something, but I didn't have an address either. Hell, I didn't even know where you were. You never told me where you lived."

"I know, that was stupid," I say. "I'm sorry. She got a friend to drive up here and get her on Wednesday night. Can you believe that?"

"She's not in favor of what we're doing, I know that," Clay says.

"I shouldn't have involved her in this. I should have brought her up here by myself."

"Yeah, maybe that's what you should've done then."

The click of his lighter puts our conversation on hold. It would've been better for me to go to Walhalla and talk to him face-to-face, not wake him like this. "Look," he says, "I talked to Coach Lambert. If she's there by tomorrow, she can work back into the pitching rotations for Saturday's game, but he can't guarantee anything else. He told me if I heard from you to tell you that."

"Okay then, I'll have Peck take her on up there as soon as he comes in."

The mere mention of Peck's name brings silence. Before I left the low country, when Clay was more a source of strength to me, I might have meant what I say next, but now I do it to break the silence, to ease the uncomfortable distance between us. "I don't know what I would do without you," I say. "Thank you for taking care of this."

"I don't know why I did it," he says. "You took all your things when you left."

"You knew I had to come up here for a while."

"I guess. I just thought you'd be back by now, at least leave something here, take the goddamn key—you know, put down some sort of a stake in all of this."

"I think the stake I put down is rather large, don't you?"

Of course this gives him pause. I can hear him inhale from the cigarette, makes me ache for one, the pack still out in the car hidden from my mother. "It's large enough," he says, exhaling smoke, "no doubt. Look, I don't mean to hurt you, Cassie. It's just hard."

"I know. It's hard for me too," I tell him.

"Are you okay with him coming up there?" he asks.

This time I appreciate his concern. Even through the distance of the phone, I can feel his worry. "I can handle Peck," I say. "It's Kelly. I don't know what I'm going to do when I see her."

"Well, she did this because of me and you. I wouldn't put too much blame on her."

"It's time she learned the world doesn't revolve around her," I say. "She needs to learn it's hard sometimes."

"Just be careful, that's all I'm saying. She's just fifteen."

I don't really want Clay telling me what to do with Kelly. It gets under my skin, even as I'm trying to be nice, trying to apologize for my behavior. Some lines don't need to be crossed, whether you're lovers or not. I'm smart enough to keep that to myself right now, shift the conversation. I tell him instead that I don't know when I'll get back to Walhalla.

"Just take your time," he says. "I got my hands full as it is."

"I'll call you soon and we can talk about everything."

"About you coming back down here?"

"Yes, about that too," I say. I wait again, this back-and-forth uneven, the whole conversation awkward from the start.

"So if I need to reach you?"

"Not this number, Clay, not yet. Please understand. I can't let you have it. I don't want a call coming to this number. I'll call you."

"And if I'm not here?"

"I can call the station."

"Then I should give you that number," he says, his words snapped off with an impatience I choose to ignore.

I know he's hurt, but he's also scared because he's put a lot into this move as well. His stake is just as big as mine, the fear of failing as a chief and having nothing after all is said and done. "Yes, please, I'll need the number," I say, trying to sound cheerful about wanting it.

I look around for something to write with and am startled to find Momma standing half in, half out of the hallway. The worried look on her face tells me she's heard the whole conversation. He calls out the number, but I don't hear it. I don't take it down, my response to Clay's voice dulled by Momma's presence. "I'll call you later," I say. "I have to go now."

I hear him say something about staying in touch, his voice trailing off as I hang up the phone. The expression on my mother's face tells me she knows what I'm up to. "You left Peck, didn't you?"

"Don't be silly," I say, pushing past her and into the kitchen. The morning's chill has yet to fade from the room. The water from the spigot at the sink is cold as I fill the coffeepot. I need a cup of coffee.

"Then what was all of that about?" Momma asks. "Who were you talking to?"

"You shouldn't listen in on my telephone conversations," I tell her. "That's not right."

"It's not right what's going on here, Cassie. You're pregnant," she reminds me. "Is that baby yours and Peck's or not?"

I feel Momma's stare pressing me, waiting for me to come clean. "I'm not pregnant," I say, though I can't imagine my words are anything more than wishful thinking.

"Whose baby is it, Cassie?"

For a moment I stand at the stove watching the sun push down along Whiteside, the deep shadows in the cove finally burned through with light. "I don't know," I say, finally. "It could be either's. This is not the way it was supposed to be this time." I turn off the stove. The coffee I need will have to wait. I sit down at the table, my head in my hands.

We stay there for a long time, Momma stroking my back as I tell her what I have done, the flood of story helping to somehow strengthen us both. I tell her of Peck and Clay, of Kelly and her land. The news of John Boyd comes particularly hard. "John Boyd's my friend," she says, hoping the words will make it so.

"No he's not," I say. "But that's what he wants you to think."

We go back and forth about Peck and Clay, her questions stinging. "Why would you do such a foolish thing?" she says.

"I'm sorry I keep disappointing you," I tell her. "I just needed something different than what I was given."

"Sometimes you don't get to choose that way, Cassie. You take what you get, and make it work."

"I'm not you," I tell her, the words hurting more than I intend for them to.

"You look at that girl of yours," she says. "You look at Kelly and then tell me again that you want something different. She's a blessing, and so is Peck. Count your blessings, Cassie."

We talk for a long time, hurt each other with more words, cry, and then fight our way through it all to find love. We stay there in the kitchen throughout the day while the sun moves across Whiteside Cove, Peck and Kelly yet to arrive, still somewhere on the road.

Peck

I NEVER THOUGHT about it before, but being a parent is a lot like being a fireman. You've got to put up with a lot of stupid mistakes, never knowing what will happen and what kind of mess you'll have to clean up. It's an around-the-clock job, always on call and you have to be prepared.

Kelly's done something about as stupid as you can do in my book, asking a sixteen-year-old to drive from here to kingdom come to pick her up—in a Volkswagen of all things. I've seen what happens to those cars when they run off the road. They're like tin cans, the trunk in front, just empty air out there, so it crumples right up into the driver's compartment.

We had to respond to a wreck some time ago where a Volkswagen had left the road and hit a tree off of 707, the front cut right down the middle to the dashboard. A young girl was killed. Some witness said she had tried to swerve to avoid hitting a rabbit. It's a shame if that's what really happened. The girl was only seventeen, a year older than Ellen. What a waste.

But that's not the scariest part of what my daughter's done. Ellen's driving up to Cullowhee by herself, and then the two of them all night to get back home, driving on unfamiliar roads that snake around, dropping off into hairpin turns and switchbacks, is just crazy. It's dangerous when you know what you're doing, but two girls driving all night is about as stupid as it gets.

Ellen Thomas's parents had no idea what she was up to. Nobody knew what those two girls had in mind. I'm pissed off that they would do something like this, pissed off at myself that I didn't see it coming. Now I have to take personal time so I can get Kelly back up to her momma, and that just pisses the hell out of me.

I'm filling out paperwork, getting the schedule figured out for a crew already shorthanded, when Goose Hetzel comes flying in here with two other men in the bed of his truck holding on to Collie Walker. They're yelling and screaming that Collie's dying, something about his arm being bit off by an alligator. Now, I've seen gators in cypress swamps off the Waccamaw River, in the freshwater ponds over at the state park, so I know they're out there, but this worries me because Collie Walker is as good an outdoorsman as there is.

He owns a charter boat and should've been out on the water today while a boatload of seasick tourists tried to catch barracuda or some big-ass fish they could mount on a wall. If he was hit by a gator, no telling what's going on, so I throw my pencil down and tell Lori to call this in. I yell at J.D. to pull his kit from the Pirsch and get the hell over here.

I give Collie the benefit of the doubt until I get close enough to smell his breath, then I almost don't give a shit anymore. "He's drunk," I say.

"We been down on the river," says Goose, all out of breath. "We've been drinking, but he ain't drunk."

"Well, where the hell did he get bit like this?" Collie's arm is gone to the elbow, not a clean cut like he might get off a saw down at one of the mills, but jagged and torn, ligaments hanging, arteries pumping blood right out of his body. The boys have a belt wrapped around the upper biceps to try and stop the bleeding, but they did a piss-poor job.

Collie's losing lots of blood, already white as a corpse. He's wet too. They're all soaked to the bone. "Why is he so wet?" J.D. says. "Ya'll fall out of a boat?"

Everyone looks at each other like they know what to say, but don't know which one ought to say it. "He was fishing," Goose says.

"He was what?" I ask.

"He was fishing in the Waccamaw."

I look around to see if anyone else is going to add to this. It's obvious they're going to let Goose do the talking. He was the driver, so I guess that makes him the captain here. "You mean he was in the Waccamaw fishing with a pole and some alligator just came up and bit off his arm?"

"Nope," Goose says. "He was using his arm."

"You mean he was noodling?"

"Yeah, he was," Goose says. "He hit a hole inside one of them cypress trees, went under at the roots and then up inside to his shoulder. He got a gator instead of a catfish. It weren't that big." Goose says this like that makes it better. "Pulled it out and whacked it around real good, then it let go."

"Well, it did a little more than let go," I say and then yell for Lori to call an ambulance. J.D. has a tourniquet applied and an IV going to try and ward off any shock. "Why didn't you take him to the hospital?" J.D. asks, his impatience with the boys obvious.

Goose looks at the group, replaying the whole trip in his head. "You was closest," he says.

"I think Conway was closer," J.D. says. "You came the wrong way."

I look up to find Kelly behind Partee, her face white, her hands at her mouth like she's forgotten to breathe. She shouldn't be looking at a man without his arm. "Take a breath, girl," I tell her. "Go see if Lori needs anything. Now."

J.D. checks the man's vitals, adjusts the IV flow, and then gives Collie a shot for the pain. He's pretty frustrated at them for bringing him to the station. "I don't know if a hospital will do him any good now," he says. "He's lost a lot of blood."

"He's going to need a tetanus shot, ain't he?" Goose says.

J.D. just shakes his head. "That'll about do it, Goose, that and about three pints of blood."

Billy Jackson sticks his face down into what's going on and says, "We got the arm," and that stops everything.

"You got the arm?" I say. Partee comes over to see what he can do. Billy glances over like Partee's the school principal and needs to be told the truth.

"Gator let it go," Billy says, "floated right out in front of us, so we brung it along. It's in the bed of the truck, behind that tire." He points in the general direction of Goose Hetzel's truck. We all turn to look, but no one volunteers to get the arm. I finally have to yell at Partee to go do it.

"Go with Billy and get the goddamn arm, get it in a bucket of ice, fast."

"Where am I getting ice in this heat?" he asks. It's obvious Partee's got a problem with Collie's arm lying in the back of Goose Hetzel's truck. We always keep several bags of ice in a freezer out back. Partee knows where the hell the ice is.

"Well, you can walk on down to the pier, if you want to, and pick some up," I say, "or maybe go right out there in the ice box. Your pick, Partee."

He stands there for a minute more like he's really thinking

about the pier, but I know he's just pissed off. Finally, he turns to Billy. "Get the arm," Partee says, and then walks off to find a bucket big enough to hold the thing.

I've been an outdoorsman all my life, shot duck down on the marsh, been deer hunting, bow and rifle, every year. Pops taught me to shoot a gun when I was twelve, and I learned how to bait a hook when I was six. I know all about noodling, been along a couple of times when I was a teenager, but I never saw any use in such a thing, none at all. Blind leading the blind's what it is.

Usually gators aren't down in holes like that, but with the heat being what it is, I guess this one was just trying to stay cool and Collie came in and woke it up. Every one of these boys holding on to Collie or watching him suffer has been warned not to noodle in the Waccamaw. It's dangerous and yet they still do it. This is what can happen, even worse.

When we stand up, I'm dripping in Collie Walker's blood. The ambulance attendants arrive and load him onto a stretcher, J.D. right alongside. I look up at Partee, stare real hard as he passes. He's got the bucket and a bag of ice, headed toward Goose's truck. "What?" he says when he walks past me, but I don't give him an answer. He's noodled in the swamps back there too. Partee's waded into that murky water, hung on to cypress roots, and felt around for a goddamn catfish.

J.D. helps get Collie in the ambulance then walks over to tell me he wants to ride in. "We'll take him over to Myrtle Beach," he says. "They got a real trauma unit there, not just emergency. Maybe they can do something with that appendage."

"Fine," I say. Partee brushes past me smelling like he's been working hard, even though he didn't like what he had to do. He puts the iced-down arm in the front seat of the ambulance.

"You follow them in, Partee. And keep your arm out of holes,"

I tell him. "See what can happen? I can't have you looking like that."

"Ain't the right time for noodling," he says like he's the authority on all this. "Them boys ought to know better. They been drinking, not thinking."

Kelly stands with Lori, still watching what's going on. "Get her in the office, Lori," I yell. Then I give Partee another hard look. "I didn't ask you to explain these boys' mistake, I told you not to noodle." Partee shuts up after that, looks like my yelling hurt, but I don't care. Nobody's listening to me anymore. The whole goddamn place feels dangerous and out of control.

One thing a fireman needs to feel is control, even when it's not there, even when he's surrounded by danger. If you lose that, fear can seep in, and fear is a cancer in this line of work. Everybody snaps back fast when I yell. It's something I don't do often, so they know I mean it. Then the station falls back in line, the ambulance leaves, and Partee gets in his Mustang to follow them up to Myrtle Beach. Calm settles in and I go change my clothes.

In the bunk room, I toss everything into the trash. The clothes are ruined. There's a pair of pants and a uniform T-shirt that will get me back home where I can put on regular civvies. The trip up to Meemaw's is going to take us the better part of the day, and I'm already exhausted, still have one more stop to make before we can get out of town.

When I'm dressed, I collect Kelly. She's sitting in the office with Lori looking at a magazine, their heads leaning together, lost in some picture of a boy who's on television. My gut seizes up when I see Kelly with Lori. They are interchangeable. Kelly could be working down here in a couple of years. But as much as I love Lori and how well she does her job, I do not want my daughter settling for something like this. I want her to get out of here one day.

I don't want mistakes to determine her life. I want *her* to determine it. "Let's go, girl," I say.

Out in the drive, Phil Roddy is cleaning up Collie's mess. "Hey," I say. "You know of anybody who can come in for a couple of days?"

Roddy sits up on his knees to think about it, then says, "Call Johnny Cash. I don't think he's working this week."

"He's probably off making a record in Nashville," I say, smiling, thinking it's a pretty good joke.

"Naw," Roddy says. "This one makes a much better fireman than a singer. Hell, he can barely read." He laughs at me and then gets busy cleaning up Collie's blood.

When I call Johnny Cash, he's available, tells me to take my time, that he's got the days to give. All these boys, all the volunteer firemen, are good as their word. They train more than they fight fires, but they come when they're called, Phil Roddy and now Johnny Cash. I thank Johnny on the phone and then hang up whistling "Ring of Fire." I feel a little bit easier about taking time off, but still, I want to get back as soon as I can. I'm still chief.

AT THE HOUSE, I throw together a small bag of clothes, toss it into the back of the truck along with Kelly's gear. She snuck out late Wednesday night after everyone was in bed and sat on the steps of her dorm waiting for Ellen to show. "When did you call her?" I ask. "That's a long way for her to come on such a short notice."

"I called from Clay's on Sunday," she says, confirming everything I already know. Still, my heart sinks.

"Did you call collect?" I ask.

"No, person to person." And then she smiles because she knows it cost Clay money for the call.

I chuckle when she tells me this, but that's it. I won't give her any more. I don't want her thinking she's clear and free from what she's done.

Ellen told her momma she was going to a friend's to spend the night. Then she drove to the state line and found a gas station that sold maps. Someone there helped her figure out her route and then she showed up sometime after midnight. It took her a little time driving around the campus to find Kelly but she did and then they had traded off driving all night to get back home. Said they ate M&M's and drank Pepsi-Cola to stay awake. Kelly hung out at Ellen's house before she came down to the station. Called some boy who said the surf was good, so they left to hang out at the beach and wait for me to get back from the trailer fire.

All the time they were driving, I was drunk in the back end of a truck watching grown men throw firecrackers out into dry fields. I have no idea what Cassie was doing, but I can bet she wasn't paying attention either. Seems no one's making good choices right now.

I know that my little girl is growing up, that she does things that I'll never know anything about. She's never had a steady boyfriend and I like that. I don't worry about anything happening to her like it did to me and her momma, at least not yet. Kelly's going to get into things. It's just the nature of growing older, finding your own way. I just want her to be safe. I want her to have a good head on her shoulders. "Look," I say, "what you did really stinks."

"I know that," Kelly says.

There's something about my attempt at moral high ground that feels pretty low. Still, I push on. "No, I'm serious. You could've been killed driving that far with Ellen."

"I could have been killed surfing. I could have been killed riding the school bus. I could have been killed by a line drive in a softball game." Kelly folds her arms and stares out the side of the truck like that should be enough to put a stop to my lecture.

We drive on for a bit, the air starting to smell like smoke. "Look, all I'm saying is I love you, and I hope I've taught you better, so next time—"

"Daddy, please," Kelly whines. "It's not like you're Mister Perfect."

"What does that mean?" I ask. The road across from the power-plant reservoir is packed with traffic going into Conway, so I have to be careful.

"I know what you and Teddy do out in the water."

"What?" I ask.

"You know, smoke pot."

I nearly run off the road when I hear this. It brings a smile to Kelly's face, her hands on the dashboard as I guide the truck back off the shoulder. Not too long ago, I told Teddy to be careful with bringing pot to the beach, that Kelly was surfing with us now and that she was old enough to understand. But Teddy doesn't have kids. He had no idea what I was talking about. "We don't do that much anymore," I say, "and besides, we're adults, something you're not yet."

"It's still against the law," she says like she'll forever have this on me, a get-out-of-jail-free card.

"Yeah, it's against the law," I agree. "I can't argue that. But that's not what we're talking about here. Teddy hasn't offered me smoke in I don't know how long."

"Daddy, I don't care what you do, just don't be a hypocrite, okay?" She sits back and puts her feet up on the dashboard like she's over this conversation.

Kelly looks so much like her mother sitting here, the way her hair falls into her eyes. That summer I met Cassie, she would sneak out of the church camp and meet me at the pier. We rode around in Pops's truck, Cassie sitting like Kelly listening to the radio out of Myrtle Beach, nothing in our way except the roads we drove every night. I would take her to places up north, Ocean Drive and Windy Hill, Atlantic Beach, where juke joints played the best beach music along the strand.

"Your momma would kill me if she knew we were talking about this."

"I'm not talking to her," says Kelly.

"Well, me neither," I say, smiling.

Kelly winks an eye, sealing our allegiance. I see Cassie even more in her face when she looks at me. It hurts deep, so all I do is turn my eyes back on the road and keep moving.

I follow 501 into Conway, crossing the Waccamaw backwater and then the river, the bridge swooping us down onto Main. Kelly looks at me. "Are we going to see Pops?"

"Yeah," I say. "He needs to know that I'll be gone for a while. It won't take long."

"He won't even know you're there."

She's right. There's a good chance he won't, but I still need to go. "I at least got to let the nurses know where I'll be," I tell her.

I pull up in the parking lot off Fourth Avenue, the air acrid, tasting like smoke. "Damn," I say, looking up into the sky.

We walk up to the door, go inside, Kelly holding my hand as we walk down the hall to Pops's room. We find him in his bed in near dark, small jaundiced slices of light cutting through the Venetian blinds. Margaret is there again, looks up when we push back the door, smiles wearily then gets up.

"I'm glad you came today," Margaret says. She sees Kelly and her smile grows bigger. "And you brought the child. She has grown, Mr. Peck."

"Hey, Margaret," I say. The television is off, not a good sign. "Is he asleep?"

"He might be," Margaret says. "He's been coming in and out lately. More out than in, I'm afraid." She looks at both of us like we should understand what this means. "I been telling them to call you, Mr. Peck. I don't think he's doing too well. Ever since you were here the other day, he's been sort of going down."

I walk over to Pops's bed and look at him, lay my hand on his. "Pops, you awake?" I ask. His face is bloated, his skin pale and thin. The room is hot, the windows closed because of the smoke outside. There's a smell of urine floating up from his sheets. "I think we need to change the bed, Margaret," I say.

She sighs heavily when she comes over to stand beside me. It's like she's checking a baby's crib. One hand goes under the covers to rub up beside Pops's body. "Yes, mercy," she says. "That's the third time today. Don't know where it's coming from. He ain't drinking a thing."

I'm not sure he knows who I am, even after I open his blinds to let clean light into the room. I ask Kelly to step outside for a moment and she's out like a rocket shot to the moon. Margaret brings in fresh sheets and I help her move Pops around, his body bloated more today. When I was here last time, it was only in his feet and ankles, now it's everywhere.

"I just can't get up to go to the bathroom," he says, his words strong when he speaks.

The hospital gown he wears is soiled too, so I ask him if he wants Margaret to leave before he changes. "I ain't got no modesty left," he says. "She knows that." Margaret just smiles, leaves with the soiled bedding while I help Pops get the clean gown around and tied in the back.

All the commotion around him helps as his eyes brighten, his mind catching up. I tell him about Collie to keep him engaged. "Do you remember Collie Walker?" I ask.

Pops is fumbling with the gown, getting it to cover his privates while I try to hold him there on the side of the bed. "Collie Walker," he says like he's throwing the name back into his memory to see if something comes up. "Where's he from?"

"Over here, I imagine," I say. "He's got that '63 Hatteras he runs out of Murrells Inlet."

"Is that the Jarvis Walker family?" Pops asks.

"I don't know, Pops."

"Well, I've been out fishing with Jarvis Walker," he says. "Bet that's who it is."

"Probably is then," I say. "Well, Collie got his arm bit off by a gator out here in the Waccamaw today."

"Today?" he says. I swing him around, feel his stomach protrude from the gown.

"Yes sir," I say. "He and some of his buddies were out in the Waccamaw noodling."

"Noodling?" Pops says like it's the first time he's ever heard of such a thing.

"Yeah Pops, stuck his arm up a hole in a cypress stump and there was a gator waiting instead of some big old catfish."

Pops gets a big laugh out of that, his body shaking as I lay him down. "Guess he'll use a hook next time," he says.

"If he wants to keep the other arm," I say. "Any way about it, he's going to have a hard time putting bait on a hook." I don't tell him what happened when they brought him to the station, all the blood and the severed arm, the near cost of life. I just let him hold on to the funny part of the story, get Kelly and ask her to come back in.

"Pops, you remember Kelly?" I put her in front of the old man, tell her to say hey.

"Hey, Grandpops," says Kelly. She pushes against me, leaning back for support. It's hard for a young girl to be around age like this. They have no history, no understanding of who the person was before they came to this point in their life.

He smiles at her, but I don't think he gets it. "Yes, um hum," he says and then turns to look out the window.

"I'm taking her up to the mountains today," I tell him.

"You are?" he says, turning back to us. "That's a long ways away, ain't it?"

"Pretty good distance," I say. I nudge Kelly, push her to move closer. "Tell him what you're going up there for."

She's hard to move, but I get her to finally open up, her face a sweet smile. "I'm going to camp, Grandpops. I'll play softball up there."

Pops holds out his hand for hers, then coughs so hard I'm afraid he's messed his bed again. I don't say anything about it. I just let Kelly stand there holding hands with her Grandpops for a moment. "You be careful and don't fall off one of them mountains now," he says.

"Okay, Grandpops, I'll be careful," Kelly says.

Then he lets her go, points with a crooked finger to his night-stand. On it sits a picture of Mom and his wristwatch. I look at the face of the watch, almost one o'clock. I know how late it is going to be when we get into the mountains, so I need to get us out of here soon. His finger points to change on the nightstand. "Give me that," he says.

Kelly looks, tries to follow where he points. "What, Grand-pops?"

"That penny there," he says.

I know what he's doing, so I reach over, pick up a penny and give it to Kelly. "Here," I say, "stick this in your shoe."

"You take one too, boy," Pops says, like I don't have a choice.

Kelly grins at me when I have to put a penny in my boot. Pops's thing, always has been.

He smiles then, says, "You go on. Let me know when you get back."

"Will you be all right?" I ask, knowing the question's a stupid one.

"I'm fine, boy," he says. "Now you go on. Come by when you can."

Kelly's hand slips into mine. "Let's go," she says, her voice a soft whisper.

I wanted Kelly to see him today on the way out, wanted her to have a moment with her grandpops. She's never seen him that much anyway. She was too young to bring over here when he first moved in, and by the time she was old enough, Pops was getting sick. At one time, early on, Cassie wanted him to come live with us out on the creeks. That seemed a bit too much, and then time just got away, everybody too busy with living life. I'm glad we came here today. There won't be many more times, I'm afraid.

Outside, we climb into the truck. Kelly smiles. "He called you *boy*," she says, then goes digging for the penny she has in her shoe.

"Yeah, he's always called me that," I say. "I don't think he ever knew my name."

"Daddy," Kelly says. She rolls down the window, asks if we can stop for ice cream on the way out of town.

At Barker's Servicenter I fill up with gas, think about Goose

Hetzel and Collie Walker's arm, figure it's all about over by now. They either saved it or Collie will work his boat with one arm for the rest of his life. Either way, the man better be thankful he's got a life to live.

I pay for the gas, let a boy I don't know check under the hood, top off my water and oil. I look inside where my daughter is paying for her ice cream, the poise she has, the way she holds herself at fifteen. She counts out her change, uses Pops's penny to make it exact, smiles when she's coming out the door having caught me staring at her.

She needs to be in Cullowhee, to let people see her talent. I'm getting her back up there for that camp no matter how much work I might miss. I'll get her through college whether it's with a soft-ball in her hand or not. She's going. She'll be first generation, but by God, she's going.

"You used Pops's penny for the ice cream," I say.

"Yeah," Kelly says. "I was a penny short."

"Then it worked," I tell her.

"What?"

"The penny," I say. "It brought you good luck."

Kelly shrugs at Pops's superstition, her feet on top of the dash-board while she eats the ice cream cone. When we pull out of Barker's, she looks at me for a moment. I can feel her eyes. It's like Cassie's on me when she says, "I'm sorry that I did this. I know it wasn't right."

"I know that," I say. "You're not the first teenager to do some-thing stupid, won't be the last."

She sits up in her seat, the white cream melting faster than she can lick at the cone. "I love you, Daddy."

The sun is moving too fast for us to have any chance of getting into the mountains before dark, but I'll push it as fast as I can. I watch Kelly for a moment, melting ice cream running down her fingers. "I love you too, baby," I say, "but you do this again, and you'll be dead meat on a bone. Do you understand?"

The girl doesn't look at me. She just licks her fingers, tosses the rest of the cone out the window before leaning back on the seat, her legs against the dash, eyes closed. And then just like her mother, she smiles.

WE ARE DEEP into the mountains after dark. Kelly has withdrawn, all balled up in her seat watching the road before us, the dashboard lights washing her face pale. I ask her to keep an eye out for the turnoff to Meemaw's house. But by the time we see it, it's too late. I'm going too fast, the fog hiding the road until I pass it by. We drive on into the white dark looking for a turnaround. I can sense the truck is out near the edge of something deep and dangerous, but I can't see a thing. "Hold on now," I say when I find a shoulder wide enough to pull off.

A creepy feeling rises in my body, headlights reflecting off the white air. I pull across the road and drive slower now heading what feels like up, but it's hard to tell with fog covering the road like a pillow.

"Don't miss it again," Kelly orders.

"Then you see it quicker this time," I say, trying not to let her see I'm nervous about all this too.

Finally, Kelly sits up straight and points out into the swirling light. "There," she says, "there it is, slow down."

"All right," I say, "I got it this time." We make the left onto Meemaw's road. The headlamps fight the fog, passing houses and then oddly into open space, the land torn up, trees cut and stacked along the roadside. "They're doing something out here, aren't they?" I say, but Kelly's not listening. She knows what's coming at the end of this road, her legs drawn back up into the seat, arms holding her tight again.

Past the last house, we drive into pitch black, the land filling in around us again. The truck's headlights shine down onto the damp earth following worn tracks that lead us around a curve and then a right onto gravel, Meemaw's house in front of us, finally. The light from the windows draws us in, soft halos muted by the fog. I see Cassie's car in the yard, pull in beside her, and kill the engine. Meemaw is standing on the porch, her silhouette small against the lighted opening. "Go on," I tell Kelly. "I'll get our bags." She sits in the truck still tucked in her ball, head laid over to the side looking out her window. "You go on now," I say. "You might as well get it behind you." Then like a firecracker, she releases her grip, pushes open the door, running barefooted up to the porch, Meemaw waiting with a hug.

I work on the bags, taking my time, letting everybody have a minute together inside. From the porch I hear Cassie and Kelly talking, finding some kind of truce they can live with. I stay put, light up and smoke my first cigarette of the day. I've been so preoccupied by the drive, I haven't even thought about a cigarette. It feels good to draw smoke into my lungs, to taste tobacco on my tongue again.

The air is black, filled tonight with sounds of tree frogs and crickets. If I was to walk out ten yards past my truck I would be unable to see a hand in front of my face. It's dark and cold here, my body not expecting such a change in climate. In Garden City Beach, the heat makes you want to take off all your clothes and sit in a tub of ice. I saw reports right before I left that warned fire departments along the beaches to be aware of rogue brush fires, not only those started by an act of God, but ones started by careless tourists, cigarettes thrown out of windows, or pop bottles that catch the light just right to magnify it into a spark.

Up here it seems like a different world, the land so wet and full that nothing could burn, no matter how hard it tried. A chill pulls at my body, making me dig into my pack for a sweatshirt. I'm not used to this weather, not ready for such change. It all makes me feel just that much more like an unwanted guest, a stranger here among what is supposedly my family.

I don't know what to say to Cassie. Don't know what to expect. It's too late to take Kelly on to Cullowhee tonight, too dangerous to be on unfamiliar roads. If I could, I'd take her back to that college and then drive straight home, because I don't believe I should be up here, not with the way everything's falling out. I want to give Cassie room because I want her to come back home. All I ever wanted to do was love that girl, provide as best I could, but maybe all that will turn out not to be enough. When your own soul's lost, nobody else can find it for you. Cassie's looking for hers, and I feel like my being up here intrudes, makes her job all that much harder.

Before I can finish my cigarette, she's there at the screened door. "Hey," Cassie says. "You made it."

"Yeah, guess so," I say. "But if Kelly hadn't been there, I'd probably be in Tennessee by now."

She smiles at that, pushes the door out, joins me on the porch, her arms wrapping a sweater around her body. "Well, I'm glad you're both here, and safe," she says. "The fog really set in fast."

"Yeah, well, we made it," I say, and then we fall quiet for a moment until the space between us grows too uncomfortable. "Did Kelly apologize to you?"

"She did," Cassie says. "She's in there with Meemaw now. I apologized too. It's not fair what I did to her."

"What did you do?" I say.

Cassie reaches over and takes my cigarette, pauses while she pulls a long draw. "I made her come up here for that camp," she says, exhaling the smoke. "Maybe she should have stayed down there with you. If I'd known all this was going to happen . . ."

"Naw, she needs that camp," I say. "That's a good thing. What she doesn't need to do is what she did. I don't care how much she hates where she is. She needs to stay put."

"Well, I found out she can go back, finish out next week. The coach wants her there tomorrow."

"Bright and early," I say. "I'll get her there, just point the way."

She takes another drag off my cigarette, holds the smoke deep before letting it go, the fine line disappearing into the black air above us. "I thought we'd both take her back up, if that's all right with you?"

I look at her when she says this, the night hiding anything from her face that might give meaning to her words. "That's fine with me," I say. "I just don't want to be in the way up here." I take the cigarette back, touching her hand for the first time in a while. "I don't want to be crowding your space. You seem to need it."

"I'm just glad Kelly went home and didn't run off somewhere else," she says. "You know how kids are today. What if she had just taken off?"

"Yeah, well, Kelly's pretty stupid for what she did," I say, "but she's not dumb. She's too much like her mother in that regard."

Cassie smiles at this, leans against the porch rail to look at me. "You put credit in the wrong place, Peck. I'd expect her to be long gone, if she was like me."

"Well, I don't know about that," I say. I want to go to her, stand in front of this woman and tell her she can come back too, if she wants, but I don't. There's more going on here than I can begin to understand, not sure I even have a say in it, so I let it go. "Do I need to go find a motel around here or what?"

"No, of course not," she says. "Bring your bags in. Have you two eaten?"

"No, not since lunch," I say, "and I don't even remember where that was."

"Momma's got some fried okra and sweet potatoes. She cooked a ham so there's plenty of food."

"So what's Meemaw saying?" I ask, the intent of the question understood.

Cassie waits for a minute, choosing her words carefully. "We've been talking, Peck. She knows that I'm going to be up here longer this time."

"How long?" I ask, unable to help myself.

"Let's don't talk about this now," she says. "I thought we could do that tomorrow, after we drop Kelly off. Maybe drive around or walk somewhere. Let's don't do it here, tonight. Okay?"

Though I don't want to give her this, I do. I'm tired, need to rest after this all-day affair. Here I am in the mountains, hours away from home, looking at the woman who is my wife, the mother of my daughter, trying to understand what it is that I have done to chase her away. After all these years, all the work we put into living a good life, we are here in this cove unsure of which way to turn.

I agree with Cassie about the night, let her take one last draw off the cigarette before I toss the dying ember out into the drive. I touch the small of her back as we turn to go inside, the shape familiar and soft. We walk into the light of Meemaw's small house where it is warm and dry, good food waiting to comfort us all.

––––––––

ON SATURDAY MORNING I lie in bed listening to thunder and the sound of Cassie throwing up in the bathroom. I barely slept at all, thinking of her in the room next door, Kelly beside her instead of me. I tossed around, heard the crickets and tree frogs give way to wind and thunder, then rain drumming against the tin roof of Meemaw's house. I lay quietly until there was a dull light in the sky and then I heard Cassie, the door flung open on the way to the bathroom. Now she's in there, and I need to get up. I have a long day ahead of me.

I stumble out of bed, throw on a pair of pants, then walk to the door frame of the bathroom. She's on her knees dry heaving. "You all right?" I ask.

"I'm okay," she mumbles. "Something didn't set right."

"Can I get you anything?"

"No, just close the door."

I do as I'm told, and then look in on Kelly. She's sound asleep, the covers over her head. I pull the bedroom door shut, then go to the kitchen looking for coffee. Mavis is out on the front porch, the rain coming off the roof slapping into puddles. It's been pouring for a good while now—rain like I haven't seen in months. I want to think it's going to roll off this mountain and have enough left to get to the coast. But I have my doubts.

It's already seven o'clock, and I don't want Kelly missing another whole day of camp. I imagine with all this rain there's no real hurry. Nobody's playing games today. But I'd like to get Kelly back up to Cullowhee. I'm just antsy about being here, that's all. I'm anxious about how still this house is, like it's afraid to breathe, afraid of what might leak out at the seams. Cassie goes back into her room when she's finished being sick, and closes the door. I take that as a sign to stay away. Instead I go out on the porch with Meemaw, sit in a chair, shirtless, with hot coffee warming my hands. Meemaw is on tiptoes clipping flowers, trimming her ferns.

"You must be exhausted from that drive up," Meemaw says.

"It's a haul," I say, "especially when you're not expecting to do it like that." I take a sip from my cup, hot coffee burning my tongue. "I forget how far back in here you live, Mavis. We about didn't find it last night with all the fog."

She stops and looks out into the distance like she's finding her words. She's surrounded by her plants, each basket fresh with color fighting against the drab morning light. "We've been here a long time," she says. "You need to come up more often."

"I wish I could," I tell her, "but it's hard to get away."

She sits down in the chaise lounge, her shears placed in her apron like a holstered pistol. "Well Peck, you should've tried," she says.

It doesn't get past me the way she says this, the past tense of her statement. "Cassie seems to like it up here just the way it is," I say.

"She's going to need some time now. I'm afraid it's come to that."

Inside, we hear Cassie heading for the bathroom again. Meemaw watches the door like she's afraid what might walk out.

"Cassie's sick," I say.

"I can hear," Mavis says.

I wait then, watching the rain come down, a straight sheet of water. I want to see if Mavis will offer without me having to pry. "She just told me to shut the door," I say. "That's as far as I got to finding out anything."

She ignores my words, points out at the graveled curve that

bends toward the main road. "Did you notice what they were doing to the land down below?" she says.

"I saw something going on," I say, "bunch of earthmovers pulled off along the side of the road."

"Well, they're trying to get my land."

"Trying to buy you out?" I ask.

"I don't know if it's buy out or take out," Mavis says. "Cassie can tell you about that. I don't know what to think." She looks at me then, her guard coming down for a minute. "You know John Boyd Carter."

She says this like a fact. It's a name I recall from years ago, someone mentioned in all the craziness when Cassie and I got married.

"The name's familiar," I say. "Is he a friend or foe in all this?" I ask.

"Cassie tells me he's a foe, but I can't believe that," she says. "The church gave us this land. John Boyd and Parker worked it all out before he died."

It's like she's trying to use her words to convince us both, but hell, I don't have an opinion about this. I have no idea what she's talking about. "Then you don't have anything to worry about," I tell her. "Parker took care of you." Mavis likes what I say, the idea that Parker is looking after her even from the grave. She smiles at me for reminding her of this, while inside, Cassie calls.

"Well, I better go check on her then," Mavis says. She gets up slowly from the chaise lounge, bent a little more now like a weight is holding her down. When she walks across to the door her arm touches on my shoulder. "Parker would ask you to put on a shirt," she says. "He didn't believe a man should be naked like that in front of God and all."

I laugh a little under my breath. "Not naked, Mavis," I say. "I just don't have on a shirt."

She squeezes my shoulder then. "Well, I'll bring you one when I come back out," she says, and then disappears into the house.

I fish around in my back pocket, find cigarettes crushed in a crush-proof box, light up, and let the smoke fill my lungs. Something is familiar about all this, sitting here with Cassie inside, Mavis warning me about Parker.

Years ago, after Cassie called and said she was pregnant, I drove up overnight, came in during the morning when Parker was up at the mountain. I stood right here on this porch smoking a cigarette while Cassie stayed in the bedroom. It was pretty bad. Cassie was upset, Parker was livid with her, and Meemaw was just trying to find something in between to hold them all together. When Parker finally returned, he was shocked to see me, then angry, all fire and brimstone. He made me wait out on the porch until Cassie packed her things. There was more grief and pain in that afternoon than I ever thought this old house could stand up to.

I wasn't a fireman yet, so I'm pretty sure I looked a sight to the old man. I was a lifeguard when we met with no big plans, especially concerning marriage and starting a family. Nobody ever plans to have to get married. But one thing Pops taught me was that consequences mattered. I was foolish when I was younger, but I learned quick that if I did something bad, Pops would box my ears good. He had a sixth sense for that sort of thing. It was hell growing up knowing that when he got home from Georgetown on Friday evening or Saturday morning, I was going to get beat like an old rug if Mom had any trouble to report.

Even though I know the whole thing hurt Mom and Pops bad, they respected me for standing up and marrying Cassie. Life-

guards at Myrtle Beach were organized and run by the fire department at the time. Surfside was hiring a firefighter, and it just
seemed the right place to go and stay after Cassie and I got married. There wasn't any training back then. They just put a hose in
your hand and turned on the water. It was smack-upside-the-head
on-the-job training.

I never came back up to Whiteside Cove while Parker was
alive. Cassie reconciled as best she could, and after her father
died, she started going back in the summers. She used Kelly as her
excuse, when I know the real reason was that she just couldn't
stand living in the low country. I could feel it building all year,
every year, each time I'd come off rotation. By the time the heat of
summer was on us, Cassie was miserable. The first time she went
back to visit her momma, it lasted only a week, but later, two
weeks stretched into three or four until I had to plead with her to
bring Kelly back home.

I can count on one hand the number of times I've been back
here—once when Parker died, a few times in the summers since
then, once in the winter when Cassie wanted Kelly to see snow.
It's been some years now, but standing here looking off the edge of
the porch toward the mountain, the cove stretching out behind
the house, it feels strangely familiar as if I am waiting, watching
for Parker to appear along the rise, his measured steps bringing me
news that his daughter has done it again, and that this time, we
are both betrayed.

Inside, Kelly's finally up rummaging in the kitchen for something to eat. If Cassie's not feeling up to it, I'll take the girl to camp
myself. Cassie said we would talk after dropping Kelly off, but that
was last night. Who knows what she'll want today, if she'll even see
me at all. I know she's been with Clay, maybe in ways I hadn't figured on. I could've asked Kelly driving up here. She tried to tell me

in her own way, but I didn't want my daughter telling me things like that about her mother. I can read between the lines, or maybe I should say between trips to the bathroom. I've been here before.

Breakfast is quiet, Mavis cooking too much good stuff, ham and bacon, eggs, and buttermilk pancakes. Cassie is nowhere to be found until we're done and the dishes cleaned. When she comes out of the bedroom, she's dressed, ready for our trip. I look at her, but she's not taking the bait. When I ask if she'd like a piece of dry toast, that gets her goat good. She knows I know, but we don't talk about it there. We'll have time after Kelly's back at camp.

We let our daughter say good-bye to Meemaw and then head out. The rain never lets up, thunder rolling across the mountains as we drive to Cullowhee. It's slow going on a two-lane road that drops into the middle of the earth before rising up, twisting and turning us until all our stomachs are knotted. Cassie looks like she's going to get sick again, so I pull off the road, the Tuckasegee River running alongside us. I don't think she notices where we are. She's too busy dry heaving, squatting outside her door, where she spits into the mud along the shoulder, but I know exactly where I am.

After Parker kicked Cassie out, we drove all day through the mountains, spending time in Highlands and then heading back down to Cashiers. We parked in the lots of the local tourist traps, waterfalls and mountain overlooks, trying to figure out what to do next. That afternoon, we drove in the opposite direction, further north to Cullowhee. Cassie wanted to show me where she had started school. There was still hope in her voice that once the baby thing was over—that's the way she would talk about it, the baby thing—she'd be back in school, just like nothing had happened.

We drove on to Sylva after Cullowhee, ate at a small café on Main Street, went to a late-afternoon matinee at the movie house, and then had dinner in the same café, sitting in the same window seat, where we watched the rain pick up again, the dirty gray sky weighed down with clouds. Cassie tried to call home all day, but Parker wouldn't let her talk to Mavis, told her just to go on, pray that God would forgive her. They finally stopped answering the phone when she would try, so we were on our own sitting in a café in Sylva with no idea what to do next.

We'd have stayed there forever if it hadn't closed, the manager sorry that he had to kick us out. We left Sylva in a downpour, headed back in the direction we'd come. It was dark by then, and I was so tired from being up nearly twenty-four hours that we started looking for some cheap place to stay. "Cheap room for cheap people," Cassie said. She was trying to punish both of us, but I just told her we'd be all right. I was trying to do the best I could. I saw no reason to stay in the mountains, but she wouldn't leave.

."How?" Cassie said. "How can we be okay?" She started crying uncontrollably then, the darkness crawling into the mountains much sooner than it ever would along the salt creeks.

I was so tired my eyes started playing tricks on me. Tar lines came alive in the road, snakes skimming across in front of the truck. Trees bent heavily on both sides, and I overshot the motel when it came up on us, the lighted sign almost disappearing in the fog. I slammed on the brakes, hit the steering wheel with my hand. I was pissed at Cassie's father, a minister of all things, for sending us out like this.

Hell, Pops drank liquor and beat the tar out of me when he thought I needed it, but he'd never have done anything like that. It wasn't right to let kids so young and messed up wander along dangerous roads in dark so black headlights found it hard to open it up. I put the truck in reverse, stuck my head out the window, and backed up the fifty yards, telling Cassie to watch for head-lights bearing down on us from behind until we were safely in the motel parking lot. Then she broke down again, cried real hard there in the seat. It had been a pretty goddamn rough day, worst in my life at the time.

It's odd remembering all of it now, this road fifteen years later. Kelly's sitting in the back of the car reading a *Sports Illustrated* she talked me into buying her on the way up last night. I try to get her to look at me, but she's not going to do it. She's just acting like she couldn't care less that her momma's throwing up in the mud alongside the road.

By the time we get moving again, the rain has lightened up, a breeze pushing at the clouds to clear the air. It all makes the final push to Cullowhee less treacherous, the mood lighter in the car as the rain begins to leave the mountains. I let Cassie take Kelly to her dorm, then wait as they walk down to the gym to join the rest of the girls working out inside. It's easy to think about Cassie as a student here, makes me wonder what she would have been like if she had finished her college degree. Where would she be today?

That summer when she left the beach, there were promises that we'd write, maybe a trip up to visit her at college that fall. But, hon-estly, I wasn't betting on it. I thought I'd probably never see her again. I imagine she would have written letters for a while, maybe a phone call or two to talk about the next summer. Then it would have all stopped. Cassie wanted me to come up here and work, said there were lifeguard jobs at summer camps or maybe in Highlands at a country club. They boarded the summer help in Highlands, she said, so I'd have a place to stay. We talked all summer about the mountains and how we could be together after Myrtle Beach was over. It was fun to talk about, but I don't think either one of us re-ally thought another summer together would ever happen.

When she reappears, Cassie is by herself, hurrying down the street toward the car. Her sundress presses against her legs in the breeze, her shoulders covered by a white sweater, flip-flops on her feet. She looks like she belongs here. She should have gone to school. We could have figured it all out in a different way after Kelly was born, but we didn't, and so when she opens the door, it hits me hard, my breath taken away like my air tank has just emptied out. I can't keep her. I'm going to lose Cassie this time. I'm going to lose her for good.

Cassie

"THERE," I SAY, flopping into the seat of the Bel Air, a weight lifting with Kelly back in her dorm.

"She going to be all right?" Peck asks.

"Yes, just fine," I say. "I talked to Coach Lambert and he said they would start games this afternoon if the weather holds. She's missed a lot, so she won't start, but she'll get to pitch."

"That'll piss her off," Peck says, his attention turned to starting the car. "Teach her not to run away."

"I don't think she'll do that again, do you?" I ask.

"She's got her own mind now, Cassie. She sees things."

Peck rolls the car away from the curb and I think maybe it's time. He knows what's going on, I can tell. "I was thinking about going into Sylva," I say. "I need to go to the courthouse. It's open until noon on Saturdays, so if we hurry, I think we'll make it." Peck laughs at that, just a little under his breath, but I hear him do it. "What?" I say.

"What what?"

"You want to let me in on the joke I just made?" I ask.

"There's no joke that I can see," he says. He's looking both ways like he's not paying any attention to what I'm talking about, but I know he's pissed off. A few trucks come and go, but the roads are mostly clear; no need to squeal tires the way he does when we leave the campus. He rolls his window down, stays quiet then, and that's what always angers me about Peck. He keeps everything inside, never talks without a fight first. I don't want to fight today, so I keep steady, let Momma's story occupy our conversation.

"I need to go to the courthouse to look up Momma's land," I say.

"What's wrong with her land?" he asks.

"John Boyd came over and told me it wasn't hers."

Peck's eyes cut over briefly before going back to the road. "She told me about that this morning," he says. "Said you think this guy's bad."

"I think so, but I don't know. I need to look at the land deed, see what it says. I have to go to Sylva to do that, so I thought since they're opened till noon, we could start by driving over there. That's all I meant."

The curves to Sylva are easier, two narrow lanes widening out to four. Peck looks at me again, longer this time with some kind of a shit-eating grin on his face. "What?" I ask.

"What what?" he says, really pissing me off this time.

"Dammit, Peck, don't do that to me."

But of course, he does. He smiles that grin again, says, "Want to renew our vows while we're there?"

"You think that might help?" I say, looking out the window. The land out here is more open, not as severe as the road in from Cashiers.

"I don't know," he says, "you tell me."

"I don't have an opinion about that," I say. "You're the one who brought it up—"

"No, you did," he interrupts. "You're the one who brought up the courthouse."

It's like we're teenagers again, a tit-for-tat fight over silly notions, emotions out of control. I try to let it go, ignore his taunting.

"Let's just look at the deed first," I say. "One mess at a time."

He laughs again, a pissed-off kind of thing. "Mess, that's a fine word for this," he says, "a goddamn mess."

I look at him hard. For the first time, I don't feel threatened. I feel I can stand up to Peck on my own. Maybe it's because we're here in the mountains, my turf, not his, maybe it's the distance the days have put between us. I don't know, but I'm not going back to the way I used to be. "Don't start with me," I say. And he seems to listen, shuts up. I pop the glove box, remembering my cigarettes, pull out a half-smoked pack of Winston's, offer one to Peck first while I push in the lighter.

Coming up Main, the courthouse looms high above the town. The big white building sits perched on a hill like the law is looking down on anyone who comes to Sylva. Today, the steps in front seem nearly impossible, so many and so steep. One hundred and seven, a climb I have not forgotten in fifteen years. When we came here to get married in 1954, we parked on the street below and walked up. Today we drive a road that wraps around the hill, rising quickly to a parking lot. We are in a hurry. It's late, almost noon when Peck turns off the engine.

The courthouse shadows our car, and I begin to feel nervous. Police cars are parked out front, along with an ambulance and, believe it or not, two horses tied up alongside the building. "You need help with this?" he asks.

"I've never looked for a deed before, have you?"

"Nope," he says. "But it's all public record. Can't be that hard, can it?"

"I guess not," I say when I open the door. "I'll be back, don't leave me."

"Where would I go?" he says. Then, as soon as I close the door, I hear Peck's open.

"I can look over your shoulder," he says. "Two sets of eyes look twice as hard." He walks ahead of me to the door, opens it when a woman gets confused, pulling at it rather than pushing. She's disheveled, her dress worn and faded, an oversize army fatigue coat draping her body, unlaced boots scuffing the ground. "Here you go, ma'am," he says. "Looks like they forgot which way a door's supposed to open." The little woman doesn't even smile, just shoots inside, climbing stairs toward the courtroom.

"That's probably her horse out there," I say, and we both have a good laugh.

Inside, I feel the history, the day returning to me from memory fifteen years old. The magistrate who performed the ceremony wasn't friendly at all. I think he figured out what was going on and disapproved as much as my father. Momma paid for the license, gave Peck money to pay for that horrible motel room. She stole food money from the jar kept in the kitchen cabinet, money my father gave her once a month for seasonal canning. When my father found out, he refused to give her more to make up for the loss. Folks from the church helped her fill out the shelves in the kitchen that winter. It's confusing standing here now, looking for directions, feeling emotions I haven't felt in years.

Peck finds a security guard who points us in the right direction, and we head downstairs where land records are kept in the Public Registry. Through double doors we enter a dark room that takes up most of the basement. It feels more like a musty library than the place where all the land transactions in Jackson County are carried out. I feel intimidated, walking into the room ready to search legal documents, surveyed boundary lines that, when found here today, will help to decide Momma's fate.

Inside, Peck gets the attention of the clerk, a man in suspenders, a tie loose at his neck. He still wears a tweed coat though
the weather has warmed. The man looks at the clock, perturbed
for having to work right up to closing. Peck tells him why we are
here and he leads us farther back into a small room to a table and
chairs. Windows near the top of the ceiling filter in light from
ground level, soft beams hitting against white walls, fluorescents
humming above us. I'm given a piece of paper, a request form to
write down the address to Momma's house in Whiteside Cove.
The man smiles when he sees my request. "Lots of people interested in this tract lately," he says, but I let that go. Peck nudges me
to ask who might be nosing around, but I don't say. I'm not here to
accuse. I just want to see where Momma stands.

It takes no time for the book to be located, the tract to be
found, the description of the land described in Deed Book 387,
page 239. Numbers of longitude and latitude, compass directions
and natural markers I recognize on the land. The "double oak at
the curve of Whiteside Cove Road" where the old church property
ends and Momma's begins, and on the other side "the existing cor-
nerstone intersecting Whiteside Cove Road and Garnett Hill
Lane." It's an old Cherokee marker that has been there for as long
as I can remember. The base of Whiteside is mentioned as a plot
point east and west, the distance my father used to walk daily for
his meditations and prayers, land included that John Boyd said
was never part of the deed. "This is a lot of land," Peck says.

"More than I thought," I say. "It goes all the way to Whiteside.
John Boyd told me it was only to the ridge where the tree line begins."

"John Boyd's a liar," Peck says.

"I guess so," I say, and then scan the page to find out who owns
the tract, the legalese like a foreign language. When I see it, my

heart jumps. On the deed is John Boyd Carter's name, but how could that be?

"So John Boyd owns the land, then," Peck says. "Not the church."

"No he doesn't," I say. "Momma owns it."

"Well, this says John Boyd Carter owns it," he says while pointing down at the page.

I look at Peck and he raises his hands, surrendering. "All right, all right," he says. "How can this be, then? I thought it was church property." He points to the page again like it's convicting evidence.

"I don't know," I say. "I need help here."

The man in suspenders and tweed comes over to hear my story. It shocks him. He looks doubtfully at the book, his mouth puckered up as if he's waiting for me to finish so he can kick us out. It flusters him more when I tell him that my mother has owned the land for ten years and that his book is wrong.

"No," he says out loud, his voice stronger than it needs to be. We are right across the table from him. "The books are right," he continues. "In fact, this parcel was recorded sixty-five years ago, and it's never been changed. The Carter family has owned this property since 1905. I understand some surveys are being conducted right now out that way, but this," and he looks into the book to get the name correct, "this John Boyd Carter has held the deed since it was transferred over in 1935."

"Is it possible this is a mistake?" I ask.

"No," he says. "Such a mistake or failure to report a transfer or sale would be illegal, fraudulent even. You can check with the tax assessor to see who paid taxes all this time, but that will have to happen on Monday. It's noon, closing time." He smiles then like he's proud of himself, an office well kept, his duty done, time to go home.

Then there's a second where he seems intrigued by the possibility of something more. "Now if," he says, and then pauses to think it out clearly before giving anything sinister a life. "If there is another deed that was never posted, then you might have something here. If a deed was signed, but never delivered, then it could be owned by someone else, but it means a fraud's been committed. But of course you would have to find the second deed and bring it in."

I look at Peck. "Why would he do that?"

"Who?" he asks.

"John Boyd. Why would he lie about who owns the land?"

"I don't know that he has, Cassie."

"Momma said the other night that there was a deed, that my father brought it home to show her."

"The original?"

"No, a copy, I believe."

"If it was a copy," the man says, "it would have to have all signatures *and* the county seal to be valid." He is impatient with the information now, the clock showing minutes past closing.

"I think it did," I say looking at Peck, his face doubting the possibility. "I think she said it was signed, maybe it was the original."

"Cassie, look," Peck says, "your mother never dealt with any of this stuff. Parker did it all for her and then, I guess John Boyd's been doing it ever since Parker died. I don't see how you're going to get anything more than this."

"The deacons deeded the land, Peck. I remember that. I remember Momma talking about it after he died."

"Well they didn't, if John Boyd owned the land. Maybe Parker misunderstood what John Boyd and the deacons did."

"No," I say, *my* voice rising this time. "That can't be true. That's not it at all."

"All right then," Peck says. He looks to the clerk, smiles, closes the book in front of me. "I think we've done all we can here, right?"

The man smiles in agreement with Peck. It pisses me off that he would just close the book and try to take over like this. "Find the deed," the man says. "We reopen for business on Monday, eight A.M. sharp."

"I will," I say, pushing the book hard across the table. It slides into the clerk's chest, catching him off guard, the shock on his face showing his disapproval. I'm out the door, climbing the stairs two at a time while Peck tries to catch up.

"Hey," he says, "wait up."

We're outside when I swing around, stopping him with a hand on his chest. People leaving the courthouse are watching us, but I don't care. "If you can't help, don't talk," I say.

"What did I do?" he asks, arms spread out like he might just try and fly.

"Nothing, Peck. You didn't do a thing."

"Then why are you all pissed off at me?"

"Because, Peck, you didn't do anything that helped. You made that little shit look like he knew what he was talking about."

"He did, Cassie. He was right. You have to have a deed."

"I have a deed," I say.

"Well, where is it?"

"I don't know," I scream.

"Then you don't have one, Cassie."

"Not yet," I say, and then I stomp back toward the car.

Peck trails behind, yelling at me like it's my fault he's such an asshole. "Okay, not yet. But don't get all bent out of shape at me because of this. It's not me who wanted to come up here in the first place."

I turn and face him again, try to measure my words. "Then next time, don't close the book in my face."

"The courthouse was closing down," he says. "You ran out of time."

"I was inside, Peck. They can't lock the door if I'm still inside." I'm seething over this when I open the car door, the driver's side car door.

"You driving then, I guess?"

"If you think I can, Peck."

"Jesus, Cassie." He tosses the keys into my hands.

We get into the car, both doors slamming shut, rattling windows. There is no more talk as we drive down the hill and onto Main, then back out Highway 107. I want to say I'm sorry, but Peck is looking out the window, his whole body turned away from me.

There are more questions about the deed I want to talk over with him, but he has checked out, given up on me, probably on us by now. I don't blame him. I've given Peck good enough cause to never speak to me again. None of this is easy. I drive on, pushing up the mountain, wondering why it has to be so hard between us, hoping I won't get sick again, hoping I won't have to stop and finally tell Peck that I am pregnant.

BY THE TIME we are back in Cashiers, the wind has cleared the air, and I have turned onto Highway 64, Peck sitting up in his seat now as we climb toward Highlands. It feels like the first time we drove along these very roads trying to decide what we were going to do—two lost teenagers. I don't bring this up. I'm afraid it might confirm the suspicions I know he has about me, so I point out the window to our left, the looming cliffs of Whiteside rising through the trees. "Maybe we should take a hike," I say. But Peck remains silent. He's hurt by the way I behaved in Sylva. "You feel like a hike?" I ask, a question this time. He looks out at Whiteside flickering at us through leafed branches, his hair mussed up by the flurry of a strong breeze pushing through the car from windows rolled down.

"You're wearing flip-flops," he says. "You can't hike in flip-flops."

I run into slow traffic moving along Highway 64, a flatbed truck carrying large earthmoving equipment up toward Highlands. The going is tedious, stopping and starting, a line of cars snaking behind the truck, inching along. "We have to walk the old road, anyway," I say. "The trail's been gone since they tore up Wildcat Cliffs."

When I was a child, my father held Easter Sunrise Service on Whiteside. He would invite his congregation to meet on top of the mountain, to hike in from the campground while he took the old Kelsey Trail alone from Highlands. It was his way to get right with God, I think, just like his daily prayers at the base of the mountain.

The Easter that I was nine, he let me go with him, Momma's prodding getting the best of his solemn nature for once. At first, I don't think he minded the idea, but the five-mile trail was cold and icy, extremely long for a young girl. That early April morning, I struggled to keep up, his pace brisk and direct. My father could walk the trail in the dark because he knew it so well. I did not, and when the slope began to rise, when I had to navigate rocks and steep inclines, I slowed him down. He became impatient as if I was somehow interfering with God.

When we passed Highland Falls, I wanted to go down to it, to feel the spray of water dampening the air. The trail led us through primeval forest, trees that seemed to hold up the sky, red maples and tulip, yellow birch. Hemlocks were giants among the rest, so big around that together my father and I could not have held hands and circled the tree with our arms, even if he'd been willing to try. We passed landmarks that my father would call out, not to let me know where we were, but to tell himself how much farther he had to go. The falls, Wildcat Cliffs, Garnet Rock meant nothing to me, but with each point made, he would increase his pace and put more distance between us. The trail ended at an old campground, a quarter mile from the summit. There was light in the sky by the time we arrived.

We joined a small group from the church that had ridden in wagons to the campgrounds. They were ready to hike the final distance, but my father was visibly upset that we were late, that others had gone on ahead and were already on top. When the service was over, he asked Momma to take me down with her; he would walk back to Highlands alone for the car. I took this as a rebuke, that I had somehow failed him at his most important moment, the high mark of the church calendar, the resurrection.

From that moment on, his disapproval extended to every aspect of my life, and I began to feel like a second-class citizen. I remember thinking then how I would hate to be my mother and have to live with this man for the rest of my life.

It was only a few months later in 1946 that logging began around Whiteside and the trail we had followed was gone forever. My father joined with others in trying to stop the destruction of the old-growth forest. The logging broke the quiet, filled the Cullasaja River with silt, and browned Mirror Lake for what seemed like forever at the time. It angered him to see God's good earth destroyed, tractor skid trails and logging roads scarring the very land he had walked while carrying on his lifelong conversations with God.

When the logging was exhausted, the giant hemlocks and the backside trail forever gone, my father refused to go to the summit of Whiteside again. Even after a road was cut through to bring tourists to the top, a road that would have made the service more agreeable to his congregation, he never went back. He remained faithful to his walks to the southern base of Whiteside, but once the logging began, he refused to go on top and have to look down at the mutilation that was taking place along the northern slope.

Traffic gets the better of Peck and he agrees to a hike when we see the turnoff to Whiteside Mountain. I park the car in a small lot that is left over from the days of the tourist trade. It is rutted and muddied from the rain. "The road will be better," I say, looking at my feet, the rubber flip-flops already covered in muck. Peck is in boots. Except when he surfs, he is always in boots. He comes around to my side of the car. Peck Johnson, always the gentleman, lifts me up, carries me to the remnants of the old road, the ground there no better than the parking lot.

"This isn't going to work," he says.

"Sure it will," I say. I have him put me down along the edge where wild grass and moss cling to the ground. I am able to walk along this sedge, the north slope drop-off pitching steeply as we ascend. Up here the air is crisp with the wind blowing in against the trees. The smell of fresh earth, the sweetness of Catawba rhododendron and flame azaleas, bush honeysuckle after the rain, is like God's candy to the mountains. It lifts my spirits, even as luck runs out and the mud thickens along the road. When I run out of anything to walk on, lose a flip-flop, I look at Peck nervously, afraid he might end this hike before we get to solid ground. But instead, he picks me up again, surprises me with a back ride as we climb the rest of the road together. The silence between us

is still there, though I can feel it loosen as we make the old parking area near the summit. There the earth is drier, with wild grass
and shrubbery thick along the bluffs of the northeastern face. The
view is toward the headwaters of the Chattooga River watershed
and all the land beyond.

Because of the storms, we are alone on Whiteside today, no
one else attempting the muddy climb. The wind is fierce, gusts
pushing at us as we climb toward the summit past Devil's Courthouse and the old tower overlooking Fool's Rock. We hike the final
distance along a narrow pathway, ascending eventually to a slab
that is carved with Whiteside's altitude. The roughly etched numbers set the elevation at four thousand nine hundred and thirty
feet, "above sea level," Peck says as he looks down into the cove.
From here we are protected against the harshest gusts of wind, the
sky above us the deepest blue I have ever seen. Giant puffy clouds
push fast across us almost at a height that I think I can touch, if I
would just reach out and try. We sit on ancient limestone rock
along the Eastern Continental Divide, riding the backbone of the
Smoky and Blue Ridge mountain ranges. Whiteside Cove spreads
out before us some two thousand feet below.

"I can see Mavis's house from here," Peck says. In all the years
we have been married, he has never been to the summit of Whiteside until today.

"You can see everything from here," I tell him. "I can't believe
you've never been up here until now." It feels good to be the one
showing something to Peck rather than the other way around. He
stands and walks to the edge, a rail preventing him from going too
far.

"Parker walked down there, through those fields," he says.

"Yes he did, every day," I say. I rise and join him at the edge.
Below us a hawk rides the air currents like a curving mountain

road. It dips and turns, rises and falls until it is near enough that we can see its eyes scanning the clumps of rhododendron clutching the mountain face. I point downward to the fields below. "There's Momma's house, then the fields," I say. "You see where the line of woods starts?"

Peck nods, points himself. "There?"

"Yes," I say. "Follow the line of woods to the left and then look out into that field. Can you see it?" Below my finger, the distance through air to earth, I can see a faint vein cutting into the green patch. "I think that's it," I say.

"What?" he asks.

"I think that's the old trail my father walked to Whiteside."

Peck's eyes try to focus on what I think is there, but he doesn't see it. You have to grow up in the mountains to understand where and how to look for things. Peck is a low country boy, the geography of this place too different from the land of his own life. I can feel his uncertainty, confusion over why he is here, why I'm here in a way that doesn't include him. It's how I felt for fifteen years living in the low country, so I guess now it's his turn. "Do you understand me now?" I ask. But this just confuses him more.

"How is that?" he says.

"You don't like this place any more than I liked Garden City Beach."

"That's foolish, Cassie."

"No it's not, Peck. How often have you been here since we got married?"

"You know I can't make every trip," he says.

"Four times, Peck. You've been here four times. I could understand it when my father was alive, but he's been dead for ten years. Ten, Peck, and you've been back up here only four times."

"Well, I don't count like that," he says.

"Maybe you should."

"Look, you know why I don't come," he says. "I know how much you want to be up here. I let you come to give you room."

"Peck, you can't stand this place any more than I can stand the mud in the marsh. What if I said you had to move up here if we were to stay together?"

It takes him a minute to answer this. His eyes focused somewhere off into the empty air. "I'd say tell Kelly first," he says. "She's the one I'd worry about."

"No you wouldn't," I say. "Kelly's young. She wouldn't know the difference in a year or two."

"Cassie, in a couple of years, she'll be a senior. She'd be devastated to leave her friends and the beach."

"No, Peck, I think you'd be devastated." I watch his jaw clinch, his hands tighten on the railing.

"Look," he says, "I know you need time. I want to give you that. I don't need to be up here because I'm just in the way. I'm in the way right now." He leaves me then, walking farther up the trail. That's the way it is with Peck. I challenge him and he walks away. I have things to tell him, things he needs to hear, so I follow him until he stops at another overlook. It reaches out to reveal the curvature of the mountain, a rough-hewn semicircle of rock that looks like ancient cathedral walls descending below us.

"We need to talk," I say.

"Then talk." Peck sits down on a small outcropping where the sun is warm, the wind quiet. I join him there, letting the silence of this place wash over me as I try to decide what he needs to hear. What I want him to know.

"I don't know what I'm going to do," I say finally. "I know that doesn't help, but that's as far as I've gotten. I haven't been here long enough to decide anything else."

"I can understand that," he says. "I wasn't planning on visiting you."

"Momma's said I can stay with her as long as I need to. And with all this going on with her land, it seems the right thing to do."

"Have you thought about Kelly?" he asks. "Have you asked her about any of this?"

"No, and if I did, she'd say she wants to go home. That's obvious."

"She won't do that again," he promises. "She'll stay put."

"She can spend a week here with Momma after camp, and then I'll put her on a bus or something. She can go back to the beach and have her summer like you want her to. Besides, she doesn't need to be in the middle of all of this. I was stupid to do that to her."

He laughs a little under his breath. "Kelly would hate it up here if you tried to pull her out of school."

"I know that," I say. "She's more you than me anymore."

This brings a smile to his face. "She's hardheaded, if that's what you mean," Peck says.

We sit in silence once more, high clouds beginning to dull the sun. It feels like rain might be coming in again. "What about Clay?" he asks.

"I don't know about Clay," I say. "He's in Walhalla."

"He needs to step up here, don't you think?" Peck says. "Does he know about the baby?" His eyes search mine, waiting. I'm shocked to hear the words come from him, but then after this morning, after what we have just said to each other, why should there be any doubt?

"No," I say. "I don't think it's his."

Peck stands up like it's my answer that pushes him off the rock. "Goddamn it," he says. "Goddammit."

At first I don't understand, stupid me. Then I realize what has just happened. He didn't know. He was fishing for something. He didn't know I was pregnant, and I just gave it to him, just like that. I'm mad at him for doing this, testing me, playing his little game. I'm mad at myself for not seeing it coming. "That's not fair, Peck," I say, staying put. "Stop manipulating me like that."

He turns around at the rail, all of Whiteside Cove below him. "You tell me to stop manipulating you, and here you are saying you don't know whose child you're carrying. One thing we know for certain here is that it might be someone's other than mine. It might be Clay Taylor's."

I hide my face, start to cry at his words. It's not so much the cruelty of them as it is the truth. "Stop it," I say. Out before us, clouds build near Chimney Top and Rocky Mountain. "I don't know what to do," I say. "I don't know what I *can* do. I didn't come up here because I was pregnant. I came up here to get away, Peck, to see what it might be like to not be Peck Johnson's wife anymore, or Kelly Johnson's mother for that matter. I wanted to just be me again, me, Peck. Fifteen years ago, I put me in a drawer when I packed away all my plans for college and whatever I would have done with that. Well, fifteen years is a long time, and I think I'm due. I didn't want to get pregnant, I just wanted to get away."

I watch Peck from where I sit, the wind shifting, picking up around us. He turns to face me, his eyes sad this time. His hands rub against his unshaven face, pull through tangled hair while he remains exposed on the edge of the mountain. "Well, what the hell are we going to do then?"

In all our arguing, we have failed to notice the storm. It's odd when one blows onto Whiteside and you're still on top. It can come up and over or stay below and leave you alone. This one hasn't made up its mind where it will land yet. We watch as towering thunderheads climb along the cliffs, push upward on the draft of wind. It's like being in an airplane watching lightning ignite and run throughout the dark clouds below, no doubt pushing powerful bolts toward ground we cannot see.

The storm silences our differences and we move hurriedly back along the trail, expecting the worst to push up and over the walls of Whiteside. Peck pulls me into an old run-down structure off of the parking area. The makeshift shelter is a small building with fading words painted on its side claiming it's the world's smallest post office, remnants of when the top of Whiteside was a tourist trap. We climb over debris, pushing aside rotted boards to huddle in the small space, waiting for the storm that never comes. To the north, the air is clear, above us the sky blue. It's the southern face that is taking all the beating. "We need to leave," I say. "Momma is in all of this."

"Let's wait it out," Peck says quietly, his arm hovering above me holding on to the small roof we squat beneath. "It'll be over soon enough." I'm drawn to think about any other time that this might have occurred. Peck would have held me. But in the close quarters of this shelter, I sense he is holding back, keeping his distance as we wait for the storm to clear.

When it is over, we walk back to the car, slipping and sliding, my feet thick with mud and Peck not offering me his back this time. I let him drive us home in silence and do not offer anything more. There is nothing that I can say.

On Whiteside Cove Road, it is apparent the storm has caused damage. Downed trees and a few electric lines straddle the road. Men are already out with chain saws and axes clearing the fallen timber. We turn off pavement to find the road to Momma's house rutted and soft, Peck slipping and sliding when traction falters. He guides us past the earthmovers that have gone silent, the land lying in huge heaps and piles where the earth has been cleared away. We pass John Boyd's house, a few trucks sitting in his yard, a station wagon there with some realty company's sign painted on its side.

"I've got to find that deed," I say, but Peck is not listening to me. When I look at him, he is just watching the road, and I feel distinctly that he has already left, gone back to the low country where his world is flat and understandable to him. "When are you leaving?" I ask.

"Soon," he says. "Tonight."

Before us, Momma's house comes into view. There is a tree down in the front yard, a large one that has come up by its roots. Momma is walking out of the house. "It would be nice if you could stay long enough to make sure she's all right," I say, but Peck is silent.

I look out the window to Whiteside Mountain, the face dark gray now that the sun is moving behind its peak. It stands there like it always has, a sentinel, angry and hostile one moment, forgiving and soft the next. Its paradox is as ancient as its beauty. I look at Peck and ache for him. I want it all to be different, but it can't be anything more than it is. I know that.

When I get out of the car, Momma is already in the yard surveying the damage. I can tell she is glad to see us, glad that Peck is here to take care of things, to take care of both of us. And for the moment, at least, I am happy about this too.

Before we can join her at the downed tree, John Boyd is turning into our drive. There are several other men in the car with him, and though I could be wrong, I don't believe they are coming here to help with the tree. Peck walks up beside me, looks out at the drive. "You know these guys?" he asks.

"It's John Boyd Carter," I say.

The car pulls up behind Peck's truck, doors opening before the wheels have even settled. John Boyd gets out, waves, a friendly smile on his face that makes me think he's going to try and sell us something. The other men wait by the car. They are talking among themselves, lighting cigarettes. One man has a large roll of paper under his arm, blueprints for Arnold Palmer's golf course, no doubt. They are all dressed in suits but wear boots like they might be planning a little walk around Momma's land.

"Mavis, you all right?" John Boyd asks, his smile drawn down into concern. He stands in front of her, ignoring me and Peck for the moment.

"I'm fine," she says. "I was all right the whole time, John Boyd."

"That storm sure hugged onto the mountain," he says. "It just hit it straight on and stayed there. Haven't seen one like that in quite a while." He looks at me then, keeps the charade of concern going. "I wanted to come on up here in the middle of it to check on her, but it was just too bad," he says. "Martha wouldn't let me near the door. But I'm glad you were here for her. I'm sure that helped."

"I wish we would've been here," I say, looking at Peck. "We were up on top. It never came over, just wind and sunshine up there. We came down here as soon as it passed." I hear thunder rolling along some distant ridge, too early to know if there will be more for the cove. "John Boyd, I don't know if you remember my husband, Peck."

He looks to Peck finally, smiles. "I do," he says, "but it's been a while."

Peck reaches out to shake his hand. "Time slips," he says. "Hard to get away from work."

"I know that," John Boyd says, looking back to the men standing around his car. "How long you going to be up?"

"Not long," Peck says, turning his eyes on me. "Maybe until to-morrow now, until I can help get this out of here."

Peck's words draw John Boyd's attention to the fallen tree. "Mavis, you just lost a red oak here."

"Is that a red oak?" Momma asks. A worried look shadows her face as if she has just been told of the death of a good friend.

"I'm afraid so," he says. "This'll take some time to cut apart, Peck. I can have some men over here this evening, if you need the help."

"I think I'll be all right," Peck says.

"There's a bow saw around here somewhere, but you'll need a chain saw to cut it up. I can help out there." John Boyd looks back to the men standing by his car, then up to Whiteside, the shadows darkening, painting the air deep blue. "You ain't getting this cut up tonight though," he says. "I'll bring the saw by first thing in the morning."

Peck looks at me then. "You want me to stay and cut this?" he asks.

I watch his eyes. He's not going to do it if I don't want him to. He'd leave if I said go. "If you got the time, it would be helpful," I say.

Peck looks back to John Boyd. "I'll find the bow saw and start cutting these limbs back tonight, look for the chain saw tomor-row."

"Bright and early," he says before glancing at Momma. "Now Mavis, I'll drop that saw off before dawn tomorrow, so don't go shooting me full of rock salt, you hear?" He laughs at his joke, but Momma is more confused than anything else. She has lost a red oak, part of herself here on this land.

"I don't own a gun, John Boyd." She turns in a huff to go back inside.

"Momma, he was joking," I say.

"I know he was," she says, her back to us. "I don't want to look at it no more, just makes me sick." She turns at the top of the steps like she's forgotten to tell us something, points out to John Boyd's car where the men wait smoking their cigarettes. "These men want to walk the land," Momma says. "I thought that would be all right."

I glance toward the men, who have not moved from the car, and then back at John Boyd. It's hard to hold back anger, not tell him I've seen the deed. "I hope Martha doesn't mind you staying out after dark," I say.

He smiles, but it's not all that friendly this time. "She'll hold dinner for us. But thanks for asking." He winks at Peck like he's in on the joke, reaches out to shake his hand again. "Peck, it was good to see you. I'll have that saw here in the morning."

We stand by the fallen tree watching John Boyd walk away. Thunder is getting closer, though the sky above us is azure blue, nightfall approaching. The men gather at the car, huddle momentarily, and then traipse off through the opening in the fence, walking briskly like they have an intended direction.

"What was that all about?" Peck asks.

"He's an asshole, that's all," I say.

"Think you can find the deed?" he asks.

"I don't know if there's time," I say. "I looked some, but no luck. I just have no idea where it could be."

Peck turns to me then, the fading light finding its way into the blue of his eyes so they shine. "Try again, Cassie, you find that deed," he says. He walks off then, heading toward the outbuilding behind Momma's house to find the bow saw.

I stay and watch John Boyd lead the men out into the fields. Just off the fence line, the men flush a covey of quail, the sudden explosion of wings startling the men. At first they seemed stunned, but then raise arms like young boys carrying invisible guns. The man with the rolled-up paper aims it at the lifting birds, pretending to fire. They laugh, pat each other on the back, and move on, John Boyd leading the way, pointing off in the distance toward the line of trees. Someone in the group says, "This is incredible land."

"Of course it is," John Boyd says. The laughter that follows feels poisonous to me. It hovers, abrasive, refusing to leave even as the men become silhouettes against the dying light.

Peck

Cassie came to my room last night after we had all gone to bed, quietly asking if she could crawl in beside me. "I'm empty," she said. "I don't know what to do anymore."

She stood in the dark waiting, nervous at the silence that followed. "God, Peck, I'm sorry. I'm sorry I hurt you like this."

Hours earlier, I had cut most of the big limbs off the trunk of the red oak before it got too dark. Meemaw cooked dinner, went to bed early so Cassie and I could talk. We sat on the front porch and smoked cigarettes, tried to figure out what Kelly was feeling about our separation, how her running away was some kind of acting out against us both. We talked calmly about Clay and the baby and what it might mean if the child was ours, and if it wasn't. We kept our voices low, sat close, and spoke without hurting each other. When we came inside, Cassie told me she missed Kelly and me, that her life was unraveling in front of her.

"I don't know if I can do anything about that," I said. "What if Kelly hadn't run away? I wouldn't be up here, and we wouldn't be talking. Would you still feel the same way?"

She stood in the living room, her arms wrapped against the

chill that followed us in off the porch. "I don't know," she said. "It's hard for me to know that, Peck. That's what scares me."

"It scares me too, Cassie." I went into the bedroom then, closed my door wondering if I had accomplished anything over the past two days other than bringing Kelly back to the mountains and finding out that Cassie was carrying a child that might be some- one else's. I can't explain why she came into my room, no more than I can explain why I let her in my bed, but I lifted the covers and extended the offer. We touched, but there was nothing ex- pected from it, just Cassie's familiar body next to mine.

IT'S EARLY, BARELY ANY light in the sky, as I push myself up and out of bed. I slip into my pants and then out of the room not wanting to wake Cassie. She's on her back, legs bent, tenting the covers with her knees, lightly snoring. It's like there might be another chance now. Fifteen years have given way to this moment. Maybe, if we want to, we can find a way to start all over.

Meemaw's sitting at the kitchen table, smiles when I walk in.

"Did you sleep well?" she asks.

"Like a dead horse," I say. "I need some aspirin if you've got any." I pour a hot cup of coffee while Meemaw rummages around in a drawer and comes up with a small tin of Bayer. I take four, hoping they'll work fast and help me get through the rest of the wood that's waiting for me out in the yard.

"John Boyd left the saw for you," Meemaw says, "some oil and gas too."

"Thank you, John Boyd," I say, washing down the aspirin with the coffee.

"You want something to eat?" Meemaw asks.

"Only if you're going to fix something for yourself," I say. "I don't want to be any trouble."

"I'll wait until Cassie's up. If she's feeling like something, I'll eat with her. But if you're hungry now."

"I can wait," I say. "Let me get a good piece of that trunk cut, then I'll be ready for something hot and greasy."

Meemaw smiles at that, touches my hand. "Peck, you're a good man," she says, then gets up to walk to the sink. She washes a few dishes from last night, carefully drying each one with a towel before replacing it in the cabinet.

"I'm afraid those are mine," I say. "I needed something more before I went to bed."

"It's good to eat," she says, "but I'll need to go to the store if you plan on staying around."

I take a sip of coffee, the bitter taste of the aspirin still lingering in my mouth. "I wish I could," I say. "But I need to get back. We got fires inland and I don't know what's going on right now."

"Well, it would be nice," she says. I can tell she's worried about me and Cassie from the way she stays longer at the sink twisting the extra water from the dishrag, but she won't bring it up. Pain is plentiful in all of this, carried in different ways by each of us. Mavis and I stay together in the kitchen, remain quiet while I finish my coffee.

Before I go out and look at the tree, I call the station to check on things. Partee answers, and even though it's early, he sounds awake like he's been up for a while.

"What do you hear?" I ask.

"Not good," he says. "Depends on the winds. Right now, it's coming our way. They've put us on alert, Peck. It'd be best if you got on back home."

"I'm working on it," I say.

"How's the weather up there?" he asks.

"You don't want to know," I tell him. "The place is soaked to the bone."

"Jesus." I can hear him sigh on the other end, frustration and fatigue for always coming up short on the rain. Then Partee tells me about the makeup of the fire. There were actually three small ones at first. One was a campfire that escaped out of its pit; the second was alongside a road, a cigarette or something thrown into dry grass. "The third looks just plain stupid," Partee says. "Some guy pulled a trailer with a chain sparking along the shoulder of the road for miles. They just started investigating it, but it's getting too big to be worrying about its source just now. Plenty of time for that later."

"I'll be home today," I say, "but it might be late."

"Late works," Partee says. "They're holding all of us on call, but nothing's happening until the fires join up and cross county lines, or they call us in to support Georgetown. You get home tonight, and you'll have plenty of time to play fireman with the rest of us."

I smile at Partee's humor, tell him to hold the place together. "I will," he says, "if you promise to bring back some of that rain."

"Loading it up as we speak, partner." When I hang up, I see Mavis has been listening. She's standing at the doorway to the kitchen, a worried look on her face. "Guess I better take a look at that tree," I say.

She points through the hall toward the front porch. "John Boyd's saw and gas are out there," she says. "You better get busy if you're driving back today."

The fog is thicker than I imagined, the air so wet that when I walk off the porch with the chain saw, I can feel my face dampen like rain is still falling. I haven't felt this kind of weather in over a year. I want to believe it's headed east, but nobody's saying anything about rain coming into the coast. We're just stuck in bad luck, that's all.

But out here, I need to be careful with the chain saw, cut with safety. I don't want to end up like Collie Walker, armless and spilling blood everywhere. John Boyd's saw is old, but it's sharp and well tuned. Still, it takes me into mid-morning to finish the tree. I section the trunk, then quarter it, having found a maul in the shed alongside the bow saw. I stack the split wood while Meemaw and Cassie rake the bark and sawdust up into piles. "I'll get that later," Meemaw says, looking at her watch. "You need to get on the road, Peck. It's getting late."

Meemaw cooks up a breakfast while I shower and shave. I'm anxious to leave, so I don't wait around any longer than I have to. It's going to take me the rest of the day to get back to the low country, so I'm packed and in my truck by noon. "At least it's all downhill," I say, joking with Cassie when she pushes the door to the truck closed, leans in like we're dating, like I'm her boyfriend all over again.

"You be careful going home," she says.

"I will," I say. "You be careful up here."

She smiles at that, touches me on the arm, squeezes it to hold me there. "Peck, I'm sorry about all of this. Sometimes I wish I'd never—"

"You go on," I say. "Figure it out. I'll just be at home." I start the truck's engine, the cab feeling empty. "Tell Kelly I love her. Let me know how she does next week."

"I wish we could go see her play," Cassie says. "I know she'd love to see both of us there."

"That'd be nice," I say. "But you can let me know. That'll be enough this time." Cassie sticks her head into the cab, kisses me lightly on the lips before whispering in my ear. "If it's ours, Peck, what then?"

I look into her eyes, hold her there, wanting Cassie to always be mine. "I could live with that," I tell her. "After everything that's happened, I could live with that."

She kisses my cheek before walking back to stand with Meemaw.

I put the truck in reverse to turn it around so I can head out, but instead I'm backing up until I am near the porch. I lean over the seat, yell out the window. "You find that deed, Cassie. Mavis, turn this house on its head, if you have to."

Cassie smiles, puts her arm through Meemaw's. "Just waiting for you to get out of here so we can get to work."

"Yes ma'am," I say, dropping the truck into first. I watch the house through my side-view mirror, Meemaw and Cassie on the porch waving. When I take a curve, they're gone.

At the end of the dirt road, I turn right onto hardtop snaking back through the mountains until I hit Highway 107 and leave Cashiers. I head out of the mountains toward a low country that is boiling hot and dry, fire beginning to eat up the land. Partee seemed worried when I talked to him on the phone, so I find myself accelerating, pushing the truck a little harder than I should coming down out of the mountains.

I go through Walhalla, think about finding Clay so I can drag his ass back to Garden City Beach just to make him work as hard as I'm going to work when I get back down there. But instead, I push straight through, find the line of least resistance, drive roads that take me through small hamlets and towns, two-lane highways that are off the Sunday tourist routes so I can get home fast.

I start seeing the smoke several hours later outside Bennettsville. It tricks the eye, towering into the sky like giant thunderheads. I don't smell it until I'm outside Florence, the late sun a soft white spot that is covered by a layer of smoke, the smell of campfire hovering in the dead air. It's hot, the heat oppressive even while I'm sitting at a stoplight. I can feel the smoke scratching at my eyes by the time I reach Galivants Ferry crossing the Little Pee Dee River. It's early evening by the time I'm in Aynor sitting in summer traffic. I stop for gas, call the station, and Lori answers. "What you doing there this late?" I say.

"They got us all on extra duty until they figure it out," she says. "It's not looking good. There're new fires breaking out all over the place."

"I see the smoke," I say. "It's pretty thick up this way."

"And you're not even in it yet, Peck," Lori says, with tears in her voice.

"I'll be there in about an hour," I say. "I'm coming straight down."

There's a pause on the other end of the line, Lori talking off the phone and then back to me. "I hate to tell you this, Peck, to add more to what's already there. But I need for you to go somewhere else first."

"Where?" I ask.

"Over to see Pops. He's had some sort of accident. That's all I know because they wouldn't tell me anything else. They've been trying to reach you since yesterday."

"I'll go there first then," I tell her. "If anything happens, if we're called in, you call the home, let them know so I can get the information when I arrive. Got that?"

"Okay," she says. "And Peck?"

"Yeah."

"I'm sorry about having to tell you all this. God, it's insane around here right now."

"We need rain, Lori. That's all it is. We just need some goddamn rain. I'll see you soon."

In Conway, it feels like I'm in dirty clouds. I pull into the Kingston's parking lot. Inside, Margaret tells me Pops has been transferred to the hospital in Myrtle Beach. "We moved him when he was stricken," she says, her face worried.

Everybody's coughing because of the air outside. The windows are closed, fans on in the hall and in the rooms, but there's still smoke in here. I'm glad Pops has been moved. The Myrtle Beach hospital will be better for him, the ocean breeze keeping the smoke from settling in. J.D. reminds me every day about the trauma center, says it's the best in the low country, so I'm hoping everything else is just as good.

Margaret follows me into Pops's room. His chair is there, empty, his crutches too. "Should I take these to him?" I ask.

"You can if you want," she says. "I don't know if he's able to walk or not, Mr. Peck. They couldn't tell at the time if he was having a stroke or something to do with his insulin." She points to a space beside his chair, says, "We found him right there on the floor, got him cared for as fast as we could." I thank Margaret for her kindness, then gather Pops's robe, his crutches, and the picture of Mom before heading down to Myrtle Beach.

If there is a disaster coming, you wouldn't know it by the tourists. The smell of smoke is everywhere. The light filtering through paints the sky in streaks of orange and red. Land is being lost, maybe lives too, but the season down here goes on. Nothing gets in the way of a good time. Near Myrtle Beach, the air clears a bit and I am able to roll down my window, let the air from the beaches fill in around me. I need to get ready to be a fireman again.

When I arrive at the hospital, I find Pops in intensive care, a new ICU that's just been built on. There's nothing much in the room but machines and a bed. The temperature's kept so low that I shiver when I enter. I've got five minutes, that's all they're giving me. The doctors won't allow anything more.

Pops has all these wires running out of him, a catheter, an IV, and a tube in his nose. He's breathing hard, a nurse volunteering that if he can't keep it up on his own, they're going to put him on a respirator. It's hard to recognize the body lying here as my father. He's so bloated now. I walk over, stand at his bed listening to the machines around him. I watch his heart beat, his pulse, listen to him struggle to breathe. "Hey Pops," I say. "How you doing?"

They've removed his teeth, his mouth drawn down into a desperate frown. He's not moving, his eyes closed like he'd rather just sleep, his skin chalky. I push loose strands of hair off his forehead, stroke his cheek. Pops was a big man years ago. His life has worn him down, whittled away at his body until what remains in this bed is only a small part of who he was. He could have taken better care of himself, but he lived like he wanted, did what he could, what he had to do. I'm proud of him for that. I lean down, whisper in his ear. "Be strong, Pops. Do what you can. I'll see you soon." I take his hand in mine, kiss it, and then lay it underneath the sheet. I don't want him to be cold. I ask a nurse, "Is he cold? It's so cold in here."

She comes over to his bed, looks at the machines, touches his forehead with her hand, feels his arms. "He's all right," she says. "When you're fighting like he is, the body is better off in a cool environment. He's doing okay."

I kiss Pops on the forehead, his skin like a thin layer of paper. I put the picture of Mom on the small table beside his bed, the crutches in the corner, hand the robe to the nurse. A doctor who looks younger than me explains what the stroke has done to Pops, a bleeding stroke that has paralyzed his left side. He says his chances aren't good, too many complications going on between the stroke and his diabetes, that he might be blind when he wakes up—if he wakes up. "He hasn't lost the will yet," he says, "but I don't know how much strength he has left. There's just nothing else we can do. It's going to be up to him now."

I tell him to let Pops decide, not to go to any extremes over this. "He would want to go when he's ready," I tell him. The doctor agrees. I explain where I'm headed, how he should call Lori if things take a turn, and then leave without looking back at Pops's room. I didn't say good-bye to him, not a real good-bye. I just couldn't do that. He has the right to fight, if he wants to. I want to give him that much. It's the least I can do.

I head back out, wanting to stop at home before I report in to the station. I work the surface streets to get to Highway 17, make the marsh in good time, and find the house quiet, untouched since Kelly and I left on Friday. It's Sunday evening now, just two days later, but it's hard to get my hands around everything going on—Pops sick, Cassie pregnant, and a fire burning up the low country, the likes unseen in years down here. I go inside, drop off bags and gather some extra clothes, two uniforms from the closet. I pull out a knapsack and canteen, a compass I've used when Kelly and I have gone camping. It's all I need to bring. I'll depend on Strachen to provide the rest.

I make the station by seven-thirty. The Quonset is all lit up, the Pirsch gone. I worry I've missed the call, that my crew is already out in some field fighting fire, and then I see J.D. still inside working on his supplies. I pull around back, park, and get out. J.D. smiles when he sees me. "About time," he says.

"You know," I say when I walk up to shake his hand. "I leave you for a couple of days and the whole county goes to shit."

"Lesson learned, then," he says. "Never take a vacation again."

"Or just never come back," I say, smiling.

We walk back into the Quonset. J.D.'s lugging his EMT packs. "You got to come back," he says. "You don't know how to do anything else."

"Give me time, rookie, I could learn."

J.D. laughs at that.

"You got everything you need here?" I ask.

"I'm not sure I need any of it at all in a wildfire."

"Never know what's going to be out there," I say. "Just keep it portable. It's got to go on your back when we get there. It's going to be mostly burns and cuts and broken bones, so pack accordingly."

Partee pulls up in the Pirsch, having filled its tank off a nearby hydrant. He smiles big. "Welcome back, Chief."

He kills the truck's engine, climbs down out of the cab, tossing me the keys. "I'm officially giving you this place back," he says. "I don't need to be chief no more."

"Not sure I want it either," I say. "What's the latest news?"

Partee tells me that Roddy and Johnny Cash are already gone. Surfside called in all the volunteers to go fight so that online firemen could stay in their stations. "But it ain't getting no better," he says. "Strachen wants the chiefs to meet Tuesday morning. He'll tell us then who's going, said be ready to leave right from there, so I figured that gives us tonight and tomorrow to get all our equipment packed and ready to go."

Lori comes out with fresh coffee, smiles when she sees me. "How's Pops?" she asks.

I take the hot brew from her hands. "Not good," I tell her. The news seems to work on everyone. "I'll keep checking in for you," she says. "Let you know if anything changes on that front."

"I'd appreciate that, Lori, thanks." I follow her back to the office so I can see the latest reports, the news on inland fires. She's standing there looking at me, the radio popping off in the background behind us. "How's Cassie?" she asks.

"Fine," I say. "She's pregnant." When I look at her, Lori's watching the boys through the window, her cup of coffee held in both hands like she's trying to get warm. "Says it's probably mine."

"That's good then, right?" she says.

We look at each other for a long moment, no words, but I know she's thinking about the shit Cassie's putting me through, how she could do a lot better given the chance.

"Yeah, it's okay," I say.

She smiles then, looks down at her coffee. "You sure about that?"

"Yeah, pretty sure." J.D. sticks his head into the door, tells me he needs Lori for a moment if I'm finished with her. He looks at me, then at Lori, then back to me, says, "But I can come back in a minute if you want."

"No," Lori says, "we're done here," then pushes past J.D. to get out of the room.

J.D. looks at me. "You ready, Chief?"

"Ready for rain," I say. "Tonight, lots of it."

J.D. leans his shoulder hard on the door frame, his head tucked down to his chest like he's trying to remember something. When he looks up there's a big smile on his face. " 'Thy fate is the common fate of all, into each life some rain must fall.' Henry Wadsworth Longfellow."

I smile, give him one better: "I want rain as thick as fog, gully washers, cats and dogs. Author unknown."

He pops the frame of the door like a high five, laughs out loud, and then leaves the office. I watch him through the window walking quickly toward the Pirsch, Lori following close behind. He needs to do something about that girl before I do. I'll talk to J.D.

about that when all of this is over. He needs to know what's right there in front of that big nose of his.

Partee's figured right about the time it will take to get our supplies ready, air tanks filled, everything in backpacks. We take off the truck what we won't need, all the water rescue equipment, my surfboard, the inflatable raft. I look in the office for any notes or manuals we might have that will tell us what to expect in a wildfire. To be honest, I haven't been in a fire like this before.

I can tell you how to fight a structural fire, how to ventilate it, open up a building so the heat and smoke can escape. I can show you how to fog the nozzle, get down on all fours and crawl through hot black water to face a fire, not walk away into cooler air, but face it straight on, get to the source and hit that son-of-a-bitch with everything you've got. I can do that with confidence, tell the fire it's not going to win because I've been there many times before. I've punched out ceilings and walls, opened doors to find fire waiting for me, its fingers leaping out to grab hold and do me harm. I know the kind of fire that consumes buildings and houses, mobile homes and cars.

But in my time as a fireman, I have never been in a wildfire like the one burning out of control in Horry and Georgetown counties right now. I can't really tell you about its nature except to say it burns as hot and is as full of surprises as any other. By Tuesday morning, Partee, J.D., and I are going to go fight that fire because that's what we do. Pops always said that the measure of a man is made by the dangers he faces straight on in life, how he conducts himself in the face of unknown odds. There's just no way to know what we'll get until we arrive on scene and put our feet on the ground. We'll just have to wait and see.

Cassie

On Monday morning, I get motivated. All the pantry drawers are emptied, my hand sliding across the bottom of each, feeling for evidence of a deed. I look in the cabinets, take out Momma's china, dishes and bowls that are as mismatched as we are against someone like John Boyd. They are cracked and chipped, some that she brought with her when she was married, tin plates like out of some pioneer movie, many that were given to her over the years by members of the church, cups and bowls, pans and baking dishes. There is nothing in the cabinets, nothing stuffed at the back of a drawer or in the pantry. I have pulled all the canned goods out, looked behind the refrigerator. Nothing.

Momma is in the living room going through drawers and finding my father's hand-scribbled notes for sermons he preached without writing anything down. A note or two was all it ever took to get him started, then the hand of God would take over and my father could preach all day. Sometimes after the sermon he would not remember what he said, the words coming out of him like he was in a trance. Sundays wore him out, his hikes up to Whiteside in the early morning and then preaching way past noon. He would come home exhausted and sleep all afternoon, only to rise for an early dinner and then lead Vespers until late in the evening. My father was a man of God, good or bad, but he also took care of his family, and so I know that deed is here, if we can just find it in time.

"Parker?" Momma says, like my father might be somewhere in the house. When I hear this, I worry. I walk into the living room and find her standing in front of the bookcase. It's as much a mess in here as in the kitchen, papers strewn everywhere, cushions out of chairs and the loveseat. Momma's looking into her hand like what she holds is a precious jewel. "Parker?" she says again as if she's calling for him to come see this too. She's holding my father's small tarnished cross, sees me looking at it in her fingers, the chain broken at the clasp.

"Where did you find it?" I ask.

"It was in the small chest on the shelf next to Parker's Bible," she says. "I had forgotten all about it."

"Of all things for you to find right now," I say.

Momma's face warms. "It's a sign, Cassie. Parker's here with us."

I come over, hug Momma tight, her small frame fragile in my arms. "Tell him not to be angry," I say. "Tell him that I need him to love me this time."

My careless words pull her away. She looks at me with tears in her eyes. "Cassie, your father always loved you. What happened back then broke his heart. Don't ever think he didn't love you." I kiss her on the forehead, touch the cross held tight in her fingers.

"Maybe Parker can help us," she says, her voice quiet, calm.

"That would be nice, Momma," I say. "Just tell him to point to where the deed is."

She laughs at me, then, "You tell him," she says. "He never listened to a word I said." We both can laugh at that, and when I raise my arms, ready to summon my father's spirit, Momma is horrified. "Cassie, no," she says, embarrassed by my mockery, "now stop that."

We give up on the living room for now, start in on the hall closet just as a car drives up to the house. It's John Boyd. "What does he want?" I ask.

"His chain saw, no doubt," Momma says, rubbing the cross between her fingers. We watch John Boyd get out of his car and walk toward the door. "Come on," she says, pulling me toward the front porch. "He doesn't need to see any of this. He doesn't need to know what we're trying to find."

We meet him on the front steps. It is noon, lunchtime, the air warm, the high light flat and full on Momma's front yard. It shadows John Boyd's face, makes him look like the monster I think he is as he puts a foot on the bottom step, his hat in his hand, face cocked upward to smile at Momma. "Hey, Mavis," John Boyd says. He looks at me then, dragging his smile along. "Hey, Cassie, looks like Peck did some good work over here."

"It took him awhile," I say.

"Well, it don't look like he needed any more help from me than that chain saw." John Boyd nods at the saw and his gas and oil sitting on the steps beside his foot.

"No," I say. "He finished up and got out of here early yesterday afternoon."

"I've been reading about those fires in the low country," he says. "We're blessed up here this year. Lots of rain, so we won't have to go through that. I hope he's safe, Cassie. I know you probably worry."

"All the time," I tell him.

"Do you ever get used to it," he asks, "the danger like that?"

I don't like talking about something so personal with this man. I don't want to show him my feelings. He's the enemy now, and I just want him to go away so we can get back to work. "It wears on you," I say, offering nothing more.

"Well," he says, picking up the chain saw. "Let's just hope you don't have to worry too much this time. Peck seems like a good man."

Better than you could ever be is what I want to say, but I don't. Momma and I stand like sentinels ready to do battle if he tries to get by us and come inside. John Boyd begins to get it, to sense something is wrong. He smiles at Momma. "Mavis, you're awful quiet, cat got your tongue?"

"No, John Boyd, just don't have anything to say."

I step down to pick up the gas, help him leave. "Let me get this for you."

"You don't have to do that," John Boyd says. I hand him the gas and he starts to turn around. "Can I have a word with you, Cassie?"

I look at Momma, then to the door behind which papers are scattered like a bomb has gone off in the house.

I smile, take his arm. "Sure," I say. "Let's talk while I walk you back to your car."

At the trunk, John Boyd puts the chain saw down, searches for his keys. "Have you had a chance to talk to Mavis yet?" he asks.

"We've been talking," I say.

"About the property?" John Boyd's eyes shift back and forth when he speaks, looks around like he wants no one else to hear us.

"We've had some discussion on that," I say. "But she says the land's hers."

This seems to deflate John Boyd, his sigh pulling his shoulders down like an old dog that's just lost a scent. "Well, she needs to understand, Cassie."

"She will, John Boyd. Just give me a little more time."

"Time's short," he says. "One day a bulldozer will head up that drive and there won't be a thing I can do about it."

"I know that," I tell him. "But you said August, didn't you?"

"I said maybe August," John Boyd says to correct me. "They're moving fast and might be here sooner. Now you've got to explain to Mavis about the land. If you don't, then I'm going to come up here and do it myself, but that won't be pretty and Mavis will just die if I have to tell her."

"Like I said, John Boyd, I told her. She thinks the land is hers."

"And like I told you the other day, there's no deed. Now will you please tell her that?" The smile on his face is frozen, forced.

He comes so close, I can feel him breathe. It scares me, his eyes dark, sweat trickling down his temples, running until it disappears into gray sideburns. "I'll keep talking to her, John Boyd. That's all I can promise right now."

He pulls away, fiddles with his keys until he finds the one to open the car's trunk. Once the saw and gas are safely stored, he turns to push at me one more time. "Cassie, you need to talk to Mavis, now," he says.

"I told you I would, John Boyd."

He looks at me hard, tries to push me away with his stare, but I won't give him that. He won't win this time. "I'll let you know when she's ready," I say. "It'll be by August, just like you said." I start to walk away.

"Sooner," he says, his voice rising, but I don't stop. I keep going, my back to him as I meet Momma on the steps.

"Come on," I whisper, "and don't look back at him."

We go inside, the screened door slapping against the frame. From the window, we watch John Boyd get in his car, spin tires, the back wheels tearing up Momma's grass.

In the end, the house does not yield a thing. Neither does the attic, where Momma stored boxes from the church after my father died. Out in the shed, there are files and notes, several ledgers from the church. I am hopeful when we find these, dust covered, the edges of the pages nibbled by field mice. But in the end, there is no evidence of the land being conveyed to my father before he died. The ledgers are filled with his handwritten reports on pledges and tithes, church accounts that offer nothing more than proof my father was the pastor for over twenty years.

Momma's hope fades the longer we look and come up empty-handed, her fingers stroking the cross, its tarnished surface little help in making the deed real. "It's not here," she says. "It's just not here."

"Is there anywhere else we could look?" I ask.

"No," she says flatly. "I need to stop this. I don't feel well."

We take iced tea in the backyard, sit in chairs, and watch the sun pass over Whiteside. "Maybe John Boyd was right," Momma says. "Maybe I'm just imagining there was a paper because I want there to be one."

"We've turned the house upside down," I say, "that's for sure. I really thought the ledgers would help out."

"He was a very meticulous man," she says, looking at the cross like my father is there in her hands. "He would have had a deed if we were supposed to have one." Momma gets up from her chair. "It's two-thirty," she says, surprised by the late hour. "We need to eat something."

Sitting here watching, I realize how tired I am, how exhausted I have become in all this searching. I want to blame myself for not being a better daughter, for not understanding the terrible ordeal I put my parents through when I got pregnant and they were forced to make choices. I have made decisions all my life, none that were any better than those my parents made. Just look at what I've done lately. Who am I to judge my father, or Momma, or Peck for that matter? I have been able to live my life free of self-judgment by keeping everyone so far away that no one was ever close enough to know me for who I really was.

I can't even tell you one person in Garden City Beach whom I could call my best friend. I have been invisible for the past fifteen years, a chameleon that blended into the background, too afraid because of what I might actually see when I revealed myself. I may have thought Clay Taylor was my way out, but he's really not. I know that now. Our relationship was just me and Peck all over again. Now he's in Walhalla hurting like everyone else. I am sorry for my life, for the way I have treated those who loved me. Searching for this deed has proven fruitless. I don't want that to be the conclusion to the rest of my life. I've got to try to be better with Kelly and this baby growing inside me. I've got to try and work it out with Peck.

I hear the screened door slap shut, Momma's light footsteps bringing her back to the shade of the oak trees where I am ready to apologize for the years that I have been invisible. Momma looks at me with clear and steady eyes. "Come," she says.

"Where?" I ask, my legs tired and sore.

"Just come with me."

We walk across the yard in silence. She holds my hand, her other reaching across to clasp my arm and pull us close. She's smiling, the cross held in her fingers, touching against my arm. When we reach the back door to the house, she stops and looks at me. "When I came in, I started thinking about things," she says. "I was sitting right there in the kitchen and was thinking about Parker and all this mess, and that's when it hit me."

"What hit you, Momma?"

"The deed," she says. "I asked Parker out loud just like you told me to."

"But Momma, I was just—"

"No, Cassie, listen to me. I asked him where the deed to this property was, and then I thought, well, if I go to the Bible for guidance, like Parker always did, maybe the answer would be in the scriptures. Maybe Parker would speak to me through scripture. And there it was."

"What are you talking about, Momma?"

"The deed was in the scriptures. It was in the Bible." Momma laughs likes she's crazy, doubles over in silliness. "Parker's Bible," she says again, "the deed's been there all this time. I just never thought to look."

When we walk into the kitchen, the deed is on the table, the original deed, not a copy. It is folded and slipped inside a watermarked envelope. When I remove the deed, the paper is crisp, the edges sharp. It is as if the document had just been signed and sealed the day before, no age on it at all. John Boyd's signature is there, written in dark blue ink. And that's not all. With the deed is a letter that John Boyd wrote to my father explaining the conditions of the land exchange, how he would remain the pastor of Whiteside Cove and that in consideration of his duties, the land would be his. It is a general warranty deed, signed and notarized, May 24, 1961. Two days before my father died.

"It never was recorded," I say.

"What do you mean?"

"The deed. It was never recorded because he died before taking it to Sylva."

"He never told me it had to be taken anywhere," Momma says.

"Of course not," I say. "He was planning to do it himself."

It starts to make sense now. John Boyd gave the deed to my father to register in Sylva. But when he died, that didn't happen. John Boyd let it go, never followed through himself, and now he's trying to cash in. I look at the time. It is three o'clock, time enough. "Get your purse," I tell her.

"Where are we going?" she asks, a worried look crossing her face. "I'm not dressed to go anywhere. I'm all dirty and my hair's a mess."

"I don't care," I say. "We're going to Sylva. If John Boyd finds out we have this, he and his cronies might try to stop us, so we have to hurry."

It takes a lot more to get Momma into the car, but we manage to leave the house by three-thirty. I don't know if the Deeds Office is open past four, but we have no choice. We have to go. The road out to Highway 64 from Momma's runs red with mud, the storms having turned the scarred land bloody. No one is home at John Boyd's—at least all the cars are gone. It worries me a little seeing this, wondering if he has gone to Sylva sensing something wrong, the way I talked to him this morning. I should have kept my mouth shut and not aggravated him. He might be taking some kind of action right this minute to render this deed null and void. Momma watches out for his car along the way while my eyes are glued to the rearview mirror, hoping he hasn't found us out.

We travel behind logging trucks most of the way. Momma sits in the passenger seat with worry all over her face. She twists the cross in her fingers, nervously fidgeting, as I drive too close, taking curves recklessly. When the last truck pulls off of 64, I find empty road in front of me the rest of the way to Sylva.

The courthouse doors are still open, but the basement is dark, the Deeds Office having closed at four. I pound on the door until a light flickers on, a man worriedly coming from the back office to see what all the commotion is about. It's the same man who showed me the deed plot two days ago when Peck was still here. He's in shirtsleeves this time, caught frumpy and unraveled. "We're closed," he says, waving his hand to go away.

"Wait," I yell, holding the deed to the window. "I found it," I say, "the new deed." He stops for a moment, squints toward the doors until he finally recognizes me.

"We're open tomorrow," he says. "Eight o'clock sharp."

"No," I yell. "That won't do." I point against the glass door to the clock on the wall next to him. "It's only four-fifteen," I plead, "and we can't come back tomorrow. You said if I found the deed . . . well, here it is. You said it could be a case for fraud."

I think it's the word *fraud* that captures his interest. He stops for a moment, his eyes staring at the deed I have plastered against the glass door. He rolls his fingers across the counter, looks at the clock, pats the marble top twice, his mind made up, the key in his hand to let us in. I present the document for recording. He checks the signatures, the notary, and then tells me it will be filed first thing tomorrow morning.

"But it's official, right?"

The man takes out a county seal, stamps the document, records the date and time, 4:00 P.M., though it is nearly quarter to five, and then looks up over his glasses at me. "It's official, yes."

I turn to Momma, take her in my arms and hug her tightly. "The land's yours," I tell her. "All of it."

She seems lost by what we have just done, the cross tight in her fist. "The Arnold Palmer's golf course?"

"That too," I say, smiling at the man, "if you want to let them build it."

He smiles at Momma, tells her the deed still has to be filed. "But," he says, "for all practical purposes . . ." And then he nods his head.

"Can I have two copies?" I ask.

He doesn't like having to do more, but he takes the deed and walks quietly into a back room where I can hear a machine warming up, then laboring to print a copy. When he returns he asks for a dollar, points to a sign that reads *50 cents per copy,* and so I fish out the money from my purse. "Thanks," I say. "You were great."

The man smiles, follows us to the door to make sure he gets it locked behind us. I stand in the basement of the courthouse for a minute longer, looking at the copies of Momma's property deed. It is proof of my father's good work, proof of my mother's ownership of the land.

When we leave the courthouse, I am suddenly tired, Momma remembering she never made us lunch. She spots a small diner on Main Street in Sylva. It's near closing time, but the young waitress is patient, let's us sit and take our time. My stomach cramps a little to take away my hunger. Still I try to eat and not let Momma see that I don't feel well. I think of that night when Peck and I were just starting out, how different this dinner is, yet how they are connected in so many ways, both trying to change misfortune into something good. I want to enjoy this for a little bit longer, so I remain quiet, picking at my food.

When we are done, I pay the bill, and leave a big tip for the young girl who waited so patiently. We walk to the car, the copies of the deed held tightly in my hand. I tell Momma that there is one more thing I want to do before we head back to the house. "We need to pay a visit to a dear old friend, I say."

"Who?" she asks.

I take her by the arm, hold her close. "You'll see." And then we walk in silence.

When we are in Cashiers, off Highway 107, I slow down and look for John Boyd's house. It sits in the darkness like it has been abandoned, all the cars missing in his yard. I pull over, stop in front, and tell Momma to wait while I go to the door. I cross the front yard, my eyes scanning the property, afraid at any moment John Boyd will jump out from one of the dark shadows and catch me trespassing.

My hands are shaking when I reach the front porch and then deliver to the mail slot the best piece of bad news John Boyd will ever get in his life. I fold a copy of the deed like a letter to be mailed, write bluntly the words *Don't trespass on Momma's land again,* and slip it quickly through the mail slot. The feathery sound of paper hitting floor inside assures me that the message has been delivered. "Thanks for taking care of Momma," I whisper.

I run back feeling like a schoolgirl. Momma's face is lit by the dashboard lights, her eyes glaring out into the dark, worriedly searching for me until I reach the car and unlatch the door. As I slide into the driver's seat, she says, "Are you sure we should do this?"

"Momma, it's your land," I tell her.

"I know," she says. "But it seems so reckless the way John Boyd can be."

"What's reckless is what he did to you. It's your land and John Boyd needs to know that, right now, right this minute."

The distance we put between the Bel Air and John Boyd's house eases Momma back. I can feel her relax as she touches my arm, breathes deeply before she speaks. "You know, I'm glad you did this," she says.

"Momma, you don't need—"

"No," she interrupts, "you need to hear this, Cassie. I'm telling you this from me and your father. You did a good thing today."

"Well I don't think John Boyd's going to be all too happy about it," I say. "Probably best not to answer the door when he comes to visit next time." I accelerate down the road, the Bel Air slipping underneath us in the mud. "In the morning, I want to find a good lawyer," I tell her. "I have a feeling we're going to need one."

We are quiet the rest of the way, exhausted from all that has happened. I think about calling Peck to tell him about the deed, but also to talk about us—how the adventure of the past two days has revealed all that is good in my life. I keep this to myself, though. I don't want to share it with Momma right now. I drive on, silently keeping to the road as best I can until my headlights find the front drive, and we are back at Momma's house.

Peck

Nobody sleeps. There's too much adrenaline tonight, too much unknown about this one. We usually don't know when something catastrophic is coming. Most of the time the fire bell rings, we get up, take the call, and are off to some sort of disaster that five minutes ago we had no idea even existed. I've been doing this long enough now to sleep easy in the bunk room. It's almost my first home. If you can't settle down while on rotation, you're going to burn out. I've seen it happen more than once. You make your call, do your duty, and then let it go, come home to clean the equipment, fill out the paperwork, or climb into bed and sleep. That's what we usually expect of our lives down here. But this thing inland is different. It's all over television, the local news making big hay over the fire, so we know before we're even told whether or not we will go in that it's bad out there, one of the biggest fires in the history of South Carolina. Mark my word, we're going in.

Still we try to act like it's nothing different. J.D. takes one of the cots out of the bunk room and gives it to Lori. She's sleeping over the next couple of nights because Strachen's told everyone they have to stay on duty. She'll run dispatch out of the station, keep the line open with Surfside so we can stay in touch. When we settle down, there's a lot of tossing and turning in the dark. No one says anything. No one wants to be accused of keeping anyone else awake, but we're not sleeping—nobody, not a single fireman.

It gives me too much time to think about things, Pops and Cassie. It's all so twisted and messed up, everything balancing on an edge that I can't get to. I can't reach out, grab them and pull them back. I can't stop any of it. I don't think Pops is going to make it. He didn't look good when I saw him tonight. And then there's Cassie and Clay. I'm so frustrated by what they've done. I put it out there to Cassie before I left, that we could work something out if she wanted, but I don't know how a baby would fit into all of that. I guess it can't if it's Clay's baby. Although if I let myself imagine it, I can see us raising that child as ours, no matter who the father is.

It's hard to put it all together with all the heat and fire that's out there. But Cassie's my wife, and there's something that brings our bone and blood together. It ties us tight and makes cutting her loose something akin to tearing half my soul out of my body. It just can't be, I keep telling myself. I need my soul whole, I need Cassie back home.

At first light on Tuesday, I ease myself off the cot and walk out into the station in my underwear. Lori's already in her office, and I can smell fresh brew as I head out the door to find old cutoffs in the bed of my truck. She catches me in my boxers, smiles, and when I act like I'm going to shoot her the moon, she doesn't even flinch, almost challenges me to go ahead and do it. But I chicken out, slip through the door acting embarrassed, waving a finger in the air, a playful scolding for looking at me like that. It feels good to play with Lori. It eases the tension that's already building with the morning heat. Outside, I change into the cutoffs and then grab my board, walk back in to tell Lori I need some time at the beach before we go in to fight this fire. The station is ready, everything packed and loaded. "I'll come get you, if I need you," she says, handing me a paper cup full of hot coffee for the walk down.

All along the beach, the air is smoky like the fire is just on the other side of the marsh, but I know it's a long way inland from here, no chance of it getting all the way to the coast. We'll have to go to it this time. So far, nobody's died, but thousands of acres have been singed and burned. The television news showed us houses last night, farmland burned away, a trailer park that was destroyed. Everyone made it out, the fire slow enough in its movement that emergency personnel were able to evacuate and keep people alive. There's talk of the winds changing. A southwesterly shift will keep the fire from coming toward the beach, but it will also fuel the flames inland. Everyone who's going in is getting his mind right for the changing conditions. Fast fire is just too unpredictable, too hard to contain.

The sun peeks out from the horizon down toward Myrtle Beach, its rays a colorful plume. I've never seen such beautiful colors, the way they reach out of the water, yellow and orange, deep reds and purple streamers, smoke-filled air giving the whole strand a show. When I get to the water, there is a lone body already waiting. Teddy's beat me again. I wave, throw on some fresh wax, and hook up with him before he can catch his first ride in.

"Thought you were in the mountains." Teddy's looking back over his shoulder, watching the swells form.

"I was," I say, "but I came back."

"To surf with little old me?"

"Yeah man, is there any other reason?"

"Not that I can think of." He pushes off, paddles fast, but pulls back when his move is too late to catch the front side of the swell. "You get Kelly back to camp?"

"I did," I say. "There's been a lot of rain up there, so she hadn't missed too much."

"Lot of rain, huh?" Teddy's shaking his head. "Did you bring any of that back with you?"

"Nope," I say. "I was hoping it would just roll on down here behind me, but looks like that didn't happen."

We both catch the next wave. I'm on the inside of the break, let my arms extend to hold me above the board, guiding it, edging down into its trough before I set my feet. It closes out fast into foamy soup, the ride short as I kick out. Teddy works the wash for a little more distance in and then he kicks out, dropping down on his board to paddle back out beyond the break.

We sit there in the early light, quiet for a moment just thinking about surfing, looking for the next ride in. "You should have brought some of that rain back, bro," Teddy says, finally. "It's getting serious down here."

I nod in agreement, tell him we're going in later today.

"Where to?" he asks.

"I don't know yet. Strachen's going to tell us in a couple of hours."

"Goddamn, Peck, you better be careful. They're saying ten thousand acres are burning, thirty maybe, before the rain gets here."

"Is there rain coming?" I ask.

"Hell, I don't know," he says. "They've been talking about rain since Easter." He looks out behind him, sees something good coming. His eyes widen, his face pulls all that skin up into a big smile. "Jesus," he says, "now there you go."

When I look back, I see it, a wave much larger than the rest, a rogue wave that pulls both of us up as we paddle onto its front. I'm up fast, make a cutback, pull off the top, and let my board slide down the face. Teddy's right behind me. He's on a long board so he's just cruising, whooping and hollering. I watch him go low to try and take me out, to swing around me, make me pull up and kick out of the best wave I'll ride today, but I'm not having that. I cut back at him. The surprise move loosens his feet, throws his balance off, and then wipes him out, the words "Son of a bitch!" lost in the wave that pounds along the beach. I laugh at Teddy when he finds his feet, his pants nearly at his knees. "Fucking A," he says, his middle finger high in the air, so I know the bastard is all right.

"Never try to cut off a fireman who knows he's going into fire," I say, walking up the beach to get Teddy's board. "You need to wear a leash," I tell him, but I know he never will. Teddy's old-school out here. He just smiles.

"I'll get a leash when I get a dog," he says. We laugh hard. I love Teddy like a brother. I'd walk through fire for him and he'd do the same for me. We paddle back out into the surf together.

I figure I've got a couple more rides, if I want to wait, and then I'll head back to the station. Lori will tell Partee I'm on the beach, but he always figures that one out for himself, so I'm not worried I'm being missed right now. I tell Teddy about Lori seeing me in my underwear, and the story turns his face into a grin. "Bro, you be careful with that one," he says. "You've got to fight fire today."

"Hell, I could be talked out of doing that," I tell him.

Teddy looks for something out beyond us to ride in, but the water's flattening under our boards. "Leave the young to the young, bro," he says. "Lori's too good for old waterlogged civil servants like us."

"Probably so," I say, "but I'm not that old." We get a good laugh talking like this, feeling the ordinary trying to seep back into our lives. I need that. I need Cassie and Kelly back home. I need Pops well. I need the ocean smooth and predictable again.

After a few short rides, the waves die out and we call it quits. Teddy ties my board to his patrol car and gives me a lift back to the station. Everybody's up when we get there. Partee's been to the pancake house up on 17, so there's good food waiting for us all. Teddy, of course, invites himself to the meal. The coffee's rich and hot. Teddy changes clothes right there in the Quonset, in front of Lori when she dares him to do it. She should know better than to dare Teddy to do anything. She runs and locks the door to her office, pulls the little shade over the window before he can get his pants down. We're all standing there laughing our asses off when the call comes in, giving us the time to report to Surfside.

It all gets serious after that. I go inside, take a shower, put on a pair of blue khakis, standard issue, and a station T-shirt. I don't even look for the button-down and my lieutenant bars. Today, I'll be a fireman. I'll fight like everyone else. If they need me to be a lieutenant, then I will, but I won't ask for any favors because of rank.

Before I leave the bunk room, I find one of Pops's pennies. I roll it around with my fingers then let my eyes drift out the window toward Myrtle Beach, some seventeen miles away. "Help me be lucky, Pops," I say. I slip the penny inside my sock, feel it rest snug against the arch of my foot, then I tie my boots tight.

We load up into the truck, say good-bye to Teddy, who pops his siren for us a couple of times when he spins out, headed toward Surfside for his own roll call. I let Partee drive, J.D. ride shotgun. I'm in the third seat when we pull out. The roads near the beach are already filled with traffic, but I don't mind it this time. I'd rather not get there at all because I know after the meeting, we'll go fight fire. I tell Partee to take it easy, to not be too anxious. "We'll get there when we get there," I say. He looks through the mirror at me like he thinks I'm joking, but I'm not. I nod, tell him to keep his eyes on the road.

It's nearly ten by the time we show up, hot as hell, barely any wind coming off the water. I hear someone say that might be a good sign and we're all encouraged until Strachen tells us the weather's going to change over the next couple of days, high winds and heat until the rain can get here. Then he levels with us. "We'll all get a turn at this," he says. "I've been working with Georgetown County. We're going to blend our crews up and down the strand." He pulls out a rolling blackboard, the one we use when there's a training class, search and rescue, or first-aid safety. This time he's attached a map, black lines and colored sections dividing it up like the thing might be carved, cut up, and served to us for lunch.

"The state's brought in some fire jumpers from out west," he says. "They won't work as a unit, but will split up in the worst areas here to lead local fire crews. There's a handful going in up off Highway 9 out of North Myrtle. But most of them will be down here where the fires are burning the worst."

When someone objects to the plan, some commonsense reason that we all understand since we live and work down here, Strachen holds up his hands to quiet us down. "These boys might not be homegrown," he says, "but we're going to let them run this one since they got the experience. Local rangers will get you to your location where you'll meet up with these guys. They've already been fighting fire for a couple of days, but there's still a lot to do. You need to be careful walking in."

I ask Strachen if we're taking the trucks in. "We spent a lot of time prepping yesterday," I tell him. "I'm hoping it's not all for nothing."

"You can drive down to the access points of course, but after that, it's a walk in. There will be supplies waiting for you, equipment you'll need in hand to work on a fire like this. It's beyond putting water on it, boys. We're just trying to control it until either rain comes or it decides to burn itself out."

He pulls out another large piece of paper, tapes it over the map to show us the schedule he's come up with. How, I have no idea. "Litchfield and Surfside are going to stay put for now. Garden City Beach, you're going in with Pawleys Island to fight fire." He points to an area I'm not familiar with, something way off Highway 378, past Pee Dee Crossroads. The area is shaded bright red, a hot spot burning out of control right now.

"Garden City Beach and Pawleys will pull out on Thursday night, Litchfield and Surfside will go in, three days in, three days out until we extinguish this fire. Peck, when you get back, you'll be responsible for working any emergency down toward Murrells Inlet and Litchfield. It's hot and smoky and still dangerous everywhere around here. Nothing is out of reach of a spark, so everybody stay on their toes. Peck, you boys be careful and come back here safe. Listen, keep your heads up and fight a good fire."

We all mill around, talk about things that don't have a connection to what we're about to do. Teddy shows up with a small stray pup he's found wandering Highway 17. It's peed on his seat, but he doesn't give a shit. It's got fleas, ticks sucking blood off the soft meat of its ears, probably needs to be dewormed. He's feeding it half of a Krispy Kreme donut.

"You're going to kill that dog if you feed it shit like that," I say.

"This little thing just ran across Highway 17," Teddy tells me. "A truck and two cars nearly flattened the little fellow. He can eat a donut, Peck." I smile at Teddy. It's funny to see such a big man holding something so small and feeding it. "You can keep it out at my place if Mo gives you any shit," I say.

"Hell, she'll probably want to keep the dog and make *me* stay out there," he says, his grin pulling his face up into wrinkles. We laugh about the dog, the little pup chewing on Teddy's finger, but then something hits him. He looks at me hard. It's a seriousness I don't often see coming from Teddy. "Peck, you got to be careful out there," he says. "Lot more fire than any of us are used to seeing."

We shake hands, Teddy pulling me in close. Strachen comes out of dispatch, and when he sees we are still here, starts in on us. "You should've been gone fifteen minutes ago," he says. There's no screaming, just Strachen being Strachen. "There's a crew waiting for you, so get out of here."

I pet Teddy's head, the dog's too, tell him I'll be back. We climb in the Pirsch and I ride in the third seat again, let Partee and J.D. get us to where we're going. I sit behind them with a lot on my mind. I'd like to call Cassie, tell her where I'm headed, let her know I love her and Kelly real bad. Pops is there too. I feel lost without everyone even though I'm sitting among men I call my brothers. I pull the radio, let Lori know that we are 10-76, moving and responding. "You all be careful out there," she says, her voice strong and full in the radio's speaker.

"10-4 that," I say and then hang the mike back up.

We turn on our emergency lights because we're on a call, but don't use our siren. The inland traffic is light—maybe the fire is getting to people down here after all. It's almost noon and it's pretty much a clear shot out to Conway. Partee moves without effort, something that seems strange to us all, though no one remarks openly about it. We just watch the road, look at each other when we pass an intersection where there should be a fist of traffic. We move up Highway 707, much farther inland than we've ever taken a call, hook up with 544 and then 501 into Conway. I think about Pops when we pass Kingston Convalescent Home, but he's not there, not now anyway. He's safe in Myrtle Beach.

The smoke in Conway is thick, no wind yet. It hugs the ground, building into a dense cover that's almost impossible to see through. We make the turn onto 378, going slower now because of smoke. When we pass Pee Dee Crossroads, it doesn't take long for us to run up onto the first roadblock. They're not letting anyone through here right now except firemen and locals who live up and down this road. No one's been evacuated in this section, but it's near impossible to breathe good air, so I know the call is coming soon.

We're waved through, the Pirsch crawling along the road, our emergency lights bouncing off white air. The smell of fire is starting to burn our throats and noses. We cross the Little Pee Dee River and things get worse. The staging area shows up near the intersection of Highway 378 and 41, an old cornfield already plowed under because of the drought, the crop a total loss. Partee pulls up alongside trucks and emergency vehicles from Pawleys and other stations working out of three different counties. A lot of firemen have already gone out into the field. It's a walk in from here.

The scene's really nothing like Strachen said. There's no crew waiting for us, only a ranger, a boy who seems too young to be telling us what to do. He's wearing a yellow hard hat and is covered in ash, his face marked with black soot. He's been here awhile. There's little equipment, most of it already out in the field, we're told. The boy shows us where we can pick up side packs. There're canteens full of water. We hook four around our belts as we are told to do. He hands us drip torches, hand-held fuel tanks to be used for starting backfires. "We're headed out in a few minutes to set a fire," the boy says. Then he gestures to our air tanks. "Won't do you no good to carry all that. It'll just slow you down when the fire starts to run." He points to buckets on the ground filled with dirty water. "You might want to get a couple of bandanas over there and soak them down real good."

At the truck, Partee comes up to me with worry on his face. "This don't feel good, Chief," he says. "Who's in charge out here?"

"The fire," I say. I look around, see signs that tell me we're not where Strachen told us we'd be. "You know we're in Marion County. I didn't hear Strachen say this thing was all the way out here, did you?"

"Not a word," Partee says.

He's shaking his head about it all when I tap him on the arm. "Don't worry," I tell him. "We're going to set a backfire. In my mind that sounds pretty good. At least we won't be trying to knock one down."

"Have you ever done this before?" he asks.

"Nope, never." I test my air mask, make sure the flow is properly regulated, then I look at Partee and J.D. "We're carrying air in," I say. "Rather have it on my back than fire in my lungs. Get hooked up and let's go see what the Boy Scout wants us to do."

A triage unit is set up in a small field. There are men coming out who are burned, one man carried on a stretcher with a broken leg. J.D. looks over and I can see he's interested. "Hey," I say, when J.D. looks my way. "Go over there, see if they can use your help."

He looks at the triage unit and then back to me. "I think I ought to be fighting fire today, don't you?"

"I think you ought to do what you do best, show them who's boss." I smile, tell him we got the fire handled. "You'll have your chance a little later. We'll go set this backfire and then come get you if we need you. How's that?"

"Whatever you want, Chief," J.D. says.

"Well I want to go surfing, and I'd love to see Kelly throwing a softball right now, but that ain't going to happen, is it?" He smiles at that and then leaves me and Partee with the Boy Scout ranger. I watch him for a moment longer, the triage unit happy J.D.'s there.

The boy tells us then that we're going to hook up with a crew that is already out in the fire. "There's a main burn coming from the south," he says, pointing out in front of him, "back over behind those trees. It's going to get them, no doubt, so they want us to start a backfire, see if we can use the woods to contain it all, burn it out if we can."

"Is that all the fire?" Partee asks.

"Hell no," the boy says. "This thing is more than thirty thousand acres, I've heard."

I look at Partee. "Big fire," I say.

"You could say that," the boy says when he thinks I'm talking to him. "We're trying to contain it until the rain comes, but we're having little luck. The timber's too dry. It's like we're walking on top of matches out here."

I look down and see a fire rake and a bush ax on the ground, pick them up, tossing Partee the ax. "These might come in handy," he says.

"That's what I was thinking," I tell him. Then I look at the Boy Scout ranger, smile like I'm really happy to be here. "Well let's go start a fire," I say.

The boy nods, "All right, let's go," and then he radios that we're walking in from the north perimeter, headed into smoke.

We seem to be doing all right, the boy recognizing the lay of the land as we move out. There are hot spots along the way that we take care of, Partee smiling when I rake over one that's right in front of him. "This looks like it might be okay, Chief, fighting fires without water."

But the boy looks concerned that we're finding hot spots. He stops and looks around, and for the first time I notice that we're standing on burned land, black soot-filled dirt that crunches under our boots when we walk. When we start to backtrack, it makes me think that I need to pay closer attention to what's going on. We end up in trees that are scorched, not the fresh land I thought we were supposed to light afire. "This land we're supposed to burn," I ask, "has fire already come through it?"

"No," he says. "Not that I'm aware of."

"Then we're in the wrong place," Partee says. "This ground's been burned over already."

The boy pulls out his map, reaches into his pocket for a compass. Out in smoke, there is no direction, hard to tell what's east from west, north from south. There's a small holly bush that somehow has been spared from the fire. We've passed it before. That's the only way I know where we are. When the boy sees it again, I can tell it bothers him.

He can't find his compass, so I give him mine. "Keep it," I say. Just figure out where we are."

I hear fire close by. The heat makes our turnouts feel more like ovens. Lightning flashes around us. Partee says, "Is that rain coming in?"

"No," the boy says. "It's coming from the fire, static electricity or some shit like that." The boy kneels to the ground, works the map, finds his coordinates, radios back that we have missed the mark and need to backtrack to reestablish our proper direction.

"Where's the crew?" I ask.

"We got to double back," he says. "We overshot them."

"You mean they're behind us?" Partee is standing beside me. I can tell he's pissed off.

"Yeah, just back that way." The boy throws a thumb over his shoulder as he folds the map. He tucks it all, map and my compass, in his coat, starts to move fast back in the direction we have just come.

I look at Partee. "We keep following this kid and we might never fight the fire."

"I could live with that," he says.

The smoke is getting so thick now, it's hard to breathe. I tell Partee to put on his respirator if he needs it, but it seems foolish to waste air until we know where we are. We hold off, wrapping wet bandanas around our faces for now. When we catch up with the ranger he seems even more confused, not even looking at the map now, just walking in a little circle like he can't find a landmark that should be there. What worries me is the ground we are on. It's still smoldering. The fire's just been through here. We were on old burn a minute ago, but the only earth I see around us now is black and smoldering, trees that are burned, but not down. It's like the fire raced through here too fast to finish it off. I didn't pay close enough attention to the land to notice this, so I'm a little confused, standing here waiting for the ranger to come up with a direction.

The wind picks up, swirling the smoke. "Shit," the boy says.

"Where are we?" Partee asks, his impatience with the kid too much. I put an arm on Partee's shoulder, pull him back. "Where do you want to go?" I say, trying to help the kid out. "Where would the crew be waiting for us?" But the boy doesn't answer. He looks panicked.

By the time we start to move again, the wind is brisk, coming from the south. "Should we walk north?" the boy asks.

"That might work," I say. Even when you are a seasoned firefighter, been in buildings with flame surrounding you, places so dangerous that if you stopped to think about it, it would freak you out, there are still moments when fear creeps into your bones. That moment comes to me when we walk directly into an exploding wall of flame. I'm not sure where it comes from, a backfire set or the raw burn of fire out of control, but it rises up in front of the three of us, just startles the shit out of me. "This might be a good time to get in your air," I tell Partee.

We double back, find fire on three sides now, moving quickly in the one way that offers us egress. It doesn't feel right walking this way either, the wind in our face, which makes me feel we'll find flame sooner rather than later. But hell, there's no other way to go. I hear a voice crackle across my radio.

"Peck, where the hell are you?" J.D. says.

"Not sure, bro," I say, pulling my mask off to talk. I look at the ranger, his eyes glassed over, coughing smoke. He won't be much good to us like this, but I have to ask him. "Any idea where we are?" I say.

The boy pulls out his map like he's looking for a place to pull over and eat. I get back on the radio. "We're lost," I say. "Give me a second, J.D. Let me look at the map."

I go over to the boy, take the map and compass from him, let him use my air while I look at coordinates, find north, and plot a direction out of this mess. I click my mike. "Looks like we walked north, maybe east and then back south," I tell him. "We just went in a circle. Now it looks like we might have gotten between the crew and fire, might be smack in the middle of the whole god-damn thing."

"I got a map, Peck," J.D. says. "Can you see a road near you?"

It's getting smoky again, the boy and Partee huddling over me. "Yeah," I say. "I got the road. It's about a hundred yards to the north."

I wait for J.D.'s reply. Behind us there is flame in the trees, sixty-foot sticks of fire breathing down on us. "We got to move, J.D.," I say. "We've got flame coming up behind us."

There is a crackle over the radio, J.D.'s voice ominous when he comes back to me. "Peck, you're in the middle of it. The wind shifted, it's coming back over you. Can you move north? There's a crew north of you on an old logging road."

It takes me a moment to register what J.D. tells me. I look at Partee and the boy. "We're in the middle of it," I say. "We're fucked."

"Can you go north?" J.D. asks again.

I look at the map, but it's not doing me any good now. The compass points north and I can see smoke, but no fire. "We'll try," I say. "I'll get back to you." I jam the map and compass into the ranger's hands, tell him to tuck it away, and we start to move, our pace brisk. We're using up air fast, spreading apart too far because we're panicking. We come up on fire moving in from the east, and then see it following us. We start moving randomly then, everybody getting confused out here.

I was taught early on as a rookie to keep perspective, to stop and survey the scene, make sure proper procedure was in order, things done in a way to ensure maximum safety. I have always done that, pulled myself out of a fire or a bad accident to take in the scene, find potential dangers before they become deadly. I didn't do that today. I didn't lead. I followed. I rode in the third seat, and then let this Boy Scout ranger lead us into fire. Now we're in a world of trouble.

Because we are not following a road, or taking any definite path, we separate and I can't see either Partee or the boy after a minute or two. I hear them yelling, but I can't find them, smoke and flame coming in on me. I pull my mask again, get on the radio. "Where are you, Partee?" I say.

"We're out," he says. "We found a break. I thought you were right behind us."

"Nope," I say. "Which way, brother, I need to get out of here."

"We went east," he says, "due east. There was a little fire, but nothing big, just run through it when you get there. It goes into an open field."

I reach for my compass, realize I gave the goddamn thing to the boy. "Jesus," I say. Then I just have to laugh at this. "You'll have to bring me my compass," I say, the joke's timing perfect to me, but no one else gets it.

"Goddamn, Peck," J.D. says. "Where are you?"

"Well I'm not east," I say. "And I got fire coming in on me." I look up, but there's no sun to help me find a direction. It's all blotted out, heavy smoke starting to roll in, hot fire boiling the air over me. Suddenly there's a large boom as a bolt of lightning streaks in, exploding just outside the flames, my eyes spotted blind. It shuts me down for a minute, a precious minute that does me in for good. There's nowhere I can go. The heat and winds are creating a huge thunderhead that feels like it's right over me. "I got to go down," I tell J.D. "Somebody's going to have to come get me."

"Cover yourself, get your mask on," he says. "Partee, you going in?"

"We're moving now," he says.

I find my fire rake, try to use it to dig a hole in ground hardened by fire and drought, but it's useless. The flames roar in closer now, heat making it hard to breathe even with the respirator covering my face. I give up on digging the hole because the fire's right on top of me, the lightning too. One or the other's going to get me, if I don't get low, get covered fast. I pull the fire blanket from my pack, throw the drip torch as far away from me as I can, sling it high and deep into the encroaching flames so it won't blow up anywhere near me.

The blanket looks like something an astronaut would use, silver, light, though I'm told it will hold off hot flame. Guess I'll find out now. It's gathered along the edges like a fitted sheet for a bed. I pull the air tank off my back, tuck my feet into the blanket before pulling it over the rest of my body and gear. I don't know how much air is left, the cumbersome tank making it hard to stay covered, but I need to breathe. It's hugged in tight to my chest as I try to secure the edges of the blanket so flame won't find a seam.

The radio keeps chattering, J.D. telling me to keep covered, Partee yelling that it's too hot, the fire coming too fast. There's a call to pull back, J.D.'s voice calm in all of this when he tells me to hold tight, that they've got to pull back for a minute. I let him know I understand, two clicks on the mike to say that I'm good to go. Then I shut it down, turn the radio off because I don't want to hear it anymore.

What's left is the roar beside me, the heat making its way into my turnout, my mask fogging when I start breathing hot air, the last of the tank finished. I can feel the soles on my boots starting to smolder, Cassie's ring blistering my finger, even in the gloves I wear. It's like an oven—no, maybe an open flame—inside my suit. It's hard to explain. I just hunker down, hold on to the sides, yell out that I'll be okay, that I'll make it.

It's like night inside this little oven, so hot I want to pull off the blanket and run like a motherfucker, find Partee and that Boy Scout. Hell, I want to run all the way back to the beach and sit out in the waves for the rest of my life, cool my ass off forever. There is great pain across my body, fire in my lungs as the storm rushes in on me, and then there is no pain at all.

I find sudden quiet, the worst of the firestorm having passed. I think about Kelly, close my eyes and see her standing on the mound, two outs, bases loaded. She winds up, delivers a ball that has sparks coming out of it. The girl waiting at the plate swings, but the ball just burns right through the bat. They win the game and Cassie is there jumping up and down in the bleachers, my father too. I look at him and see he's whole, both legs on the ground, and he's looking good, the way I remember him when I was a boy. The place goes crazy over my little girl. I smile, hoping when all this is over, I'll be able to tell Kelly about my dream. Tell her what I saw in the fire that ate the earth around me.

When I figure the worst is over, I peek out and find the ground around me untouched by fire. There are footsteps coming, my eyes adjusting, so I don't know if I'm dreaming or if this is real, J.D. and Partee running in after me. I feel a tap on the shoulder, hear a voice familiar and good, so I lift up, shade my eyes from the white light, and see Pops standing there above me.

"Well, hey," I say. "What are you doing here?"

He smiles, a strong full set of teeth in his mouth. "Hey yourself. Now you don't look no worse for the wear. You okay?"

I pull myself up, sit on the ground like I've just been awakened from sleep, the blanket down around my waist. I check my body, find nothing missing, the turnout clean, my boots and fingers cool. "Yeah, I'm okay," I say.

"You made it, then," he says.

"Yeah, I made it. I'm all right."

"Then you were lucky today," he says, smiling, "Let's go. Let's get on out of here." He holds his hand out, offering to pull me up, and we walk side by side off into air that is clean and cool and fresh. "It's like riding a wave," I say, "it feels like magic." Pops just smiles at me again, tells me to hold on as he takes me by the hand. And then, we are gone. We are long gone.

Cassie

By Wednesday morning John Boyd still has not driven by. He doesn't call. He doesn't come looking for us, doesn't send one of the development boys over here to try and break our legs. For all practical purposes, I might as well have not slipped a copy of the deed through his mail slot. It's like it never happened. Still, I'm excited and can't help myself when I call Peck at home and then try the station, though I know he won't be at either place. The fires are big down there now, so I imagine he's busy doing what he does best. I let it go, wait to leave the house until it's time to watch Kelly pitch in an afternoon game.

I'm worried about Momma. Since we delivered the deed to John Boyd's front door, she's been frightened of what might happen. I woke up this morning to find her sitting in the living room, her watering can beside her on the loveseat. "I can't go out there," she said. "What if he comes by?"

"Smile and tell him it's a lovely day," I said. "He's not going to know what hit him."

Momma cooked breakfast while I made phone calls looking for a good lawyer. I had no idea where to start, so I got in touch with Kimberly Jordan's parents in Cashiers. Kimberly's father was in real estate for years, so I figured they'd know a good lawyer or two. They told me Kimberly was married to one, that her married name was Holton now, and that she was living over in Asheville.

When I called that morning, Kimberly cried. She was so happy to hear from me after all these years. I tried to explain why I never got back in touch with her after that summer in Myrtle Beach, how I had started to call her a thousand times, but felt ashamed and disappointed about what I had done while at the church camp. She stopped me before I could finish and said, "That was when we were still children, Cassie. I'm just glad you knew you could call."

She laughed when I told her I needed a good lawyer. "I know the perfect guy," she said, then put her husband on the phone.

Bit Holton knew John Boyd, said he was a tough character, that he was in cahoots with developers all over Jackson County, but that he would gladly help me with the deed or whatever else might come up. "I'll be in Sylva on Thursday," he said. "Maybe we can have lunch." When we were finished, Kimberly took the phone again. "I wish I could see you, Cassie," she said. "It's not right we lost touch like that. Life's too short." I wept after I hung up the phone, Momma sitting beside me holding on tight while she kept an eye on the road looking for signs of trouble.

It all feels like it's going to work out now. John Boyd never shows and we are out and on our way to Cullowhee before noon. The day is beautiful. A cool breeze blows through the car with all the windows down, the radio catching AM signals whenever we start climbing out of the gorge along Highway 107. We arrive early at Western Carolina, plenty of time to see Kelly before she plays.

She is beautiful, so sure of herself, skin tanned, her hair pulled back in a ponytail. She runs up when she sees us walking to the field, hugs me hard, all giggly and excited that Meemaw gets to see her pitch. "I wish Daddy was here," she says. There's no poison in her words, just a longing to have Peck watch her play.

"He sends his love," I tell her. "He's thinking about you." It's all good, the best I have felt in years. I touch my tummy, feel a slight swelling, and know that soon I will need to talk to Kelly, let her know she is going to be a big sister. It feels right, this baby inside me, it feels like Peck's.

Coach Lambert walks over and I introduce Momma. I thank him for all he has done for Kelly. "She looks wonderful," I tell him.

"Kelly's settled in," he says. "She's a natural." He's cordial, but there is something there, a brief glint of sadness in his eyes. He tells Kelly to go warm up, asks Momma and me to come with him. "Is this about Kelly?" I ask.

"No," he says. "But someone is here who needs to talk to you."

Coach Lambert walks us up a hill away from the field. White clouds float across the blue sky like giant islands in an azure sea. I think about that first summer at Myrtle Beach, Kimberly and I not much older than Kelly. We rode together in a car with other girls from surrounding churches, screaming like it was Christmas morning when we first saw the ocean. When we got to the camp, I ran straight down to the pier, stood at the end barefoot, the skin on the bottoms of my feet blistered from the scorched wood, and gazed out onto something I had never seen before. The white-capped water—its vast flatness took my breath away. The smell in the air, the deep white sand as far as I could see, the hot wind on my face made me feel I was in a strange and exotic new world.

Now, walking up the hill so far away from that place and time, I suddenly feel like that girl again, and Peck is there with me, a subtle breezy whisper, so close that I almost turn to see if he is beside me. *Be strong,* he says, words of reassurance, even in his saddened voice. It feels odd.

Coach Lambert leads us to a concession stand, a small cinder-block building that is closed except for the door entering from behind. When I walk in, I find Clay waiting, sitting on a stool, his head bent, his hands limp in his lap.

"Clay," I say, trying to feel surprised. My anger starts to grow because I think he is here for the wrong reasons, to expose us, to finally make me commit to the life he has planned in Walhalla. A life I know now will never happen. "What are you doing here?" I ask. I look at Momma, worry pushing against her face. I hold her hand to strengthen us both. "This is my mother, Clay. Momma, this is Clay Taylor."

She is kind, cordial when she shakes his hand. "I'm sorry I haven't been back in touch," I say. "It's just been one thing after another. Kelly ran away—" But then I stop because I realize we have already had this conversation.

He smiles, looks down at the floor when Coach Lambert turns to leave. "Take as much time you need," he says, then closes the door behind him, leaving us in dim light, the smell of stale popcorn and spilt Coke spoiling the air.

When I turn back to Clay, I see something else in his eyes, a kind of hurt that I've never seen before. I want to ask again why he is here, but before I can find words, he tells me that Peck is gone.

At first, his comment is funny. I think he is asking *if* Peck is gone, and I tell him yes. "He left day before yesterday."

But Clay just shakes his head, smiles nervously. He gets off the stool, stands nearer as if he needs to be close to deliver the news. "No, Cassie," he says. "Peck is dead. There was an accident in the field and he didn't get out."

I don't feel my legs give way with Clay's words nor his arms catching me when I fall. It is like my body understands what I have been told, but my mind won't allow it to be true. Peck gone?

No. "It's not right," I say. "He was a safe fireman. He wouldn't get himself into something he couldn't get out of."

"He got separated and the fire turned back on him," Clay says. "That's all I know right now. They're still trying to figure it out, put the pieces together. And no one can believe it, Cassie, the incredible coincidence of the timing." I look at Clay, not understanding what he means, and then he tells me about Pops, that he is gone too—Peck lost within the hour of his father's passing—and then I feel my life empty out of my body.

How DO YOU tell a fifteen-year-old, so full of life, just ready to begin living in this world, that she will have to do it without a father? There's no good way, I know that now. But at the time, my thought was to pull myself together and let Kelly play the game, let her be a girl for one more afternoon before her life would change forever. Momma wasn't sure about that, whether I could keep up the appearance long enough, the burden of Peck's death so strong. "I'm good at appearances," I promised her, and then we walked out from the concession stand into unforgiving light.

It was harder than I thought, though, to sit there and watch Kelly pitch, her arm tough against girls two, maybe three years older than she. But as I watched her on the mound or at the plate when she was batting, it was like I was watching Peck, the very image of him standing there, his strong shoulders and back, the sleekness in his legs. I gazed down at the shadow on the ground, Peck's image if I allowed myself to believe it, connected to Kelly by the sun and the ocean sky and the rich red dirt of the pitcher's mound and baseline paths. Always with her, I thought. Peck will always be with her.

After the game, when I told Kelly that Peck and Pops were

dead, I lost my daughter too. She blamed me for it all, cried when she collapsed against the counter inside the concession stand, this the only place that afforded us the privacy we needed. She promised to hate me forever, never wanted to talk to me again. Momma helped Kelly gather her things from the dorm room while I walked with Clay out to his car. I told him I appreciated that he had been the one to bring the news.

He came closer, a hand on the small of my back that seemed misplaced. "I should never have left the station," he said. "Maybe I could have done something to help."

His words provoked me, my anger boiling up into tears. "I think we both did enough to Peck," I told him. "Don't apologize like that."

"That's crazy talk, Cassie." he said. "We didn't cause him to die."

"No," I said, stopping him there. "If Peck had not been worried about me, about what I was doing with you, maybe he would have made better decisions, maybe he would have lived, Pops too for all I know."

Then I told Clay that I wouldn't be coming back to live with him in Walhalla, that it was over. I asked him to leave so that I could go find Kelly, try to salvage what was left of my family. He started to get into his car, but stopped short, his eyes narrowing, his throat tight against his collar. "You tell me this then," he said, wagging a cigarette in my face. "If Peck was still alive, would you feel the same way? Would you be telling me to leave?"

I could not in good conscience continue after that. I told Clay I was sorry, but that he needed to go. I never told him that I was pregnant.

DEATH AND ALL ITS DEMANDS surround me. Conway Funeral Home is taking care of Peck and Pops, both cremated, so it will be a few days—time enough to have pitiful little arguments about how and where they will be buried. Kelly wants to spread their ashes in the ocean, but I don't know about that. "I want to be near Peck," I tell her, but she's not buying it.

"Last time I looked," Kelly says, "you were trying to get away from him."

I don't know how you explain such a thing to a child, the complications of a life rearranged. I want to hold her, but she won't come near me right now. I let Momma be there because I just don't have the strength to fight for her.

J.D. and Lori are with me most of the time, helping sort through the paperwork from the fire department. There's life insurance to file, forms the county requires. I let them push me through it, my hand signing papers that I don't even read. I could be signing away my life for all I know, but J.D. is thoughtful, Bob Strachen too. They all tell me how much they loved Peck, how he made sure Kelly and I would be taken care of. Lori is there to hold my hand all the way through. "Peck loved you, Cassie," she says, trying not to cry, not to make it any harder on me. "No matter how much trouble you two were having, he loved you all the way through."

And then as if God slaps me in the face, it starts to rain. By Thursday afternoon, the land that killed Peck is saturated, the fires gone. All in all nineteen thousand acres were burned, Partee says, five houses lost, a whole trailer park, a couple of cars, all the livestock in one barn. Seven firemen were injured, but only one lost to the fire, Peck Calhoun Johnson, thirty-five last week, a birthday I forgot about until I was asked to verify his age for the death certificate.

I am ashamed of myself, the way I am doted over, how my actions are excused, excused by everyone but Kelly. She holds my hand to the fire. When Conway Funeral Home calls to let us know the remains have been returned, she faces me defiant in her desire to put the ashes in the ocean. I tell her Pops will be buried in Conway beside Grandma Cealy, but she can make the decision about Peck. It is a fair compromise, I think, one that seems to soften her hatred for the moment.

Pops's funeral is first, a small, quiet graveside service. He never attended a church, never was baptized. Still, the funeral home found a preacher to help put him in the ground. We stand on earth that is trying to recover from deep drought and listen as a stranger offers encouraging words that we will find each other on the other side, that Pops is there already, waiting, watching us, smiling down now that he has completed the circle, his ashes the final sign of our short time here on earth.

Ashes to ashes, dust to dust. I am on my knees near the edge of the grave. Kelly kneels beside me, our hands together holding the urn as we let Pops go, the ashes poured quietly into the grave. Most in attendance are from the fire station, Pops's friends having dwindled and passed on before him. Margaret, his nurse, is smiling, certain that Pops is standing right beside Peck today, knocking on Heaven's door, though it's hard to feel such assurance through all the pain. Someone in the small group begins to sing "Amazing Grace." Not everyone knows the words, but they make it through well enough, and Pops is laid to rest next to Cealy.

"Meemaw's all I have left," Kelly says, kneeling at the grave while everyone sings.

"You still have me," I tell her, but she won't take her eyes from Pops's ashes, which spread to whiten the dark black earth inside the hole.

Later that night, we are back on the marsh, Kelly sitting alone on the dock, Momma watching from the screened porch. "Why don't you go talk to her?" she pleads.

"What more can I say?" I ask in return. "She thinks I'm the cause of everything bad in her life."

"She's fifteen, Cassie. That's what you told me not too long ago. Go, go talk to her. Even if she rejects you now, she'll remember that you tried. She'll come around." Momma walks over to stand next to me, her hand wrapping into mine. "Go talk to your daughter."

I walk barefoot through wet grass. At the edge of the yard, I stop and wait to see if Kelly will acknowledge me. When she doesn't, I look back, Momma standing on the porch, an encouraging wave to push me on. "Mind if I join you?" I ask.

Kelly turns then, her face dull, lifeless. "I don't care," she says.

I walk to the end, sit on the edge of the floating pier, let my feet dangle in the black water of a high tide. "God, I can't believe the heat's broken down here," I say. I look at Kelly. She's sitting on the small bench leaning against the rail, her eyes cast down, focused on nothing. "Peck always said that we just needed rain. I guess he was right."

"I don't care what he said," Kelly says, her voice no more than a whisper. "It's too late, it rained too late."

"I think Peck would say that it wasn't too late," I say, choosing my words cautiously. "It put the fires out and saved lives and property. I think he would feel good about that."

"You think so?" Kelly says, her words snapped out, angrier now. "You really think Daddy's feeling good about things?"

"Yes I do, Kelly," I say. "I think Peck is somewhere good and he's resting well with Pops because the fires are out, his crew safe. That's what he always worried about."

"Well that's good, Momma," Kelly says, "I'm glad you feel that way. We'll all sleep better now knowing Daddy's dead, but his crew is alive and safe." She stands up then, looks at me hard, the anger in her eyes becoming hatred. She wants to hurt me. "Don't ever tell me what Daddy's thinking," she says, the words spewing from her mouth. "What gives you the right to come back here and act like you actually cared about him, that his death is even important to you? It's embarrassing when I know how you really feel."

I try to stay calm, remember like Momma that Kelly is just fifteen, probably the hardest age to deal with something as tragic as death. Her anger is no different than what I felt for my father when I was pregnant and kicked out of my own home. I think that's what Kelly is feeling right now, that somehow she is being denied something that she should never have to give up—a life with her father. "Kelly, you can't judge me like that," I say. "It's too easy to just paint it all black and white. Your father and I struggled, and I know I made it hard on him. I won't deny that. But what I lost, the opportunity that I squandered so long ago, has sat heavy on my heart for years. It was suffocating. I had to leave your father to breathe again."

"Well, I wish *you* were dead," Kelly says. "That would make more sense to me."

"That's unfair," I tell her.

"What you did is unfair," Kelly says.

"What I did, you'll understand one day," I say, "especially when it's your turn to do it."

"I'll never do something like that," Kelly says, her voice trembling with hate. "Clay Taylor is disgusting, you two dangling your feet in the water, running off and dragging me along with you."

I stand up then like I've been caught, my legs wet to mid-shin, embarrassed that she remembers Clay being here that afternoon. "We didn't drag you anywhere," I tell her. "You were given a great opportunity to play ball at a wonderful camp and Clay Taylor helped get that for you."

"If I had to choose, I'd take the beach any day," Kelly says. "I never want to set foot in the mountains again. I hate the mountains."

"No you don't," I scream.

"Yes I do," Kelly screams back at me.

"No, you hate me." And then as if my words pull my feet from under me, I fall, crumbled against the pier weeping, my body shaking uncontrollably. "You hate me, you hate me," my mind lost, the record broken. "You hate me."

I can feel the warmth of arms, Momma's words, "No, no stop, both of you, just stop it." When I look up, Kelly is running toward the house, Momma holding me. I weep in her arms. "I tried," I say.

"I know you did," Momma says. "I know."

"There's nothing left," I scream, my mouth wet with tears as I try to get loose.

"There's everything left, Cassie. You've got to fight for her."

But I have so little left inside, that I just don't know if I can. My daughter hates me, blames me for Peck's death as I blame myself. There is nothing I can do to stop the grief, my sadness so complete that I can no longer breathe.

In the early hours of the morning after restless sleep, I find Peck in the room, his clothes fresh, face clean shaven, his hair back out of his eyes. "You need to stop all this now," he says.

I sit up in bed, watch him, pray that he is real. "I can't help it," I say. "I miss you."

"I'm good," he tells me. "No more fires. I'm with Mom and Pops. It's better. You can go on."

"Kelly's hurt by what I've done," I tell him. "What can I do?"

Peck walks over, sits on the end of the bed, but I don't feel him there. I just see him, all white and clean, sweet. "Give her time," he says. "Death's hard."

"Are you sad?" I ask.

He smiles a little, shakes his head, "No, I'm not sad." He lifts himself from the bed, walks over to where I sit, leans in close. "Go on, Cassie. You go on now."

I touch him but feel nothing. "I can't feel you," I tell him, tears filling my eyes.

"You will," he says. "Now go on."

And when he lowers his head to kiss me, I close my eyes, waiting to feel the warmth of his touch, but he is gone and I am there awake for the first time, straining in darkness.

A figure comes through the door, Kelly shuffling her feet to the edge of my bed. "Mommy" she says, her voice desperate, small.

I lift up, open my arms to take her in. "What is it, honey? Are you all right?"

She folds herself into me. I push over in the bed, make room for her warm body to lay next to me. "I dreamed I talked to Daddy," she says, "but when I woke up, he wasn't there. God, I loved him so much."

"I did too, sweetheart."

"I know you did," she says. "He said you loved him." We hug tightly in the gray light of this morning. I kiss her on the cheek, spoon up next to her. "Do you think it was him or was I just dreaming?" she asks.

"I don't know honey, maybe a little of both."

"It was a gift," she declares. "I hope he does it again sometime. I want to talk to him always."

"You will, if you want to," I tell her. "Now go back to sleep. We have a lot to do later today."

Kelly falls silent in my arms. I don't tell her that Peck was here with me too. I want to keep that for myself, but before I drift off, I thank him for giving me my daughter back. I thank him for being there for both of us. *Always,* his word still in my head when sleep takes a tight hold on me until late morning, the sun leaking in through turned-down shades to warm the room.

Momma comes in, surprised to see Kelly in my bed. She smiles at us, lifts the blinds to flood the room with good light. "It's time," she says. "Folks are here. They're waiting to take Peck to the beach."

Peck's funeral is a pretty big thing. We gather at the station, firemen from all over the state in attendance. The fire chaplain from Conyers is there to lead the service inside the Quonset. I don't remember the station ever looking this nice, the way chairs are placed on the drive out front, the whole place draped in roses and magnolia. Everything is shiny and bright, Partee and J.D. wearing dress blues and white gloves.

I notice Clay standing near the back. I'm glad he's here to pay his respects, though I don't have anything else to say to him. I hold on to Kelly for support, Momma's arm over my shoulder as I slump in my chair, Peck's ashes on the back of the engine—the black urn sitting on sparkling chrome, waiting for the final journey to the water.

I make it through the eulogies, Bill Strachen and J.D. remembering Peck and his life as a fireman. The chaplain is kind with his words of everlasting light, a fireman's work done, his rest a just reward. At the end of the ceremony, J.D. carries a folded flag, leans down, his hands covering mine when he presents it to me. "Peck would have thought all this was too much," I whisper.

J.D. smiles, his eyes red, tired. "No doubt about that," he says, "but don't you think he would have liked the way we all cleaned up?"

The crowd around me chuckles, J.D. finding a way to heal us all. I reach up, kiss him on the cheek. "Thank you, J.D. I think he would have been very proud." I hug the flag to my chest, accept his salute, and then we are done.

I'm good until we move to the water, until Kelly and Teddy bring Peck to the edge, having shed their clothes for swimsuits, their boards ready to take him to sea. Partee joins them there as we all do. It's late afternoon, the crowds giving way for the moment, affording us all some time alone on the beach to say our good-byes. There is a huddle over the surfboards, Kelly and Teddy holding on to each other, crying over Peck's urn as if they are anointing the ashes with their tears. I walk to the water, hug Teddy, his grip on me strong and full of sorrow. And when Partee lifts his voice, Teddy has to hold me up because I have nothing left, the words sung by a man who literally walked through fire to try and save my husband.

The water is wide, I can't cross over,
And neither have I wings to fly,

> *Build me a boat that can carry two,*
> *And both shall row, my love and I.*

I am handed to Phil Roddy, who helps me down onto the sand where I can rest and watch as Teddy and Kelly push out into the waves, Peck's urn carefully carried under Teddy's arm. I don't know what this man will do without Peck. They were like brothers, and I'm ashamed I never understood that, never tried to understand. But as I watch Peck carried out, I am brought to smiles to see Teddy in the surf taking him home, taking him to his final resting place.

> *A ship there is, and she sails the sea,*
> *She's loaded deep, as deep can be,*
> *But not as deep as the love I'm in,*
> *I know not how I sink or swim.*

When Kelly and Teddy are out past the break, a good distance beyond the length of Kingfisher Pier, Phil Roddy helps me stand. The distant figures on the water trick me for a moment, and I see Peck and Teddy out there playing as the boys they've always been. But it is only for a moment that I hold this image because I know the figure with Teddy is my daughter, and when she holds the urn high above her head, I wave, smile, and say one last prayer for Peck, that he forgives me my life with him, and that I remember his love for me, always.

> *Love is handsome and love is fine,*
> *The sweetest flower, when first it's new,*
> *But love grows old and waxes cold,*
> *And fades away, like summer dew.*

The chaplain stands along the water's edge, the tide wetting his pants, but he doesn't seem to mind. He waves to Kelly. Beside her, Teddy raises his hand, giving the sign of peace as Peck flows into the water, his ashes scattered in the very place he loved so much. Kelly sets the urn in the water as I told her to do, lets it fill and then releases it to sink to the bottom, deep enough that the tide will never bring it in, yet close so that whenever she is on the water, she will be near it. She will be there with Peck always.

Give me a boat that can carry two
And both shall row, my love and I.

When Partee finishes, he comes over to hug me, his strong able body not enough to save Peck from this moment, but his voice beautiful enough to help him go across. I am grateful for the friends I have here, friends I never understood until now. We watch as Teddy and Kelly find a wave, pull up on it at just the right moment that it catches them, Peck somewhere out there molding the surf into perfect form, the wave breaking easily to bring Kelly and Teddy back to the beach. When they are on solid ground, when we have huddled and cried our eyes dry, there is nothing left to do but go home.

JULY 1970

Cassie

After my father died, I hurt for a long time. I tried attending church in Murrells Inlet, a small Methodist chapel nestled beneath a grove of large oak trees and next to Oliver's Lodge, but it didn't help. Peck and I argued constantly. I left him at home, taking Kelly and staying with Pops and Cealy for days on end. I went back and forth to Whiteside Cove where Momma's grief was overwhelming. In the years that followed, I failed to find a way to reconcile my father's loss. What I regretted most was that he had never seen his granddaughter, never held her, never had the chance to know what a wonderful child she was growing up. I was angry at him for excluding her from his life. I didn't care about me, our battles were different, but Kelly had done nothing to deserve exile. It wasn't fair and I let him know it in the form of letters and phone calls, in which I begged Momma to tell him to call me. If Kelly could at least see him, I was sure she'd win him over. There was no doubt in my mind he would fall in love with his granddaughter just like Peck and I had when she was born. But my father never called, never wrote a letter, and so he died never knowing this wonderful child.

The spring that Kelly turned five, I came back home from a

drive that was intended to take me away from the marsh for good. It was late and Kelly was still asleep in the backseat of the car. I came into the house, exhausted and lost, Peck sitting in the living room. He was off duty, and had found my note, one of many over the years. He had read the cruel words I wrote, my desire to leave him and my life along the marsh spewed all over the paper, and he still stayed up waiting for me to return.

"How did you know I'd come back?" I asked.

"I didn't," he said. "I was just hoping you would."

I started back out to get Kelly, but Peck stopped me. "Let her sleep," he said. "She won't know the difference for a while longer."

He took me back to the bedroom, undressed me, and we made love while Kelly slept in the car outside our window. It was a desperate act, two people trying to find a way to hold on. Peck was more willing than I was. He tried so hard, and there were times that I welcomed it, needed him to work hard for me. But there were others when I just didn't care. That night, it was somewhere in between, and afterward we were exhausted. We lay in the bed holding on to each other, watching out the raised window just in case Kelly woke up. "Why do I hurt so much?" I asked.

Peck stayed silent for a moment like he might not know the answer, then let go of me, raised up on an elbow. He stroked my forehead, brushed the hair away from my eyes, looked at me and said, "Because you miss your father. Too much left unsaid, I guess."

"It's all too painful," I confessed.

He turned over, lit a cigarette, blew the smoke out into the room, let me have it and then lit his own. "I don't imagine you ever get over the loss of a parent," he said. "I just think you learn to live with it." In two years' time, Peck would lose Cealy when her heart gave out while cooking a Sunday afternoon dinner. Peck would find her, alone and laid out on the floor in the kitchen.

And then he said something I have never forgotten. Peck rose up even farther, almost to hover over me and said, "Cassie, if you just let go, great healing can come out of pain." He waited there long enough to see I wasn't going to argue about that, then kissed me on the lips, a soft, sweet kiss before he got up to bring Kelly in from the car.

Since Peck's funeral I have been drowning in pain. I cannot forgive myself for the choices that I made, choices that left Peck alone at a time in his life when he needed me. Even if I had been with him, I know Peck would have still gone to fight that fire, the young ranger would have led him in, and mistakes would have been made. That knowledge, however, does not stop the hurt. I have lost Peck forever, something I never imagined when he was alive. Peck was too good, too smart to die like that.

It seems foolish to have these thoughts, to play the events of the past month over and over trying to reconcile something so irreconcilable. I know this, but I have had a lot of time over the past couple of weeks to think on my own, alone for the very first time in my life. I say alone for the first time because that's exactly what it is. I was born thirty-three years ago, and I have always lived with someone who took care of me. First it was with my parents until I was pregnant with Kelly, and then with Peck. Neither house offered me much of a say in how my life would play out. Now I will have all the say. After fifteen years, I will have to learn to take care of myself.

I came back up to the mountains alone shortly after Peck's funeral, Momma telling me to go away for a while, agreeing to stay with Kelly at the beach so I could have some space to breathe and work things out. I needed to be in Sylva in early July because of the land dispute, John Boyd Carter and his stable full of lawyers making a run for the land after all by bringing an action to quiet title the property. "He can do that?" I asked Bit over the phone from Momma's house. The machinery around the cove sat silent, the digging stopped until the dispute was settled.

"Yes he can," Bit said. "He's claiming now that the land was conveyed as a gift deed, and those are void after two years, if not properly recorded. Obviously it was more than two years old when you filed it. John Boyd's saying his contract to sell the land to the development company is in jeopardy and that the delay will cause irreparable harm if the courts don't act quickly to settle this."

"How quick?" I ask. "Will we have a chance in this?" I could feel my hand trembling holding the receiver to my ear as I waited for his reply.

"Cassie," Bit said. He drew my name out long and slow over the phone just to make the point. "This case will pour as slow as molasses in winter, if you want it to. You had the original deed, a general warranty deed signed, notarized, and submitted to the Register before John Boyd could get the land sold off. You have a letter setting out the terms and conditions of the deed that John Boyd signed.

"For whatever reason, he was trying to get you to go along with something he didn't have to. He could have transferred the deed that existed, sold the property, and that would have been that. It was his mistake to wait, and now, he's trying to fix a bad deed done, no pun intended, of course. Cassie, we've got him for as long as you want him."

When I heard those words, *We've got him,* I just sat down on the floor in the hall of Momma's house, no longer able to hold back my tears, joy and sorrow all mixed up into one bad heartbreak. Kimberly got on the phone and told me not to move, that she was on her way.

I stayed with her at her parents' home in Cashiers through July

4th, hiked the old trails, and sat on outcroppings of Chimney Top Mountain, the sun melting away in front of us. We watched fireworks explode over High Hampton after dark and I told her about my life with Peck, how it had fallen apart and then come back together, but not soon enough to tell him before he died. We sat in silence, traffic moving along 107, the distance great between me and the rest of the world. "This is what it feels like," I said.

"What?"

"Losing Peck, everything. It's like being lifted up onto the top of some great mountain and left there alone. I can see all the life below me, but I can't get to it. I can't be part of something that's going forward, not right now, not yet." Kimberly looked at me then, reached over, and wiped away my tears.

I spent the next afternoon sitting out in Momma's backyard remembering the cove, my father, and the life we led here so many years ago. When I became restless as a young girl, when I could no longer stand living here, that great wall of rock hemmed me in, left me a prisoner. When I sat there on that last day I would for all practical purposes live in Momma's house, Whiteside was like old blood running deep inside of me. It stood quietly, the one constant that would never change, always here to mark the lives of those who lived below its ancient walls.

I closed Momma's house up, left Whiteside Cove after that. For the past couple of weeks, I have been on my own, driving endlessly through the mountains of North Carolina and Tennessee thinking, crying a lot, but mostly thinking. In this time I have been a stranger on sidewalks of small mountain towns where I walked, ate in restaurants, and slept in motels, all of it done alone. I have lived anonymously. I haven't said two dozen words to anyone since I left Whiteside Cove, sort of an unintentional solitude.

It's mid-July now and everywhere I go, Chattanooga, Asheville,

Cherokee, there are posters for Tallulah Gorge and the great Wallenda's tightrope walk. It haunts me seeing posters of a man walking across a narrow strip of words. ACROSS THE AWESOME GORGE, it says, the slight image of man holding a large stick balanced on top of the word *awesome*. This is where Clay had promised to bring me and Kelly, a celebration that was to mark the beginning of the rest of my life.

In the Asheville newspaper there was a picture of the rope, a cable actually, of spun steel that had been fabricated in Georgetown. It was being hauled up to Tallulah Gorge on a flatbed railroad car, each stop along the rail documented by pictures and commentary. An editorial inside the paper criticized the need for such a spectacle that would no doubt erode the pristine nature of the gorge. Everyone has a point of view these days, but nothing, I have learned, is ever black and white.

My plan was to have returned to the low country by now, but instead I piddled around long enough that I ended up in Franklin, North Carolina, about the time of the walk, too close to find an excuse not to drive the short distance to Georgia and the gorge. And so, here I am, July 18th, having paid my five dollars for a ticket, endured crowds ten times worse than any in Garden City Beach during the summer season. Someone near me has said there are twenty-five thousand people here to watch this walk. I have been camped out in a single spot all day, seated along a makeshift rail constructed so no tourists can fall into the gorge and kill themselves. Only the Great Wallenda will be allowed to do that today, if it is to happen at all.

I wonder as a lady sings "America the Beautiful" how many of these people here actually want to see Wallenda fall. Peck always said that people love a tragedy more than they do a miracle. He was always concerned about those who stopped to witness accidents and fires, afraid someone would end up hurt because they just couldn't keep going and stay focused on their own lives. They had to try and watch the heartbreak of others.

I also worry that I might see Clay Taylor among the crowds. I have not talked to him since I thanked him for bringing the news of Peck's death to me. At Peck's funeral, we kept our distance. I plan to do the same if he is here. I'll leave if I have to. I don't want Clay in my life anymore. That whole idea was dead even before Peck was.

I rub my tummy, the curvature more recognizable, a baby growing inside me. I'm not sure of the exact date. I haven't counted the days, looked at a calendar to figure out when I will deliver, because I'm not ready for what is happening to me. I can't get excited about bringing a new life into this world. I want to believe that this baby is Peck's, but I know there is a chance Clay is the father. What a mess I have made of my life, I think. I have made such a spectacle of it that I wonder if I ought not to be put on display, a sideshow folly at some county fair where people would pay a dollar to come in and see me.

I am just about to give up, stand and walk away, disgusted by my self-pity, when the whole place falls quiet. We turn collectively toward the steel cord stretched out across the gorge, the walk about to begin. I am on the south rim, so Wallenda will walk toward me, toward the thousands who line the edge over here, everyone holding their breath as the small frail man on the other side steps gingerly out into thin air.

When Bob Strachen brought me all of Peck's belongings, he hesitated with the last item. He stood there a bit uncertain about what he held, but then he showed me a penny. "I don't know why he had this," Bob says, "but they found the penny in his boot—well, in his sock actually. It was against his foot."

I smiled when he handed it to me, almost like a sign from Peck, a last little bit of himself handed to me, a gift. "It was something Pops always did," I told him, "a penny in his shoe for good luck." The irony of what I had just said was not lost on either one of us. Bob shook his head. "I'm sure going to miss him," he said. I held the penny in my palm, let the near weightless coin sit for a moment, and then I said, "You take this."

Bob looked at me, his eyes sad. "No," he said. "It's yours. Peck would have wanted you to have it."

"No," I said, "he would have wanted a fireman to have it." I put the penny in his hand, closed it, and walked away.

I remember this now, sitting here on the side of Tallulah Gorge because just as Wallenda is in the middle of the wire, he stops, a gasp rising from the crowd as he trembles briefly. I look down because I cannot watch him fall, if that is what he is about to do. There has been enough death this summer to last a lifetime. I don't need the burden of another on my mind, so I turn away. And when I look to the ground, between my feet, slightly dusty, tarnished, and beat up, I find a penny lying in the dirt, the date 1954, the year Peck and I were married. The year it all began. The coin brings me to tears, though I try hard not to let those who crowd around me see that I am crying. I take the penny in my hand, hold it tight, and feel Peck there beside me, the touch of his skin, the smell of his body.

That's when I feel the first kick of our child. Just when Wallenda bends over to rest his head on the wire, to lift his legs up and over into a headstand, I feel the baby inside my tummy kick like it's trying to say, pay attention to what's going on here. It's impossible, I know that. It's only a little over three months along, but I swear it is there. I am breathless after it, tears streaming down my face as I feel the certainty of life inside me, Peck's child, I know

now for certain, already eager to get on with it, to grow and be born, to fight and fight harder to live in this life, to be our child, to be Peck's child.

Wallenda ends his walk, stepping onto the tower on the south rim, after a mere eighteen minutes of stunned silence. And then cheers across the gorge, some yelling for him to do it again, to walk back across. All the shouts and cheers are met with a wave from the little man hanging off the tower by an arm, and then he disappears into the throng, the spectacle over, someone behind me careless with their words. "That's it? Kind of a rip-off, if you ask me."

I stay at the rim long after Wallenda is gone and stare at the wire, feel the wind begin to bring a storm that's been waiting to come up the gorge all afternoon. I close my eyes and promise Peck to raise this child as well as we raised Kelly, but I'm afraid it won't work without him. "I need you, Peck," I say, my fist tight on the penny in my hand.

A young ranger walks to where I sit, leans over, and asks if I'm all right. The sudden attention is embarrassing, pulls me up quickly as I wipe my face with the back of my hand. "Yes, I'm all right," I tell him. "I'm fine, really." And then I hurry away.

I catch the last shuttle back to the parking lots, trying to be invisible, wanting to do nothing more to draw attention. When I am at my car, I search my pockets for the keys, find them, and open the door. It's then I realize the penny is gone, no longer in my hand. I look around the car, search my pockets, pulling them inside out, retrace my steps around the parking lot looking frantically for the small piece of Peck that I have no doubt lost.

When the storm finally blows in, it is a sudden outburst of darkness and torrential rains that move through fast, leaving the parking lots steamy and wet on the other side. It's silly being chased into my car by rain, sitting here looking down at empty hands thinking I have lost Peck again. If he was here next to me, I'm sure he would be laughing, telling me to start the car and be on my way.

What comes next begins as small waves, warm touches across my body like I am being held and comforted. I close my eyes and remember the morning of Peck's funeral, the desperate need to feel him again, his comforting words from my dream. *You will, now go on.* The heat doesn't last long, but the touch remains, my body relaxed, quiet for the first time since I found out Peck was dead.

By the time the sky clears, I am restless to do just what he said, to go on. I start the Bel Air, roll down my window, the air fresh and sweet, the smell of rain filling the inside of the car. It is enough for now, I tell myself, to be on my way, to simply leave the parking lot on this mid-July afternoon, to see behind me shadows on the ground covering the distance I have already crossed, the way out in front clear as the Bel Air holds me balanced and steady toward the state of South Carolina, moving on, taking me back to where all of this began. Home.

Awassa

Acknowledgments

It seems a fitting place to be here in Garden City Beach, South Carolina, looking out on the Murrells Inlet Marsh in early August, writing acknowledgments for a book that found its inspiration in this place only two short years ago. I have just finished reading the galleys for *The Fireman's Wife*, the last chance I will have to touch the lives of Cassie and Peck. It will be up to them now to go out into the world to tell their story. My job is finished.

Looking back on this journey, I have traveled far and wide to gather in Peck's and Cassie's lives. From the low country of South Carolina to the high peak of Whiteside Mountain outside Highlands, North Carolina, I have traversed the geography of their lives, meeting folks who were able to add authenticity to their story through a strong sense of place. Without the help of these lovely people, Peck and Cassie's story would not have been possible. I am indebted to them all.

In Garden City Beach, there are the usual suspects, the ladies at Seawatch Inn at the Landing, the place where I wrote most of Peck's life. Renata Beebe, Kim Saunders, Kim Herriot, and Virginia Blake have always provided a quiet, lovely space for my storytelling to come alive, not to mention the homemade cookies to nibble on. In addition, Paula and Wade Nichols, longtime residents of Garden City Beach, treated me to a lovely dinner in Murrell's Inlet, where they were able to confirm my suspicions about the marsh and surrounding geography during the 1970s. It was a warm and enjoyable evening with new good friends.

Carolyn and Bob Riordan are very special. They opened their lovely mountain home to me on numerous occasions, so I could learn about Cassie's life, the land she traversed as a child, the college where she would dream of going one day until that fateful summer of 1954 when she visited the low country of South Carolina. This book would not exist without *Awassa*.

To backtrack in 2007 to a time that is completely gone from the mountains required some conversations with those who have lived in the coves and towns all their lives, or long enough at least to know where all the bodies are buried. I was lucky enough to find several people in and around Highlands and Cashiers, North Carolina, who opened their homes, allowing a total stranger the chance to "pick their brains" about a lost time and place. My thanks go out first to Suzannne Roweton, whom I met along Whiteside Cove Road. She offered to introduce me to the "caretaker" of the land that I wanted to hike, land that would help me understand Cassie better. That caretaker was Suzanne's father! Kenneth and Linda Smoak allowed me (and my dog!) into their home so I could learn about the country in and around Whiteside Cove. Kenneth invited me to hike on private land where Cassie's father would have walked during his visits to Whiteside Mountain. The next day I made the six-hour trek that would reveal much about Cassie's life and help me to create authenticity in her existence. The hospitality shown by Kenneth and Linda Smoak and Suzanne and Kenneth Roweton helped me feel that this place I have always visited is now part of my home.

Debra Rogers of Ashburn Real Estate was gracious enough to sit with me for an afternoon, offering her impressions of Highlands, North Carolina, back in the 1970s, and when I needed to go back further, I was blessed to meet Sue Potts from the Highlands Historical Society. She stayed with me until early evening one cold February day after I had been out traipsing around the mountains alone and uncertain about what I was looking for. A lifetime resident of Highlands, Sue sat and told me wonderful stories, some of which found their way into this book, albeit altered or fictionalized to make them part of Cassie's life before she met Peck.

I would be remiss not to mention my good friend Bit Holton, who helped me navigate through the legal issues of real estate law in the 1970s. He helped me devise the devious plot John Boyd Carter brings to bear on Meemaw and Cassie. Bit is one of my closest childhood friends who, along with his wife, Kim, have remained dear to me even as the years have grown between us.

There are those in Atlanta who have stuck with me over the years. George and Jayne Cavagnaro, Andy and Shelley Rogers, John (Goose) and Kelly Hetzel have always been loving and kind in their support of my writing. Debra Marlow and Barbara Antley are two women who have read my early drafts and always supported me with kindness and love toward my work.

At Georgia Perimeter College, I want to thank our president, Dr. Anthony Tricoli, for the vision and direction he has set for our college and his understanding of my place in it. Rob Jenkins, the director of the Writers Institute, who has been my most ardent supporter during the writing of this book—thank you, Rob. And Pamela Parker, who has been there from the start and continues to this day to support my writing, you have always been ready to read and critique my work. Thank you.

Without Stella Connell's love for my work, this book would never have been published. And without Jane von Mehren's belief in Cassie and Peck, I wouldn't have been blessed with Robin Rolewicz, who saw the story even before I did! I am thankful to Millicent Bennett, who, as my editor, worked unendingly to make this book shine for Ballantine. And last but certainly not least, my agent, Amy Hughes, who saw the story when it was raw and fresh and still knew what it could be. You took a chance, and for that I am indebted to you.

Finally, to my parents, who stand deep in age and wisdom. You have been steadfast in your love and belief in me. God bless you.

I don't know what will happen to *The Fireman's Wife*, but I know that the journey is over. The lives of these characters and the real people I have met along the way have been woven into a rich tapestry that is now a part of my life for always. I can let Cassie and Peck move out into the world knowing that they are ready to go, that their lives are complete, their story finished. It is up to others now to decide what will become of Cassie and Peck, good people with a story they would like to tell you.

August 2008,
Garden City Beach, South Carolina

THE

FIREMAN'S WIFE

Jack Riggs

A Reader's Guide

Connie May Fowler and Jack Riggs
Discuss The Fireman's Wife

Connie May Fowler: What was your inspiration for the novel?

Jack Riggs: You know, sometimes the stories that we end up telling aren't the stories that we intended to tell. That certainly happened when I sat down to write my second novel. I spent about two years working on a book that Ballantine decided not to publish. It was a hard time for me. *When the Finch Rises* had been such a wonderful experience and suddenly I really wondered if I ever would publish a second novel. The next summer, while I was trying to figure out my future, I was down at the beach south of Myrtle where I concentrate on my writing—a noisy, crowded, boisterous family beach just like in *The Fireman's Wife*—and my agent got a hold of me and said Ballantine was still interested in something new.

I was thrilled, but what would I write about? For some reason, I had been thinking a lot about Larry Brown lately. I had read him very early on and became friends with him even before I was published. I would talk to him from time to time, and he was always so gracious with his words. When he died, it was just devastating to me, as it was to many others. I had recently reread his memoir *On Fire,* and was thinking about how Larry had been a fireman years ago, when I noticed a fire truck from the station next door to my condo was heading out on a call, and for whatever reason all those thoughts and impressions coalesced into one at that moment and I thought, *What the hell, at least Ballantine is still asking*. So I told my agent that I was working on a story about a fireman. I asked her to give me a week and I'd send her something when I got home. And that's when I started writing *The Fireman's Wife*. It came out of a great confluence of emotion and need, of failure and desire to begin again. That was the seed, but of course there was much more.

CMF: Do you feel like you chose this story and these characters, or did they choose you?

JR: I always feel like the characters choose me. Peck was the first to come on board. He found me down there at Garden City Beach, beat up and needing rescue. Cassie came a bit later. She was the hardest to understand. Maybe it's because she's a woman and I'm a man and it was harder to communicate, I don't know. I started with Peck's story, and as I went along and Cassie began to trust me more, the story really became hers. Peck's story is about other folks' disasters and how he tries to help the victims survive, but it's Cassie, on the other hand, who's in trouble, she's the character in transition. She needs rescuing. I just didn't know it early on. She pretty much demanded that her troubles be front and center, so that this becomes a story about how she is trying to right a wrong life. Her choices are certainly suspect, but the attempt is true and real. Peck is there to support her as well as he can and to give her room to breathe. He finds his own peace while Cassie attempts to find hers.

CMF: What prompted you to write this novel from both Cassie's and Peck's perspective?

JR: That's a good question. When I started looking at Peck's and Cassie's lives, I wanted to make sure I did both of them justice. What we forget is that there are always two sides to any problem and usually both sides have a degree of validation to them. Peck is a strong man who understands, to a certain degree, what his wife is doing. But Cassie is sympathetic too, even as you can see that she's a bit out of control. I wanted to explore the idea of a relationship caught in the tides of change. It is 1970 and women's lib is pretty intense, so I wanted there to be an undercurrent of that running through the book, and I wanted to explore the confusion on both sides of the relationship in that context. Look, Cassie got pregnant at eighteen, lost her chance to go to school, was kicked out by her father, and has lived the last fifteen years of her life in an area of the country that she doesn't really understand, the low country of South Carolina. We have to be in her head to understand why she becomes so restless, and we have to be in Peck's head to see the impact of her choices on the rest of her world and the people she loves. It was just apparent early on that I would have to look at this story from both characters' points of view. It made the book tough to write because I always had to be thinking from both perspectives. It took longer to process information and character motivation, but in the end, I think it worked well.

CMF: Was it difficult for you to slip inside the voice and viewpoint of a woman?

JR: It was more difficult to slip from one point of view to another and keep the story moving forward, but if I have to answer that question, yeah, it was harder. I'm not a woman, never have been one, never will be, so I had to consider my own sensibilities and filter them with extreme care to make sure I found the right voice.

In some ways, such as human nature and emotions, men and women are the same. But our actions and thoughts are often in stark contrast. In this particular case, Peck moves quickly, decides and takes action. Cassie spends lots of time deciding on things, is careful with her words, moves quietly to begin her journey to self-discovery. To juggle those two patterns of thought and behavior was difficult, but I enjoyed Cassie the more I got to know her. She became a strong character for me, especially after I spent some time near Highlands and Cashiers, North Carolina. Once I understood her terrain, the geography of where Cassie grew up, then she became much more real to me. I was able to write her then.

CMF: Did you do anything specific and intentional in order to shape-shift into a woman's point of view?

JR: It's funny, but early on, I wrote Cassie's story without the use of contractions. I wanted her thoughts and her dialogue to seem more proper in a way. It gave me a starting point for a voice. I found pictures of women who could have been Cassie, thought about the type of clothes she would have worn, her skin type and such. I listened to and observed my own wife. She helped me a lot with mannerisms and dialogue; how to write it so it sounded and felt real. I thought about her language patterns and behaviors, watched my daughter and noted her body language and behavior around the house. Madison is younger than Kelly, but she's entering the stage of her life that I think is timeless, that teenage period where she's too cool. It was fun to watch her and it was fun to think about my wife in Cassie's position. She'll be surprised to hear this, but it's true.

CMF: You do something very brave in this book; you detail an issue that is present in the lives of many women but is hardly ever spoken about: Cassie resents her daughter. What is the source of the resentment? Do you believe her resentment is justified, or do you see Cassie as a flawed and perhaps even bitter woman?

JR: I think Cassie is a woman in transition, and people in transition sometimes do things that appear crazy and inappropriate to others. We go crazy for a while and then the ship rights itself and we go on with our lives like nothing out of the ordinary ever happened. Cassie has been coming to this moment for a long time and now will not let anything stand in her way. She does love her daughter, even though we see her use the girl in some ways. From a distance we might see her as a bad mother, but I don't think that's true. In Cassie's mind, Kelly and Peck stand in the way of her freedom to live her real life, that life she left behind when she got pregnant and had to get married. She wants to get back to what she believes is her true life's road, and to do that she will have to let some things go: like Peck and Kelly, if necessary. Does Cassie resent Kelly? Probably on a real silly, immature level, but deep down, she's a mother and a good one at that. I think Cassie is bitter, yes, and flawed. Her life, in her estimation, has been one of captivity. Like she says, when she returns from a visit to the mountains, she feels like she is a cornered animal. All human beings need to feel like there is an opportunity for growth in their lives. If we lose that, I think we lose the will to live. So Cassie is fighting back, albeit in a way that is less productive than she hopes.

CMF: Cassie is resentful of Clay, saying that "Sometimes Clay will just take over," yet she leaves her husband for him. What does Cassie truly want?

JR: I think Cassie just wants to be herself and, as long as she feels trapped, she is struggling to find who she is. I also think Cassie wants to have one final chance to understand why her father did what he did those many years ago. Clay is a means to getting out, and as the book begins, we get the strong impression that Cassie knows that going with Clay is just "trading a fireman for a fireman," but she has no other way to do it, and so she sticks with it. But interestingly enough, as she begins to free herself, she drifts further from Clay, too. I think as Cassie gets further away from Peck, the more she begins to understand him and what her life with him really means. Of course things happen and it's not easy to just say "my bad" and go back to normal. Cassie's actions bring about consequences that have devastating results. She learns a very hard lesson before the book is through. And though she was looking for this rearranged life, in the end, the completeness of that change is incredibly powerful, is beyond anything she ever imagined.

CMF: When you were a little boy, did you want to be a fireman when you grew up?

JR: I think all boys pretend to be things like firemen and soldiers. I don't think I particularly thought I would ever be one, but I certainly romanticize that type of character. When I was growing up, I remember visiting fire stations, and listening for the fire siren that always announced where a fire was burning. There was a page in the back of our telephone book that had all these fire codes, and when the fire horn would blow, it sent out a series of blasts that would correspond to one of these number codes. You could look that code up on a map of Lexington and find where the fire was burning. I remember once, we heard the fire horn and checked the map and realized it was Dixie Furniture, the local furniture factory where many in Lexington worked. It was a huge and expensive fire, one we all drove downtown to watch.

Like I said, the early ideas of this book came from being at the beach and hearing a fire engine go out. And then there's Larry Brown and my impressions and thoughts about him. Of course there is 9/11 and all the firemen lost in that event. But one moment that affected me most came in the summer of 2007 when nine firemen lost their lives in a blaze in Charleston, South Carolina. Ironically, I was back in Garden City Beach with my family on vacation, taking a break from writing, when the news of this huge fire came on the television. As we watched, the number of firemen grew until the news began to report that nine had died when the roof collapsed. It was the worst fire disaster since 9/11. I found it terribly poignant that I was writing a book about firemen in South Carolina, and here in Charleston nine lives were lost on a summer evening while we were all enjoying the beach. It left its impressions on me and colored the thoughts Peck had about summer vacationers at the beach and the type of calls his crew eventually went out on.

CMF: The firefighting information is so real and detailed. What kind of research did you do in order to achieve the level of verisimilitude that is present in the novel?

JR: Well, here you go. I wish I could say that I was a fireman for a month, that, for research, I walked through flames alongside my brother firemen. It would be nice to be able to say that I am a volunteer fireman or something like that, but alas, I am not. My father was not a fireman. My brother is not a fireman. I have a couple of friends who are firemen and I've been to a fire station with my son's Cub Scout troop. But having said that, I will tell you that I did a lot of research on fires and firemen. I read tons of material until I felt comfortable enough to write about it. It was all researched and then written and rewritten until I felt I had accomplished an authentic feel. For me, the story must feel real. In *When the Finch Rises* I had a character that was bipolar, and so I had to arrive at a degree of verisimilitude before I felt like I could believe in her disease. In *The Fireman's Wife* the same level of authenticity had to be reached or else I could not have written the story. Of course, my worst nightmare is that some fireman will read this book and say, "That's not the way it happens at all." My only retort to that will be, well, maybe that's the way they did it in 1970! It helps to write in a time well past, but that also presents its own set of problems. You have to know what was available at the time, and how procedures worked nearly forty years ago. But it also helps to ease the reality of the moment. I hope I have connected in a real and authentic way. I think I have.

CMF: Are you a surfer?

JR: Yes! Now I can say I am. I learned this summer. It's the one thing I always wanted to try, and I think I need to thank Peck for giving me the incentive to try. I was a snow skier, but I haven't been on skis since 1992. The one thing I remember about skiing was how free I felt sliding down the mountain. It's something that would stay with me even after I came off the slope and went to bed. I loved snow skiing, but I am transfixed by surfing. It is so much more a self-contained sport. You don't need a ski lift to get you to the top of a wave. You just need to paddle out and wait. And then the motion, the drop off the lip of a wave and skimming along the trough just seems like the most organic activity in the world. I liked surfing as a metaphor for Peck—this idea of being one with the ocean, one with the low country, seemed fitting. It was the perfect sport for Peck, too, because it gives him a sense of being a bit alternative. At first, my editor didn't like that Peck surfed and smoked pot, but as I showed her drafts of the final story, she bought it totally.

CMF: Setting in the novel is very important. You quite successfully juxtapose the opposing nature of mountains and beach. In what ways are these symbolic of Peck and Cassie as opposites?

JR: Setting is always preeminently important to me. When I write I have to have three elements in order to really get going on a story. First, I have to have a strong, believable character who will trust me with his or her story. Second, there must be conflict, and third, but equally important for me, is a strong setting, or as I like to call it, a strong sense of geography. And of course in this story the geography is almost a character itself. I have juxtaposed the mountains and its feeling of a lush wetness against the low country and a hot sandy dryness. I think the contrast speaks for itself.

Symbolically, both geographies have dual meanings, I think. For Cassie, the mountains represent her childhood and John Boyd Carter and all that she endured during those dark days, but it also represents all that she lost, the opportunity to go to college and accomplish something with her life. The mountains, especially Whiteside Mountain, represent something that is old and transcendent; Cassie needs the mountains to complete her. She needs them for internal strength, and she needs to be in the mountains as a way of fulfilling her life, taking up where she left off fifteen years earlier.

For Peck, the mountains represent foreignness, a sense of

being landlocked. When he is up in the mountains, he isn't familiar with things, can't pick out the nuances in the landscape that Cassie can see from high above on Whiteside Mountain. It represents a threat to him as long as Cassie feels the need to stay in the mountains and not return to him. Still, at the same time, he recognizes the mountains in Cassie's life in much the same way that she recognizes the low country in his.

For Peck, the low country is life as he knows it. The marsh and the beach are the marrow in his bones. It's as if the surfboard and the waves complete him. For Cassie, a fair-skinned woman who doesn't understand the flatness of the marsh, the low country is like a desert to her. For each, the other's geography imprisons. For each, their own geography is freeing.

CMF: How is finding the deed a form of redemption for Cassie?

JR: One of the subplots that drives the story is the land deal that has gone bad for Cassie's mother. When I discovered this in the story, I realized that the deed and the problems surrounding it are really a metaphor for Cassie's battle with her dead father. In *When the Finch Rises*, it was the photograph of the lynching that became the symbol of struggle between father and son. In *The Fireman's Wife*, it's the deed that brings out the struggle between Cassie and Parker. It is also the vehicle that helps Cassie understand herself, a way of finding her own inner strength. It is the accomplishment of finding the deed and the way she resolves the issue with John Boyd Carter that helps Cassie grow into her own.

CMF: It seems to me that Peck is surrounded by death and, early in the novel, he is particularly surrounded by the death of young people. How does this proximity with mortality affect Peck?

JR: I think Peck sees his own life in the victims he has to confront. Clay likes to think of himself as a "thinking fireman," but Peck understands the raw nature of the beast and is always prepared. Fire burns and changes everything it touches, and the resulting deaths teach Peck lessons for his personal life. I think death builds a strength and understanding of the human condition in Peck that allows him to continue to try with Cassie. He sees her flaws. He sees his own flaws and because of it, I think he's more patient with Cassie and her behavior. His work preoccupies him because of the danger and death that is always present, and that probably works against him at home. But it is something that makes Peck the man that he is.

CMF: Cassie's father cast her out of the house and church when she got pregnant out of wedlock. It seems to me that this exile was deeply wounding to Cassie and may be at the crux of her general resentment. How do you view this banishment in Cassie's life?

JR: The banishment is definitely the seed of Cassie's problem. Without Cassie's being cast out of church and home, and without her being forced into marrying Peck and moving to the low country, the story becomes something entirely different. This is the most important back story material in the book. It sets up Cassie's struggle with her father, with John Boyd, and eventually, with herself. Of course in the end, we all know that we can't go home again, so for Cassie the moment of banishment is directly connected to the moment of return when she leaves Peck. It all culminates into a revelation for Cassie. The problem is that in doing this, Cassie sets in motion a series of events that will eventually bring her to her knees. It's all part of the same thing, the full story, if you will, that begins the day she finds out she's pregnant with Kelly and then is banished for good by Parker.

CMF: Do you think readers might see this story as antireligious?

JR: I worried that it might come off that way, yes. But I don't think that's the way it looks now at all. I was trying to make a subtle suggestion about the restrictiveness of this type of religion, but when I started working with this part of Cassie's life, I was afraid of cliché and the type of character that ends up being too much of a broad stroke and not subtle enough to feel authentic. I think, though, that Parker comes off pretty real and I'm happy about that. I also like the idea that John Boyd Carter is involved in the banishment, and I think it deepens the divide between Cassie and John Boyd when we get into the land deed battle.

CMF: Are the religious themes intentional or do they simply flow from your own experience and convictions?

JR: If you are familiar with my first book, you know that religious themes are intrinsic to the story, and I am always conscious that my characters in the end are on some sort of theological journey. After all, as thinking and reasoning human beings, we are seekers. We want to have answers or maybe we want to avoid the answers to the questions that have always been there. What is the meaning of our existence? Is this really all there is? What is my destiny? Simplistic questions, but ones that have in one way or another defined us. Cassie is the most obvious seeker here. She is the one stepping out onto the metaphorical tightwire when she leaves Peck. There's a little prodigal son metaphor here, and a bit of the idea of costly grace. A type of understanding, if you will, that only comes to us through great sacrifice and suffering. Cassie is on that road and it is a road that has to be taken, if she is to find herself. The problem with her journey, of course, is that there are dire consequences that she cannot imagine. In that regard, the story is like a biblical parable. Or at least, that's the way I see it.

I try to show a theological journey while at the same time take a look at the darker side of organized religion, or maybe I should say the more complicated issues of organized religion. I don't want to condemn religion, but with Parker, Cassie's father, I wanted to show that religion isn't always clean, that sin and redemption are messy sometimes. When Cassie reminds us what Parker feels he is providing his congregation when he has Meemaw take those young girls back into the mountains for abortions, we can understand more clearly what Parker feels is his battle with the devil. What he participates in might seem criminal to most, but I love the way he looks at the issues he is dealing with. It's complicated, and it's uncomfortable, but then many stories in the Bible, when they aren't sanitized or "child-proofed," are uncomfortable.

CMF: When you started the novel, did you know what Peck's fate would be? If not, when did it become clear to you?

JR: When I started this book, I knew Peck much better than I knew Cassie. I always figured Cassie would have an affair, get pregnant, go for a back-alley abortion, and then die. I started the novel with that idea in mind, but as I continued to discover Cassie's character, I started liking her, and doubting that she would die. Then my daughter and I went to Tallulah Falls right before New Year's Eve, 2006, and I discovered that Karl Wallenda walked the gorge in July of 1970. As soon as I learned of Wallenda's walk, it was almost as if Cassie spoke up and said, "Hey, you can't kill me because this is where I end up at the end of the story. I'm still alive." And I knew then that Cassie wouldn't die and that I would have to figure out the issues between Peck and Cassie if the novel was going to work properly.

Now I know that my answer seems to have nothing to do with Peck's fate, but in reality, it has everything to do with it. I realized I needed to understand Cassie and her fate before I could realize Peck's. In fact, when Peck finally revealed his fate to me, I couldn't buy it. I didn't like it, and I didn't want to write it. But I learned with *When the Finch Rises* that I don't have a lot of control over what my characters tell me to do.

CMF: The Great Wallenda plays a quiet but important role in the novel. How do you see his importance in Cassie's life?

JR: Well, as I have just mentioned, when I discovered Wallenda's walk across the gorge during a visit to Tallulah Falls, I learned that Cassie wouldn't die, that she would live and be there when Karl Wallenda did his thing. It also became a wonderful metaphor for Cassie's own life, the idea of walking her own tightrope of life as she tries to find herself and deal with leaving Peck and somehow remaining a mother to Kelly. The last chapter where Cassie is there at the gorge watching Wallenda on the tightrope brings the whole novel into focus for me. The frail acrobat moving through great danger, balanced there a thousand feet above the gorge, walking toward safety on the other side, is precisely Cassie's life.

CMF: I think Cassie's great peccadillo is her ingrained resentment. What is Peck's?

JR: Ah, her "peccadillo." I like that word. Peck? He's perfect, I think. But really, if you want a serious answer, I think Peck's peccadillo, his sin, is his inability to see Cassie's suffering for what it really is. He's so busy with his life as a fireman, he can't see what Cassie's unhappiness is doing to the relationship. I think Peck feels deep down that Cassie will always come back because she always has. He's guilty of letting things get too far out of hand and not seeing Cassie as someone who needs to have her own life and her own identity in that life. It was something that happened to a lot of women in the seventies, and as a product of that time, I saw many of my friends' parents, those who were important role models in my life, get divorced and move on into new and different lives. It was unsettling to me at the time, but I came to understand what was going on, how women were subjugated in their lives, and I think that has happened to Cassie. Toward the end, I think Peck makes headway in understanding what he has done to Cassie and her life. When he is with her at Western Carolina, he sees what she missed, and understands, I think, his responsibility for some of Cassie's loss.

CMF: I think that one of the things a novelist has to do is love his or her characters—even when they are dastardly. Was it easy for you to love Cassie or did you have to work at it? Or perhaps the better question is: Do you love Cassie?

JR: I do love Cassie. I love her so much that I couldn't kill her! That sounds funny, but it's true. I will have to say, though, my love for Cassie came gradually. Not that I hated her. I never thought what she was doing was wrong in an evil sense. Cassie is human, just like the rest of us, and humans struggle with life and love. Cassie is struggling. She is a seeker looking to find herself again, and when we participate in such a life's journey, someone is always going to get hurt.

As I said earlier, I didn't really know Cassie very well until I spent some time in the North Carolina mountains where she grew up. While I was up there, I talked to people, hiked some beautiful country, saw the church that I imagined Parker preached at while Cassie grew up. I could see her on the land and I could feel her presence there, especially in the eyes of the folks I talked to. And I came to understand her journey as being the lifeblood of this book. She is a fighter, just like Peck, and they compliment each other very well. I think Cassie comes to understand that at the end of the book. She is authentic, and yes, I do love her.

CMF: Writing a novel is such an organic process of discovery. What discoveries did you make while writing this novel that surprised you?

JR: I'm always surprised at the fragility of the story, how, if you are not careful, you will miss things that are vital to the success of the story. In *Finch*, it was the photograph of the lynching and a section I put in very late in the revision process where I explained the return of the finches to Finch Creek. Without that, I think the book misses a very lyrical moment, and a thread that pulls the novel toward its conclusion. In *The Fireman's Wife*, it was discovering the story itself, how it moved from being Peck's story to Cassie's and how Cassie came alive to me. If I hadn't been prepared for anything to happen, if I hadn't been sensitive to the story changing in midstream, then I might not ever have finished it. It sort of oozes out, and what I have learned is that it is a 24/7 job. I have just started to rest and to let go of the intensity involved in telling this story.

The other thing that surprised me about this book was how hard it was to write it. I mean, it's been five plus years since *When the Finch Rises* came out. I wrote a second novel that did not get published, questioned myself as to whether or not I would ever publish again, flew through editors like a hot knife through butter, until I finally landed on a good one, wrote and wrote and wrote and wrote until I couldn't write anymore and finally, after it was all done, I looked up and a book was waiting at the end of this incredible journey. It was hard, really hard to get it right this time, so I hope people will read it and come away understanding the story of Peck's and Cassie's lives together. I say it's Cassie's story, but really it's a love story.

CMF: What is next for you, Jack?

JR: Sleep, lots of it, I hope.

Really, I don't know. I want to write another book, so I'm looking now, testing a few ideas. I teach at Georgia Perimeter College, a great two-year college in Atlanta, and will continue renewing myself through my students. They are wonderful, especially at the two-year level. They have no idea what they can do but when the light goes on, man oh man, that's something to behold. I love teaching, so that sits in front of me, the one good constant in my life. But I'll write more, I'm sure. I need to get this book to bed and then clean my palate, so to speak. I'll keep you updated, sweet Connie May, that's for sure.

Questions and Topics for Discussion

1. Early in the novel, as Cassie is about to leave with Clay, she hesitates. "Clay Taylor is a fireman too, and what good would it do to live with him, trade one fireman for another?" Do you think she's running away from Peck himself, or from his way of life? In what ways is Clay a better, or worse, choice for her? How would Cassie and Peck's marriage have been different if Peck hadn't been a fireman?

2. Cassie feels trapped by the low country in which Peck and Kelly thrive, while Peck is uncomfortable at Meemaw's house in the mountains. Talk about the ways in which landscape and environment affect and define each of the characters in *The Fireman's Wife*. How do you feel your own life and personality have been shaped by the environment in which you grew up?

3. The book begins, and ends, with Cassie thinking about the Great Wallenda's tightrope walk across Tallulah Gorge. What symbolic significance does this event hold in the novel? How does the meaning of the tightrope walk change for Cassie by the end of the book?

4. Cassie explains, "Peck always told me that in a fire there's nothing good for anyone, not those caught in it or those that have to fight it." What larger significance does this statement have for the events of the book? In what ways does Cassie's decision to leave Peck resemble this kind of fire?

5. There are several different kinds of parent-child relationships in the novel: Cassie and Kelly, Parker and Cassie, Pops and Peck, etc. Even Peck and Cassie have very different approaches to parenting their daughter. How do these family relationships affect the individuals involved, and how could each be improved? What do you think makes each of these parents and children treat each other the way they do? What lessons can be learned from these relationships?

6. "Momma used to say children were empty vessels that we fill." Do you agree with this statement? What evidence does the story offer for and against this idea?

7. Peck's first emergency call is for a child who died because his parents weren't paying attention—ironically, this call takes him away from an important moment in his own daughter's life. In what ways do the series of fire calls narrated in the book reflect on Peck's and Cassie's own lives? How do they add to and deepen the meaning of the novel?

8. Clay tells Cassie, "I don't think anything could make you happy." Is that true, do you think? What is Cassie looking for? Do you think she'll ever find it?

9. Peck is surrounded by old friends like Teddy, and an alternate "family" of sorts at the firehouse; Cassie spends most of her time alone, or clashing with Kelly. How do you think this influences their different outlooks on life?

10. Meemaw, Cassie, and Kelly are each very different women. Discuss the ways in which their passions and personalities represent the worlds in which they came (or are coming) of age.

11. What do you think attracts Cassie to Clay? Do you ultimately think he is a sympathetic character? Why or why not?

12. When Peck apologizes for taking Pops to a nursing home, Pops explains that "a man builds his home in his heart." How true do you think this is for the other characters in the novel? What symbolic role do physical houses—Cassie and Peck's house on the marsh, Clay's rented cottage in Walhalla, Meemaw's little house on the disputed land in Whiteside Cove—play in the lives of their inhabitants?

13. The story takes place in the summer of 1970. Why is this timing important? How would Cassie's and Peck's lives be different if their story were happening today?

14. Cassie is a headstrong character, with stubborn opinions of her own—yet she is always quoting the thoughts and comments of the men in her life. In what ways is she passive, and in what ways is she active? How does her passivity contribute to her frustration, and is there anything you think she could have done to resolve it without leaving Peck? How does this frustration play out in her relationship with Kelly?

15. Cassie says, "I've come too far, even if I fail, to give up trying now." She says this about running away with Clay, but could it be applied to her life with Peck as well? Do you agree with her statement? Is it a good principle to live by? Why or why not?

16. The novel's title is *The Fireman's Wife*. Ultimately, whose story do you think it is—the fireman's, or his wife's? In what ways is it accurate, or not, to define Cassie as mainly a "fireman's wife"? Does this change as the novel progresses?

JACK RIGGS's first novel, *When the Finch Rises,* won the Georgia Author of the Year Award, and was chosen by *Booklist* as one of the Top 10 First Novels of 2003. Riggs is the writer-in-residence at the Writers Institute at Georgia Perimeter College in Atlanta.

About the Type

This book was set in Fairfield, the first typeface from the hand of the distinguished American artist and engraver Rudolph Ruzicka (1883–1978). In its structure Fairfield displays the sober and sane qualities of the master craftsman whose talent has long been dedicated to clarity. It is this trait that accounts for the trim grace and vigor, the spirited design and sensitive balance, of this original typeface.

Rudolph Ruzicka was born in Bohemia and came to America in 1894. He set up his own shop devoted to wood engraving and printing in New York in 1913 after a varied career working as a wood engraver and as an art director and freelance artist. He designed and illustrated many books, and was the creator of a considerable list of individual prints—wood engravings, line engravings on copper, and aquatints.